# KEEPERS OF THE EARTH

Olivia Diamond

Copyright © 2023 by Olivia Diamond

All Rights Reserved.

No part of this book may be reproduced, stored in a retrieval system, or transmitted by any means, electronic, mechanical, photocopying, recording, or otherwise, without written permission from the author.

Cover Design by Christian Nelson

mountainofdreamsbooks.com

ISBN: 9798377913443

*To Marianne Diamond Stephens*

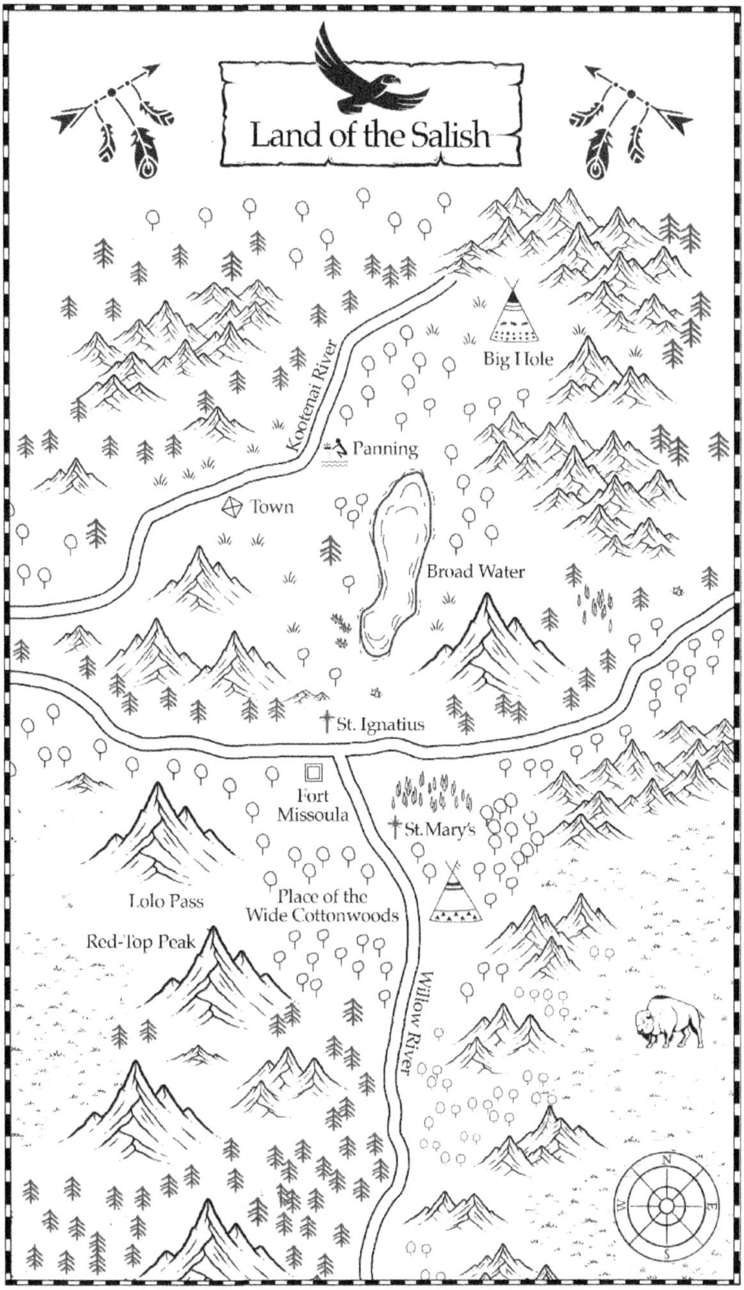
Land of the Salish
Big Hole
Kootenai River
Panning
Town
Broad Water
St. Ignatius
Fort
Missoula
St. Mary's
Lolo Pass
Place of the
Wide Cottonwoods
Red-Top Peak
Willow River
N
E
S
W

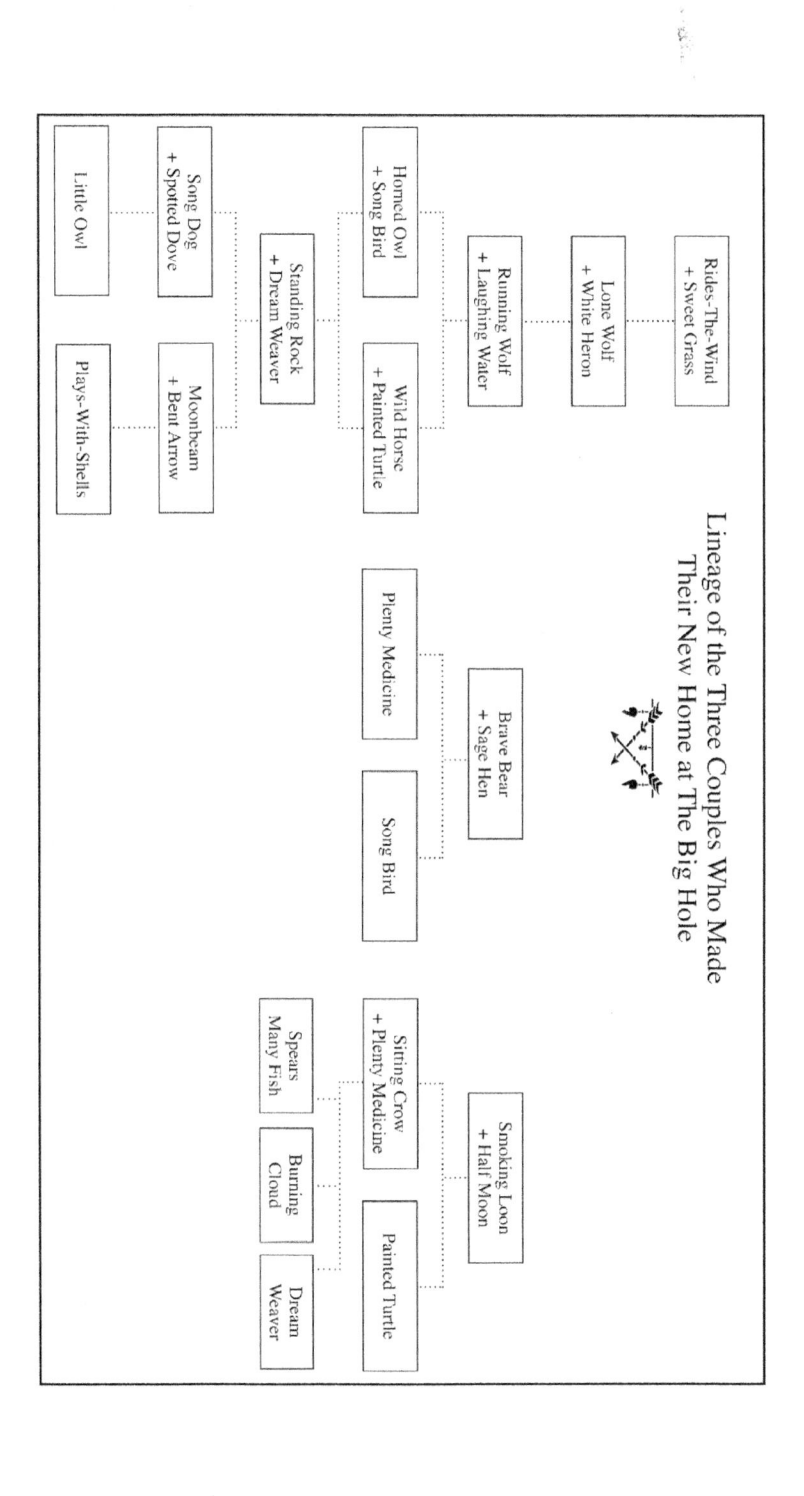

# Lineage of the Three Couples Who Made Their New Home at The Big Hole

- Rides-The-Wind + Sweet Grass
  - Lone Wolf + White Heron
    - Running Wolf + Laughing Water
      - Horned Owl + Song Bird
        - Song Dog + Spotted Dove
          - Little Owl
      - Wild Horse + Painted Turtle
        - Standing Rock + Dream Weaver
          - Moonbeam + Bent Arrow
            - Plays-With-Shells

- Brave Bear + Sage Hen
  - Plenty Medicine
  - Song Bird

- Smoking Loon + Half Moon
  - Sitting Crow + Plenty Medicine
    - Spears Many Fish
    - Burning Cloud
    - Painted Turtle
    - Dream Weaver

*Everything on the earth has a purpose, every disease an herb to cure it, and every person a mission. This is the Indian theory of existence.* — Mourning Dove, Salish woman writer, 1888-1936

**Note to the Reader**

The reader, especially the Native-American reader, may object to a white woman of European ancestry presuming to write about Native-American reactions to the white men's encroachment on their land and the destruction of their way of life. Because this book may be considered another arrogant appropriation of what does not belong to me, I wish to state the impulse that made me write this fictional history.

Sadness and shame have always overcome me whenever I have read the history of the European conquest of the native populations of North and South America. I wished it could have been different. I wanted to rewrite history. I began to ask: What if a few Salish had managed to live in isolation from 1855 to 1920 and maintained their traditions? I live in Montana so I was familiar with the ancestral homeland of the Salish. The Salish are unique among American tribes because they numbered only a few thousand and avoided war against the whites, knowing they would be overwhelmed. They lived in a protected valley in the Rocky Mountains away from the Oregon Trail. They refused to ally with the Nez Perce to fight the United States cavalry in 1877.

I imagined a band of twelve Salish Indians separating from their tribe and retreating to a remote corner of northwestern Montana after the 1855 Hellgate Treaty at Missoula. In this alternative history, five generations of Salish, disturbed by the destruction of the earth, recount their first meeting with Lewis and Clark in 1805, the Black Robes' arrival, the theft of their land, the decision to shelter in a hidden valley, their survival in isolation, and the band's eventual return to their ancestral homeland in the Bitterroot Valley. What motivates them to emerge from seclusion? The ultimate realization of any people that neither warfare nor separation can permanently guarantee peace. We must learn to live together as brothers or die together in fear and hatred.

There are abundant reasons to carry bitterness from one generation to the next, but it cannot repair the damage. What reparation can be made? It is a simple answer, but one difficult of attainment. Resolve to respect all creation and walk gently upon this earth. And ensure economic, educational, and social justice to the First Americans. Finally, preserve the environment for future generations.

**Contents**

Rides-the-Wind ..................................................................1
Lone Wolf ......................................................................27
Running Wolf ................................................................103
Horned Owl ..................................................................207
Standing Rock ..............................................................279

**Rides-the-Wind**

His back straight as a lodgepole pine, Rides-the-Wind sat astride the appaloosa stallion festooned with feathers, quills, and painted rawhide trappings, and peered into the morning haze. The Salish sub-chief had ridden north that early fall morning to scout for possible horse thieves in the valley. He intently studied the horizon. A party of about twenty men gradually gained definition approaching through the upper valley. Two men mounted on horses rode in front, and behind them walked bedraggled men wearing strange clothing and leading a few packhorses. At first bewildered, he stared in shocked amazement, wondering if he should immediately return and alert the village or ride out bravely to confront the visitors. He did not doubt they belonged to the race of men, because they had the shape and form of all people who walked upright on the earth. As they moved along, they looked from side to side, surveying the terrain to the west walled by a mountain range that had sheltered his people since Coyote had killed all the monsters to make the land habitable for the Salish. They were not men of any tribe Rides-the-Wind had ever seen before. They were not Nimiipuu people, the great horsemen who lived to the west; nor were they of the Niitsitapi tribe who terrorized the eastern plains and who some called Blackfeet because the soles of their moccasins were blackened. Whether they came as friend or foe, he did not know; whether a hunting or war party, he could not determine. Taken together, they appeared lost, as if they did not know where they were going. Or why did their heads turn in every direction as they moved? He surmised they had entered the valley and descended from the peaks that safeguarded the camp's eastern side. As the party drew closer, he nudged his horse around and rode back toward the Salish encamped a few miles south along the river. He rapidly dismounted and ordered that their herd of horses be led to graze in a well-hidden forest clearing.

Chief Three Eagles, hearing the commotion, emerged from the central teepee in the ring of teepees and asked Rides-the-Wind, "What did you see?"

"A war party advances from the north. They are not a great number, but we must prepare to meet them. Mount up, and we will ride there to face them." Not hesitating, Chief Three Eagles, the second sub-chief Woodcock, and several other braves leaped on their horses. Warily, they trotted toward the strange travelers now in view, determined to discover if they came in war or peace. Drawing ever closer, the Salish exclaimed, "What strange clothes!"

"They are cold. Look at their pink faces," Woodcock said.

"They must be mourning. Their hair is short," Rides-the-Wind added.

But all the Salish fastened their gaze simultaneously upon one creature who stood out in the group. They stared wide-eyed at the tall man with charcoal smeared over his face, his neck, and hands. A few yards from the party, the two men they presumed were leaders, dismounted. One had hair the color of the red stone; the other leader's hair, cut shorter, was the light brown of a bird's nest. None of the men had the dark black hair of their people. Who were these people who fearlessly approached, seemingly in friendly greeting? Chief Three Eagles decided for the moment to consider them harmless until proven different. If they showed themselves hostile, the Salish outnumbered them. The chiefs followed suit and strode toward the strange men who walked toward them with their hands upraised in greeting. Their pallid expressions and short hair made Three Eagles believe they had been attacked and defeated in war. Members of their party must have been killed, and they mourned their loss. Maybe the black-faced man had painted his face to prove he had been the bravest in combat. Maybe they had met the Nittsitapi or Blackfeet, fierce warriors on the east side of the mountains, who, unlike his people, possessed fire sticks.

He spied a woman with an infant in a cradleboard strapped to her back, which made him think this certainly could not be a hostile party because they would not have brought a woman and child along. She stepped forward, and he recognized her as Shoshone, a friendly tribe. The woman, shorter than the two leaders, approached from the rear of the group and began to use sign language that confirmed his belief that there was no cause for fear. The leaders extended their hands to indicate that they came in peace; they came in search of a trail over the mountains to the sea. The chief shook their hands in greeting. None of the strangers knew the Salish language, and the Salish did not know the Shoshone speech. Amid several attempts to communicate in different tongues, Woodcock moved toward the black man and tried to remove the charcoal from his face with his fingers. Startled, he examined his fingertips and muttered, "The sun has burned his skin black."

The brown-haired leader turned to Woodcock and said something unintelligible. The Shoshone woman pointed to the black man and attempted to explain the phenomenon, but Woodcock did not understand. Salish of the western bands had told them they had seen pale faces before, but no one had ever told them stories of black faces.

Then Chief Three Eagles spoke to his people, "We will bring them to our village and do them no harm while we discover what they are about." He then invited them to his camp in his own tongue and signed the message to the Shoshone woman, who in turn conveyed the invitation to the strangers in sign language.

When they arrived at the village, the strangers unpacked their horses, spread their gear on the ground, and camped outside the circle of teepees. Soon after, around twenty other white men approached, apparently having split up to search the valley for rivers that might provide access over the mountains. They had additional run-down ponies that carried their supplies and one mule. Three Eagles motioned for the two leaders to enter his teepee. The Shoshone woman also joined the circle of men around the center fire. The chief proceeded to light the pipe and pass it around. The *suyapi* on his right smoked first, then Rides-the-Wind, the sub-chiefs, and other principal men of the village, ending with the red-headed *suyapi* who sat on the left of Three Eagles. They began calling them *suyapi*, meaning upside-down people, because they had hair at the bottom of their heads, or beards. Both *suyapi* were taller than most of the men of the tribe, but were as rugged and well-muscled as his people. Although he did not fear them, Three Eagles was cautious and wary of their purpose. Who were they? Where did they come from? Why did they enter their hunting grounds? He began to question them. He was curious about why they brought the blue jay, the name the Salish applied to a man who painted his skin black in preparation for the war dance. Clearly, this black man was a brave warrior and meant to dance for his victory in battle. He wondered when the black man would dance.

The red-haired *suyapi* may have been the lesser chief, because he spoke less than his companion. Three Eagles directed his questions at the other leader with the short, light-brown hair seated on his right. A Shoshone boy who lived with them—an orphan recently adopted into their tribe—attempted to translate from Shoshone into the Salish language, although he had yet imperfectly learned their tongue. The boy's efforts met with more confusion and consternation, although Three Eagles was persuaded that these peculiar creatures meant them no harm, and he would provide the hospitality that travelers to their camp deserved.

"Why do you bring the blue jay with you?" Three Eagles asked.

Every attempt to communicate failed. Neither party understood what the other meant. The custom of gift-giving between host and guest was the only meeting point. Even then, misunderstandings occurred over the exact meaning of the gifts. Three Eagles gave the *suyapi* buffalo robes, dried meat, and camas cakes made from the mashed bulbs of the plant. At first, the white men flung the robes across their shoulders and refused to sit upon them. They did not eat the food the women offered them.

Woodcock suggested, "They think it is the bark of trees."

Rides-the-Wind said, "That cannot be the case. They must have eaten the pemmican of other tribes on the way to our land."

"It is rude," said Three Eagles. "I do not know why they should behave so. We took their necklaces and flags." He pointed to the medallion with the profile of an unknown man pressed upon the bronze surface.

Through the sign for horses, the Shoshone woman made them understand that the *suyapi* needed many horses to continue their journey. They had lost most of their horses and only had a few weary ponies and the two mounts for the leaders.

"I will give them thirteen to help them cross the mountains," the chief promised.

The white men rested for three days. The Indians brought forth thirteen horses—elegant steeds. There were several appaloosas in the bunch that the Salish had obtained from their friends, the Nimiipuu, with whom they frequently combined in hunting trips for buffalo on the edge of the plains. In fact, they were waiting at the southern tip of the valley for some of their band to join with their people for the seasonal hunt to the eastern plains. Other Salish bands from the other side of the mountains to the northwest would also be joining them. Many hands were needed to butcher and process the meat before it spoiled.

As the sickly, ashen-faced strangers prepared to leave, the black man they called blue jay brought the seven tired ponies forward and handed their lead ropes to the Indians who stood around, watching the white men pack up. The Shoshone woman signed that the animals were in trade for what the Salish had given them.

Chief Three Eagles jutted out his jaw. "We do not trade. The earth gives what we need. We have enough. We keep only what we need."

No one could translate this for the *suyapi*. Even if someone had the language skills, the chief wondered if they would have understood. He shook his head; their behavior was so inexplicable. In silence, he watched them pack up and head north up the valley. For what, he still did not know. He did not know why they did not take the robes with them. He still did not understand why they did not wear them around their shoulders. They would need them when they crossed the mountains. Already, in early fall, there had been snow flurries. Soon the mountain tops would be robed in white. Soon snow would be blowing in the passes, so thick a man could not see beyond his nose. He hoped that the Shoshone scout could help them. He hoped they would find what they were looking for. For their safe passage, he sent one of his scouts to lead them to the Lolo Pass, a well-traveled route west to the Nimiipuu people.

Rides-the-Wind, as confused as Chief Three Eagles about the strange behavior of their guests, felt uneasy in his bones. A cold west wind began to blow. He sniffed the air that smelled like early snow. The strangers would not have an easy time in the mountains. Woodcock stood shoulder-to-shoulder with Chief Three Eagles and gazed at the sky.

"May the Great Spirit bring us a good hunt. We leave to chase the buffalo. Their hides grow heavy with fur for the winter. Scouts have gone ahead to look for them at the foot of the eastern pass. We must get to the buffalo grounds before the Blackfeet reach there," Woodcock said.

"Ah, my brother, we have seen in the last seasons their hunters use the fire sticks the traders gave them. They will not be at the cliff where we drive the buffalo to their death," Rides-the-Wind responded.

"Maybe not, but they want to drive us to our death. They do not want to share the buffalo."

"The herds are smaller because they trade hides for guns, blankets, tools, and trinkets from these strangers." Rides-the-Wind walked to his teepee, which was constructed of tule reeds that were bound together in square mats and then attached to the lodgepole conical frame. The women had already taken down these summer teepees, burned the tule, and put up the warmer winter teepees covered with buffalo hides. When they left on the hunt, his wife would burn their teepee. He undid the flap, bent, and entered through the opening. His fifteen-year-old son, Lone Wolf, was fastening the freshly sharpened flint arrowheads with sinew to willow shafts. He would join the men on the hunt. His mother, Sweet Grass, sat next to him, sewing shells on a buckskin shirt. Born the season when they camped on the Great Plains during the buffalo hunt many moons ago before the Blackfeet came to dominate the region, she was named for the abundant grass that grew there.

The men continued their conversation. The boy listened attentively to what his elders thought about the guests who had just left.

"The time of the fulfillment of my great-great-grandfather's words dawns," Woodcock pronounced solemnly. Rides-the-Wind and Lone Wolf knew what he referred to. Everyone had heard the story around the winter campfires since they were old enough to understand speech. Woodcock was descended from the honored and beloved Shining Shirt, the great prophet who died before the first horse appeared in the valley. Shining Shirt had emerged from a vision quest with astounding revelations and had not said when his predictions would come true. In the generations since the prophet's passing, the cycle of the seasons had progressed in their predictable round of tasks—births and deaths, hunting and gathering the fruits of the earth, singing and dancing.

"Shining Shirt said that we would not always live the same, that our lives would change. When—he did not know—but we must look for the arrival of men with fair skins who wear black robes. These men will be known as Black Robes and will give us new names and new prayers. In his vision, he was given a sacred sign, a rock with a cross scratched on it. He always signed us with the power of this metal whenever he went into battle or ventured on the hunt. He prayed to a god he called He-Who-Lives-on-High. That God made us, the trees, plants, rivers, and mountains. An evil being we must avoid also prowls the earth. Whoever does evil will end up in his land beneath the trees. Shining Shirt was a powerful medicine man. The Black Robes will teach new ways of doing things. He said we should not shed blood. In time, the country would be overrun with white men, but we must not harm them, but welcome them and try to learn their teachings." Woodcock sighed. "I believe Shining Shirt's vision. These men we just met are the advance scouts. I do not know how soon the Black Robes will arrive, but my great-great-grandfather's vision is true."

"True that Shining Shirt was believed and respected," Rides-the-Wind added. "His power was great, and we have not forgotten him. The pale faces are few. We must watch if others come. No matter, we are keepers of this earth."

"Maybe they will perish in the mountains and not be seen ever again," Woodcock said.

"I felt a foul wind blow when they entered our camp. It did not go until they left. I fear it was the evil one from the land under the trees," Rides-the-Wind said.

"The Nimiipuu say they have seen other white men who look for beaver. Do you believe they will reach the great water they seek that the Shoshone woman made known through signs?" Woodcock asked.

"We know of the great water, but none of us have journeyed that far. We are happy in our hidden valley. It has everything we need. The white men search and never find happiness. This is what I believe. They cannot bring us happiness," Rides-the-Wind affirmed, defiance in his tone. "I am glad they only stayed three days and departed."

Lone Wolf's heart constricted at his elders' words. He did not want life to change. He had listened to tales of Shining Shirt's visions many times. He knew the name of the evil one who lived underground was Emtep and believed that anyone who did evil would join him. Until the Black Robes came to tell them of the true name of God who lives in the sky, they should pray to Amotkan, who is found above the earth. Although Shining Shirt had taught his people not to fear, Lone Wolf sensed future danger. Usually, he felt strong and safe in communion with his family and every member of the tribe. During his recent initiation rites into manhood, he had experienced his first vision quest and had returned to the village in possession of an ancient knowledge that gave him access to a spiritual realm. Fasting and praying in the cedar forest glen had brought forth his spirit guide, the lone wolf that stood before him between two trees, head slightly bent, its slanted eyes peering at him unafraid. Lone Wolf smiled, and fixed his gaze upon the alpha male for a long time. The wolf did not flinch; neither man nor beast moved. The wolf seemed to smile back at him, then slowly and gracefully turn and lope into the screen of trees. He had not been afraid of the wolf. Why should fear flash through him? He was a man now, prepared to accompany the men on the fall hunt.

While Rides-the-Wind and Woodcock talked, Sweet Grass crooned her sewing song, but Lone Wolf knew she had taken in every word the men had spoken. His mother, a woman of few words, was recognized for the fine garments she made. In early spring, she dug for bitterroot bulbs in mountain meadows. Later, with the other women of the village, she prodded the earth with digging sticks to harvest baskets of camas roots. The peels of the bulbs had to be removed before the bulbs were cooked for a long time in pits of hot stones until they lost their bitterness. Finally, they were mashed and patted into tasty cakes. In summer, the round of berry picking ensued in regular order as each variety of berry ripened—chokecherries, elderberries, serviceberries, huckleberries. Her hands were always occupied, a smile always on her caramel-colored face and ever-singing at her task. He would seek a cheerful worker like Sweet Grass to be his wife.

Some of the people would remain behind here at Big Clear Place, their winter camp, while hunters and the women skilled in butchering, skinning, and drying the meat made the seven-day trek over the eastern range to meet where the prairie met the foot of the mountain. Every abled-body man, woman, and child was needed in these tasks. The women loaded the equipment for the hunt on travois, which on the return trip would serve to carry hides, skulls, hooves, bone, and meat back to the Waters of the Red Osier Dogwoods, the long valley where they would camp at the confluence of the smaller water with the larger river that flowed north through the extent of the valley. There were two main passes over the eastern range where the buffalo grazed. One was at the southern end of the valley where they were camped. The trail dropped down and bent around a high peak following the Waters of the Pocket Valley and then led north to the open plains. The other was farther north, where the confluence of two big rivers met at the Place of the Big Bull Trout, then over a less treacherous pass to the Place of the Small Bull Trout, which opened onto the sweeping prairie. Proceeding west to the prairie for a while, they veered north to the buffalo jump. Three Eagles said they would take the northern route and then west over the wider pass. Judging by the weather and what he believed would be an early snow, that was the wiser way.

 The last of the bands they had been waiting for arrived in the camp to join the hunt. The whole village now readied for the hunters' departure. The women disassembled teepees that would shelter them on the prairie during the hunt. Every season, fresh hides were cured to make new teepees because the old hides were too worn for protection against the elements. They packed enough pemmican for the journey along with implements for removal of the hide, stripping the meat into slices to smoke, and scraping the bones clean. Parfleches to hold the meat and sturdy bark baskets were added to the supplies. Before their departure, the village gathered to bestow good luck with hunting songs and dances. Then the hunting party, both men and women, mounted horses. A string of extra horses trailed behind them.

Lone Wolf chose his best horse, a buckskin, to ride proudly behind the leaders, his father ahead of him on a white horse, and the chief on his favorite appaloosa. The river rippled along the trail they followed over the mountains, sometimes disappearing in a canyon and then re-emerging around a bend. The pastureland for the horses was plentiful for the horses at night when they camped along the riverbank. Fortunately, they encountered no snow in the pass, and at the higher elevations, only patches from the flurry the white men's expedition must have experienced when they crossed the mountains. They hoped the mild weather would hold for the duration of the hunt, but they could not count on it. The Salish knew how to read the weather well, the clouds and sky. They could interpret the odors in the air, the slightest movement in the wind or change in light. The Great Spirit, whose power they invoked, would grant them a speedy and successful hunt, although increasingly, that fortune had occurred with less frequency, and the scouts had to look longer for the diminished herds. The Blackfeet had impinged on their traditional hunting grounds, fierce competitors for the game. More ominous were their weapons. The Blackfeet did not have to track the buffalo and stampede them over a cliff or sneak up on them disguised as buffalo calves to spear them at close range like in the olden days. Today they did not have to be at close range to kill them with bow and arrow or lance, but could shoot them from a distance without dismounting from their horses. The Salish knew that the Blackfeet had obtained their deadly weapons from white fur traders. They knew they sold the buffalo hides for the fire sticks. Chief Three Eagles was adamant about not trading hides to the white men, but he did not know how he could obtain the guns without doing that. For the present, the Salish people thanked the Great Spirit for the gift of the horse. Since acquiring the horse, they had learned to use the fleetest horses to outrun the buffalo along with the horses that were unafraid to approach the big animal at close range. Bending low, they loosed arrows in quick succession from their bows straight into its lung on the buffalo's right side. After an arrow pierced the exact fatal spot in the lung, the buffalo ran a short distance and collapsed. Other times they might steer the herd on horseback and stampede them over a cliff as they did before the coming of the horse. Other times, they corralled them into a fenced-in area. The scouts were now able to cover long distances tracking the animals and then cornering them for the kill. Each hunter needed five extra horses, fearless and fresh, to pursue and kill the buffalo over the course of a few days. But the herds were becoming scarcer and harder to find with each passing season. Were the Blackfeet killing too many of them for the traders? Were the white men taking more than they needed because of their great greed?

Lone Wolf had listened to the elders tell of their great-great-grandfathers' time when Shoshones appeared at the outskirts of the village mounted on horses. They stayed in the village many moons and showed them how to train and care for these huge dogs. They taught them to ride the horses. The grandfathers marveled at the wonders the Shoshone performed. Quick learners, they implored the

Shoshone to bring them more horses. The Shoshone obliged, saying they had thousands and knew how to breed them to increase their numbers. They taught the Salish everything they knew about horses. Old Chief Red-tailed Hawk, at the time of their coming, had asked how the Shoshone men obtained the horses and where the animals came from. The Shoshone answered that a desert tribe far to the south had traded with them. The Shoshone had also brought horses to the Nimiipuu. The Salish admired the prized spotted horses of the Nimiipuu, who had also mastered the breeding method. Their appaloosas were greatly coveted, and the Salish made certain to barter for these animals. Chief Three Eagles was inordinately proud of the appaloosa he had obtained from this tribe of skilled horsemen who inhabited the region west of the Red-topped Peaks. Since the arrival of the horse, it had become common as well for tribes to steal horses from other neighboring tribes. Stealthily, they crept into an encampment, cut the hobbles, and led the horses away on moonless nights.

 Lone Wolf thought of all these things as he trailed behind his father through the pass to the plains, his confidence enlarged with the accomplishments of the men who had lived before him. From a very young, the boys were trained to handle the horses and ride them without spurs or saddles, controlling them merely with a click of the tongue or a nudge of the foot, keeping their hands free to wield bow and arrow or spear. Practice with the bow and arrow hunting small animals began soon after they could walk and talk. Lone Wolf would comport himself well on this buffalo hunt.

On the afternoon of the seventh day, they topped a promontory and paused to survey the grasslands that stretched as far as the eye could see into the distance. Lone Wolf reined his horse parallel to his father's mount.

"Four more days of riding, and we reach the hunting grounds," Rides-the-Wind said to his son. "The weather holds good."

Lone Wolf had gone on other hunts to help with the care of horses and setting up camp. This hunt was special because he would prove himself as a marksman. He was confident of his horsemanship as well, for was he not the son of Rides-the-Wind, recognized as the best horseman among all the Salish bands? His father had taught him all his skills to ride and shoot on horseback. Father and son possessed the fastest horses. For these reasons, they were expected to pursue and kill sufficient buffalo. Lone Wolfe's anticipation grew as the party moved to descend toward the plain. He felt the full weight of his responsibility to his people. A few days more and they would meet the scouts who had gone ahead at the designated camp known as White-Colored Waters.

Their sure-footed horses descended the slope and reached the scouts' camp the afternoon of the fourth day. Cheerful greetings were exchanged. Two hundred buffalo had been sighted a few hours' ride to the northeast. With luck, they could overtake them, looping around in the direction they were heading. Some of them could drive them over the buffalo jump while others could spear them on horseback, assuring them of a sufficient game. Lone Wolf's father, the acknowledged rider and marksman, naturally was to pursue the herd on horseback while another group veered into the herd, cutting into them from two sides to force them into a stampede that angled them toward the cliff. The plan was perfect. Either way, they would kill enough buffalo to meet their needs. While the men rode off to their assigned duties, the women began to erect racks for drying the meat. They assembled the scrapers and bone tools they needed for butchering the carcasses. Everyone was excited and ready for the communal work, the countless days of processing the meat.

Lone Wolf, in high spirits, mounted his buckskin and trotted after his father and Three Eagles. His chosen weapon was the bow and arrow. Strapped to his side by a leather thong, hung his quiver to which he had attached a red-tailed hawk feather. A finely sharpened lance sat upright in its rawhide sheathe on his horse's withers, which he would use later to finish off any downed animal. Through the grass, they trotted over knolls presenting broad views, following the trampled trail and tracks the buffalo left. Ascending a rise, they spotted the herd grazing in a bowl formed by the surrounding hills.

"Ready?" Three Eagles glanced at Rides-the-Wind, who nodded. With a kick to his white stallion, Rides-the-Wind whooped and galloped at breakneck speed toward the nearest animal. He gripped his bow as he careened toward his target. Three Eagles, not far behind, rushed toward a buffalo that stood apart from the main body, thinking he could easily outrun the laggard. Within moments, the buffalo realized the danger of his isolation and bounded forward to rejoin his brothers.

Lone Wolf raced into the herd, at first not identifying his target. There were just too many, but at the first opportunity, he would take a sure shot at the closest animal. He did not intend to miss; he must be certain that he could aim well and accurately to strike at the fatal spot. Flanking the herd, he scanned the stampeding herd to carefully select the most vulnerable animal. Then he spotted the cow, a good-sized one with a calf desperately trying to keep up with its mother in flight. The cow would provide the choice meat. He was only ten horse-lengths behind her. With a lash to his horse's flank, he gained on the cow and pointed his drawn bow squarely at her chest. He could not be mistaken in his aim. He leaned sideways over the horse's shoulders while his thighs and shins ably hugged its flanks. Exactly parallel to the lung spot, he powerfully released his arrow into the animal. The shaft was halfway exposed. He reined in his mount, and the tail end of the herd thundered past him. He turned to watch the cow slow and collapse a short distance in the rear. The dust settled around him, and he trotted to the fallen cow. He dismounted and pulled his arrow from the animal. With uplifted hands, he praised the Great Spirit, and then with bowed head, he thanked the animal for giving up its life to feed his people. He saw a group of women and children running toward him, scalpels in hand. The work now began to butcher and quarter all the animals. Wind River and Three Eagles added four animals to the slain that day, each killing two more buffalo. And this was only the first day.

  Rides-the-Wind congratulated his son on his kill. Lone Wolf knew what to do next; his father's gaze told him to proceed. He had witnessed the ritual performed many times before. Now it was his turn to enact it. His chest swelled. He unsheathed his knife. The women knelt beside the buffalo, four clutching the legs while two other women sliced open the body from throat to anus and cut through the sinew and organ linings. Then Lone Wolf took his knife, cut the vessels to the heart, and extracted the heart from its cavity. He held the bloody mass in his hands, lifted it to the sky, again thanked the animal for the sacrifice of its life, pressed the heart to his mouth, took the first bite, and then each man and woman ate of the organ. Next, the women cut out the tongue, a prized delicacy, thanked the Great Spirit, and handed it to the men.

It had been a successful day. The women chattered happily about the other hunting party that had driven the buffalo over the cliff. Eighty carcasses to skin and butcher lay at the base of the cliff, which they called Deep Blood Kettle. Added to the twenty slain by the hunters on horseback, the hunt had secured a hundred carcasses to process.

Inevitably there was some waste because they could take only what they could carry back. They did their best to save every part of the dead animals. In some ways, killing the animal was the easier part; more difficult was the work after the slaughter. Now it began in earnest. All hands joined in every phase of the task. Their haul of buffalo, although less than in former days, did not produce a surplus of hides, but was enough to meet their needs for food, shelter, and clothing for at least a year. The grueling work took days, but it was made less arduous by singing together. Each phase of the operation required communal effort. Lone Wolf did not stand idly by but joined in the butchering and spread the larger cuts of meat for the women to strip into smaller pieces, which they hung on the racks to dry. Bones were scraped, and sinews were saved for use in countless ways, sewing, bowstrings, lashings, and ties of every sort. Brains possessed essential properties for tanning. Fat was meticulously preserved to mix in with ground meat to make pemmican. The hooves and horns were saved for rattles and headdresses. Scouts kept watch on ridges and patrolled the perimeters of the camp for unfriendly tribes who might try to rob them of their goods. There would be time for rest and celebration upon their return to the village at the other side of the mountains.

Finally, the labor completed, the Salish prepared to decamp. Lone Wolf helped bind the bundles of hides and then secure them to the packhorses. The women loaded the travois with bones and parfleches of meat. Younger children sat upon the laden travois. With luck, they would not encounter heavy snow on the return journey. If they did, they knew what to do. Pitch their teepees and huddle in them until the snow stopped. Lone Wolf rode beside his father, tall upon his mount,

"Son, you did well on the hunt. You will join the men in the dancing. The Great Spirit has blessed us. We must give thanks."

Lone Wolf felt pride grow in his breast. Strength flowed through every muscle of his body. He gazed at the tallest peaks, snow already capping them. He inhaled the rich aroma of the pines and heard the chatter of squirrels, the drop of cones from the limbs, and the small creatures skittering to recover them for their winter nests. All the animals were preparing their dens and nests for winter, as were the people, those the Great Spirit had appointed keepers of the earth.

Just then, an eagle soared high above the treetops, swooped and circled, glorying in the grace and power of its flight. Father and son watched its flight, sharing in the eagle's beauty, and they did not need to say anything. Silence was the best acclamation and appreciation of what the Great Spirit had granted the bird. Only the clop-clop of the horse's hooves on pebbles broke the reverent silence. Rubble broken from a cliff was scattered on the trail. The horses with travois had to skirt the area with the fallen rock. Travel was not easy in the mountains with travois, but the Salish had discovered less difficult trails over the mountains.

Unexpectedly, Rides-the-Wind mentioned the strange seekers of the sea they had encountered before they left on the hunt.

"I do not wish to see the pale faces come again. I feel a chill in my bones when I think of them, and dreams have come to me that I will not see the last of them."

Worried, Lone Wolf looked at his father. He knew him as fearless. How could his father fear anything? He was a tamer of horses; he was the rider with the wind. No furious wind could blow him off his horse.

"I did not like them either, Father. Do you believe the tales Shining Shirt told like the other elders do?"

"He was a great medicine man. His tongue was straight. I do not wish to believe his visions, but I do because he was honest and true, brave, and just in all his words and deeds. That is what has come down to us through the generations. We trust our grandfathers and their fathers and the fathers before them."

Lone Wolf knew he trusted his father. His words disturbed him, but he resolved to watch and learn of his elders. He would be ever-vigilant. His strength would not elude him because the power of the wolf coursed through his body. Endowed with the wolf's wariness and keen eyesight, he would be able to guard and defend his people.

Lone Wolf and Rides-the-Wind trained their eyes on the landscape ahead, their horses proceeding at a gentle trot.

Suddenly, as they rounded a bend in the trail thick with pine on both sides, six Niitsitapi warriors leaped from the undergrowth, stripes of red and black paint smeared across their cheekbones, whooping and firing their guns. The women and children scrambled behind rocks and bushes, and the men jumped from their horses to combat their attackers. Foolishly, their enemies thought their fire sticks gave them the advantage, and they would quickly have the Salish hunters fleeing in disarray, but they fiercely engaged the six Niitsitapi, aiming for their throats and hearts with drawn knives. They were out of bullets and could not reload. The blows of the Salish knocked two of them to the ground, and the four others turned tail and ran into the forest. But the war party had done its cruel damage. The lead scout, Black Bull, lay in the middle of the trail, blood seeping from his mouth. Everything happened so fast that Lone Wolf could not take it all in at once. He had witnessed his first ambush, and there had been no time for him to prove himself in a fight. It was all over before he could strike one blow in defense of his people. The women immediately took up a wail.

"This will not go unavenged." Chief Three Eagles swore. "If they come again into our land, we will capture and torture one of the Niitsitapi. They have their land, and we have ours."

Two of the other Salish men had flesh wounds in their arms. The women applied healing poultices to their injuries. Black Bull's body was borne upon his horse to where they found a place to bury him in a mountain meadow. No marker was placed. He belonged to the sky.

The band left his spirit to walk the skies, although his body was buried in the earth.

The band sadly continued westward, the sun a golden blaze in its descent behind the peaks. They found a spot along the river to camp for the night. Much of Lone Wolf's glory in the successful hunt paled as he stared into the campfire that night. A brave man had gone to the spirit world where all must journey one day. If one must die, it is good to die bravely. Yet Lone Wolf prayed to live a long life, to grow old, and to go off to fall asleep beneath a great tree in the forest. No one had words that night. No one wanted to tell stories. Only the shaman came forward and began a death song for Black Bull in the firelight while the people sat around in somber silence. He sang:

*Over our head; Under our feet.*
*We weep. We weep.*
*Where is our brother?*
*Where is our brother?*
*Over our head; Under our feet.*
*Ah Eee Ah Eee. Ah Eee.*

The plaintive syllables repeated; sounds of grief and of faith that the fallen warrior would follow in the footsteps of his forefathers into the spirit world that surrounded the living and encompassed the dead.

After seven sunrises and sunsets they descended into their home valley and reached the river running north to south through it. A few men checking their willow traps for fish spotted them first and quickly spread the news to the rest of the village downstream. The Salish kinsmen came out to greet them, rejoicing at their safe return and eagerly inquiring about the hunt. The bundles on the packhorses told them all they needed to know. Embraces were exchanged all around, and they escorted the hunting party back to the circle of teepees. Sweet Grass, who had stayed behind, leaped up from where she had been weaving a basket. She joined the others who were already unloading the harvest of buffalo.

That evening they celebrated the homecoming around the blazing fire, the hearts of every man, woman, and child gladdened with their return and the bounty they brought. The men leaped to their feet to dance in mimicry of the flames. Rattles made of antlers and skin drums accompanied their rhythmic movements. Woodcock, wearing a bison headdress, emerged from the circle of men to lead the dance, while voices rose in sing-song fashion to chant the praise of the hunt.

>  *Beat with feet like the buffalo.*
>  *Now with cries.*
>  *Now with hooves.*
>  *Trample the earth.*
>  *With curved horns.*

Over and over, the words were chanted until the men receded and resumed their seats around the fire to make room for the women and young girls to rise and sing their dance of thanksgiving.

>  *Above beauty.*
>  *All around beauty.*
>  *The earth gives bounty.*
>  *Daughters give thanks.*
>  *Above beauty.*
>  *All around beauty.*
>  *The earth gives bounty.*
>  *Daughters sing always.*

The drums and rattles continued as they spread their arms, the buckskin tassels on the sleeves of their dresses sweeping the ground and then swooping up like the eagle's outspread wings. Among the dancing women, Lone Wolf watched a girl about his own age, taller than some of the adult women, and lithe like an otter sliding in and out of the line of dancers, her long braids flapping from side to side. Her lips were shaped like the petals of a delicate flower, her arms slim, and her nimble feet in high boots of tanned deerskin. Her nose was finely shaped, neither too fat nor too wide, and her face bore the sheen of sun on clear waters. The women's joyful dance ended, and all were comfortably settled around the fire again. Then, stories from the heart enlivened the rest of the night, with warriors boasting of their bravery and equestrian feats as they flung spears into the sides of stampeding bulls. Laughter rippled through the group. Close calls with raging buffalo were relived. Mishaps were made light of, regaling the tribe. Everyone stayed up late, far past the time the moon had receded beyond the western peaks. The children finally fell to sleep, their heads on their mothers' laps. The littlest ones were lifted and carried into the lodges where their mothers tucked them under fur blankets.

 The men lingered around the campfire a bit longer. In the flickering firelight, Lone Wolf eyed White Heron seated across from him. She had not followed the other women to bed. He tried not to stare, but he could not help turning his gaze toward her ever since she had stopped dancing and resumed her place around the campfire. During the evening, she had not spoken a word but had listened intently to all the tales that were told. He could not resist bragging about his own feat, purposely regarding her reaction. She had the manner of a gentle bird, the modesty and possession that his own mother, Sweet Grass, possessed, a woman who would not bedevil a man with a carping tongue. He hoped she was suitably impressed with his valor and could only hope that he was not mistaken about the admiration he detected in her doe-like burnished brown eyes. He could not be mistaken once their eyes had met. Embarrassed, she quickly looked down at her lap. This could not be mistaken for disinterest on her part. Yes, she was attracted to him. She did like him. He did not misinterpret her liking. He must tread lightly and search out her inclinations. In the daylight, he would reveal his intentions.

White Heron yawned and covered her mouth so that she gave no audible sound. Quietly, she rose to go to her family's lodge. Lone Wolf followed her movement away as her form became just a slim dark shadow. Tomorrow, he would seek her.

But could he capture the heart of Woodcock's daughter? He treasured his daughter, and he would be certain to place her price high, of course. But Lone Wolf had something to offer in fair exchange. He was the son of a sub-chief and a valued horseman. Of the five hundred head of horses the Salish held, his father had trained most of them and claimed as his own fifty of the finest. Rides-the-Wind would make it happen.

The festivities broke up; the older men gathered their instruments, robes, and other belongings and retired to their beds. Lone Wolf followed his father into their teepee. Nestling under his bearskin blanket, he fell asleep dreaming of a Salish maiden with lustrous black braids who stood in the marsh among a flock of white herons.

**Lone Wolf**

By day there were no idle hands in the camp. While the light lasted, every man, woman, and child old enough to help was making and doing, especially in the winter when clothes had to be sewn, lodges repaired, and food stored for the cold season. Bows were made of willow and flint sharpened for arrows and tools. Lone Wolf helped his father with the care and the pasturage of the horses. They braided rope from the fiber of plants and animal sinews. The women fashioned rawhide into various items—moccasins, leggings, trappings for the horses, parfleches, and pouches. As soon as the first rays of light penetrated the opening at the top of the teepee, the women rose, stirred the embers in the firepit, and the chores began. Gathering firewood was a major task for the women.

    Lone Wolf accompanied his father to the grove where the horses were sequestered. Tending to the horses was their first task of the morning. They devoted attention today to a two-year-old colt. By degrees, a bond was being built between the horse and man. Rides-the-Wind slowly approached the bay with black mane and began to sing. Since he was three years old, Lone Wolf had observed his father's method of gentling a horse. Rides-the-Wind walked around the colt. His song asked for the horse to walk with him in beauty and harmony. Somehow the singing soothed the animal and dissolved any fear he had of the man. Sometimes his father came closer to the animal and stroked its side from neck to rump, and then he backed away and resumed his song. Again, his father walked in a wide circle around the colt. The fearlessness of the man transferred to the colt. If his father changed direction, the horse also changed direction. Lone Wolf saw the results of this procedure. Trust was built over time by his father's imitation of horse behavior, particularly in the use of his legs. His father approached the flank of the horse and, with a deft movement, playfully curled his lower leg around the horse's foot in the way one horse would kick another horse. The colt did not take offense, but let the man wind his limbs around his hind legs. After these affectionate gestures, Rides-the-Wind resumed his relaxed walk-around, singing soothingly and with confidence that a friendly relationship had been established between horse and man. This continued for a while until the magic moment occurred, when the colt followed behind the man, turning when he did, stopping when he did, attuned to his direction and command. Rides-the-Wind let this follow-the-leader game go on for some time. Now he thought the moment right, and he again approached the colt and slung a foot over the back of the horse, but not fully mounting. That would come when the horse could bear the full weight of a man. His two feet implanted on the ground, Rides-the-Wind, stroked the nose of the animal. He placed his nose against the horse's flesh, inhaling its spirit. Next, he held the colt's muzzle and exhaled his breath. Lone Wolf, who had witnessed this ritual from early childhood, knew this represented a spiritual bond between rider and mount that could not be broken.

Rides-the-Wind signaled to Lone Wolf to draw out another colt and do the same things while he stood aside and watched. This one was a dappled gray. Lone Wolf had worked him before and confidently pursued the technique he had learned well from his father. It was important not to startle the animal, to do everything slowly and deftly, and to let the animal see where the man was. In that way, they would become as one later when the man rode him. In another year, he would mount the horse and ride bareback, guiding him with his calves and heels, without saddle or bridle, clinging only if necessary to the horse's mane. Exquisite balance and symmetry were gained from a walk, to a trot, to a canter, to a lope, to a full gallop. By twelve years old, Lone Wolf had mastered every riding skill.

"Well done, my son," Rides-the-Wind praised him after the session. "In the spring, several mares will foal. You will be responsible for them."

Lone Wolf liked working with the horses. There was not a Salish who did not love the big dogs and thanked the Great Spirit for them. So indispensable, so valuable, and so beloved to the people in every phase of their life. Lone Wolf also loved the solitude of the forest-covered mountains, the beauty above and around, and the marvel of each forest creature, beaver, otter, blue jay, and bear that talked to him without words. He realized words were powerful too—simple words—like the words in their songs. A few words said much. That is how the Salish spoke.

"Come, let us return to the camp and taste what Sweet Grass has prepared for us now that we have seen the horses fed and watered."

"I will follow a little later. I want to gather some branches for a bow," Lone Wolf said.

"As you will." His father left him in the grove by the riverside.

Lone Wolf had clear intentions for wishing to linger. Not far upstream, he knew where White Heron would be collecting dried driftwood on the sandy banks. With luck, he would find her alone with a bundle of kindling because the women and girls often separated to search for wood at different locations. He walked quite a distance, scanning the area in hopes of catching a glimpse of her. He had studied her habits for a long time to increase the chances of finding her alone. This could be the day he could talk to her privately and empty his heart. He almost despaired of seeing her when suddenly, like a bedded doe's head popping up in a field of tall grass, he sighted the figure of a girl emerge from behind a bush. It was White Heron! She did not see him. He rushed toward her. Hearing the rustle of his feet through the grass, she turned her head and recognized him. She smiled shyly as he slid to a stop beside her.

"Here, let me carry that bundle for you. I will help you gather the wood."

"No, it is women's work. I am almost done."

"Two can carry more."

She let him help. There were several pieces of dry wood nearby. She set her bundle down to pick up the wood. Lone Wolf seized the bundle into his arms and let her retrieve the wood. As she placed three more branches on the bundle, she avoided looking into his tender eyes.

"That's enough," she said.

"White Heron," he pleaded, "before we go back to the village, I must speak my heart."

She stopped in her tracks to listen but peered at her feet.

"Look into my eyes. You must know my feelings for you. Someday you will be my wife. That is what my heart says."

"We are too young to speak of those things," she said.

"But not forever. In a few seasons more I will take my place as a man among men in the council of the people. When I am called to take a wife, I will ask your father for you."

Then she giggled, which surprised Lone Wolf. Did she find his declaration funny? But then he also laughed. He realized it was a giggle of approval, of delight, and of pleasure. She was not displeased. A smile brightened his face, and they walked side by side to the village. He realized then that White Heron was as tall as he was. By the time they married, he believed he would have grown taller than her.

Trust makes peace and happiness possible, Lone Wolf thought, as the couple approached the camp. He felt a bond of trust growing between him and White Heron. Speak softly to the woman, do not startle her. His father used these methods to train the big dogs. Lone Wolf was happy as he handed the bundle to White Heron to separate before they entered the village. He must be about a man's business, and she must be about a woman's business. In that way, tongues would not wag if they saw him doing her work. No parting words were necessary. Understanding had been established.

Lone Wolf raised his eyes to the eastern peaks. A cold wind blew, swaying the topmost branches of the trees. The snow was coming. The bears had retreated to their dens. The rabbit's coat was changing from brown to white. Soon its fur would be completely white. The village was hunkering down for the winter. The women had prepared an abundance of camas and bitterroot. Plenty of jerky was stored, but the men would still hunt deer and elk over the winter. Their hides and antlers provided multiple uses, decorative and utilitarian, from clothes to tools, adornments, and musical instruments.

He was not wrong in his suppositions of imminent snowfall. The next morning a layer of snow blanketed the valley. The work of repairing weapons and implements continued while the women sewed and mended clothing. Baskets were woven, and bark buckets carved. Lone Wolf looked forward to the evenings when, snug in their lodges around the fire pit, the elders would tell stories of the beginning of times, of how people came to live in the valley after the ice melted and the monsters were slain. Many of these stories he had heard countless times, but they were always told with vocal expression and gestures to make them come alive. He loved the way the teller would change his pitch from high to low, depending on whose lines he was speaking. Lone Wolf listened, enthralled no less now than when he had first heard the tales. A great flood occurred that left the broad lake north of their valley. Coyote then roamed the land and transformed the gigantic creatures, the people-eaters, he had slain into the many rock formations that marked the Salish territory. Huge canyons, great rocks, rivers, and hot springs took shape, and smaller creatures replaced the monster animals. In this way, Coyote made the land habitable for the people. The Salish had dwelled here from the earth's creation and were entrusted with its keeping, the elders concluded. Lone Wolf believed with all his heart and with every sinew of his body that eventually he would be transformed into the earth from which his people originally arose. The glorious cycle of stories contained the history of the world and a spiritual geography embedded in his bones.

The cold season was also the perfect time for the festival during which the blue jay ritual was enacted. The shaman, Spirit Talker, was preparing right now for the ritual. At dawn he had traveled outside the village to a wooded outcropping that overlooked the valley from the west. There he built his sweat lodge of wattles and bark. In several days, he would return to the village to conduct the ceremony. Lone Wolf understood that the blue jay was the messenger from the afterlife. The shaman, in the guise of the blue jay, communicated with their dead ancestors. Nature slept in winter like the dead, but only on the surface, for even under the cold ground, new life stirred again, and in spring it would burst forth. The spirit of the ancestors inhabited the lakes and rocks of the land. Even in the dead of winter, their ghosts walked the earth. Yes, the dead were always with us. They surrounded us and gave us courage and hope that the land would sustain us through fat and lean times. These were the truths Lone Wolf held precious, as did every Salish who was ever born and died.

The day of the mid-winter festival arrived.

Along with the rest of the village, Lone Wolf expectedly waited at sunset for the ritual to begin. Every inhabitant crowded along the perimeter of the great circle where the ceremony would be performed. Spirit Talker, purified and spiritually prepared, leaped from the shadows into the center of the village. His face and limbs smeared with charcoal, he whooped and stomped, the deer-hoof rattles jangling around his ankles. In imitation of the blue jay, he stopped and flapped his arms like wings, then jumped and uttered wild gibberish, crazily bounding back and forth, even shimmying up a tree. Seated on a limb, he hooted and hollered. Spirit Talker, thoroughly possessed by blue jay, flew from his perch, landing solidly on his feet. Flapping his arms, he skittered toward the fire and flung his robe off his shoulders. Vigorously, he flailed the fire with the robe and smothered the flames, leaving smoldering embers. Then he ran into the trees, squawking his unintelligible chant while Lone Wolf, mesmerized, watched the ritual. He knew that the shaman, transformed into the blue jay, would jump from the woods without a moment's warning again. This time he reappeared to heal the sick of the village with his powerful medicine. Soon he burst forth from the darkness, less frenzied, and ducked into a lodge where a sick man lay. Minutes later he emerged to resume the blue jay dance, which continued for a while and ended when he climbed a tree, perched on a branch, and jumped to the ground to merge into the dark woods for the rest of the night. The ceremonial dance continued for several more nights during which the blue jay blessed the ceremonial food and issued messages from the dead that were considered prophecies. Spirit Talker ceased his gibberish and pronounced intelligible words that astonished Lone Wolf with the potency of the message. The words he knew would be forever emblazoned on his mind. They also momentarily stunned all the Salish, although they hoped his words would not happen during their lifetime or their children's lifetimes. Spirit Talker stood still and spread his arms wide and then raised them to the full moon that shone silvery white the last night of the ritual, and he intoned the dead ancestor's message.

"Shining Shirt has spoken to me. The Blue Jay Dance will be no more. More powerful medicine comes. Another dance will be danced. The dead will be many."

What did all this mean? Men shook their heads. Women shivered, and children clung to their mothers' sides. Spirit Talker exorcised their confusion as he began his restless movements around the center of the village, jumping and hopping from one spot to another. His dance became more frenzied. This was the point at which a second shaman, the wizened Big Cloud, came forward to subdue the spirit in Spirit Talker. The old shaman of weather-wrinkled face, with the help of two young braves, wrestled the blue jay dancer to the ground. Two warriors restrained him, one taking hold of his arms and the other pinning his ankles down while the shaman smudged him with cedar incense from head to foot. Soon Spirit Talker ceased his writhing, and the blue jay was seen to rise from his chest. No one saw this occur except the shaman, who exclaimed, his hand uplifted, "See the blue jay ascend into the night." Lone Wolf gazed in the direction the shaman pointed and thought he saw a swirl of smoke in the shape of a bird, likely an emanation from the smoking cedar sprig. In any case, Spirit Talker was restored to his senses. The men released their hold on him. He stood up and signaled the feast to begin. The sick felt better and joined everyone to partake of camas cakes and slices of roasted deer. As the villagers feasted, they forgot the blue jay dancer's prophecy, but it lingered on Lone Wolf's mind so that he could not completely savor the meal. It took days for the bitter taste of those words to recede to the back of his mind. He was young and vigorous, with fresh blood coursing through his body that yearned for achievement.

His thoughts returned to White Heron, dwelling on her beauty and grace and dreams of the stature he would gain as a man among men of the Salish people. He wanted to tell his father about his desires, plans, and ambitions. His father was his north star. They were often together, whether caring for the horses or reconnoitering the area for game or marauding Niitsitapi. They did not like these neighbors to the northeast. They were warlike; some evil spirit had gotten into them, causing them to harry neighboring tribes. Why it was so, he did not know, but he and his father had to be on the lookout for these troublemakers and horse thieves. As if the Great Spirit had not given them enough horses of their own, they had to prey upon their neighbors. What evil possessed them? Fortunately, the Salish had good relations with the Shoshone.

Lone Wolf brought up the subject closest to his heart one day when they were setting rabbit traps.

"When it comes time for me to take a wife, I know who will be mine," he began.

"Already? You have some years to go before that. Your fancy may change in several seasons. My taste was fickle, too, as a young buck."

"Mine is not. My gaze will not swerve from White Heron. She shines the brightest in my eye."

"Aha, I have seen how sweetly you look at her."

"How could I not? Her temperament is like my mother's."

"Ho, I remember how I desired Sweet Grass many moons ago. She has been a good wife."

"White Heron will be my wife. I ask you to tell her father, Woodcock, of my desire."

"In due time, in time, my son. You leap ahead of yourself. For now, I give you the four spring foals to train. From them, a fine string of horses will grow. When you have trained them to ride, then that will be the time to marry. Then you will have something to offer Woodcock worth his beautiful daughter. No?"

"You are right, father. I will work for that."

They hooked forearms together to confirm the deal.

The future was promising; one thing rankled Lone Wolf's memory. With the prospect of many horses and an attractive wife, suddenly the ominous recollection of the blue jay prophecy disturbed his pleasure.

"Father, do you remember what the blue jay said?"

"Yes, I do, but I want to forget it, and so do all our people. Think no more of it. The Great Spirit will not let it happen."

"I do not want things to change. I do not want the blue jay dance to stop."

"Our customs have endured since the ice melted. The people will keep their traditions as they were founded from the beginning of the earth. Ho, I say it."

His father's vehemence reassured Lone Wolf. He trusted his father's wisdom; he trusted his knowledge. Furthermore, no other man could speak without words to horses as his father could.

When he arrived home, Sweet Grass was sewing a dyed porcupine quill to a deerskin shirt. She greeted him, and he sat beside her to watch her work the needle of sharpened bone threaded with buffalo sinew. He wanted to share his plans with his mother.

"Father has promised me the spring foals."

"That is good. Horses will help you obtain a wife." She smiled, not at him, but at her handiwork.

"I have chosen a girl."

"That is good. She is White Heron."

"How did you know?" he asked, surprise spread over his face.

"A mother knows. A mother sees. She knows her son like she knows how to thread a needle."

Lone Wolf broke into a laugh and said, "You are wise, Mother. Do you agree that White Heron is a wise choice?"

"I could not have chosen better if I had chosen her myself." This time she looked up from her needle and smiled at him."

They spoke no more. A mutual understanding persisted between mother and son. Until he matured to marriageable age, they trusted together that he would grow in wisdom and knowledge.

The women had taken down the buffalo-hide teepees of winter and replaced them with the tule reed ones of summer. Carrying baskets, they hurried to the sunny mountain meadows to dig the white roots of the camas plant. White Heron was among them, long-limbed and tall, as she strode foremost among the laughing women. Lone Wolf watched them climb a slope and then dip below to where the plant was known to grow profusely in early summer. They had camped farther north to take advantage of the plentiful bitterroot and berries that would proliferate as the warmth enveloped the earth. There was much to do in tending the horses. The new foal scampered in the lush grass around the camp, the two-year-old colts needed training, and young boys practiced their riding skills under the tutelage of Rides-the-Wind and Lone Wolf. Since his father had given him the foals five years ago, they had developed into fine mounts, fit to ride in the hunt over rugged passes and timbered trails. They confidently forded streams and did not spook at thunder or lightning, but they did lunge when they heard the fire stick emerge from an enemy attack, for over the years, the Blackfeet raids had increased in frequency and ferocity. They carried more of the fire sticks. Despite their firepower, the Salish put up a fierce defense only because they could launch arrows more rapidly at their attackers than the Blackfeet could reload their guns. In these summer moons, the Salish had to be constantly vigilant for their neighbors' sneak attack. It had come to a point where a guard was assigned to watch over the horses at night.

    Lone Wolf walked among the herd, stroking each animal and chanting a song of friendship. It was a ritual he followed every morning. This morning was special because he planned to select the mare that he would present to White Heron's father. Five cycles of the season had passed since he told his parents of his intentions. "Ah, this one," he murmured as a three-year-old mare, a golden color like the flowers of the field, nickered at him and nuzzled his hand. She knew he held wild carrots in his curled fingers. She came from southern stock brought by the people of the painted desert. The temperament of this horse matched the sweetness of his intended wife. Pliant and gentle, intelligent, and responsive to his touch, Daughter of the Sun would make a perfect mount for White Heron. He mounted the mare and took her through her paces. He loved the feel of the breeze on his cheeks and the smell of the pines as he whisked past them. The earth, vibrant with new life, spoke to him. He was a young man about to procreate like all things alive and well. Yes, his three sisters had already given birth, married off to men of neighboring bands to the northwest of the Red Top mountains. Sometimes they came to visit with their men, who would hunt the buffalo with them or share information about game and other tribes. Unlike his sisters, he chose a woman of his band. He coveted no other distant maiden. His mother, Sweet Grass, approved; his father approved; their approval satisfied him. What remained was the approval of White Heron's father. When the women returned from digging bitterroot, he would approach Woodcock. For now, there was horse work to do. He trotted back to where the young boys on horseback were shooting arrows at a circle carved on the bark of a birch tree. He joined them in their exercise, offering advice.

  He had returned to the camp and was seated outside his tule teepee when he saw the women approach from the west, carrying their heavily laden baskets. They had peeled the roots in the field. Immediately, they began to prepare the firepits with heated stones where the roots would be baked for days followed by the tedious work of mashing the roots. The women pounded the baked roots into a pulp on stone mortars with pestles made with round stones tied with rawhide cords to wooden handles. And when the berries were ripe and picked, the women mixed them into the mash to make healthy and tasty patties. White Heron glanced at Lone Wolf as she made her way to her family's teepee at the far end of the camp. He smiled to himself in the knowledge that soon he would accomplish his desire and take his place as a man among men.

In the evening, Lone Wolf lingered with the other men outside their teepees. He did not talk but listened to the other men tell stories of times spent and of the wily deeds of Coyote. This early summer night was unusually warm. The moon had waned completely, and a wind came up in the valley that rustled the leaves and sent up a sighing of trees as their trunks bent in the high winds. Lone Wolf gazed at the dark sky, sniffed the air, and studied the night. Would it rain? Would it thunder and lightning strike this moonless night? It would come but not yet, probably before dawn.

"Ho, the clouds will open soon," Three Eagles announced and stood up, yawning. "Sleep calls before the thunder sounds." The other men followed suit and drifted toward their respective teepees. Lone Wolf entered his family's teepee and stretched out on his deerskin blanket. Within minutes, he was sound asleep.

It was not thunder that aroused him in the predawn hours, but the shriek of a brave, shouting the alarm to arms; Blackfeet warriors had penetrated the guard and whisked away several horses. Lone Wolf and Rides-the-Wind, instantly alert, jumped to their feet and raced to the area where the horses were pastured. They needed daylight to track the thieves. Silently, the intruders had crawled close to a cluster of horses, and only the rumble of hooves on the ground had alerted the guard who had dozed off for a moment. Lone Wolf and Rides-the-Wind counted the herd and determined that Daughter of the Sun, along with three other mares and two stallions, had been stolen. Lone Wolf was crushed, then his anger erupted. He would brook no delay. He wanted to pursue the thieves immediately.

"Wait, son, soon the sun will awake, and we will follow their trail. We will get Daughter of the Sun back. I know they will head west over the Place of the Small Bull Trout. It is the easier way with the stolen horses to the Place of Water Falling Over a Rocky Ledge back to their home northwest on the prairie. We will capture them and torture them before we kill them," Rides-the-Wind swore.

"But what of their fire sticks?" Woodcock said.

"I am not afraid of their fire sticks," Rides-the-Wind declared with an upraised clenched fist.

"Neither am I," Lone Wolf added. "Let me go now."

"Not long, not long, we will follow them. Let them think they are safe, unpursued, for a while. They will drop their guard once they reach the canyon. We will catch up to them. We will trap them. We will corner them like dogs in a cage. Rest. Prepare for the battle." Rides-the-Wind withdrew his medicine bundle from under his buckskin shirt. "Here I invoke my guardian spirit. He protects and strengthens me." The rest of the men did the same. Lone Wolf recognized his guardian spirit. The wary, keen-eyed, white-coated wolf that appeared on his vision quest would guide and defend him in battle.

Before daybreak, the clouds burst open, and a furious downpour drenched the earth. The men covered their heads with their buffalo robes.

"Ah, the sky has spoken, but his fury will be spent quickly," Rides-the-Wind murmured. The other men's silence acquiesced with his judgment. They recognized the cloudburst as one that came suddenly and furiously, emptying itself all at once and stopping almost as quickly as it began. Six men mounted their horses to pursue the thieves –Chief Three Eagles, Bear Tooth, Woodcock, Big Hawk, Rides-the Wind, and Lone Wolf.

Soon a thin line of light broke the eastern horizon, and they moved forward mounted on horses while the best tracker among them, Big Hawk, walked ahead leading his horse behind him, studying the ground for the tracks of man or horse, as well as bent grass and broken brush on all sides. Picking up the thieves' trail assuredly was rendered more difficult, but Big Hawk's keen vision still managed to discern the subtle signs of human passage as the daylight pierced the forest canopy, brightening the path.

"Here are horse droppings," Big Hawk pointed in the direction for them to go.

They traveled a little farther, each of the ten warriors intent on every sound or movement that might indicate the Blackfeet were within range.

After a while, Big Hawk spoke again. "There are eight of them." Each of the Salish absorbed his pronouncement but did not flinch. They were six in pursuit of eight. They accepted Big Hawk's estimate. Lone Wolf could not recall a time when Big Hawk erred in his count of how many men or how many animals they pursued.

Anger simmered in Lone Wolf. With his own hands, he would kill the thief who had stolen Daughter of the Sun and pummel him until he was squashed like a bug. But no, he wanted to bring him back alive, whip and shame him in the village, strip him naked, and flog his back until the blood soaked the ground. Thievery was to be punished in the most horrible manner possible. Picturing every cruel torture he could inflict upon his enemy, Lone Wolf trailed behind his father as the troop of Salish warriors pursued the horse thieves. Signs were visible to Big Hawk along the way. They rested only to water and feed the horses and then silently resumed the pursuit.

In the middle of the second day, Big Hawk, who had scouted a distance ahead of them so that he was no longer in sight of the company, came into view and signaled for them to halt. He walked to meet them and announced, "They are a short way ahead of us. We can ambush them if we circle above the trail and approach from the east in front of them. There are several rocky ledges from which we can shower our arrows down on them. When those in the front engage the thieves, some of you stay behind, and when they are busy with the frontal attack, you hit them from behind. Others grab the stolen horses and head back. The ones still alive, we capture, bind, and take back to camp. That is the plan."

Stealthily, the warriors moved forward. Slowly, they guided their mounts through the woods, trying not to disturb a branch or crack a twig on the ground. In single file, they moved forward. Big Hawk indicated how to go in a wide circle to prevent even the slightest sound from carrying. When he judged they had come full circle around the thieves, he halted the men. Some dismounted to take up positions on ledges, while others remained mounted to confront the thieves who would also be mounted. Lone Wolf sneaked up to a ledge and positioned himself to take aim. He saw the party of eight mounted Blackfeet with the string of six stolen horses. Daughter of the Sun was the first one in the line behind the thieves. Their fire sticks were in sheathes strapped to the horses' withers. They looked secure and oblivious to danger, satisfied they had accomplished a successful robbery.

The Salish were outnumbered, and the Blackfeet's superior arms required they surprise and slay as many of the eight Blackfeet as they could before the thieves realized what was happening. Do not give them time to reload the fire in their thunder sticks, Lone Wolf thought. From past skirmishes, he knew that eventually the fire would run out, and they would have to pause and add the deadly material, whatever it was, into that hollow space in the stick. If he had that weapon too, waiting in ambush, he could make even shorter work of those devils; but they had not yet stolen one from the enemy. Rumor was that the Blackfeet traded buffalo hides for the arms and the fire they put into the sticks.

In rapid succession, Lone Wolf released four arrows, toppling four warriors from their horses. Three Salish jumped down upon two mounted Blackfeet about to unsheathe their fire sticks, wrestled them to the ground, and deftly planted knives into their chests. Lone Wolf scurried down the side of the ledge and grabbed Daughter of the Sun's lead rope. He leaped upon her back and rushed into the foray where the two remaining Blackfeet were firing their weapons at the four mounted Salish who had launched a frontal assault. Shouldering his fire stick, the Blackfoot struck down Bear Tooth. At the same time, Lone Wolf let loose an arrow into the back of the Blackfoot warrior who had just fired. An arrow penetrated deep into his flesh, and he fell forward over his horse's neck and slid to the ground. Only one thief remained, engaged in combat with five Salish. Overwhelmed, the horse thief was powerless to aim his fire stick effectively at any of them. Then Chief Three

Eagles lifted his war club overhead and squarely crashed it down upon the skull of the Blackfoot.

No thief remained standing to take back to camp and torture. It would have been better if they had one alive to teach a lesson, to humiliate before the entire tribe, and to make suffer for his deed. That would have been justice. Death was the easy way for these devils. Whippings and dismemberment of tongues and fingers would have been the proper manner to mete out punishment. Next time he would shoot to disable and not to kill, Lone Wolf thought. He patted the mare's neck. "Well done, Daughter of the Sun." He dismounted and joined the rest of the party, who were stripping the men of clothing. They recovered three fire sticks, for not all the thieves had been armed. It was a precious commodity that not all warriors possessed. Chief Three Eagles gathered the fire sticks and tied them in a bundle to the back of a horse.

"There's not much we can do with these until we have the fire and learn how they work."

"How will we get that knowledge?" Rides-the-Wind asked.

"The Nimiipuu have told us they have seen the white traders," Chief Three Eagles said. "They have come to their lands beyond the Red Top Mountains, asking for pelts of beaver, mink, otter, and the fur of every animal. I think it will not be long until they come for more. Their mouths and stomachs are big."

They buried Bear Tooth, but left the bodies of the fallen Blackfeet for the crows and rode home with considerable booty for their efforts—the six stolen horses, the eight mounts of their slain enemies, and the belongings of the dead thieves.

Triumphantly, the party entered the village a few days later with the horses and the booty they had taken off the dead bodies of the thieves. Lone Wolf had proven himself both in battle and in the hunt, so he did not delay approaching Woodcock regarding his daughter White Heron. Woodcock was witness to his bravery. In addition to his valor, he owned a string of fine horses—no small matter when a man made his case for a wife. Confident of success, he led Daughter of the Sun to Woodcock's teepee. Rides-the-Wind, who had previously advised Woodcock that they wished to meet with him that morning, walked beside his son. Woodcock, aware of their purpose, waited outside his teepee. With few words, they sealed the bargain dependent on White Heron's agreement.

Woodcock opened the flap of his teepee and summoned White Heron to come out. Meekly, she stepped outside, wearing a white buckskin dress, a ring of shells sewn around the collar and hem, and a belt of porcupine quill chips dyed red. Her hair, lustrous as raven wings and parted in the middle, hung down her shoulders in two braids tied with rawhide thongs. A cap of woven willow reeds fit snugly on her head. Smiling shyly, she stood before her father.

"Do you want this man, who brought you this fine horse, as your husband?"

Nodding, she answered, "I do."

"Take her into your teepee. It is good," Woodcock said.

A broad smile illuminated Lone Wolf's face. Life was good. Everything was as it should be. There was no ceremony, no other ritual but to continue life together in the round of seasons as it was in the beginning, as it was now, and as it ever would be. He took his helpmate by the hand. They entered the teepee of tule his mother and some other women had erected as his own dwelling as a married man. Willingly, White Heron accompanied him into their new home. Happily, she submitted to his will. There was no fear or anxiety because it was the nature of man and beast to mate, to increase, and to labor in tandem, each assigned their respective tasks in the grand design of the universe.

"Are you happy?" Lone Wolf asked after they had consummated their union.

"My heart is as big as the mountains; I am as full as the moon," she answered.

"I am happy too." Lone Wolf stroked her cheek. "You are beautiful and strong. We will have many children."

"So will the Creator grant," she whispered.

White Heron was big with her first child when the fur trappers and traders came down from the western mountains with a string of packhorses laden with goods—glass beads, metal tools, pots, kettles, fabric, woolen blankets, ribbons, buttons, and other gewgaws and gadgets the Salish had never seen. There were two bearded white men and a half-breed Walla Walla of the northwest plateau in the group, along with Ignace La Mousse and his son from an unknown tribe called the Iroquois. They wore fur caps with long ear flaps, heavy sheepskin coats, woolen leggings, and high leather boots. The half-breed served as interpreter. The white men spread their goods before the wondering eyes of the people. The women picked up the pots and pans and knew instantly that they wanted to cook with these utensils. The tin cups, metal ladles, spoons, and knives were immediately recognized as of inestimable value. No longer would they have to labor countless hours to make bowls and other implements of bone, leather, and wood. The traders showed them flour, sugar, and coffee. They prompted the women to put sugar on their fingertips and lick it off. Expressions of amazement and pleasure covered their faces. "Sweet," they murmured in their native tongue and dipped their fingers in the white crystals for more. Then one of the traders took a coffee grinder from his pack. With a spoon, he scooped some coffee beans from a sack and poured them into the grinder. The women watched, intrigued, as he ground them into a fine powder. He pulled a coffee pot from his bag of goods and asked that it be filled with water. A woman returned with the pot filled. The trader added the ground coffee to the pot and set it to boiling on the firepit. White Heron was the first to take the tin cup, sip the brew and affirm her approval, saying it was as good as any sassafras or other herbal drink she had ever tasted. She passed it to the next woman, and the coffee made its round among the group of fascinated women.

"If you like, you can add sugar to it," the *suyapi* trader said and proceeded to demonstrate, placing a spoonful of sugar in his cup and stirring it.

When the trader was satisfied that the women thoroughly coveted his goods, he turned his attention to the men.

The men stood in a circle examining the metal arrowheads, axes, and knives. Several of the trappers knew the Salish language and explained how much more effective and deadly sharp the metal arrowheads were. They listened courteously and attentively for a while. "Twelve beaver belts for the lot," the trader said. The tribesmen were shrewd bargainers. Chief Three Eagles turned away from the group and walked toward his teepee, leaving his men to haggle with the trader by themselves. He entered his teepee and emerged a moment later with the three fire sticks in his arms. He approached the trader seated on the ground and dropped his load at the man's feet.

"We want the fire for these sticks. Show us how they work."

Astounded for a second, the trader then chuckled and invited Chief Three Eagles to sit next to him.

"You mean the black powder. The ammunition for these rifles. Well, well . . . now we can really talk business. He stood up and took one of the rifles from Chief Three Eagles. He opened the powder horn slung on his shoulder and measured an amount which he poured into the bore of the rifle. He pulled the ramrod from the side of the barrel and inserted it into the bore, pressing the powder compactly in the barrel. He then took a linen wad, wrapped it around a lead ball that he withdrew from a leather case around his waist and shoved that into the barrel. Finally, he stuffed another linen wad into the barrel and pressed it firmly down with the ramrod. Holding the rifle vertically, he added powder to a pan under the matchlock. He explained the firing mechanism, the trigger, and how to shoulder the rifle. The second white trader walked forty paces to a tree and carved a circle on the trunk. The trader with the rifle then took aim at the tree, placed two figures on the trigger in the large guard, and fired. Thunder ripped the air, and puffs of smoke rose from the barrel end. At the outburst, the women clapped their palms to their ears, but the Salish men, accustomed to the roar of their enemy's fire sticks, stood stalwartly gazing at the hole torn in the tree trunk. Several of the Salish moved to the tree and closely examined the spot where the ball had hit.

"That killed a deer," the *suyapi* said smugly and sat down again. "Twenty-four pelts for one rifle," he said. "Twelve beaver pelts for lead and powder."

Throughout the demonstration, the Walla Walla interpreted and continued as the bargaining commenced.

Chief Three Eagles pointed to the serpent on the stock plate above the trigger.

"We want only rifles with the serpent."

"Twenty-four beaver pelts," the white trader repeated, "and we will bring you rifles with the serpent."

"Twenty pelts," Chief Three Eagles said.

"You drive a hard bargain, Chief," the trader said. "You bring me 125 pelts this winter, and I will bring you six rifles along with powder, lead, and molds to make the balls."

They smoked the pipe to seal the bargain that night in the chief's lodge. It was a pleasant evening of banter and stories.

Before the trading party left, the traders showed the Salish how to heat the lead and pour it into a mold to harden and shape into the balls to load into the barrel. He furnished them with some ready-made balls. The traders told them a *suyapi* had established a trading post upriver to the west near the falls where the rivers converged and where they could bring their pelts in exchange for many wonderful and useful items—all the supplies they needed to live happily and prosperously forever. The man who ran the trading post was David Thompson. He was fair and would treat them well.

When it came time to pack up and leave the Salish village, Big Ignace LaMousse did not want to go.

"No better people have I met in all my travels," he told the white traders. "This valley is mild and beautiful. I feel these people will gladly receive what I tell them of the religion the Black Robes brought the Iroquois. I want to dwell among them and be their friend. I will trap here and take my catch to David Thompson's post."

"As you wish," one of the white traders said. "What about your son? Does he come with us?"

"He wishes to live among the Salish too." Big Ignace looked at this son to confirm that was his decision.

"It is true," not-so-little Ignace said. He was a grown man, well beyond marriageable years. "This is a good place to live. This is a good place to die. My father and I have traveled far together, from the great inland seas, over vast grasslands and mountains, even to the edge of the earth where monster sea creatures spout water. These people have welcomed us and are eager to hear the story of our people who listened to the words of the Black Robes many years ago and have held it ever since in their hearts."

Then Big Ignace held up a metal cross on which the almost naked figure of a man was fastened, his arms stretched out and pinned to the horizontal cross beam. Chief Three Eagles wondered what the man had done to deserve such torture. The punishment resembled the torture they inflicted on captives, piercing their skin, and stringing them up by leather thongs drawn through the holes in the skin. Big Ignace held the cross to his head, his heart, his left side, and right side while he intoned an unintelligible prayer in a language that was not his, the trader's, or the Salish's.

"What is he saying?" Chief Three Eagles asked the half-breed Walla Walla translator.

"He is saying the Our Father prayer he learned from the Black Robes. He blesses their journey. Big Ignace turned and said something to the half-breed, who in turn spoke to the chief. "Ignace says he will teach you this prayer to the Great Spirit of the *suyapi*. Their god is all-powerful and all-knowing. Their god has made them strong, stronger than any other people on earth. That same power can be yours if you listen to his words."

Chief Three Eagles looked thoughtful, but did not express curiosity about the *suyapi's* religion. For a while, the Salish men and women watched the trading company recede into the distance.

"Come, my people, let us assemble and take counsel of these matters." The elders and sub-chiefs gathered in his lodge. Lone Wolf and Rides-the Wind took their places in the council. The women brought in bitterroot patties, pemmican, and buffalo bladders of water. They placed the food and drink before the men and then huddled against the sides of the teepee. The chief sat against a backrest of woven willow branches. Everyone waited for him to speak first. Lone Wolf was anxious to hear his wisdom. So much had happened in so short a time to baffle him that apprehension lay beneath his overriding feelings of curiosity and wonder at the merchandise the white men had brought.

Chief Three Eagles raised the talking stick, indicating he would speak first. When he finished, he would recognize the next speaker and pass the talking stick to him. Two owl feathers were attached to the stick at one end, and wolf fur was wrapped around the end the speaker held.

"We have the fire stick, but to what use will we put it? It makes us a match for thieves who would sneak into our village and steal our horses and women. It will be good to hunt deer, elk, and buffalo. If a big war party comes upon us, it is not so good in battle. It takes too long to put the black powder in. It will be good for warriors in hiding to shoot from behind trees and boulders. The traders ask us to trap more animals for more fire sticks, powder, and balls. They have shown us how to make balls from lead. I think we should give them the pelts for balls. Much easier. It saves us the trouble of making them. What say you?"

Woodcock extended his hand for the talking stick, "I say we get many pelts for the *suyapi*. This is good for our people. There is plenty for all. The Blackfeet cannot beat their chests and claim they are the strongest now. There is power in the *suyapi's* way." Woodcock passed the stick to Rides-the-Wind.

"Brave words. I had a dream that bravery will not stop the traders and trappers from asking for more. They will not stop with twenty pelts, a hundred pelts, or pelts piled as high as Red Top Mountain. My dream is true. They breed like rabbits and will overrun the land before our grandchildren grow old and die."

Woodcock took the walking stick. "How do we know your dream is true? Coyote in the night came to fool you. The fire stick is good and not the only good thing the white men bring us. Our women do not have to work as hard tanning hides and sewing clothes. They bring fabric and warm blankets. The *suyapi's* axe cuts down trees better than we can with our old tools. I say everything they have is useful."

Rides-the-Wind took the talking stick again. "I do not feel right. I cannot say why I have this uneasiness. My spirit tells me there is something in the spirit of the white men that will devour every fish, bird, and four-footed animal in our land."

Woodcock claimed the walking stick. "Calm your fears, my brother. You cannot stop the wind. We must heed where the wind blows, go with it, bend with it, and we will not be broken."

Chief Three Eagles reclaimed the walking stick. "Fine words. I agree the things the traders bring are good for us. It is easy for us to get the pelts. We can control the number of animals killed. When we have what we need, we will not take more pelts."

He passed the talking stick to Rides-the Wind, "They will not want to stop when we want to stop. I ask if you can trust their words. We do not have enough experience with them to know for certain. We must be cautious."

Listening to his elders speak, aware he was a younger man, Lone Wolf was reluctant to share his own misgivings. His feelings leaned toward the ones his father expressed. Caution was necessary; they must act carefully and observe the white men's actions, for wisdom taught that a man's deeds spoke truly regardless of what words his tongue spoke. He would listen and learn, observe and beware before he pronounced final judgment.

The village resumed its round of activities, but the men became more intent upon gathering the fur and hides that would buy them the goods they wanted. Not long after the trader's visit, White Heron delivered a healthy, chubby baby girl. So round-faced and precious she was that Lone Wolf began to call her Moon Glow. She grew chubbier each day with White Heron's ample milk. As the baby grew, she began to chortle and smile; the earth as well began to expand. The snow melted and the rivers gushed. Buds appeared on the bushes, and the forest was alive with bird song. Sprigs of bitterroot appeared in the mountain meadows. White Heron swaddled Moon Glow, placed her in the cradleboard, and walked with the other women to the meadows. Tending to a child did not lessen White Heron's labor. She sang to her child as she peeled the bitterroot bulbs, cooked them, and mashed them to a pulp, which she mixed with pemmican and berries to make nutritious patties.

The Great Spirit was pleased to bless them with another daughter in the following years, two years apart, because Lone Wolf was away from the camp much of the year in chase of the buffalo and hunting and trapping long distances in search of the wary deer and elk. These hunts stretched into weeks and months as, with the passage of time, it became harder and harder to find abundant herds. White Heron proved to be a hard-working, dedicated helpmate. When Moon Glow was eight seasons old and their second daughter, Blue Bird, was six, they already had learned the homemaking arts from White Heron that would make them ideal wives and mothers. The only black cloud on their otherwise happy life was the increasing frequency of Blackfeet raids. The purpose was to terrorize them from ever venturing onto the plains for buffalo. They wanted to reign supreme over the herds and tolerated no intruders upon the supply of meat and hides the buffalo supplied. Their greed had grown strong to trade the hides to the white men for the goods they coveted. The Salish had lost too many men in skirmishes with these devils as well as fine horses. Most distressing was that the Blackfeet had stolen women and children. The captives worked as slaves for them and used them as breeding stock to replenish their people. Like many tribes in the land, they had lost many people to the *suyapi*'s spotted sickness.

"Mind your back," Lone Wolf cautioned the women. "Have a designated lookout in your group. Mount your horses and return to the camp if you detect anything suspicious."

"Do not worry. At the first sense of danger, I will leap upon Daughter of the Sun with the two girls and ride like the wind," White Heron smiled to reassure him. He knew she was clever and strong, but he still worried. Trouble stalked the land like he had not known in his boyhood. Trouble from the white men who had made the Blackfeet more dangerous, greedy, and all-around evil. He felt this disruption in their old ways and felt helpless to stem the forces. In some ways, life was better. They possessed weapons, tools, clothing, kettles, bowls, and pots and pans. But did they have a happier life? His doubts grew.

No matter how vigilant, the Blackfeet managed to surprise them sometimes. They were sly, moving soundlessly sometimes, and other times they mimicked bird chatter to disguise their presence and fool the group of Salish before they suddenly pounced. They would also descend, whooping and running headlong into an encampment, seemingly out of nowhere. The Salish men would grab spears and axes, leaving dead bodies of friend and foe alike on the ground.

It could not go on like this forever. Lone Wolf asked himself, where it would end? In one or the other tribes' obliteration? No, he swore. The Salish were too strong to be defeated.

One autumn morning, golden with the larch needles littering the earth, he prepared to track deer through the forest. The rutting bucks might not notice a stealthy hunter like him. Three hunters would join Lone Wolf on the hunt while the rest of the men remained in the village. He mounted his stallion, and White Heron handed him a parfleche of pemmican and a bladder of water for the journey. He nudged the horse forward, and his two daughters waved as he departed.

"Your father will bring back plenty of game. Then we will tan deer hide to make new dresses for you," White Heron said to her girls. "Come now, we have work to do."

The autumn light faded as they sat together and sewed buckskin shirts for the coming winter. Tired but satisfied with their day's work, they ate a small meal of pemmican and retired to their bearskin bed. In the next few days, White Heron had no time to dwell on Lone Wolf's absence or wonder how soon he would return, laden with a sufficient supply of meat to add to their winter larder. She went about her daily tasks, humming as usual, secure in the knowledge that the Salish men, empowered by their guardian spirits, would keep her from danger. She had confidence in her own strength also. The intelligence and grace of the white heron empowered her.

Near dusk, after Lone Wolf had been gone for a week, White Heron and her two girls went to the creek to scrub the cooking pots and ladles clean with sand. The creek bent around the back of the cluster of teepees not more than 300 paces from the camp. As they rinsed the pots, White Heron told the story she had told them many times about the water babies who swam at the bottom of the creek. "They are the spirit of dead babies, crying for their mothers," White Heron told the girls.

"I see one! I see one," Blue Bird exclaimed. "Over there! Swimming under the shadow by the rock."

Moon Glow and White Heron looked in the direction the little girl pointed.

"Are you sure it is not a tadpole?" her sister asked. No sooner had she raised the question, when a frog splashed into the water.

"You cannot mistake one for a tadpole, although the baby grows fins and a tail like a fish," White Heron said. "The water babies who swim here died not so long ago of the spotted disease. Sometimes you can hear their keening, but do not let them lure you into the waters."

"I feel so sad for them," Moon Glow said.

"You must not feel so sorry for them that you join them and drown."

Just then, they heard an outcry from the village and, grabbing their pots and ladles, hurried to the circle of teepees. The next moment the thunder of fire sticks and war whoops reverberated around them as two horsemen galloped toward them from the rear. Each rider slowed his mount, bent forward, and scooped a girl onto the horse in front of him, spurring his horse in the opposite direction, and racing away. White Heron screamed and ran furiously after the fleeing attackers that she knew to be the hated Blackfeet. Desperately, she pursued them on foot until she gave up, realizing it was futile. Her shrieks rent the air between the curses she hurled at the kidnappers. Hearing the tumult behind her in the village, she raced toward where the battle raged. The Salish warriors fought with axes and spears. The chiefs who had fire sticks fired and reloaded their weapons from behind teepees. The attackers were all dismounted by now and in hand-to-hand combat with the surprised defenders. The Blackfeet had attempted more than they could accomplish over the superior numbers of the Salish. Apparently, they had counted on most of the warriors being gone on the autumn hunt and the women and children left prey for their depredations. Despite the valor of the Salish, two of them lay on the ground. She saw two Blackfeet turn tail and rush toward their horses, leaping upon them and escaping the battle they were losing. White Heron ran like a mad woman toward Chief Three Eagles, who held his smoking gun aimed at an enemy in retreat. Seeing the Blackfoot was too far away for a certain kill, he lowered his rifle. White Heron rammed into his chest, hysterically screaming, "They have my daughters. We must pursue them. Bring my daughters back." Tears gushed down her cheeks and the terror of a crazed animal arose in her eyes.

"They are defeated. We have driven them off for the time being. They may return with greater numbers. We do not know how many lurk in the woods."

Wild-eyed, White Heron stared at him in disbelief. "You will not pursue them? My daughters!" she screeched.

"We live to fight another day. Then we will take two of theirs for the two of ours."

"Eeei-ow-eeei-ow . . .!" her painful cry elongated in anguish. Then she pulled away angrily from the chief and clenched her fists. "The Daughter of the Sun and I will ride and find them."

Chief Three eagles gripped her forearm. "No, you stay here. Crazy woman, they will capture you too, and do the same to you. They will have three slaves instead of only two."

She flung his arm away and headed to where the horses were pastured. Chief Three Eagles signaled for Big Hawk and Woodcock to restrain her. The two braves easily grabbed her and held her securely between them. Three Eagles approached her and said, "If you resist my orders, I will tie you to a pole until your husband returns when he can deal with you."

White Heron realized she had no choice except to obey. Her strength could not match these men, but when Lone Wolf returned, he would track the kidnappers even if he had to travel to the farthest reaches of the Northern Plains that the Blackfeet called home. From this territory, they terrorized any other tribe that ventured to kill buffalo on the vast reaches of the land they ranged. White heron submitted and supplanted her resistance with unrelenting wails. Her keening continued night and day, even as she continued a woman's daily tasks. Outwardly submissive, she plotted how she and Lone Wolf would rescue their daughters. At night, exhausted from weeping and wailing, she succumbed to sleep.

Disturbed by her abject misery, Rides-the-Wind, approached White Heron while she was bent over her sewing. How to comfort a bereft mother? She guarded hopes that were impossible to attain. She stubbornly refused to grasp the reality that stealing the girls from a distant Blackfeet camp endangered more of their people than recapture of the girls would justify. The mother could not see the situation in those terms, but he had to attempt to explain Chief Three Eagle's decision to her. If he could not do that, he must try to offer her some consolation, some solace at the loss of her children.

"White Heron," he sat beside her. "Listen to me. You must cease your lamenting. Even if we ride as far as the plains and succeed in finding the camp where the girls are, they are small, and their captors would have hidden them well. Because of their greater numbers, they would fend off our attack. We do not have the men to spare for such an undertaking. Don't you see, it cannot be done?"

"Our guardian spirits will help. Lone Wolf's strength will ensure victory," she replied.

"You would kill your husband in this vain attempt?"

"He has powerful medicine." She tightened her lips and refused to look at Rides-the-Wind.

"When Lone Wolf returns, then you will listen to what he says."

She said nothing but continued to poke the metal needle and strong thread into the linen fabric, all materials obtained from the white traders.

Rides-the-Wind rose and left her to simmer in her grief and rage. He also wished that his son would return soon and deal with the catastrophe that had befallen the family. Would his rage be as unrelenting and unreasonable as White Heron's? Would anger blind him to reality? Moon Glow and Blue Bird were lost to them forever. Their adopted family would raise them to womanhood and treat them as their own daughters, but that was not to say, they would not assign them the most backbreaking women's work. He knew their fate and could describe it completely to White Heron, but he had not. His description would only deepen her misery. In time her lamentations had to cease. Who could live with eternal grieving?

Sweet Grass also tried to relieve White Heron's lamentations. Most of the day, Sweet Grass worked beside her, allowing her tears and woeful sighs to flow. Then she began a song of healing. The sweet sounds wafted words to sooth White Heron's tortured soul. Great compassion flowed from the heart of Sweet Grass to the heart of the younger woman. When calamity struck, the silent presence of someone who loved you served best, and that is what Sweet Grass strove to provide the grief-stricken mother.

Once, White Heron paused in her wailing to say to Sweet Grass, her constant companion, "Mother, I cannot live without my daughters. I am a dead soul. If I must die, I will die rescuing my daughters. I will mount Daughter of the Sun and go myself to plead for their release. Even if the Blackfeet refuse and capture me too, at least I will be with the children I love."

"That is foolhardy. Lone Wolf will tell you so."

"No, he will not. When he comes, he will ride with me to Blackfeet country."

"Heed what I say. The girls will work hard in the Blackfeet camp, but they will not let them die. They need their hands. They will grow to womanhood among them. They will treat them as one of their own and then marry them to one of their warriors. The more women they have, the better for them. Women are valuable. Take comfort from the knowledge that they live and thrive there. If they are wily and want to return to the people that birthed them, they will plot to escape if the opportunity arrives."

"Eeeiiiooo-ow-ow-eei!" White Heron wailed, taking no comfort from the older woman's words.

One golden afternoon with the aspens aglow in the dying color of the season, Lone Wolf and the three other hunters arrived with the carcasses of five deer carried on the backs of their packhorses. They unloaded the animals, and a bevy of women scurried from all directions to begin the processing of the hides and meat. Chief Three Eagles immediately recounted the Blackfeet raid that had occurred during their absence. From inside her teepee, White Heron heard the commotion and excited speech at the hunters' arrival. She dropped the basket she was weaving and ran outside, her heart beating wildly, to greet the hunting party. She spotted Lone Wolf in grim conversation with the chief and burst upon them, shouting, "They took our daughters!"

"Talk sense into your woman," the chief said to Lone Wolf. "She is mad with grief. No one can talk to a crazy woman."

Everyone was talking at once. With all the clamor around him, Lone Wolf could not think straight. The frenzied speech bombarded his ears, and he raised his arms for silence. White Heron's shrieks did not abate, so he directed the others to feed, water, and pasture the horses while he led his wife into the privacy of their lodge. Once inside, seated on the ground, he cradled the woman and rocked her in his arms like an infant, stroking her black hair as he cooed to her like a mourning dove.

"Moon Glow saw the water baby in the stream," White Heron mumbled into his sleeve.

He did not know what to make of her words. She was hallucinating, imaginary portents running through her tormented mind. What could he say to alleviate her sorrow? He decided to let her mutter and release her emotions as she wished. After a while, she lifted her head, sat upright next to him, and gazed fixedly at him. "You must search for them and bring them back."

"Do you want me to be lost to you also? That would be my fate because they have more arms and men than I could take with me. Such a mission would end in my death and the death of anyone who dared to go with me. The Blackfeet have taken our girls to serve as their women. Yes, they will work them hard, but they are now their adopted daughters."

"How can you say that? Ride after them! I will ride with you."

"No, White Heron, it is not wise. You are crazy with grief."

"Crazy, you call me. I will show you what crazy is," and she began to pummel his chest.

He took her by the wrists. "Whoa, woman! No more of this." She ceased trying to wrench her hands free and looked scornfully at him.

"You had the courage to chase after Daughter of the Sun when the horse thieves stole her. Do not tell me you will not go after your own daughters."

"My pain is as great as your pain, but wisdom prevents me from pursuit. They are daughters of the earth. The Blackfeet consider and keep them like daughters now." He spoke this gently and kindly. He could not scold her for her grief. He shared that grief but could not give way to foolhardiness.

She quieted that night as he showed her that he still loved and held her dear. In his love embrace, she finally obtained what comfort was possible in her great loss. His strength and steadiness had helped her clear her head and balanced the tumult in her soul. Even so, she still clung to the idea of rescue. It was intolerable that her daughters should be abandoned forever to Blackfeet servitude. In the morning, she would plead again with their father, who must not consign them to that fate.

"No, it is impossible." Lone Wolf stood firm in his resistance. He left her to brood in the teepee in the morning and went to tend to the horses. He encountered Rides-the-Wind in the pasture, brushing out the mane of his white stallion.

"She still insists I pursue the captors," he said as he joined his father in the meadow where the first frost tipped the leaves of grass.

"Maybe we should ride to the plains in a show that we did pursue them. After a while, we can return and say we spotted a large encampment. A raid meant certain death with no assurance the girls were in there."

"That is practice of deceit. I could not do that."

"I suggest it as only a way to bring your woman some peace."

"Give her time. I know she will regain her senses. Deep inside she is strong. She will stand tall again," Lone Wolf said. He knew his woman well. She possessed inner reserves of stamina. As winter deepened and the snow wrapped the world in white, he observed her start to sing again as she cooked and sewed as if she wished to ease the pain and accept responsibility for her own healing. That winter of her sorrow, the white fur traders visited again, bringing fresh merchandise, ribbons and buttons, glass beads, bolts of cotton, knives and axes, saddles, and blankets. The traders knew a few words of the Salish language, having dealt with related Salish bands across the western mountain range. They were big men who stood taller than any of the Salish chiefs. They portaged from river to river as they traveled by canoe, trading and trapping between the great water and the intermountain region. The *suyapi* were very friendly and brought curious amulets and charms with them. They were eager to show and tell the Salish all about these magical objects.

That winter, White Heron felt life quicken within her womb. The child moved inside, and she thought it kicked like a boy. Just as her body enclosed new life, the valley, rich in food and game, sheltered and nourished. There, surrounded by high peaks, in the following autumn, she delivered the fruit of Lone Wolf's planting nine moons past. His newborn son in his arms, Lone Wolf emerged from the teepee, his moccasins crunching on the early dusting of snow that had fallen during the night and lifted the baby to the powder-blue sky. The elongated cloud formed the shape of a lead wolf of a pack above the rim of the mountain. He murmured, "That is good. You will be Running Wolf from this day forward." He uttered a birthday song of praise, and his feet instinctively started to dance in rhythm to his chant.

"Ho, Sun, Moon, Stars and Sky," he sang. "Ho, Winter, Spring, Summer, Autumn. Into your circle, a new son of earth. Give him, I beseech, a smooth path to breech the sacred hills. Make his heart strong, his feet fleet. Ho, Fire, Earth, Water, and Wind. Give him, I beseech a shining path to lead the pack."

He re-entered the buffalo-hide teepee and placed the infant in White Heron's lap. Her face shone as bright as the morning sun after a labor that had been easy. After the baby had been delivered and swaddled, she had combed her silky black hair, parted it in the middle and tied the two strands with a leather thong to hang neatly at each shoulder. Her caramel complexion, the Asiatic slant to her eyelids, and finely shaped lips marked her one of the outstanding beauties of the tribe. Her youth and sturdy body were made for childbearing, this delivery much faster than the two earlier ones of her lost girls. Tears welled in her eyes as she remembered them, but she quenched them to not dampen their joy at the birth of a son. A fire burned in the middle of the floor; the smoke wafted upward through the open flaps at the top where the poles met.

A few moments later, they heard footsteps outside, and a voice spoke their language in a foreign cadence of the far northeastern woodlands, a sojourner in their land for the last ten years.

"Big Ignace, here to anoint the newborn with water."

"Come in and see my son."

Big Ignace carried a flask and unscrewed the cap. "I will christen the child as the Black Robe taught me to do."

Lone Wolf stayed his hand. "No need to do that. I have already thanked the Great Spirit and invoked his protection. The blessings of the earth are bestowed upon him. I have told you many times before that our people have their rites, and they are the ones I will practice."

"The Black Robe's religion is stronger. I have seen its power. It sweeps over the land from sea to sea. You have not witnessed what I have witnessed. Their God made them mighty among the nations. By adopting their medicine, your people will survive."

"I stood outside the village to meet you and Little Ignace when you arrived many seasons ago with your black beads and crosses. Let your amulets protect you. Many of our people believed your teachings about this God sacrificed on a cross. You have convinced them of the Long Knives' powerful medicine. All I have seen is strange disease and dwindling of the game since I first laid eyes upon the fur trappers who came to barter for our pelts. We have none to trade. We have only enough for our shelter, clothing, and food. We will not kill to trade."

"The sacrament of Baptism cleanses the baby of Original Sin and grants him eternal life."

"My son is innocent. Go now. We do not need your water."

Big Ignace departed reluctantly, saying. "I will pray for you and your family."

The baby had fallen asleep nestled close to White Heron, and soon she was dozing comfortably too. Lone Wolf stepped outside, irritated that Big Ignace had intruded. He remembered vividly the day when Big Ignace and his son had appeared with the white traders, Upon the western horizon, he saw the string of packhorses approach. The women and children gathered outside the ring of teepees clustered around the river that twisted and turned through the valley. At first, they communicated with the traders through sign language and learned his purpose. Chief Three Eagles invited them into his teepee and passed the peace pipe with the travelers. Big Ignace introduced the Long Beard David Thompson, who had built a trading post at the falls from where salmon rushed downriver to their secure valley. The tribe knew tales of the great water at land's edge because Salish bands long ago had branched off from that territory. Another Indian scout Latreque, an oily-haired half-breed whose mother was western Salish and whose father was a pale face, was a translator. Thompson wanted the Salish to trap beaver. He, in return, would supply us with cooking pots, sturdy axes, blankets, and many fine things. The chiefs were impressed, handling the sharp tools, immediately realizing how valuable they were. He and his father, Rides-the-Wind had questioned the relationship. Lone Wolf had also voiced his concerns during the council Chief Three Eagles had called a council to discuss trade relations with the white men and acceptance of the Iroquois into the tribe. Lone Wolf had pointed out that already the people had seen fewer beaver and otter in the streams. Deer and elk eluded them. In the summer, they had to travel farther to the east to find buffalo. They warred with the Blackfeet over the herds. The Blackfeet had fire sticks to their advantage, and only now were the Salish able to obtain weapons more lethal than arrows from captives and in trade with the white men.

"Many of our people have died of the spotted disease, our medicine men unable to heal them. We have sufficient food to sustain our smaller numbers. Go barter with other tribes. We wish to live in peace alone. So long as the white men leave us alone, we will not harm them," Lone Wolf had said and passed the pipe to the next sub-chief.

Big Ignace had spoken of his land located many months of travel to the east, of the towns and forts that the French had built, and of the kindly Black Robes who taught him good medicine. The Black Robes had baptized him and his son with water and commissioned them to travel to the far regions of the world to preach the Gospel of their God called Jesus Christ. From beneath his buckskin shirt, he pulled out a silver crucifix strung on a leather thong. He moved the cross in four directions, muttering some words unintelligible to the chiefs. Latreque translated for them.

"He is signing you with the Sign of the Cross in the name of the Father, the Son, and the Holy Spirit."

"Ah, the same Great Spirit," Chief Three Eagles said. "All men are sons and daughters of the Great Spirit. Let me hold that cross." Big Ignace removed the cross from his neck and handed it to the chief.

"Ho, it has four points. The four directions." With a forefinger, he drew a circle around the cross. "See, I make it into the medicine wheel. North, East, South, West. The hoop."

Lone Wolf had remained impassive, but his spirit was unsettled, perceiving that the principal chief's interest was aroused.

"Speak more of the words of these Black Robes. Why do you believe their words?"

"Their medicine is powerful. They offer their God bread and red liquor called wine. The bread and wine are the body and blood of the God. It holds great power to bring them health and happiness. I have learned their rites of sacrifice and will teach them to you. They also have a Great Mother, Mary, a Virgin Mother." From a leather satchel, Big Ignace pulled out a ring of black beads with a short tail and cross at the end. "I will teach you the songs to pray on each bead."

In the cycle of seasons since the two Iroquois had arrived, the chiefs' interest had grown rather than diminished. They had stayed after the traders left and were adopted into the tribe, eventually learning the Salish language. They had enacted the rituals of the *suyapi*'s religion, and the chief's fascination with the tales Big Ignace and Little Ignace told continued to fascinate them.

"I am not a medicine man of their religion. I only know enough to tell you about it. You must have a Black Robe come. He is the holy leader."

The presence of the Iroquois had not affected their life. They had continued to live as they had always done. They wintered in the western valley, but in spring, they traveled over the mountain pass eastward to the place of the buffalo jump, where they had hunted since time immemorial. Now they did not have to stampede the buffalo over the cliff to kill and harvest every bit of the animal for food, hides, and bone for tools. They had obtained guns from the Blackfeet, and soon they had become as skilled in shooting as other tribes on the Great Plains. But competition for the dwindling herds had led to warfare with the Blackfeet. They managed to stay close to the eastern edge of the mountain range, killing the number of buffalo necessary for their needs and returning with their travois laden with the hides and their parfleches filled with pemmican sufficient to feed them until the next season.

Lone Wolf remembered clearly again the council Chief Three Eagles had called before he had decided to allow the Iroquois to dwell among them. In the meeting, Three Eagles held the talking stick and began to speak. "Big Ignace asks to stay and live with us. What say you?"

Woodcock had indicated he wished to speak. The chief passed the talking stick to him. "The Iroquois have traded with many nations. They know the *suyapi's* ways. Our friends, the Nimiipuu, have been trading with them for many seasons. Our enemies, the Blackfeet, obtained strong medicine from them. These Iroquois who want to live with us trust the *suyapi*. They say they can bring the Black Robes' powerful magic to us. Big Ignace praises their Great

Spirit and claims it is the *suyapi*'s religion that makes them so numerous and able to prevail against us." Woodcock passed the talking stick to Chief Three Eagles.

"I think what the Iroquois say carries truth. It is clear that the white men possess superior power that their Great Spirit has given them. I have heard Big Ignace say the Black Robes promise eternal life. The god on the cross rose from the dead and will give the men who believe in him immortality. Ah, that is the secret I want to hear. What say you? Shall we let Ignace and his son stay with us?"

Woodcock took the stick again, "It is clear also that the Great Spirit favors the white men. I, for one, want to hear Big Ignace speak. He and his son must stay and learn our language perfectly to explain these things." He passed the stick back to the chief.

"You speak rightly," Chief Three Eagles said. "They will live here and learn to speak our language. They babble like little children already."

Rides-the-Wind and Lone Wolf had listened with impassive faces while Woodcock and Three Eagles expressed their opinions. Then Rides-the-Wind extended his hand to show he wished to speak.

"If the Iroquois wish to live according to our traditions, let them stay, but we should not rush to change our ways. Not everything they bring is good. They bring sickness. They have pushed hostile nations to our borders that chase us from our ancient hunting grounds. Warfare has arisen among the people of the earth. Horse stealing is widespread. People are no longer satisfied with what they have. They want more. The earth is soaked with blood. The game flees from the fire sticks in the forest where we find fewer of them year after year. We must not be hasty to accept everything the *suyapi* brings. Can we say his religion is better than the Great Spirit of our Fathers? I do not see they have more honor and virtue for it." He passed the stick to Lone Wolf.

"I agree with my father. New things are not all good."

Some men had given silent acquiescence to what Lone Wolf said, while others sat impassively, deferring to the chief's opinion. None signaled they wished the talking stick, so Lone Wolf relinquished the stick to Chief Three Eagles.

"You speak well. The ills we face we can overcome with the powerful medicine we know the white men have. They promise immortality. The Blackfeet arrows will not kill us, they say. We must hear out the Iroquois and listen closely. Our numbers are small, but the strength the Iroquois offer could mean our survival. They will remain with us and share their knowledge. This is my decision, and so it is."

After the meeting had ended, outside in the light of the moon, Lone Wolf shared his feelings with his father, "A sour taste is in my mouth. I cannot explain it. Though these Iroquois are polite and pleasant, I feel their presence bodes no good eventually for our people. I do not know why." He shook his head.

"Come what will, we will endure," Rides-the-Wind replied. "It is true that the *suyapi*'s God is strong and favors them, but I do not like it. We will see what will be."

Several days later, the white traders had departed, and Big Ignace and his son had settled into the life of the village. Immediately, they took Salish wives who erected a teepee of buffalo hide for the two men. They moved their wives and possessions into this teepee and built a low table inside on which they placed a crucifix and chalice. They knelt before this altar, muttering prayers in a strange language. They had a string of black beads that they fingered one by one from the cross on a short tail back to the cross in a circle of incantations. They tried to get the people to repeat the words. The first ritual they succeeded in teaching them was a gesture that included touching the fingers to the forehead, to the heart, to the left of the chest, and to the right of the chest. The people liked doing this because it reminded them of how they waved the sacred smoking sage bundle in the four directions. Later, Big Ignace explained that he could not teach them everything. His knowledge fell short of the Black Robes because they were consecrated preachers, deeply learned in the holy rites.

"Like shamans," Woodcock said.

"Not exactly," Big Ignace said. "They are ordained priests, apostles of Jesus Christ. I am a humble servant, inadequate to spread Christ's teachings."

"Who is this Christ?" Woodcock asked.

"The Son of God. The Black Robes can explain everything."

"Aren't we all sons of God?" Woodcock persisted.

"Yes, that is true, except Jesus really is the Son of God, human and divine."

"Hmmm," Woodcock, his brow furrowed, mused. "I don't understand."

"The Black Robes will help you understand."

"Where are these Black Robes?" Chief Three Eagles asked.

"To the east."

"Will they come to us?" the chief asked.

"Someday. There are few of them. There are not enough to serve the churches there, but I will teach you what I know."

Lone Wolf, standing nearby, had overheard this conversation.

Big Ignace had made an impact on his people and was entrenched firmly in the life of the Salish in less than one cycle of the seasons. All these remembrances ran through Lone Wolf's mind the morning his son was born. He wondered what world Running Wolf had entered? He vowed to preserve the heritage of his people now and forever and stand as a shield against the influence of Big Ignace and Little Ignace. Too many of his elders were being seduced by the allure of immortality and sought to be more powerful than their enemies. His desire was only to live in peace.

While Lone Wolf had been reviewing in his mind these past events, White Heron and the baby had not stirred. He heard footsteps outside the teepee and rose, leaving mother and son to rest. Little Ignace stood at the entrance, his body casting a shadow, his back to the sun that had ascended and now peeked above the tips of the eastern mountains. The not-so-little Ignace greeted Lone Wolf and congratulated him on his son. Stockier than his father, Little Ignace shared his father's zeal for this Christ. He wore a medal around his chest. It was not a cross with the crucified Christ but an oblong medallion with an image of a woman with her head veiled, arms outstretched, and her bare feet on the head of a serpent. The Salish respected the serpent and its power to strike suddenly. This woman apparently was more powerful than the venomous serpent with flicking forked tongue. The Iroquois had talked enthusiastically of this woman and claimed she was Christ's mother. For Lone Wolf, there was no woman more powerful than Mother Earth.

He saluted Little Ignace with a "Ho," and started to move past the man, but Little Ignace wanted to talk. He talked too much just as the *suyapi* talked too much. He picked up this bad habit from the *suyapi*. It was better to speak little and listen much.

"You should let my father baptize your son," Little Ignace said.

"Hasn't he baptized enough children, the sons and daughters of our chiefs and elders? Let him sprinkle water on the ones who think that water makes them immortal."

"I pray for your disbelief," Little Ignace said. "The Black Robes can explain baptism better than I can."

"Talk . . . talk . . . all your talk is of these Black Robes. Then go and dwell with them. Why stay with us?"

"Because in all my travels, I have not met a finer or nobler race of men."

"Aha, then we do not need saving," Lone Wolf shot back and briskly walked away.

The two Iroquois, he thought, were not bad men. They were amiable and adaptable, fitting well into the customs of his people, not lying or cheating. They were not quarrelsome. Indeed, if they found children squabbling over a game, they intervened to settle disputes. They were universally liked and did not violate the tenets of the ten rules of conduct that they preached. Not only were they of good character, but they were excellent trappers. Their knowledge of animal behavior was respected and valued. Everyone counted Big Ignace and Little Ignace as valuable additions to their tribe. Lone Wolf admitted he liked them. If only they would leave off talking about the *suyapi's* religion. It was monotonous, a constant drumbeat in his ears that his impulse was to escape. In that sentiment, he was a minority in his village. Among the few that shared his feelings were Rides-the-Wind, Sweet Grass, and White Heron. But now he had a son to whom he would pass on the values of the grandfathers. He deemed it his sacred duty to transmit to Running Wolf the wisdom of the ages.

His education began immediately. With his first babble and smile, he heard the stories of his forefathers. When he started to walk, Lone Wolf lifted him in front of him on horseback and rode to all the sacred places—the rocks, trees, and springs—that figured in the legends. He showed him where the great ice field melted and where the monsters were slain. At three, he whittled his first bow and arrow for the toddler. His grandfather Rides-the-Wind gave him his first pony. Grandfather and father taught him to track the elk and deer. He went with them into the mountains at age five, mounted on his own pinto pony. Rides-the-Wind looked at the fresh-faced boy, sparkling with joy and zest for the world around him, and murmured, "He is destined to lead."

Although Running Wolf learned to ride as soon as he could sit astride a horse by himself, he preferred to feel the earth under his feet. Rides-the-Wind did not fault him for that, saying, "Each person must find their way. A man follows his nature."

With pride, grandfather and father observed the nature of the boy develop. They recognized early that his strength arose from his feet. Even at six years old, his fleetness won the foot races with the other boys of the village. They ran for pure enjoyment and sheer love of their limbs. Running Wolf's calves and thighs grew in power and agility. He joined in the fun of the boyish games, target practice and races. Not shy of these competitive activities, he still sought out solitude at a young age. At nine, he wandered from the village, distressing his mother when he did not return at nightfall.

"He is too little; the bear will mangle him," his mother cried.

Rides-the-Wind tried to calm her. "He has often been in the forest with his father and me. He is young but wise beyond his years. He sensed the movement and nearness of animals before we did. His nose and ears are keener than ours and as keen as the wiliest animal. Once, he knew a big cat was ready to pounce from a cliff. He stopped us in our tracks and pointed to where the cat was poised. We whooped then and fired our rifles. We did not wish to kill the cat, only scare him away. He turned tail and disappeared. Running Wolf was happy the cat did not attack. He will be all right, White Heron. He will find his way back, sniffing the ground, tracing the direction he came."

"I hope you are right. He is only a boy."

"But a boy who blends in with the earth," his grandfather stated.

White Heron spent a restless night. Soon after she awoke to stir the embers in the firepit, she heard a voice. "Ho, mother, I am home." Running Wolf entered the tent, holding a rabbit by the ears.

"I brought something for you to cook," he said.

White Heron was so happy to see him that she hugged him, took the rabbit from him, and immediately began to skin the animal that Running Wolf had already gutted.

"I will line the moccasins I am making for you with rabbit fur. But, son, you are yet too young to wander at night."

"There is no cause to worry. The night is not my enemy. Even in the darkness I hear and smell the creatures, who, like me, nestle for warmth under the leaves and in the hollow of trees."

"But the bear can smell you, and the mother bear does not want you near her cubs."

"She has nothing to fear from me nor I from her. We agree to leave each other alone."

White Heron looked lovingly at her son. "You are wise beyond your years. How did you come to think such things?"

"I learned them from the earth. It is foolish to fear the wilderness. The wilderness is my friend."

"But you venture alone where an enemy may hide or where no friend may hear your cry for help."

"Do not fret. My father and grandfather and the spirits of my ancestors watch my every step."

Running Wolf did not heed his mother's warnings not to venture far alone. It vexed her that Lone Wolf and Rides-the-Wind did not share her concern. They brushed aside her suggestion that they accompany the boy in his explorations. "He has no better companion than his guardian spirit," Lone Wolf countered, "the leader of the wolf pack. The wolf pads through the timber soundlessly, sniffing the wind, taking the prey he needs, and no more. His coat blends in perfectly in the shadows and against the rocks and tree trunks. He is safe, White Heron. His skills as a hunter and scout in manhood will make him famous. He is a born leader."

White Heron wondered how the men could have such assurance, but since the loss of her girls, her heart was unsteady. She could not be as brave and unswerving as Lone Wolf and Rides-the-Wind. Her nose picked up danger when they remained unperturbed over Lone Wolf's inclination to roam alone. Then she considered that it was the trait of the lone wolf that the boy imbibed from his father.

On one score, the father and grandfather shared apprehension. Neither liked the influence that the Iroquois exerted on the chiefs who permitted them to practice their religion, baptize, and talk incessantly about the *suyapi's* powerful religion. They adamantly refused to participate in the prayers and ceremonies Big Ignace conducted. He talked about a Holy Sacrifice of the Mass that he was not empowered to enact. Only the Black Robe could perform this magic.

"Then go get us one of your medicine men," Chief Three Eagles said.

"We would have to go to a place by the Big Flowing River . . . a place called St. Louis where the traders and Black Robes gather. From there, they paddle up the Ouemesourita River from the land where the people of the dugout canoe dwell until they reach the plains on the eastern side of our mountains."

"Hmm," the chief pondered. He realized the expedition presented a challenging and daunting expedition through hostile territory, and he was not ready yet to order such an undertaking. It required more thought. It needed men capable of success. For the moment, he could think of no men he could sacrifice for such a risky business.

Lone Wolf was glad to see the chief's hesitancy, believing it was a fool's mission. Running Wolf told his father, "I am bold enough to attempt the journey only to see these lands I have heard them talk about, but my heart tells me bringing back a Black Robe would also bring ill luck."

"Your feelings are true. Let us hope they speak no more of this foolhardy idea, and our leaders do not give it serious consideration."

"Yes, I think my feelings are true," Running Wolf said.

They did not speak further of the Iroquois and their influence but went about their own business with Salish life continuing as it had done for generations. Running Wolf penetrated farther into northern regions where his tribe did not usually range. They were too sacred. They were where the peaks remained snow-covered even in summer.

The women took down the summer tule teepees and assembled the winter teepees, first constructing a tripod of three sturdy lodge poles the men had cut down and shaved off the bark to make smooth supports. Then, using ropes, they lifted three additional poles between the main supports. Next, the buffalo hides were spread uniformly around the poles, and lastly, the flap for the opening on top for the smoke to escape from the fire pit in the center of the teepee. Another entrance flap was attached by cross-length pieces of wood. The Salish were prepared for the cold. This was the season of storytelling, of mining the memory for tales of courage and daring. Running Wolf enjoyed this season of hibernation like the bear as much as he loved exploration of the far northern hills and valleys.

One night, the fire flickering in the center of the chief's lodge, the prominent men gathered in a clutch of warmth, with Big Ignace and Little Ignace accepted partners in this comradeship, the conversation turned to the danger the Blackfeet posed. They had crept in a few nights ago and stolen three valuable horses. The threat of winter storms and being caught in a blizzard did not daunt the Blackfeet from their depredations. They had grown bolder and bolder over the years. The demons just hunker down in a cave, wait for the snow to abate, and then slink back to their camps in the east with their ill-gotten gains.

Big Ignace spoke. "There is only one way to deal with them, to defeat this menace. Stronger medicine."

Not again, Running Wolf thought. He is going to beat that drum. He looked at his father and grandfather to confirm they shared the same supposition. It was unnecessary for Chief Three Eagles to ask what Ignace meant. Every man could guess correctly. Ignace did not wait for a question but continued to speak.

"You all know what I mean. We cannot delay. For a long time, I have spoken of the benefits to gain from a Black Robe living among us. Their god bestows powerful medicine. If we fully embrace the Black Robe's medicine, we will be stronger than the Blackfeet. They will be unable to defeat or kill us in battle. It is past time to go to the White Father's house in St. Louis and plead with him to send us a Black Robe."

"Who is brave enough to attempt such a mission?" Chief Three Eagles asked. "Are you, big talker, willing to go?"

"No, but I have found four men who will, and they are here."

"Name them."

"Black Eagle and Speaking Eagle, who I have baptized, strong young Nimiipuu men. Two younger braves, No Horns on His Head and Rabbit's Skin Leggings listened to me and volunteered to go also. The four pray with me on Sundays, the day of our rest." Ignace was always careful to explain who could administer a provisional baptism in the absence of a consecrated priest. Although beneficial as a temporary measure for the purification of the soul of the baptized, it did not carry the full sacramental grace that a priest officiating could bestow.

"Ho, the Nimiipuu are our friends. Do they know the way?" Chief Three Eagles asked.

"I gave them the maps I have from the fur trader Letreque. They know how to get to the fort on the Ouemesourita River. From there they will meet up with traders who will take them the rest of the way by canoe down to St. Louis City."

"What say you all?" The chief's eyes circled the men, and each in succession with a nod indicated agreement—all except Rides-the-Wind and Lone Wolf.

"Speak," Chief Three Eagles ordered Rides-the-Wind. "Let us hear your objection."

"We know what the *suyapi* brings—disease and division."

"The Black Robes are different. They bring peace and brotherhood," Big Ignace protested.

"So say you," countered Rides-the-Wind. "They belong to the same race. I do not feel good around them."

"And you, Lone Wolf?" The chief looked at him.

"The Great Spirit has protected our people. I do not seek the power of the *suyapi*."

"He is wrong. His stubbornness would melt before the words of the Black Robe," Big Ignace said.

"The only way to find out the truth and settle the matter is for a Black Robe to come. Then we can decide for ourselves which of you is right. Therefore, it is my judgment that the expedition should set forth in the spring and bring back with them a Black Robe. *Šey hoy,* that is all," Chief Three Eagles finished. He had rendered his verdict with the concurrence of all save the two dissenters. Now that the chief had approved a delegation to St. Louis, Rides-the-Wind and Lone Wolf held their tongues. They harbored doubts, but they would not openly oppose the mission.

When the streams gushed again with melting snow, Black Eagle and Speaking Eagle, baptized as Narcisse and Paul, began to prepare for their perilous journey. The two younger braves, No Horns on His Head and Rabbit's Skin Leggings, selected the extra mounts and packhorses they needed. They gathered food supplies, sharpened arrows, and filled powder horns. Songs and dance preceded the departure of the four emissaries to the east. Big Ignace and Little Ignace knelt and offered prayers to their unknown god. Since they had come to live with the Salish, Little Ignace had fathered two sons, Charles and Francis, boys younger than Running Wolf, who were fully accepted into the tribe. They participated in all the childhood activities of the other boys. Running Wolf had no cause to dislike them. In all regards, he considered them equals, and they were cheerful and good-natured participants in the life of the village. They were counted among the Salish; their Iroquois paternity provided no cause for distinction.

The mission set forth, well-supplied with provisions for the expected four-month journey to the confluence of the two great rivers. Running Wolf stood with his father and grandfather watching the party fade into the distant hills. From time to time, the train of packhorses and riders looked like dark specks outlined against a treeless ridge and then disappeared around a bend in the mountain wall.

"Who knows if we will ever see any of them again," Rides-the-Wind murmured.

"Who knows how many will reach St. Louis before the Blackfeet kill them?" added Lone Wolf.

"One or none, I guess," said Running Wolf.

"I fear you guess right," Rides-the-Wind said, but did not look at the boy, wise beyond his years, who gazed at the eastern horizon. "It is a fool's errand."

"What will happen will happen," Lone Wolf said. "Who can stop the wind from blowing?"

They separated to return to their individual tasks, Rides-the-Wind to tend his beloved horses, Lone Wolf to whittle fresh arrows, and Running Wolf to the seclusion of his forest retreat. He sat upon a rocky outcropping that overlooked a waterfall that fed the Willow River. He might interpret his father's words as pessimistic about the future, but he rather thought them realistic about a man's ability to control the world. The Great Spirit had set limitations upon both man and all nature; boundaries to the waters. Even the term of a man's life had a limit. Each natural element had a set role to play in the grand scheme of the universe. Men who sought to overstep those boundaries ultimately received their comeuppance. That truth was told countless times in the escapades of Coyote. Happiness was contentment with one's possessions and station in life. Man was a creature of the environment in which he was born, in the earth from which he was formed, and here in the vicinity of the gurgling water, Running Wolf knew he belonged. He communed with the earth, and it answered in the rippling of the stream, in the rustle of the leaves, in the plaintive howl of the song dog—the coyote—the whistle of the wind through the canyon—all composed the language of the Great Spirit. These thoughts filled Running Wolf's heart to overflowing. As he grew in years and stature, his love for the earth deepened and expanded.

The busy season of berry-picking and digging for camas and bitterroot overtook thoughts of the fate of the delegation to St. Louis. The men, preoccupied with the training of horses and fashioning of arrows and bows for hunting in the fall, concentrated on the tasks necessary for the tribe's sustenance. Despite the onset of the fur trade and the acquisition of guns, Salish customs and traditions continued unchanged except for the addition of utensils and materials made of metal. They had exchanged porcupine-quill decoration for glass beads, but that was merely an enhancement of an age-old art. The important concerns of food, clothing, and shelter dominated and shoved talk of the four men bound for St. Louis into the background. The summer reed teepees were taken down and burned, and the buffalo-hide teepees for winter erected. Various bands from surrounding areas again assembled for the buffalo hunt, and the massive task of processing the kill resumed. The women tanned and sewed the softened hides into garments, which they decorated with beads, feathers, and bones. In the depth of winter, snow piled waist-high, they snuggled in their teepees around the warmth of the fire pit and again told the legends that had sustained and inspired their people from time immemorial, secure in the faith that nothing could disrupt the inexorable cycle of the seasons that Mother Earth dictated. They discerned the pattern in the stars and observed it in the movement of sun and moon.

The days lengthened and warmed again. The streams furiously flowed with melted snow from the mountains. Buds appeared on the bushes, and the hummingbirds returned. The yellow heads of flowers poked from their burial holes in the earth. Spring foals romped in the meadows. The village stirred with activity. There was much to gather. The buffalo teepees were disassembled and pieces of willow woven together to form the tule-reed teepees. Work suddenly stopped when Rabbit's Skin Leggings, weakened and thin, rode into the camp in late spring. Heads turned and ran toward the mounted brave. Excitedly, they clamored around him, asking where were the others who had set out with him two years ago. Some asked why was there no Black Robe with him.

"Patience. I will tell you all," he said. They made room for Rabbit's Skin Leggings to dismount. Chief Three Eagles broke through the crowd and greeted the weary traveler with a clasp of his forearm.

"Where are your companions?" the chief began.

"It is a sad tale. Let me eat and drink, and I will tell you all."

The women scurried to bring him food and water. Chief Three Eagles led him to a spot in the center of the circle of teepees and indicated that Rabbit's Skin Leggings should sit beside him. The chief had aged in the year Rabbit's Skin Leggings had been gone. His face was rugged and brown like the bark of a tree. He still had straight teeth in his mouth, but the skin around his eyes sagged, and lines like bird's feet traced a path around his mouth. The important men of the village gathered and joined them, seated on the ground. Running Wolf hovered behind his father and grandfather along with the women and children, anxious to hear what would be said.

"We made it to the headwaters of the Ouemesourita River and the big *suyapi* trading post," Rabbit's Skin Leggings began. There we boarded the biggest boat I had ever seen . . . it is like a *suyapi* house that floats with a big pipe through which smoke rises, but it went faster than any canoe. We heard many tongues on the boat, so many we could not understand their speech, and few were there who could understand us, but after many days we arrived at the city called St. Louis, filled with more people than I had ever seen in my life. There were four-wheeled carts, horsemen everywhere, and houses tall as some trees with openings looking out on the people and animals in the streets, drovers and peddlers, cows and pigs moving about. It was wondrous and confusing. We made it known through signs that we wanted to go to the White Father's House. They told us his name was Chief William Clark, who was said to have come to our land a long time ago, but he did not remember much of our language. Somehow he was made to understand that we looked for the chief of the Black Robes, and we were sent to the great church with a big cross on top and beautiful images inside. There was no one to make our meaning clear to this Black Robe, try as we could. Then our leaders, Black Eagle and Speaking Eagle, got very sick, so sick they could not get up. Their flesh burned to my touch. No Horns on the Head and I did not know what to do. The *suyapi* medicine man could not help them, and we found them dead in the morning. We despaired, not knowing what to do, but the Black Robes there took the bodies and buried them in their sacred ground. We were afraid we would catch the *suyapi* sickness, and decided we must return home. A party of traders and trappers was heading west, and we showed we wished to get on the boat loaded with trade goods. There was a very friendly white man on board who wanted to paint our pictures. Many days we sat still as stone as he copied our faces." Rabbit's Skin Leggings extended his arms to show how large the portraits were. "This man had pots of many colors and hair brushes he used to apply the paint. When he was done, we were amazed at our likenesses, and then we were not sure we should have let him do it, for what if he had captured our spirits and would use them for no good? No Horns on the Head then said he could not believe that of the painter who had kind eyes. I agreed and was no longer worried. When the boat reached the *suyapi* post called Fort Union at the headwaters of the Ouemesourita River, the painter bid us farewell. We were told by other travelers who understood both his language and our language that he planned to visit other peoples on the plains and paint their faces also . . . the Mandan, the Sioux, and Blackfeet . . . among other tribes he said. We were told his name was George Catlin. Shortly, after we got off the boat to continue our journey on horseback, No Horns on His Head got very sick. He could not get on his horse. I made him as comfortable as I could. He had chills and fever and sweated greatly. I placed a buffalo robe over him. His eyes swam in his head, and then his heart quit beating. I buried him and continued my sad journey. *Šey hoy,* that is all." Rabbit's Skin Leggings finished his tale.

Silence ruled for several moments. The mission had not only failed, but three of the delegation had failed to return alive. The bearer of the sad report also sat silently, waiting for the chief to respond, but he did not for a long time. Finally, in a grave tone, Chief Three Eagles spoke.

"Success was not to be, but that means we must try again. The mission failed because no one understood your wishes. Someone must go who can clearly explain our desires."

Big Ignace spoke up, "I must be the one to go next time. I speak the language of the French voyageurs. The Black Robes come from their native land far, far across an eastern ocean. In their tongue, I will make them understand our desire. My son will go with me along with his sons Charles and Francis."

"It is too late in the season to make it there before winter, and too dangerous because the Blackfeet are on the warpath, attacking hunting parties and anyone who dares traverse their territory. It is not safe. We must wait until the menace is not as great," Chief Three Eagles said.

Events intervened that delayed another mission for longer than they anticipated. Enemy raids did not lessen, and the winter proved particularly severe. Spring weather brought heavy flooding; the rivers rampaged, making fording difficult if not all but impossible. And then sorrow struck. The old chief weakened; he spoke in whispers and rarely left his teepee. One morning he said, "Take me to the sacred tree. I will sit down there to die where my spirit can fly and soar into the western sky. There I will sing my death song." Before he could be lifted unto a travois and transported to the designated spot, his eyes looked vacantly at Woodcock, Lone Wolf, and Rides-the-Wind, come to bear him away. Woodcock placed his hand over his mouth. Feeling no breath, he said, "We must sing him on his way to the spirit world."

Standing Grizzly, the son of the chief's sister, had for some time assumed prominence among the sub-chiefs because he had confronted an enraged grizzly bear that had pounced upon an elk before Standing Grizzly could reach the fallen animal he had just shot. Expertly, he had reloaded his rifle and shot the animal dead right between the eyes. Standing Grizzly now came forward to preside over the burial rites for his uncle. The women tiptoed in to prepare the body for burial. They washed the body and dressed the dead man in his finest clothes. At a fair distance from the camp, secluded among the pines, a grave was dug. No stones or other markings were placed on the plot to indicate a body was buried there for fear any marker would keep the spirit trapped in the earth and not free to fly from the body. Back at the village, his teepee was burned and his possessions distributed. His close female relatives cut their hair, and they wailed inconsolably. Standing Grizzly took his place as ceremonial leader beside the other chieftains of the tribe—the hunt leader, the war leader, and clan leaders. His encounter with the bear had engendered him with significant stature among the elders. He was respected as an accurate marksman and acknowledged as a worthy replacement for Three Eagles in the tribal council because he possessed the bear medicine that would enable him to protect the people and stand up for what was right and just.

Lone Wolf gathered to listen as Standing Grizzly presided over the death song ceremony.

*O, ho, yo, he has flown*
*So cries the wind,*

> *So cries the trees,*
> *O, ho, yo, so cry we.*
> *O, ho, yo, he goes to his mother*
> *He goes to his father,*
> *He goes to the spirit world*
> *O, ho, yo, we sing him on his way.*

The people accepted death as part of life and integral to the cycle of the seasons, represented in the medicine wheel. The black, white, red, and yellow quadrants represented the four directions and the four seasons, and the circle symbolized that all life was interconnected. So sorrow would give way to joy.

Before he assumed the chieftainship, Standing Grizzly had developed a close friendship with Ignace and his son. A seeker of knowledge, he possessed a curious and inquiring mind and believed that the Black Robes could bestow great power upon his people. Consequently, he fully supported a second delegation to St. Louis. And he was not opposed to allowing the Iroquois to practice their rites and recite their prayers among the Salish. His tolerance gained many enthusiastic followers of their religion.

"My people must learn more of your unknown Great Spirit, who you say, is unlike ours and is almighty, all-knowing, and powerful. It is clear that he has done much for the *suyapi*; they multiply and spread over all the earth."

"Ho," Lone Wolf interjected, "like locusts who eat every blade of grass in their path."

"Lone Wolf, such is the exact power we seek in order to subdue the ravaging Blackfeet. You see out of only one eye, my brother. The wise man will listen to the knowledge of other men. The Black Robe holds knowledge that we must learn. We will take what is useful, true, and good, and return the husks of the grain to him. We must think and weigh, for our senses of sight, taste, hearing, touch, and smell have been given to us by the Great Spirit. It is given to the people to learn of all creatures; everything created has a place and a purpose."

Along with the medicine of the bear, Lone Wolf recognized that Standing Bear's oratory strengthened his fitness for leadership. His uncle Chief Three Eagles had been a man of firm but few words, but his nephew explained the reasons for his thoughts. Lone Wolf did not wish to argue with him. He held his own thoughts closer because they were based on instinct rather than logic.

Big Ignace again expressed his enthusiasm to embark on a second mission.

"Patience, my brother," Standing Grizzly said, "I cannot spare you now. Our numbers have dwindled from warfare and sickness. In consultation with my guardian spirit, I will tell you when the time is right to depart, but not before I am properly directed. The mother bear guards her cubs, and so shall I protect my people. *Šey hoy*, I am finished."

Running Wolf, in the intervening years between the first and the second mission, was growing into manhood. His limbs had lengthened; he stood as tall as his father but still not as well-muscled as Lone Wolf. The adolescent Running Wolf's joy in exploration of every nook and cranny of the land emboldened him to venture farther and farther afield. His expertise in living off the bounty of the land increased. Over time, his mother's concern for his safety abated, and he always returned home unharmed from his adventures abroad. He knew every cove and island in the Broad Water to the north. On its shore, he set his willow traps for salmon and brought home baskets of fish for his mother to smoke. This lake stretched for miles, and at its northernmost tip, the Kalispel band camped. He stopped there and visited with his relatives and then, after a few days' rest, ventured north to where the sacred peaks crowned with snow glimmered in the distance. He tramped through forests of cedar, inhaling its rich aroma, and hiked along mountain lakes to towering summits, where he paused and surveyed the expansive tree-covered valleys below. What wonders he took in, what glories on the heights where eagles soared. He reached the snow fields, stretching far and wide, cutting swaths of packed ice between the mountains. Here the shaggy goats kept watch on dizzying ridges so steep no mere man could climb. They watched him warily from their distant perches, and Running Wolf eyed them in return, admiring their beauty. How the Great Spirit kept them cozy and warm under those heavy, white coats that blended in so well with their surroundings.

He made other solitary trips as he matured into manhood. These were comparatively peaceful years, punctuated from time to time by Blackfeet raids. He joined in repelling the attacks, but he preferred to wander and avoid warfare if he could, although as a youth nearing adulthood, he was expected to fight. He did not care to witness the torture inflicted on their captives, much less to suffer the indignities and inevitable execution if the enemy were to capture him. He hated the warfare that pressure from the *suyapi* moving westward had put on the people of the plains and had caused them to make war upon neighboring tribes—all in competition over the buffalo. He saw no good outcome in these events, yet he did not know what he, as one lonely man, could do to stem the tide. What he witnessed was the pressure consuming his own people, their overwhelming desire for the *suyapi*'s goods and what they perceived was the white man's more powerful medicine. It boded ill as far as he could tell, and he was no soothsayer. So he retreated to the wilderness and took what comfort he could there.

One morning, camped at his favorite spot near the waterfall, a black bear surprised him. He knew not to keep bones, remnants of meat from his meal, or food exposed for a bear to smell. The female bear stood twenty paces away. He knew not to look her directly in the eye. He must not give offense or any reason for the bear to think he would make a good breakfast. Slowly, he moved his hand to unsheathe the knife at his side just in case the bear should attack. Would she or wouldn't she? Man and animal remained motionless. His limbs stiffened with waiting, waiting for the bear to turn and lumber away, satisfied that he meant no harm. But she did not. For what seemed an interminable time, but probably was only a minute, she remained undecided and then inexplicably lunged forward, barreling toward him. She attacked on hind feet, rearing as tall as Running Wolf. But he was ready. Deftly, he plunged the blade savagely and repeatedly in the eyes. The bear was blinded but not dead. With his left arm, he attempted to strong-arm the bear while he desperately stabbed its neck and head and pressed his body against the animal to protect his chest and abdomen from its claws. He felt the animal falter and slump, but he still plunged his knife furiously into its vulnerable neck. The bear was failing, but Running

Wolf fought on, fueled by the desire to survive; the bear must die so that he could live. He felt blood from a gash across his left cheek, but the pain paled before the superhuman power surging within him. When he thought the bear would never succumb to its wounds, she fell backward, collapsing spread-eagled. Her four limbs outstretched, she looked like a human being splayed on the ground, hands pinned to stakes. Dazed for a while, Running Wolf, bloody knife in his right hand, stared at the dead sow. Then he saw the cut that ran from his left shoulder to the crook in his elbow. He had to tend to his injuries immediately. Fortunately, the gashes on his cheek and arm were not deep, but he had to stanch the bleeding, treat, and bind the wounds. He went to the nearby stream and bathed his face and arm in the cool water. Then he collected some cedar leaves. Returning to his camp, he wrapped and bound the leaves around his wounds with leather thongs. He must skin the bear before the wolves and crows caught its scent and descended upon the carcass to feast. Before slitting the bear open, he spread his arms and thanked the animal for sacrificing its life for his. He would leave the entrails for the predators. From the kill, he most wanted the claws. After he had skinned and gutted the bear, he extracted the two incisors from its jaw and the five claws on each of its four paws. What a fine necklace the teeth and claws would make!

The pain from his wounds were endurable, and was nothing compared to the prowess he felt after his victory over the sow. He slung the skin over his shoulder and packed the teeth and claws into his leather carrying pouch, and at a fast clip, headed to the village.

He joyfully presented the bear skin, teeth, and claws to his mother Sweet Grass, who beamed with delight as she accepted his treasures. "What a fine robe and necklace I will make for you. Now you have the bear medicine, just like Standing Grizzly. Soon you will be a man and stand with him."

Running Wolf had his misgivings. To stand with Standing Grizzly meant support for another delegation to St. Louis hoping to bring Black Robes to the Salish. Although Running Wolf was proud to be a keeper of bear medicine, he felt that was the only attribute he shared with Standing Grizzly, who liked to be the center of attention, articulated his thoughts clearly, and thrived in society; whereas he thrived in the wilderness surrounded by plants and animals. He loved to hear their speech and not the idle talk of men or the gossip of women. He did not hold the Iroquois in high regard as did Standing Grizzly or desire to learn their religion. He was satisfied with what he possessed. He listened more than he spoke.

He preferred to listen to the wisdom of his father and grandfather and sought their companionship rather than that of his peers. Charles and Francis, the two sons of Little Ignace, followed him around, impressed with his accomplishments and his bear-claw necklace. A few years younger than Running Wolf, they were amiable, but prattled about how wonderful it would be to accompany their father and grandfather on the next mission to St. Louis. Shoshone visitors to the camp warned that Blackfeet war parties still posed considerable danger to travelers. Storms and floods made some areas impassable. Maybe the following spring, it would be safer for travelers.

And the next spring, Standing Grizzly approved the mission with the concurrence of the elders except for Rides-the-Wind and Lone Wolf, who withheld approval. Running Wolf joined his father and grandfather, who had left the council, and climbed to a promontory overlooking the camp.

"Big Ignace is anxious to go. Now he is truly old in years. For how many more days can he walk the earth? Let him walk east and take his son and grandson with him. It is right. Let him see what he can see. He has always been confident and thinks his knowledge is better than other men's knowledge. Such a one thinks he cannot be defeated, even that he will never die," said Rides-the-Wind.

"Even he will fall off his horse someday," Lone Wolf said. "Someday, even he will be too weak to ride. It is good that he goes. My ears are tired from his talk of Black Robes."

"Do you think he will be successful?" Running Wolf asked. "Do you think he will return with a Black Robe when the others failed?"

Rides-the-Wind studied a cloud drifting overhead before he responded slowly. "I believe he will. Such a man is stubborn; he persists until he wins. But his success bodes unhappiness for our people. Behind his smiling face, I see a storm cloud."

"What can we do?" Running Wolf continued, worry creasing his brow.

"Hold fast to what we know," Rides-the-Wind answered.

After a pause to reflect on the older man's words, Rides-the-Wind spoke. "It is not that Big Ignace and Little Ignace are bad. They stir up hopes in the people—false hopes. They make them think there are better ways than our own. They make them think the magic of the *suyapi* will make us stronger and more powerful than our enemies. But all men are equal. They all have one head, two eyes, one nose, two ears, one mouth, two arms, two legs, and one heart."

Lone Wolf chuckled and said, "Only the *suyapi* has a bigger mouth than any nation."

Rides-the-Wind and Running Wolf echoed his laughter, and then Rides-the-Wind added, "And the Iroquois have learned to speak like them, making promises, claiming big things if we do this or that. Forked tongues, they have, in big mouths."

Chances were he might never see Charles and Francis again, Running Wolf thought. He felt indifferent to their fate. Perhaps they might decide they liked living among the Black Robes where the great rivers met. Truthfully, he would not miss them while they were gone. The sat on their saddles proudly behind Big Ignace and Little Ignace. Both teenage boys were skinny like lodgepole saplings. But a remnant of envy lingered in Running Wolf's soul, wishing he could go exploring with them. Then he chided himself. The Salish homeland contained the grandeur of the universe and supplied every need of mankind. He need not go wandering beyond the mountains and valley he loved. He need not seek what the *suyapi* had; in fact, he wished with all the ardor of his heart, that those white men would stay where they belonged.

The second delegation set out the following spring, amply provisioned for their long journey, extra mounts, and packhorses in tow. Standing Grizzly delivered a farewell address. Never laconic, he talked to them so long that the four travelers fidgeted, restless to depart without further ceremony.

"May the Great Spirit guide and protect you. May the winds be mild and the sun warm you. May you meet with nothing but friends on the way, and the game be plentiful to furnish you food. May the White Father welcome you, and may he grant your wish . . ." on and on he orated, loving the sound of his own voice.

"His tongue flaps like a banner in the wind," Rides-the-Wind muttered to his son. "If he speaks any longer, winter will be upon us again. Let them depart now." Finally, the pompous chief ended his speech, and the crowd bidding them farewell dispersed.

Work resumed in the village where no idle hands existed. Sometimes Running Wolf thought his mother worked hardest of all yet always cheerfully. In fact, every woman appeared to work harder than any man was ever expected to work. He was glad to be a male because the tasks assigned to men were much more pleasurable and adventuresome than female duties. Hunting, fishing, and trapping were fun. Yet he did not pity the women their roles, because in one regard they were fortunate—they could stay home while the men had to ride off to wage war. Abruptly, he remembered his father telling him of how his two sisters, whom he had never known, were abducted and carried off to work and breed for the Blackfeet. Their fate was terrible, but not as terrible as the warrior who died in battle or was scalped or tortured as a captive. The two girls were alive somewhere, still breathing and walking the earth. Some nights he had dreamed of them. They would be wives and mothers by now, weaving baskets, tanning hides, pounding meat into pemmican, carrying firewood, sewing garments, beading moccasins, putting up and taking down teepees. Growing into manhood, he must start to think of who would make a good wife for him. But not today, later . . . for he had not yet seen a girl to capture his gaze in the village. None stood out above the others. None loomed higher in attractiveness or amiability. Taken together they were all appealing, but he could not single out one maiden for personal favor.

**Running Wolf**

On a warm, cloudless day the following summer, amazement and jubilation erupted when the Iroquois entourage rode into the Salish camp. The four returned travelers appeared healthy and well-fed. Charles and Francis had added muscles to their lanky limbs. An aura of triumph surrounded Big Ignace and his son. The older Ignace's shoulder-length hair contained more white strands than gray, and his son could no longer be called young. He was middle-aged, resembling the image of his father presented when he first entered Salish country. They beamed with victory and lost no time in announcing the success of their mission.

"The head of the Black Robes said he expected several Black Robes to soon arrive from across the sea. He promised to send us one."

"How soon?" Standing Grizzly demanded.

"By next spring. He was not sure they would reach St. Louis before the winter. He had not heard yet of their boat arriving in the city of Baltimore by the sea. But he promised it would be soon. Nothing would prevent him from sending us one Black Robe among the company. I know he speaks true," Big Ignace concluded.

They feasted that evening while everyone listened eagerly to their adventures. Luckily, they had not encountered enemy tribes, and fur trappers had accompanied them overland part of the way on the return journey through the mountains. Other tribes were friendly, assuming they were traders. Charles and Francis were voluble in their descriptions of the sights they had seen—the mighty mountains, the forts of the white men, the monstrous boats with wheels and smokestacks, the fields of planted crops, the mules hitched to a digger in the earth, the towns with dwellings of planed wood, the symbols on buildings they could not read. All these were things their father and grandfather had seen in their youth back east before they came west with the fur companies. It was the foundation of their belief that the white man's way was superior and that the native peoples must acquire their power. Their Great Spirit had indisputably favored them among all nations.

Charles and Francis were formally baptized in the St. Louis Cathedral according to the rites of the Holy Catholic Church. None of these terms were intelligible or understandable to Running Wolf as they were pronounced in a foreign tongue. What were sacraments, Holy Communion, Matrimony, Extreme Unction, and the Eucharist to him? Efforts at explanations of Christian tenets failed with Running Wolf. Enthusiasm ran high among most of the tribe at the imminent arrival of the Black Robe. Big Ignace and Little Ignace assured them that only the Black Robe could explain clearly the white man's religion and conduct the white man's sacred ceremonies. Standing Grizzly remained steadfast in his support of the invitation and was foremost in enthusiasm to learn from the Black Robe when one should arrive.

Running Wolf did not like the changing of names that this new religion demanded. He thought Charles and Francis should have Salish names if they were truly members of the tribe. His spirit recoiled at assuming a name in a foreign tongue. He would never understand why anyone agreed to take a different name. If this baptism required that he put aside his Salish name, then he would never accept baptism. When a people lost their language, they lost their soul. He, for one, refused to abandon his identity. His language, his traditions, and his land composed the essence of who he was. Others did not realize that to allow these vital elements to be lost meant dissolution. It was beyond his comprehension.

Pride in his heritage animated Running Wolf. His people were noted for their hospitality. Travelers passing through their land were treated with food and shelter and welcomed to warmth around their fires. They would fight to defend their people but were not known to attack first. They desired to live in peace with their neighbors. Because Running Wolf treasured these values, he distrusted the intrusion of alien ways.

In his forays to track animals and commune with nature, he reveled in the marvelous order of creation. One destination he was particularly fond of was Wild Horse Island, situated off the southwestern shore of the Broad Water. The lake stretched a great distance in a basin north of the long valley extending beyond the Place of the Small Trout where two rivers met, one flowing down from the northwest and one flowing east. His father had conceived the idea to move several of their best horses the short span over the ice of the frozen channel to the island—a hiding place from the Blackfeet horse thieves. In winter, braves took turns guarding the herd against any Blackfeet who might have discovered their location and dared to venture across the ice. In summer, the island afforded great pastureland for the horses. Then Running Wolf would paddle his canoe across the narrow channel to the island and camp there for several days, checking on the horses and enjoying the solitude. The island was reached from the western side of the lake. A smaller island sat in the channel between the mainland and the western tip of Wild Horse Island. It took Running Wolf a scant hour to paddle across the channel and beach his canoe on the sandy incline. He then hiked to a midpoint on the island to make his camp. From there, he climbed to the highest point on the island to observe the surrounding area. From this perch, he could view the eastern shore, the sacred towering peaks to the north, and the blue arms of the bays to the south. At night he ascended to this promontory to stargaze. Then the full splendid panoply of the heavens was displayed. The spirits of the dead made a long trail across the night sky. He could see the seven brothers with a girl and spot the lone star that never walked. Most of all, he sought the crying children in the sky, best seen in the winter. The seven lost star-children searched for their parents and could not find them. A pack of wolves adopted them and cared for them. They pleaded with the Great Spirit to let them go and play in the sky. He granted their wish, and there they cry for the animals that helped them. At night they can hear the wolves howling, but the children cannot go to them. When Running Wolf gazed at the crying children in the sky, he thought of his lost sisters and imagined that they were two stars among the constellation of seven. Oh, how glorious it would be to swim among the stars for a while and then to return to earth after bathing in its rivers of light! But then he thought, that did not work out so well for Coyote, did it? For the elders tell of how once the moon was stolen and how the people asked who will take the place of the moon now. First, the silver fox volunteered to take the moon's place, claiming he could shine brighter at night than the moon. Fox went up into the sky and took his place above the earth, but he shone so brightly that he made the earth too hot. People sweltered in the heat and cried, "Stop, stop! Come down from the sky!" The people knew how clever Coyote was and asked him to take Fox's place. Coyote, always eager to help, agreed readily and hopped to it. The coyote was an excellent moon, not too bright and not too dim, just right he was. But soon the people became unhappy with Coyote. From his vantage point, he could see every bad thing the people did. Coyote cried, "Ho!" when he saw someone take a salmon from the drying rack and "Ho," when he heard a person lie." The sneaky, dishonest people came together and whispered in secret, "Coyote is too nosey. It is none of his business what we do. Let us pull him down from the sky." So Coyote was brought down to earth, and the real moon was found to replace him. Coyote came down to earth, but he was still a busybody, minding everybody's business.

    These stories meant so much to Running Wolf. They provided him humor and wisdom and endowed him with a deep appreciation of the web of life. They explained how the humans, animals, earth, sky, and water—all creation—interacted. It was not absurd that sometimes animals spoke, or that a man or woman shape-shifted into a buffalo or fish, or that he saw a child crying in the sky.

One moon followed another moon, waxing and waning, and Running Wolf was glad the Black Robe did not come. "Just wait, he will come in the spring," Big Ignace assured the Salish. But one spring came and went. Another spring arrived, and still no Black Robe. Now even Big Ignace grew impatient. How could the Chief Black Robe deceive them? How could he lie? Did the Black Robe perish on the way? Big Ignace insisted he must go and investigate. Something went wrong; otherwise surely the Black Robe would have arrived by now.

"I must return to St. Louis," he told Standing Grizzly.

"I do not have men to send with you. It is dangerous."

Big Ignace held up the crucifix at his neck. "The Great Spirit guides me."

"Then I will see how strong your dying god's medicine is. We will see if he brings you back safely with the Black Robe. This is the third time I send a man to St. Louis. Maybe this time a Black Robe will listen," Standing Grizzly said.

Running Wolf shook his head, skeptical of this third mission and astounded at the stubbornness of Ignace. So many of the elders went along with the idea of bringing a Black Robe to live with them. They were so convinced of the strength of the Black Robe's medicine. To risk another trip seemed foolhardy. Wiser to interpret the failure of the two previous missions as an omen that what they desired was not good. The wishes of the elders ruled, and they all supported a third delegation to St. Louis.

Rides-the-Wind and Lone Wolf said nothing when the council of elders gathered to discuss Big Ignace's request to go again.

"Who will volunteer to go with you?" Standing Grizzly asked the assembled men.

"Two Salish braves have volunteered and one Nimiipuu warrior," Big Ignace responded.

"A company of four to make the trip?" Standing Grizzly said.

"That is enough. They know the territory, are good scouts, and skilled marksmen if we should be attacked."

"What say you?" Standing Grizzly directed his question at all the men gathered in council.

Woodcock, now an aged elder with wrinkled jowls and raspy speech, answered first. "Ho, I say they go."

Bear Claw concurred, and in succession, Big Face, Black Feather, and the other sub-chiefs gave assent.

"And you, Rides-the-Wind, we have not heard from you." Standing Grizzly looked at the old man.

"I feel it is futile."

"Hmmm," Standing Grizzly murmured and turned to Lone Wolf, his gaze clearly indicating that he awaited his opinion."

"Leave well enough alone. The Black Robe will come of their own accord one day whether we will it or not."

Surprisingly, Standing Grizzly chuckled softly and said. "Aha, there is always at least one doubter among us. I have not just one, but two." He chuckled again. "Change comes. It is in the wind. It cannot be avoided. No one can run from it. No one can dig a hole or hide under a stone. My people must learn new ways or be rolled over by the thunder." He looked first at Rides-the-Wind and Lone Wolf and directed his next words at them. "I respect your caution. These times require boldness and a willingness to learn. You are too timid. The venturesome prevails. I say, Ignace, go with your stalwart friends."

So the third mission was dispatched. But the tribe did not have to wait long for news of their fate. Before the snow flew, two fur trappers arrived in the Salish camp on their way to David Thompson's post as they journeyed west to their destination in Nimiipuu country. They said they were Frenchmen from the land they called Canada. They brought with them the cross on a silver chain recognized as the one that had hung around Ignace's neck. The Frenchmen had traded with a party of Sioux who possessed other objects, clothing, parfleches, powder horns, rifles, and other belongings of Ignace's party. The Sioux braves had attacked, killed, and scalped the four men on the plains, but they did not pose a threat to the fur traders because the Sioux warriors were eager to establish trading relations and obtain more powder and rifles in the future.

The terrible news shook the tribe. Their shock quickly resolved into anger, and they began to curse the Sioux. When the loud denunciations of the murderers subsided, the shaman stepped forward and intoned a death song for the slain men. Little Ignace, Charles, and Francis blackened their faces and cut their hair while the women wailed, mourning the deaths for days. No one wanted to speak about the ill-fated mission for fear that the mere mention of it would bring down further evil. A gloom settled upon the village. Silently, the people went about their daily tasks. Rides-the-Wind and Lone Wolf did not dare to say that their premonitions had been confirmed. The truth, they thought, spoke in silence. Yet, to their amazement, as time passed and the people began to speak their thoughts aloud, they heard hope expressed to still secure a Black Robe to live with them. But for the time being, they went about their usual activities, and the elders did not suggest another mission to St. Louis. No sorrow, however great, could keep the people from the tasks necessary for their survival.

    The shaman who sang to the dead men on their journey to the spirit world possessed special gifts. Several years older than Running Wolf, he was a respected two-spirited individual. His grandmother recognized when Has-Two-Spirits was a little boy that he was different. Being different, he was special, and the difference bestowed respect and a semi-divine status. When he reached puberty, he was asked to choose the bow or the basket, and he chose the basket. Gifted with both feminine and masculine vision, he was a "two-spirit" in the sense that he stood as a conduit between the material and the spiritual realms. He adorned himself with earrings, necklaces, and headbands in styles that the women favored. He wore the female tunic instead of leggings and breechcloth. Even though he liked feminine activities, he joined the men in battle. Still clad as a woman, he stationed himself at the forefront of the fight and led the charge. Believed to be endowed with extraordinary powers, he served as a healer and visionary. He excelled as an artisan, creating beautiful beaded belts, armbands, and headdresses. An outstanding singer and dancer, he officiated at all the rites of passage and tribal ceremonies. Has-Two-Spirits expressed love and kindness to every man, woman, child, and visitor to the village. His voice carried a woman's soft, gentle timbre; he possessed the visionary's keen intellect.

Running Wolf was curious about the shaman's reactions to the massacre of the four emissaries and wondered exactly how he felt about the elders' undimmed desire to learn of the Black Robe's religion. In counsel, Has-Two-Spirits served as peacemaker, reconciling differences. His statements were general, largely noncommittal without taking a stance of his own, albeit his advice was always wise and encouraged a man to follow his guardian spirit wherever that might lead him. He did not directly oppose seeking more knowledge about the *suyapi* and his religion, qualifying his remarks that knowledge was power in and of itself, and with the knowledge gained, the people would be fortified to make a decision on whether to adopt the new religion.

At best, these remarks struck Running Wolf as overly cautious. A shaman who truly possessed greater vision and spiritual power than the ordinary man should be able to offer clearer direction on these matters. Vaguely, he felt that Has-Two-Spirits purposely withheld his real beliefs and had not been completely candid in expression of his opinions. For these reasons, he sought out the shaman for private conversation, sure that the shaman knew more than what he stated.

He found the shaman seated alone, beading a ceremonial breechcloth apron of a floral design. Beads of bright red, blue, yellow, and green formed the various petals.

"Ho, Has-Two-Spirits, a word with you," Running Wolf said as he sat down beside him. "Beautiful work."

"I will wear it for the winter festival dance." Has-Two-Spirits put aside his needle, and looking with kind eyes at his companion, said, "Your spirit is heavy. That is why you come to me. Is that not so?"

"These three failed missions for a Black Robe, I feel, portend greater misfortune. Is not this Sioux slaughter a sign that another mission will have the same result or worse?"

"Whether invited or uninvited, the *suyapi* will come of their own accord," Has-Two-Spirits responded. "They will bring their medicine men with them."

"We have our own medicine," Running Wolf protested.

"Knowledge is not to be feared. I do not fear the knowledge the Black Robe could bring. When we learn what they would teach us, we can act prudently. We will accept what is good and reject what is evil. Knowledge is power. The Great Spirit gave us mind and heart, and we must use both. Moreover, one must know if a man is friend or foe. If he is an enemy, he must be understood to be defeated."

"But you have vision. What do you foresee if the Black Robes come?"

Has-Two-Spirits closed his eyes and inhaled through his nostrils. He remained in a meditative position for a few moments, then exhaled deeply from his chest and opened his eyes.

"I see a swarm of locusts blackening the sky, wings whirring unceasingly over the prairies. The buffalo stampede, flee from the horde, and disappear into the underworld."

"What does your vision mean?"

"It means our numbers are too few to stave off the invasion. New ways must be learned to cope with a people who outnumber us. If we do not, we will be devoured."

The shaman's dark vision stunned Running Wolf. A carrier of such a dire prophecy should be outraged and warn the people of impending destruction. But, no, he sat there impassively.

"Then why do you not sound the alarm?" Running Wolf persisted.

"The *suyapi* have medicine more powerful than ours. For unknown reasons, the Great Spirit gave it to them and favors them. That is why I do not oppose the Black Robe coming. I open my heart and mind to discover why this is so. Because our people have been open to the teachings of the earth, we have learned over the generations to hunt buffalo for our food and learned how to use the plants and animals. The Great Spirit created every living thing, rock, water, stars, sun, and moon. The Great Spirit also created these *suyapi* and brought them to our land. As we learned in the past, so must we learn now. The way of peace exists. My mind and heart tell me to follow that path."

Running Wolf should have realized that Has-Two-Spirits would not be his ally in opposition to the tribal council's opinion. His was the middle road, never to take sides. The settler of disputes and the peacemaker, he was reluctant to stoke fires of animosity, division, and dissension. He was the grand arbiter, the healer, and soother of physical and psychic wounds. So why had not Has-Two-Spirits calmed his unease? Running Wolf left the shaman to resume his beadwork and walked toward the stream to mull over their conversation. Slowly, recollection of the shaman's soft speech had a tranquilizing effect. His presence worked like a sleep-inducing plant on his soul as tobacco and sage produced a somnolent, dreamlike state. Perhaps the shaman and elders were right. He should take a wait-and-see attitude. Nothing to be gained by constant worry and unease. Has-Two-Spirits was right to affirm that knowledge was power. Knowledge of the woods and animals assured Running Wolf's safety. Knowledge of the stars, sun, and moon directed him on his journeys. His guardian spirit was always present to protect him and his people. Serenity suffused his body and spirit as these reflections coursed through his consciousness in unison with the water that flowed gently in the nearby stream. After a while, Running Wolf stood up and walked back to the village, less apprehensive about another delegation to St. Louis.

Over the summer, fall, and winter, Big Face and Standing Grizzly, principal chiefs, listened favorably to Little Ignace's proposal to set out as soon as the snow melted in the mountain passes. This time he would take two other French-speaking Iroquois. He vowed that he would complete the journey that ended tragically for his father. Middle-aged but still referred to as Little Ignace to distinguish him from his father, he was robust and healthy for his age, capable of enduring hardships and dangers along the way. He had kissed his father's salvaged crucifix and swore this time he would return with a Black Robe.

Tragedy struck the band again when a Blackfoot war party surprised Woodcock and Rides-the-Wind while they were following a herd of elk bound for the higher elevation they sought in summer. Running Wolf had accompanied them on the hunting trip. Lone Wolf, because of his expertise as a marksman, had traveled east with another group to hunt buffalo. They tracked the elk through rugged terrain and up slopes thick with blowdown. They dismounted at times to lead their horses around the fallen timber. Rounding the blowdown, the trees thinned, and they remounted their horses for a gentle descent toward a declivity in the hills. The ground leveled into a narrow valley between two rocky ridges. A clear mountain rivulet cut a passage through the middle—a perfect place to stop and water their horses. Before they could dismount, Woodcock and Rides-the-Wind were knocked off their mounts. Running Wolf behind them saw two Blackfeet emerge from bushes and leap upon their horses. Immediately, Running Wolf spurred his horse and chased the Blackfeet, shooting one arrow after another at them with no effect. The speed of the Salish horses and the rough terrain made overtaking them difficult. Running Wolf could have pursued the attackers, but his attention turned to the older men who might be badly injured and breathing their last, sprawled on the ground behind him. He reined in his horse and galloped back to the riverside. Rides-the-Wind had propped himself up, his back against a rock, but Woodcock was unmoving, face-down, an arrow protruding from his back. Running Wolf leaped from his horse and knelt beside the prone man, rolled him over, and placed his hand over Woodcock's mouth to detect a breath; but Woodcock's glassy, staring eyes told him his spirit had already departed. His grandfather still lived, and he moved to where he sat propped against the rock.

Rides-the-Wind's left hand was pressed to his upper arm where an arrow had grazed his flesh. Blood trickled from the spot.

"It is nothing, my son. I live," he said to his son.

Running Wolf took what healing herbs he had from his medicine bundle and bound his grandfather's wound with a compress.

"Can you walk?"

His grandfather nodded. Running Wolf gave him a hand up. He loaded the dead man on the back of his horse, and the two survivors trudged back to the village, leading the horse with its sad burden. Has-Two-Spirits again was summoned to sing Woodcock's spirit on its way to the spirit world. Woodcock was greatly mourned, for he had been an important sub-chief of the tribe. With his departure to the land of the dead, Big Face assumed his position in the council of elders.

Even before the fateful attack, Running Wolf was concerned for Rides-the-Wind. He had watched with trepidation his grandfather's strength ebb. His grandfather's increasing fragility did not go unnoticed. Even though his gait was slow, his speech halting, and he mounted his horse less nimbly than in former days, he continued to care for his string of mighty horses, and was still actively involved in overseeing the foals and training the yearlings. He seemed to wobble when he walked, his shoulders sloped, and his back was no longer as straight in the saddle—the saddle he had acquired from trade at the Thompson post. Because of exposure to the *suyapi*, the Salish had adapted some of the harness and tack they used. But they also loved to adorn their horses with colorful beaded caparisons.

The flesh wound, though minor, added to his grandfather's enfeeblement. He did not like to see him age before his eyes, but he knew the inexorable course of nature could not be stopped and only hoped the day his grandfather departed for the spirit world would not come soon. When Lone Wolf returned from the buffalo hunt, he was alarmed at his father's condition. "Curses on the Blackfeet. May lightning strike them. May the earth quake, a wide crack open, and send them to the underworld," he swore. Lone Wolf recognized too well that his father's hunting days had ended – his last days to be spent warming his old bones by the fire that Has-Two-Spirits kept burning, for the shaman was charged with never letting the fire go out. Has-Two-Spirits would prepare Rides-the-Wind for the great journey he must soon undertake.

One day, Rides-the-Wind looked at Running Wolf through his lusterless brown eyes. The sparkle was noticeably faded. His cheeks were sunken, his jaw sagged, and a track of crow's feet traced a path around his mouth. His once black, shoulder-length mane of hair hung limp and thin in silvery white strands. He spoke through thin lips to his grandson.

"Time for you to find a woman. One who will give you sons. Before I go, I must see this. Take my four finest horses and get a wife."

Running Wolf had to admit that he had been thinking of doing this, but his heart had not sung yet to any maiden. He responded favorably to what his grandfather said in recognition that Rides-the-Wind spoke wisely. His mother had also raised the issue with him, but he had brushed her aside, saying the time was not ripe. He was still observing.

Winter settled in again like the white hairs of his grandfather. On frigid nights while the snow flurried outside, Running Wolf sat around the fire at the heart of their home, listening to the tales of Rides-the-Wind and Lone Wolf. Their tales went back generations to tell of the time before horses and guns, before the formation of the lakes and rivers. Those monstrous rocks shaped like huge beasts once were alive and roamed the earth. Rides-the-Wind explained how the peak grooved like the claws of a bear came to be when the bear pursued seven maidens up the side of the mountain. Sometimes people and animals were changed into stone because of their evil deeds. How he loved the cleverness of the coyote, and the industriousness of the beaver. In truth, people could be transformed into animals and animals into people. And sometimes animals spoke their wisdom to people.

"I have seen many changes in my life," Rides-the-Wind said in a weak voice. It seemed to Running Wolf that his grandfather expended too much strength to speak. It was an ancient one's voice. A man in his prime required no energy at all to speak, but how had it come to be that he sounded so old? Where were the vigor and deep male voice he had listened to as a little boy? Rides-the-Wind spoke slowly, bringing forth each word as if he were a woman giving birth with each contraction of her womb. How did it seem that an old man became like an old woman, and an old woman looked like an old man? With age, the genders melded together, and no difference in face or limb could be discerned. Running Wolf pondered this as he waited to hear what his grandfather would say next.

"Ah, I have heard Little Ignace will depart with two others after the thaw. I will live to see if they bring the Black Robe. I will not die before I know what the Black Robe has to say to my people. As a young man, I saw the first *suyapi* enter our valley looking for the big waters. Since the Iroquois came to live with us, I have heard them speak of the *suyapi*'s medicine, always talking of the wisdom of the Black Robe. Let Little Ignace set out again, and once and for all, we will know how powerful their Great Spirit is. We will finally know if Big Ignace has spoken truth all these years."

"Most likely, Little Ignace will fall into a trap, caught in its teeth," Lone Wolf said.

"That may befall him, but it would be better if, at last, he brings the Black Robe so we can judge with our own eyes."

"Yes, but my heart tells me something different," Lone Wolf responded.

"It is good to observe. It is good to use heart and mind. Both unite to judge aright," Rides-the-Wind said. "Observe the horse. I speak to the foal with song and silently with my heart and train it to move as I wish. If the Black Robe should arrive, which my heart tells me he will before I die, I will watch him carefully."

Running Wolf did not like to hear his grandfather speak of his going, yet he knew that when his body passed, Rides-the-Wind's spirit would not depart from his heart. More than ever, he wished to emulate his grandfather's fearlessness and indomitable will to confront change, prepared to judge whether it was beneficial for his people. Those qualities constituted wise leadership.

The spring thaw came, and as Rides-the-Wind predicted, Little Ignace headed the party of four to St. Louis. The village assembled and danced them on their way with the short, stocky Big Face in full-feathered bonnet presiding at the farewell ceremony. The principal elders and sub-chiefs, confident of success this time, cheerfully sang a chant for the travelers. Smiling, the not-so-young Ignace assured them he would return next spring.

Running Wolf was not so sure, but he guarded his thoughts. A man did what he felt he had to do. Little Ignace was committed to fulfill his father's legacy and determined to walk in Big Ignace's moccasins. He could not fault him for his wish to do that, because he also desired to follow in his forefather's footsteps.

That summer, while the fourth delegation journeyed eastward, another change entered Running Wolf's life. Wilderness was his first love. His wanderlust never left him; the scent of pines and the sanctity of the mountain dell never deserted him, for there dwelled his solace and comfort. In the sanctuary of the forest, he walked in the company of his guardian spirit. Somewhere behind a trunk, slanted eyes glistened. He looked in that direction, and the vision vanished. He laughed to himself. "Aha, wily brother, I know you are there, spying on me. Come closer, and I will pat your head, if you dare." His favorite haunt was the waterfall. At times, when the sun hit tumbling water as it dropped into the stream, pale colors of yellow, pink, and blue danced in the cascade. He wondered at this beauty, and then his soul sang a song. With no one around, he stood up and began to dance, singing for pure joy:

*Beauty before me,*
*With it I run.*
*Beauty below me,*
*With it I run.*
*Beauty above me,*
*With it I run.*
*On the beautiful path, I am,*

*With it I run.*

He circled, lifting his right foot, and then stepping with his toe, and then raising his left foot in the same motion as he tapped forward, repeating his song. Suddenly, he heard a girlish giggle from behind him. He stopped in his dance and scanned the surrounding trees for the source of the sound. Then a maiden emerged from behind a bush, a basket of elderberries under one arm. She wore a reed cap that fit snugly on her head and a plain deerskin tunic with tassels along the sleeves and the skirt hem. White, red, yellow, and black beads decorated the tops of her moccasins.

"You sing a woman's song," she giggled.

Embarrassed to be caught unawares, he realized then how womanish his song sounded, and he protested, "Not right to sneak up and surprise me." As she approached, Running Wolf noted red feathers attached to the leather thongs that bound her black braids. Her face was elongated, her lips finely shaped, and her nose narrow, everything in proportion, Running Wolf thought, as perfect a figurine that an artisan had ever carved. Her skin was burnished like copper, and when she smiled, her cheekbones stood out and seemed to glow.

"Go on. I liked it. Do not let me stop you now," she laughed lightly, a short trill like a bird.

"Who are you to come alone picking berries? Shouldn't you be gathering them with the other women?"

She laughed again. "I suppose so, but I like walking alone. I can think better that way, and sometimes their chatter bothers me."

This time Running Wolf laughed in response. "I understand you. But who are you to sneak up on me like a cat in the dark?"

"I know you, but you don't know me."

"What's your name?"

"Laughing Water. You are so funny, Running Wolf. You do not observe the girls, but I have been observing you all along. You have not noticed me, although I have noticed you and marked your character."

"So you followed me here?"

A smile brightened her face again. "Just a chance encounter. I have come to this spot many times myself. I like to refresh myself at the waterfall after a hot day of berry-picking."

Together they walked to the stream, bent down, cupped their hands in the cool water, and drank.

"Aha, the rushing water speaks," Laughing Water said, gazing up at the white cascade that rolled over the cliff in a shimmering scrim.

"What does it say to you?" Running Wolf asked, captivated by her demeanor.

"It says what you sang when I caught you dancing. You sang and danced like the water falls."

Recognition brightened Running Wolf's countenance. "I know you now. You are Red Feather's daughter. You have grown up."

She was a few summers younger than Running Wolf, but not too young to marry. She had blossomed into womanhood right under Running Wolf's nose. Too preoccupied with his own growing up and exploration of the world, he did not expend an idle moment to appreciate feminine charms . . . until now. In the present moment, her gaiety and beauty intensely stirred his interest. All his senses were aroused and absorbed as they conversed beside the stream. Why had she not attracted his attention before? In the future, he would not be inattentive. Residing under that screen of gaiety, he discerned a tender heart. That she should have gone unnoticed was an absurdity that he needed to correct.

Suddenly she rose and said, "My basket is half full. I have more berries to pick." She scampered away, light-footed as a doe, back to where the elderberry bushes grew in abundance.

Running Wolf lingered a while in the enchanted setting of the waterfall until he felt a few raindrops, but the sun still shone brightly past the meridian point. A downpour was unlikely. Just a light sprinkling. He started to walk home. Coming down the heights into the meadow replete with lush grass, he glanced up. In the eastern sky, a pastel arc of colors curved like a buffalo horn—the seven colors merging into each other, mirroring the happiness that brimmed in his breast.

He did not immediately act upon his desires. First, he must make his intentions clear to his father and seek the opinion of his mother in these matters. Perhaps Laughing Water was spoken for already. If so, she would have indicated she was promised to another. And did she not say she had been observing him for a long time? That could only mean she had her eye, if not also her heart, already centered on him. His hope expanded with this thought. Red Feather's opinion figured most importantly in the matter. What if he intended to give his daughter to another man, one with more horses, coup, and prominence? An older man perhaps. Oh, no . . . it cannot be. He was young and had proven himself in battle. Besides, he carried the power of the bear and the guardianship of the wolf. Obviously, Laughing Water preferred him. She liked him. He knew that. A blind man could feel she enjoyed being with him when they sat together beside the waterfall.

He consulted with White Heron first.

"She is a good mate for you," his mother said. "She can soften your seriousness with her light-heartedness. Love without laughter is blight. She is not idle either, though she laughs while she works. She will make a good wife. Watch and observe a while longer. Gather the things you need for your own teepee. As far as I know, no one else has asked for her."

Running Wolf was sure that his mother was accurate that no man had yet approached Red Feather for his daughter. White Heron would have heard that gossip among the women. Rumors were rapidly borne out to be true in the tight community in which they worked.

When he consulted with Lone Wolf, he received assurance in his course. "You choose wisely, son," he told Running Wolf. "She is yet young and needs three or four seasons to come to full maturity. I can let your desire be known to Red Feather so you will have first claim to his daughter, if he approves, which I think he will. My son is a good match for his daughter. We will pick out some foals to be ready for your wedding gifts."

Lone Wolf spoke to Red Feather about Running Wolf's intentions. He did not object to Running Wolf's interest in Laughing Water. He agreed to speak of marriage when she had attained full womanhood and sufficient size and strength to bear many children. No other brave had yet expressed the wish to take her as a wife, but he anticipated many soon would wear out a path to his teepee for that purpose. He would keep in mind that Running Wolf was the first. It remained to be seen if he would take first place in Laughing Water's heart when the time for marriage came.

During the time the fourth delegation was away on their mission, Running Wolf's ardor did not dim at the prospect of Laughing Water eventually becoming his helpmate in life. At every opportunity he observed her behavior. She was a favorite among the young girls and assumed a leadership role in their activities. She excelled in food preparation. He often spotted her tending the simmering kettles of broth or mixing crushed huckleberries into bitterroot patties. Before his appreciative eyes, she was growing into mature womanhood.

One afternoon, he returned from checking his traps, a string of rabbits on a pole slung over his shoulders, he met Has-Two-Spirits emerging from a lodge.

"The girl has died," Has-Two-Spirits said.

"What girl?" Fear gripped Running Wolf's heart that it could be the only girl he cared for.

"My medicine could not cure her. But neither could the invisible mother she prayed to."

"Who?"

"The girl the Iroquois Pierre baptized and named Mary. She caught the fever. Before she died, she saw a lady come into her teepee. She exclaimed, 'Oh, the beautiful lady dressed in blue I see is Mary, my mother. Oh, the light is so bright. I see a baby more beautiful than she is in her arms. His pudgy arms stretch toward me.' Saying these words, she fell silent, stared awestruck into the air, and appeared to be listening. I thought the sickness was leaving her, she looked so happy. I bid her describe the vision. She was all too willing to tell me, her words rapturous and her face radiant.

"Mary told me that the lady was coming to take her to heaven and that her name was Mary. The baby she held was her son, the Son of God. The lady said, 'Those you wait for, the Black Robes, bring his word to you, and you must listen to them. When they come, you must build a House of Prayer on this spot.'

"After the girl finished describing her vision, she grew still, and the spirit left her body. A white bird hovered above her head and disappeared. I burned sage and performed the smudge."

"She is only a girl of twelve summers. What do you make of her vision?" Running Wolf asked.

"Death visions carry the greatest significance and must be heeded. It is ill-advised to ignore them."

"Then you think it was not just the sickness speaking?"

"Clarity is gained as the spirit loosens from the sick body. What a person speaks then is of the utmost importance."

"Who then is this woman who appears in her vision?"

"It is the one we see on the Iroquois beads--the ones they pray on to invoke her name. She is the mother of this Jesus that they tell us we should pray to—the one we see hanging on Big Ignace's cross."

"Then you think it is right for Little Ignace to travel east to bring a Black Robe?"

"Right or wrong, it is the only way to find out if they bring good or bad medicine."

"You are wise, Has-Two-Spirits. If anyone, you are the person to perceive evil, but what I feel in my heart that their mission is not good. And now I am uncertain what to think of the dying girl's vision."

"It is a holy vision, Running Wolf. The woman brought her a happy, beautiful death and took her to her heaven. The mother with child makes a sacred sign. The vision did not shake the little Mary. An evil vision would have frightened her."

Soon the whole camp knew of Mary's death vision and could talk of nothing except the beautiful lady and child. The reported vision fortified the elders' belief that the decision to send Little Ignace to St. Louis was correct, this fourth delegation would meet with success, and it could mean nothing else. Big Face and the sub-chiefs determined to listen attentively to the Black Robe as the Mother of God had instructed. More than ever, the sentiment prevailed that the Black Robe possessed powerful medicine to benefit the Salish . . . except in one teepee.

Alone, seated around their hearth, Rides-the-Wind, Lone Wolf, and Running Wolf discussed Mary's vision. The little girl, an orphan, was impressionable and had fervently embraced the teachings of the Iroquois. The tales of the crucified god easily swayed. What motherless child would not look to a heavenly mother to rock her to sleep and love her unceasingly? This was a reasonable explanation for the three of them.

"The sickness brought delirium," Lone Wolf suggested.

"But the fog clears just before the moment of death," Rides-the-Wind said, "And then clear vision comes."

"That is what Has-Two-Spirits believes," Running Wolf interjected. "My feelings are still not good about the *suyapi.*"

"Nor are mine good about the white men coming," Lone Wolf said, "But we have had to learn to deal with them, to trade with them, and to strike bargains to get the guns, powder, and other useful things. Many things we cannot make. How do we reconcile the good with the possible bad?" Lone Wolf's question was to his father.

Rides-the-Wind replied, "We see our own visions. We pray to our guardian spirits. Mine the horse, yours the lead wolf—"

"Mine the wolf that runs," Running Wolf interjected.

"We ought not to change our names," Rides-the-Wind continued. "What does this name *Mary* mean to us? Nothing. It tells us nothing. We do not need this baptism that gives new names. I reject it."

"Their language sounds like the hissing of snakes," Lone Wolf said. "I will keep our people's language on my tongue."

"But it may be wise to learn their tongue. It is the means to understand what really is in the *suyapi* heart," Rides-the-Wind said.

"What if a man speaks only lying words? Even in our own tongue, there are men who speak lies," Running Wolf said.

"That kind of man is swiftly found out and punished," Rides-the-Wind asserted.

Lone Wolf and Running Wolf nodded their assent. They had seen liars scourged in their community. No man was more detested than a liar. In full view, they were bound to stakes and whipped with knotted leather straps. It was not cruel; it was just.

Rides-the-Wind sat hunched over the fire, holding his gnarled hands over the heat, a buffalo robe around his

129

shoulders. These days he was always cold despite fur wraps. He had whittled a sturdy walking stick, which he used whenever he ventured outside. He seemed to eat less and less, although Running Wolf constantly urged him to take second portions of food, thinking extra nourishment would strengthen him and prolong what he feared was his grandfather's departure to his ancestors.

"You make big fuss about me," he told his grandson. "I will not travel to the spirit world until these old eyes see the Black Robe so much talked about since I was a young man."

"How can you be certain?" Running Wolf asked.

The old man coughed and cleared his throat. He spoke in a weak, gravelly voice. "My guardian spirit will tell me when it is a good day to die. It is not yet, because the cloud in the shape of a white stallion's head said to me that he will gallop down from the sky. Then I will mount him, and he will carry me to the land of the spirits."

Running Wolf accepted his grandfather's prediction. He respected his foresight and wisdom. It seemed to him that he had always possessed an invisible third eye between his shaggy, white brows. He could both read the winds and ride like the wind. He never doubted his grandfather's sagacity. It was written in every line on his wizened face.

"So, you think that Little Ignace will finally succeed where others have failed and bring the Black Robe?"

"It is destiny."

Running Wolf did not know how to respond to his grandfather's pronouncement of inevitability. He wanted to protest and argue for resistance. Did this mean Rides-the-Wind could accept change even to the detriment of his people? No, Running Wolf did not believe his grandfather was capable of passive acceptance. Or did age drain the urge to fight from even the bravest of hearts? Rides-the-Wind answered Running Wolf's thought before he could form a question on his lips.

"Younger men must take up the fight. It is their turn. My role is to advise and speak what I have learned to those who come behind me. By the fire, I warm my cold bones, which in time, will dry and crumble in the earth. That is destiny too."

His grandfather's words lingered long in his mind. He vowed never to forget his teachings or the stories he had told of the people from the beginning of days. The direction of the wind could not be shifted. No man had the power to halt its blowing or the dust it swirled up in its passing. But his spirit rebelled against the changes that the arrival of more *suyapi* augured.

Cries of joy resounded through the camp one day when the valley greened with sweet grass and willow buds opened. Left-handed Pierre, one of the members of Little Ignace's party, appeared on a pinto pony, like the first hummingbird returned from the tropics. Smiling, he dismounted while the Salish surrounded him, demanding what news he brought.

"Where are the others?" Big Face stepped through the crowd. Pierre's cheerful expression belied any misadventure as every ear pricked to hear his report.

"We met a Black Robe at a place the *suyapi* call Council Bluffs far east on the plains where the River of the Big Canoes flows. I rode ahead to tell that Little Ignace will follow with the Black Robe."

Chief Big Face effusively received the news. So excited was he at the prospect of the long-awaited Black Robe that he declared, "I will lead a welcoming party to escort the Black Robe to our valley. Nothing must prevent his safe arrival. Many men will accompany to greet him. That way, we will ensure no harm will befall him on his journey. Who will ride with me to meet Ignace and the Black Robe and smooth his path to our land?"

Hands were upraised, and acclamations of readiness to go rang out. Only Rides-the-Wind and Lone Wolf held back. Running Wolf turned to his father and grandfather. "Don't you think I should go too? I want to see for myself what to expect from this Black Robe."

"Youthful curiosity speaks," Rides-the-Wind. "If I were young, I would ride with them also and witness his coming. These old legs will not let me. Go, if you must."

"I yet have the strength but will not ride," Lone Wolf pronounced. "My heart cannot welcome this guest. I will stay and guard the women and children who remain behind in the village."

"Very well," said Rides-the-Wind.

So it was a few mornings later, Running Wolf set out with two hundred Salish braves to bear witness to the event many of them had hoped for years would come to pass. They first rode south and over a steep mountain pass into the One Hole Valley, following the route Left-Handed Pierre said Little Ignace would take. There a company of two hundred friends of the Nimiipuu joined them. The news of the coming of the Black Robe had spread to the neighboring tribe, who were also eager to learn more about the *suyapi's* Great Spirit. After three weeks of riding, enlarged to about eight hundred, they entered the territory of the Green River. Running Wolf had not traveled this far east before. The stunning views of jagged-toothed mountains stirred his soul. His heart expanded with the Great Spirit's bounty. They sighted herds of elk, and one time a hump-backed grizzly lumbering through tall grass. Eagles and other birds of prey soared or perched on high limbs, scanning the ground for burrowing creatures upon which to pounce. A black bear pawed for insects at a rotten tree that lightning had severed close to the ground.

The company encamped by the river and set up teepees to await the arrival of Ignace and the Black Robe, expected within a few days, according to Left-Handed Pierre's estimate. They designated the spot Pierre's Hole in honor of the scout. At noon a few days later, three men approached on horseback. As they neared the camp, Running Wolf discerned Little Ignace and the Iroquois Paul. The third man wore a wide-brimmed, round, black hat and was clothed in the long gown that gave him his familiar name. The Black Robe had arrived! Around his neck hung a crucifix. When he dismounted his chestnut horse, Running Wolf saw black beads dangling from his wide leather belt. A kindly smile on his pale face, he saluted Chief Big Face who approached to greet him. Of small stature, he had thin brown hair, parted on the left, that reached to just below his ears. His manner was most gracious and respectful of native custom. Running Wolf stood close enough to study the Black Robe's eyes of a bluish-gray hue. To the best he could determine, his gaze held no deceit, and when he spoke, the sound did not grate on his ears as the white man's speech usually did. It had a musicality he was not accustomed to in the northwest fur traders' language. It was the language Old Ignace and his son could speak.

"Père Pierre de Smet," he pointed at his heart. "*Je suis heureux de faire votre connaissance.*"

Big Face, in a full feathered bonnet, solemn and dignified, responded, "Show us the road we have to follow to come to the place where the Great Spirit resides."

An exchange ensued in which Ignace translated between the Black Robe and the Salish chief while Running Wolf, a silent witness, hung on every word.

Despite his aversion to the *suyapi*, Running Wolf found this small man pleasant and unthreatening. His gentility and manners left nothing to dislike. Maybe his coming bode well for his people.

After the initial formalities, this father, as he called himself, began to talk to the Great Spirit. From his saddlebag, he took sacred objects. He spread a cloth on a stump and placed a golden chalice and plate on it. He intoned many prayers. Little Ignace explained when he raised a piece of bread, it was the Great Spirit's, and when he drank from the cup, it was the Great Spirit's. After that ceremony, the people started to call him "The Man Who Talks to the Great Spirit." The people were excited to acquire the power of his Great Spirit and profess their belief in his god, so they lined up by the hundreds to receive baptism in the river. The Black Robe was pleased with the people's fervor. Through Ignace's translation of Father de Smet's every word, Running Wolf learned that he praised the people's courtesy and hospitality. In turn, the Salish and Nimiipuu expressed enthusiasm to receive the blessings and power of the Black Robe's religion. Running Wolf held back and did not line up with the people for baptism. Instead, he intently watched the proceedings from the sidelines. Everyone else was so engrossed in the Black Robe's prayers and ceremonies that they paid no attention that he did not participate. He could not believe that the Great Spirit Père Pierre de Smet talked to was any different from the Great Spirit that he had communed with in the forest, on the mountain, and in the valley of his home. Furthermore, his father was not this Pierre de Smet but Lone Wolf.

After resting a day beside the Green River, the party resumed the journey to the land of the Salish, traversing the mountains, following the One Hole Pass to descend into the canyon through which the Willow River drained. Encamped there was another large contingent of Salish and Nimiipuu gathered to meet the Black Robe. The Black Robe continued to baptize and pray there for two months. He explained to the people that they must rest from their labors every seventh day that he designated "The Lord's Day." On that day, he erected his altar hewn from logs. In ornate green robes with gold borders conducted his prayers and indicated that the people should repeat certain responses in a magic language.

Running Wolf sensed that The Man Who Talks to the Great Spirit was both pleased and overwhelmed by the size of the two nations that had assembled to hear his words. Through Ignace, he made known to the chiefs that he needed helpers to teach them. He was only one man, one servant of the Great Spirit. He wanted to instruct the people not only in the word of God but how to survive the coming of the white men with their superior tools. He would teach them to grow their own food and to plant and harvest new and better crops. He drew pictures of these grains, fruits, vegetables, and the seeds that would be sown in furrows in the soil. To produce these crops, they needed plows and other implements.

"I must return to St. Louis and bring laborers for the field, men skilled in carpentry, farming, and other crafts—wheelwrights and blacksmiths. The mission needs a linguist who can quickly learn your language and communicate with the people, translating the Christian Bible into the Salish language." Father de Smet held up the Bible and a smaller prayer book he called a missal. "The children will be taught important prayers—the Our Father, the Hail Mary, the Sign of the Cross, the Act of Contrition, the Apostles Creed." He fingered the black beads suspended from his leather belt. "They will learn to pray the rosary."

The Salish stared at the string of beads, awe visible in their expressions, seemingly convinced the rosary possessed magical powers.

"I wish I could stay longer among you, but alone I am unable to provide instruction to such a large number hoping to hear of eternal salvation. I promise that I will return as soon as I collect the assistants and materials necessary."

The elders were chagrined that Father de Smet intended to leave right away and attempted to persuade him to spend the winter with them and set out in the spring.

"The sooner I leave, the sooner I can do what you ask, that is, show you where the Great Spirit dwells. In the spring, I will return with sufficient resources to fulfill your wishes, enlighten your souls, and improve your bodily welfare."

The chiefs accepted his reasoning and trusted that he would return. Their instincts told them they could trust the Black Robe. Little Ignace and Left-Handed Pierre added their assurances that Father de Smet's promise would be kept. No evil aura subsisted around his presence. His apparent benevolence and amiable manner baffled Running Wolf. For once, his uncomfortable feelings about the *suyapi* melted. The beatific smile that constantly brightened his pallid complexion dispelled any notions that he harbored malevolent intentions. He demonstrated interest in understanding Salish customs and accepted their food and gifts graciously. He observed their etiquette. Clearly, he wanted to learn their ways as much as he desired to teach them about his Great Spirit. His behavior and demeanor allayed Running Wolf's misgivings. Perhaps this Black Robe would not be as disruptive as he had feared. His presence might, after all, benefit his people in ways he could not foresee. He was inclined now to give the Black Robe a chance. He could not so easily be dismissed as an evil force. What was certain, if the Blackfeet did not kill him, he believed that Father de Smet would return. If he should be killed, he was certain that another Black Robe would eventually come to replace him. One truth he knew—the *suyapi* were relentless; they were a stubborn, remorseless race that brooked no opposition.

    He asked the opinion of Has-Two-Spirits, who told him, "I sense no evil in the man. His nature is kind and good. He inquired of my medicine, and I let him see my herbs and charms. I showed him how drumming can heal the wounded spirit. I sang a chant, and he tried to repeat the words. His heart is open; he has good medicine."

    Rides-the-Wind grunted and offered no comment when Running Wolf sought his opinion. Was that resignation to the inevitable? Could his dim eyes see farther than he could? Running Wolf pressed him, "Grandfather, tell me what you can see?"

The old man paused and clicked his tongue against his front teeth. "The *suyapi* comes whether we will it or not. Life will be different for us."

"But we can stop it if we do not like what they bring . . . is that not true?"

"Yes, you can try," he said softly. "You can also try to stop the thunder from clapping and the snow from falling." His voice trailed off.

Later, when Running Wolf was alone with his father, he asked him, "Is it fated to be that the *suyapi* bring change that cannot be stopped?"

"Watchfulness . . . assume the eagle's nature. I see no evil purpose in the Black Robe. If he keeps his promise and returns with the gifts, I will patiently observe. The good I support; the bad I oppose."

Summer was now at its height, and Running Wolf's thoughts turned to Laughing Water again. She had bloomed like the bear grass and purple flowers on the hillsides. She surprised him one day while he was setting a fishing trap. Quietly, she had approached him from behind as he was bent over the stream and covered his eyes with her palms.

"Guess who?"

"The sound of your voice is no mystery." He gently grasped her wrists, removed her hands, turned, and stood to face her. "It ripples like the water."

She laughed. "You have been avoiding me. I must track you. Since you returned from the great gathering with the Black Robe, you have been sullen, brooding like a rain cloud."

"Ah, have I? I do not mean to be. I just have had too much to think about."

"That is the problem. You worry and think too much." Suddenly, with deft fingertips, she tickled his ribs. In spite of himself, he laughed. He caught hold of her and tussled playfully with her in the grass as they rolled about like newborn fawns. Finally, their rollicking ceased, and they brushed the twigs and leaves from their bodies. Laughing Water picked a stalk of grass from Running Wolf's hair, the dimples in her cheeks deepening as she smiled at him. Her speech flowed like the river washing over rocks, cajoling him to joy and abandonment of gravity, to bound forth, free-spirited and gay.

"Ah, you are actually handsome when you smile," she teased. "Wearing that serious look all the time will turn your face to stone."

"Am I too serious for you?" A somber expression appeared on his face.

She laughed and said, "You cannot help yourself, but I can help you." She tickled his ribs again. "I know exactly the spot."

"All right, all right, you can stop now. I surrender," he laughed. She relented, and he gazed at her lovingly. After a long pause during which she returned his gaze with a countenance that sparkled like sun on quartz, he said, "You are good medicine."

"Ho, the sun has come out behind the rain cloud. Tell me why the Black Robe meeting made you brood."

"I was confused because he was not a bad man. I felt he wished us good. Even so, I am not completely at peace because I sense a tremor beneath my feet that I cannot dispel and a whirlwind gathering strength over my head. A change is coming I cannot describe. I know not what it is, but I cannot help but think it endangers my people. I do not like what I feel, but I cannot suppress it."

"Then you must live for the day, for this beautiful moment, for this bounteous valley we live in. Do not dwell under a dark cloud because it will defeat you. And you must live. I must live . . . I want . . ." She could not continue but bowed her head, growing embarrassed at what she really wanted to say. She could not be so bold as to express the deepest desire of her heart. Her heart strove to unite with Running Wolf's. How could she be immodest and blurt out that she wished to lie with him? She wished to bear many sons for him.

Running Wolf discerned her thoughts, and a smile widened on his face. "I share your desire. Not too long from now, I will speak to Red Feather. You will be my helpmate. You will cure me of my folly."

"Let it be so," she whispered.

He pulled her to her feet, and together they raced back to the village, like-minded and flushed with youthful exuberance.

Lone Wolf and Running Wolf assumed the tasks that Rides-the-Wind no longer could do. They managed the horses. Grown so unsteady on his limbs, he could not mount his favorite horse without assistance. He managed to shamble with the aid of a sturdy stick to where they grazed. He whispered to them and chanted his horse song to them as in days of old. Gazing up at the clouds, he invoked the ghost horses, all the ones he had ridden, now passed into the sky. His eyes, clouded over now, saw only with an inner vision. It pained Running Wolf to think that his grandfather was preparing for his passage to the spirit world. When pangs of his imminent loss overcame him, he clung to the consolation that only his body disappeared and his spirit then would resolve into all creation. In the seasons while he prepared for his eventual marriage, he cared for the foals he would give to Laughing Water, filling the seasons with useful work. When not tending the horses, he spent as much time as possible beside his grandfather. When the moment of his passage arrived, he wished to be by his side, hear his death vision, and whisper in his ear his farewell and safe journey.

Before that happened, Rides-the-Wind's prophecy that he would not depart before he met the Black Robe was fulfilled. The Man Who Talks with the Great Spirit kept his promise and returned the next spring accompanied by two other Black Robes and three lesser Black Robes called brothers. They found the Salish encamped at a place they called Wide Cottonwood Trees in the upper half of the long valley. He introduced his companions who had unpronounceable names. The two Black Robes were Nicholas Point and Gregory Mengarini. The brothers were William Claessens, Joseph Specht, and Charles Huet. Four two-wheeled carts were laden with odd implements, sacks of grain, boxes of seed, candles, soap, and a plethora of goods unfamiliar to the Salish. Hitched between two long wooden shafts, one long-eared horse pulled the cart. Running Wolf learned this strange-looking horse was a mule. Curious Salish walked around the carts and examined the objects being unloaded. One wooden implement that a man could stand behind and hold two handles to push forward a cast iron broad blade into the earth captured

Rides-the-Wind's attention. He tapped it with his walking stick.

"What does this do?" he demanded.

Little Ignace stepped forward to do the translation. The Black Robe Mengarini stood beside him, listened intently, and scratched marks on a white leaf. The Salish later understood this was his method to learn the sounds of their language, and he would assemble everything about their language in a book.

"It will make you farmers of the earth," The leader of the Black Robes answered.

"We are keepers of the earth."

"Farmers are keepers of the earth too. I will teach you to grow your own food so that you will no longer have to gather roots and berries. I will plant fruit trees here so that you will not have to wander to find them. Other plants will provide grain to grind into meal for bread."

"We want the medicine that will make us more powerful than our enemies," Big Face said.

"That too we will bestow with the grace of God," the leader of the Black Robes said. Chief Big Face knew this Black Robe as The Man Who Speaks with God whom he had met at Pierre's Hole and who had promised to return with more Black Robes. He called himself Father Pierre de Smet. Chief Big Face did not understand what he meant by the grace of God, but he welcomed the newcomers and accepted gifts they brought.

The Black Robe Mengarini proved a skilled linguist, who, after Father de Smet left him in charge, mastered the Salish language and conducted catechism classes for the young children. The first order of business was to build cabins for the missionaries and a church. Running Wolf and

Lone Wolf warily watched these activities, but when asked to help cut the trees and hew the logs, joined in the work. They did not wish to appear sluggards while the rest of the men labored. The location for the church received special attention and prayers. Father de Smet ventured into the meadow wet with dew not long after the missionaries arrived and directed his gaze north to where Red Top Mountain towered, praying for enlightenment and blessings upon his mission. Finishing his devotions, he turned to the circle of chiefs who had been observing him.

"I name that mountain St. Mary's Peak and this place St. Mary's Mission. Our Lady, the Mother of God, smiles upon our labors. Now to choose the site where to begin building the church in her name."

Has-Two-Spirits stepped forward. "I know the place. Follow me." Father de Smet and the chiefs did as he bid, and at a short distance, stopped at the remnants of a firepit.

"That is where Little Mary's teepee was pitched. We burned it after she died," Big Face said. "Is it good to build a church where someone died?" Ignace translated his question for Father de Smet.

"Sometimes, if the person was renowned for holiness," the priest answered. "Who was this Mary you speak of?"

Then, through the interpreter Has-Two-Spirits recounted the story of the girl who saw a lovely lady dressed in blue with a baby in her arms who spoke to Mary, telling her she was the Mother of God and would take her to heaven.

Father de Smet was visibly awed by the story. "Very well. We will build the church on this spot, for the apparition perhaps is a divine sign that I cannot readily shrug off. The story needs more investigation."

Little Ignace spoke up. "We did question the little girl. I showed her an image of the Virgin Mary, and she said the lady in her vision looked exactly like it."

"Apparitions like this have been known to occur in the past, particularly to innocent, stainless children. There was just such an instance to an Indian in Mexico."

If Little Mary's apparition awed Father de Smet, the Salish were even more astounded to learn that in other times and places, the beautiful lady had appeared to other people.

Running Wolf participated in the construction of the church. A residence for the Black Robe was attached to the back. A log cabin was built to house the chief, while the rest of the tribe preferred to keep their teepees. They were portable, comfortable, and easier to construct than the white man's house. As he helped in the construction of the new dwellings, Running Wolf carefully observed the demeanor of the Black Robes. He perceived no guile in these men. They certainly were not lazy. He discerned eagerness to share their knowledge with his people. However good these qualities, Running Wolf disliked their propensity to change the names of everything, people, and places. The name of this site remained in his mind Wide Cottonwood Trees and not St. Mary's Mission, and the highest mountain in view was Red Top, not St. Mary's Peak. He resolved that he would not have his name changed. He was who he was. Everything could change and topple around him, but he would stand firm as a Salish man.

Father de Smet did not stay long. After designating where church, cabins, workshops, corrals, and fields for crops were to be fenced, he announced he would spend the winter with them, but in the spring travel west to found more missions for the Nimiipuu over the mountains. He celebrated the first Christmas with the new converts, and before his departure at the start of the spring thaw, he appointed Father Mengarini head of the mission. The Salish were crestfallen to have him depart so soon and pleaded with him to remain longer, but he insisted he must be about The Lord's business. There were too many nations in need of His word. Father de Smet was everyone's favorite because he possessed a joyous soul and exuded love and kindness unmatched even by many of their own sons and daughters. They believed he did talk to God. A smile constantly brightened his face, and some said they saw a yellow light around his head of sandy hair. The children ran to him and wanted to sit on his knees as he rocked them as if they were riding a pony. He taught them new games with stick and ball. He showed them how to skip the rope as he twirled it from head to toe, never tripping over the rope as it circled his feet.

A steeple pointed like a spear tip, rose above the church entrance, topped with a wooden crucifix. There were no pews at first in the church. The Salish sat on the floor. To one side, a cast-iron woodstove was placed to provide heat for the new Christians huddled in their blankets, who attended the ceremony, which they were told re-enacted Jesus Christ's last supper. The Salish were enthralled with the substance and essence of the Catholic ritual as the Black Robe Mengarini elevated the consecrated host and the wine in the chalice. A Belgian lace tablecloth adorned the altar in the sanctuary center. Candelabra held candles that burned throughout the religious services. When flowers bloomed, they decorated the sanctuary in glass vases. Behind the altar was an altarpiece set against the back wall on which a large crucifix hung. The back wall of the sanctuary was painted sky-blue, beautiful to behold. The ornate, embroidered vestments of the priest also fascinated the Salish. The colors changed in a regular cycle of green, purple, red, and white for the seasons, corresponding to the people's own love of color symbols to signify seasons, directions, and moods. They were easily infatuated with Catholicism because symbols were an integral part of their traditional spiritual practice.

Running Wolf mused on these similarities. Differences seemed less harsh to him. He felt the beatitude that enveloped the small congregation during the Day of Rest Mass and the celebration of the seven sacraments that the Black Robe preached to them, that of Baptism, Holy Communion, Confession, Confirmation, Holy Orders, Matrimony, and Extreme Unction. None of the explanations of these sacraments struck the Salish as absurd or foreign, because they resembled their rites of passage in many respects. The role of medicine man or shaman was divinely inspired. Songs and dances accompanied major life events. It was fitting and proper that the dead receive prayers and incense. Food carried sacred properties, and the smoking of the peace pipe partook of a holy communion.

Catechism began immediately. The linguist Mengarini mastered the intricacies of the native language, translating the Christian prayers and principles of doctrine into terms the Salish understood. In his study behind the church, he held classes for children. For this purpose, he had a small chalkboard set on an easel. Through rote, he inculcated the rudiments of Christianity. Mengarini, an accomplished musician, also directed his talents into the translation of hymns into Salish. He was particularly assiduous in the children's memorization of prayers before a mass baptism that Father de Smet would administer to the first group of catechumens. As he passed the open door of Mengarini's lodge, Running Wolf could hear the children repeating phrase after phrase of the obligatory prayers. One child, named Little Paul, struggled to recite the words. He just could not get them right or in the proper order. His mind did not have the ability for memorization. In fact, most of the tribe considered him a bit feeble-minded. In his eleven years, he had demonstrated no skill at anything, even though he tried hard to master hunting, fishing, and the art of the bow.

A moment later, Running Wolf saw a tearful Little Paul emerge from Mengarini's class. Running Wolf took pity on the boy and approached him.

"Why do you cry? Boys must not cry," Running Wolf said.

"I cannot learn the prayers, and I want to be baptized on Christmas Eve."

"Better aspirations exist. Memorization of *suyapi* prayers has no real value. I can teach you to track."

"Tracking is not important to me. I want the good medicine of the Black Robe. For that, I must be baptized, and I cannot be baptized if I cannot recite the prayers."

Running Wolf shook his head. He could not do anything about Little Paul's gullibility. From his perspective, the Black Robe's religion did not contain any more power than the beliefs he had inherited from his ancestors. Their Great Spirit was just clothed differently. He did not need to exchange one dress for another. He was not convinced that the Black Robe medicine was more powerful than the Salish medicine. He would have to witness with his own eyes that their religion created better people.

Running Wolf forgot about the boy's unhappiness and went about his business, satisfied that he was not like that child beguiled by an alien belief. But he was jostled out of his complacency as the Christian holy day drew near. In a small community, news of unusual events quickly spread. Everyone knew everything about everybody. A secret remaining a secret for more than a day was a rarity, if not an impossibility. The downcast boy that Running Wolf could not cheer up only a week or two ago reveled in his new-found glory. To the amazement of the village, he recited his prayers without a stutter or stumble. Fluently and proudly, with fervent expression, he pronounced the Our Father, the Hail Mary, and the Glory Be.

"How did you do this?" Father de Smet asked Paul.

"The Lady taught me to pray," he replied, his face aglow.

"How could this be?"

"I walked into my teepee, and I saw her standing there. She was very beautiful, dressed in white, a star over her head, a serpent under her feet, and a fruit I did not recognize. From her heart, rays of light burst forth and warmed me. All at once the fog lifted from my mind, and I recited the prayers clearly without a pause. I knew them thoroughly."

Father de Smet presented a picture to the boy. "Did she look like this?"

"Yes, but she did not have seven stars over her head, only one star."

On Christmas Eve, Father de Smet baptized Little Paul along with a group of 150 other Salish men, women, and children. In the span of a few moons, the missionary efforts had achieved astounding results. The Black Robe was gratified by the success and believed he was leaving the mission in capable hands. More work needed to be done. There were so many native souls to save for Christ, and he was only one simple priest in the fields of The Lord. When the snow began to melt, he blessed the people, bid them farewell, mounted his horse, and journeyed to the Nimiipuu lands where he scouted sites for other missions.

Not long after Father de Smet departed, sadness visited the tribe. The light faded from Rides-the-Wind's eyes, but before passing into the other world, he opened his eyes one last time and whispered faintly, "It is a good day to die. I have lived to see Shining Shirt's prophesy fulfilled. It is done. Sing me on to the Land of the Spirits." Then the light faded from his eyes, and the loved ones standing vigil where he lay—Lone Wolf, White Heron, and Running Wolf—chanted the death song. Has-Two-Spirits, hearing the somber tones, entered the teepee, burned sprigs of sage, and incensed the prone body. Women entered to help Sweet Grass cleanse the body and dress Rides-the-Wind in his finest clothes. While these preparations were underway, Father Mengarini, clad in black cassock and a purple-fringed stole around his neck, rushed into the teepee carrying a glass vial.

"I have come to administer the sacrament of Extreme Unction."

"You are too late. He has already died," Has-Two-Spirits advised. The shaman was familiar with this

Christian rite because he had listened to Father Mengarini's catechism lessons.

Mengarini ignored what the shaman said and knelt next to the corpse. He poured an oily substance from the vial onto Rides-the-Wind's forehead, rubbed the oil on his skin, and mumbled unintelligible words.

"Stop!" Lone Wolf cried. "Go now. He has received our people's prayers and needs no anointment. Be gone from here."

Mengarini, abashed by the stern commands, stood up and hastily exited.

After his burial, Rides-the-Wind's possessions were distributed. Lone Wolf inherited his forty horses along with their beaded caparisons. Running Wolf received his bow, arrows, tomahawk, shield, and parfleches. Sweet Grass, old and wizened, cried like a mountain lioness in the night, looking for a mate. When her keening ceased, she clasped her hands to her breast, saying, "His spirit answers. Not long, and I will join him." Shortly before she lay down, never to rise from her buffalo-robe bed, she called Running Wolf to her side.

"Go with your father now to Red Feather and claim Laughing Water for your helpmate. After you do, then I go to where I, too, will ride the wind." She fell silent and Running Wolf watched her drift into sleep. It was not the sleep of death yet, for she still drew shallow breaths, and so he left her to seek his father.

He found him with the horses. An appaloosa mare nuzzled the palm of his hand. Running Wolf spotted the foals, now two-year-old colts, that Lone Wolf had given him. Fully trained, they shone as fine bridal gifts.

"Father, the time is right to speak to Red Feather. I am ready; the horses are ready. Let us go with the horses and tell him I wish to take Laughing Water as my wife."

Lone Wolf smiled benignly. "It is so."

Red Feather greeted them warmly outside his teepee. Laughing Water, smiling gleefully, hovered around her father's back. She took turns peeking around first his left shoulder, then his right shoulder. She knew what the subject of the visit was and did not intend to stand upon ceremony and demurely wait for the end of the discussion inside the teepee. The offer of the four horses was acceptable to Red Feather after he approvingly examined them from shoulder to flank. Red Feather was a lean, sharp-nosed man recognized for his strong opinions and sound judgment. Unlike his daughter, he was humorless but not cranky. He rarely displayed extreme emotions yet was never hesitant to express his viewpoint in clear, succinct terms. He had acceded to Big Face's and Standing Grizzly's decisions and had supported the delegations sent to St. Louis. When the Black Robes arrived, he listened to their religious instructions and attended their *nueimen*, or what Mengarini called the Mass. He was curious to learn the construction of their houses and climbed ladders roofing the cabins with shake shingles. He helped affix the crucifix to the top of the church steeple. Anxious to acquire their powerful medicine, he accepted baptism and was renamed Paul, but Lone Wolf and Running Wolf refused to address him by that name.

Running Wolf did not expect the proviso Red Feather would put on his marriage to his daughter. Red Feather motioned the men to sit in front of the entrance to his teepee. Laughing Water slipped down beside him. No coyness in her manner, she joined the three men as an equal in the negotiations.

"Do you want this man?" Red Feather asked her.

"With a full heart," she replied.

"Then it is accomplished except for one thing," her father said.

The others waited for him to state the missing item. What more could he want than those four superb horses? Did Running Wolf have to prove himself in some other way worthy of his daughter? As far as he was concerned, nothing remained to be done but to take Laughing Water by the hand and lead her to the new tule reed teepee White Heron had constructed for the onset of warmer spring weather.

"New ways of a man coming together with a woman are observed now. I learned from the Black Robe that to take a wife is a solemn act. The couple makes a pledge that is solemnized before the Great Spirit and all the people. For this reason, you must go to the church and pronounce marriage vows, and the Black Robe will bless your union."

"My word is good enough. When we live together, everyone knows we are tied until one of us decides to cut the rope. Nothing more is necessary. What they do in the church they built is their business. I do not accept the new way," Running Wolf asserted.

"The contract is incomplete until the Black Robe marries you. The Great Spirit does not consider you husband and wife without this sacrament."

"If you choose, Red Feather, you are free to believe that. You are baptized; I am not, so I do not believe that anything else but my word is needed." Seeking her agreement, Running Wolf looked at Laughing Water.

She chortled and said, "I am not baptized either. I accept Running Wolf as he is."

"You defy my wishes, daughter?" Red Feather asked, no rancor in his tone. Always in control of his temper, he spoke with the judiciousness and composure that marked his character.

"I do not defy anyone's wishes; I merely follow my own desires."

Red Feather conceded, "It is true I have allowed you to run where you want because I saw in you a spirit that could not be tamed. No more could I stop the rain from falling or the wind from blowing." He spoke in an even, measured tone. "You have heard my wishes. I am a Christian, freely accepting the Black Robe's medicine. I will no longer insist. I pray that your heart changes, and that you embrace the new ways."

Laughing Water's older brother, Brave Bear, approached Running Wolf and clasped his forearm. "I stand with you, my brother, in peace and in war. In choosing my sister, you decide well. Neither Sage Hen nor I were baptized or entered the church to declare we were a couple. We uphold the old ways too, and our father can do as he chooses. He is too much enthralled with the Black Robes. It is as if they worked a charm upon his heart."

"Call it magic if you will," Red Feather said, "I believe in their power."

Brave Bear chuckled, "He believes that the white medicine wards off the day of dying." The smirk on Sage Hen's round face revealed that she also considered the belief was nonsense. Short and plump, she sidled closer to Brave Bear. With wide hips and big breasts, she was built perfectly for childbearing.

Although Running Wolf and Laughing Water did not submit to the marriage rites, other young couples in the village had undergone the church ceremony. In times past, couples had merely stated their intention and started to live together, standing on no formality. When they no longer wished to live together, they separated, and the man could take a new wife, because a woman was necessary to help with skinning and tanning the buffalo hides, gathering roots and berries, sewing clothes, and cooking. No man could exist without woman's labor. The Black Robes did not like this casual practice and admonished the Salish against what they considered the sins of divorce and adultery. They also condemned the torture and killing of prisoners. Mengarini himself had interceded on behalf of a Blackfoot warrior stripped naked and flogged unmercifully. Because of his plea for mercy, the Blackfoot was set free and allowed to return to his people.

White Heron appreciated Laughing Water's energy and cheerfulness that she brought to their communal tasks. Her son had made a good choice. She waited, confident the strong and vigorous Laughing Water would soon bear fine grandchildren. Both girls and boys were welcome, because both provided hands for the division of labor in the camp. In contrast to the vivacious Laughing Water, who bustled with activity and good humor, Sweet Grass continued to wither. As White Heron tended her as she lay like a dry stalk, her heart ached for the old woman. She tried to feed her a spoonful of soup, but White Heron was too weak to part her lips and sip the small amount of liquid. One morning Sweet Grass's thin lips murmured, and White Heron bent closer to hear her words.

"Carry me into the sun."

For a moment, White Heron debated whether she should or not and then complied.

"Yes, Mother, I will put you in the sun. Sweet Grass was feather-light as she lifted her and carried her with no trouble at all.

Pointing with her bony finger, Sweet Grass whispered, "Put me down under that cottonwood."

White Heron did as she was bid and set her, wrapped in a deer hide, under the tree. The sun was already past its zenith. In midafternoon, it blazed on the western horizon. Sweet Grass gazed directly into the sunlight. The film seemed to lift from her eyes and miraculously capture the sun's brilliance for a second. Then her breathing stopped, and her chin sank into her chest. Her spirit had departed. White Heron quietly kept a vigil by the dead body for a while before she rose to go and tell the rest of the village that Sweet Grass had gone to join Rides-the-Wind in the other world. Now she and Lone Wolf were the family elders standing in wait for the next generation.

During the next season's buffalo hunt to the eastern prairie, Laughing Water, pregnant with her first child, remained behind while most of the village ventured west. Father De Smet had returned for a short sojourn with the Salish before going on to explore territory for new missions and was intensely interested in the conduct of the hunt. He joined the party, eager to share the hardships and labor. The Salish respected him for his willingness to learn. Running Wolf and Lone Wolf, as usual, went on the autumn hunt. They were leery that the Black Robe possessed the stamina or the valor to fend off a likely attack from their enemy, the Blackfeet. The buffalo numbers had diminished, and it was rare not to confront a hostile Blackfeet hunting party. The hunt was successful, and after the slaughter of forty buffalo, the women began the processing of the kill. As they prepared to depart with their pack animals and travois laden with meat and hides, the Blackfoot attacked on horseback from a ridge, whooping and shooting their arrows. The priest watched, unflinching, but did not join in the combat. In fact, he emerged from behind the flank of his horse, and with upraised crucifix, attempted to pacify the combatants. The tide of battle was swift, and the Salish were able to drive the attackers away due to their greater numbers but certainly not because of the priest's peacemaking efforts.

One Blackfoot, not mortally wounded, remained on the ground, clutching his bloody shoulder. Several Salish seized him. They dragged him, tied him to a stake, and then flogged him. The Blackfoot did not cry out in pain but grimaced every so often, hurling curses at his torturers through clenched teeth.

"Enough!" Father de Smet approached, holding the crucifix aloft that hung from his neck on a silver chain. "Christ enjoins mercy. Do unto him as you would have him do unto you if you were in his place. Unbind him and let him return to his family." De Smet's radiant countenance gave the floggers pause, and they lowered their whips. "Peace upon you. Christ said, 'Peace I give to you; my peace I leave to you.' So you must free this man."

Surprisingly to Running Wolf, the men did as they were told. Once freed, the Blackfoot bounded forward, fleet as a buck, toward home.

Lone Wolf grumbled about the release of the prisoner and swore the Blackfeet would only attack with greater force. Father De Smet tried to settle his misgivings to no avail, although his assurances of Christ's blessing upon their merciful act placated the chiefs.

"I will go with peace offerings to the Blackfeet. I have long wanted to visit them because on my journey along the Missouri, I heard they were also anxious to learn the Christian religion."

Big Face and Standing Grizzly looked askance at this proposal. Not pleased at all by the Black Robe's intention to preach to their enemy, they grumbled. They had a proprietary claim to the power of the Black Robe's medicine and did not want to share it. During the past few years, they had been mainly victorious in their skirmishes with the Blackfeet and had suffered fewer losses in battle. They had succeeded in foiling theft of their horses for the most part and had continued to hunt buffalo despite the efforts of the Blackfeet to frighten them off the plains. They attributed these successes to the Black Robe who talked to the Great Spirit. They did not place the same confidence in the other Black Robes who were not as likable and amiable as Father de Smet. It was an affront to their sensibilities that he wished to visit the Blackfeet, but they made no effort to stop him. Father de Smet saddled up and directed his mount to the northeast of the mountain range while the Salish headed in the opposite direction.

On his return, Laughing Water greeted Running Wolf with a baby in her arms. "Your son," she announced as the infant's chubby face and head of thick, black hair appeared above its swaddled body. Big, dark brown eyes, open and alert, peered at him. Strands of the baby's unruly hair stuck out like small horns on either side of his head.

"Horned Owl," Running Wolf exclaimed, "You look like a curious little owl."

His mother laughed, "That's exactly right." He keeps me up at night, hungry and restless."

Thereafter he was called Horned Owl, their beloved firstborn.

It had been a fruitful season, too, for Brave Bear and Sage Hen, for during the fall hunt, Sage Hen gave birth to their second daughter, Song Bird, a healthy child who began to coo like a bird at a few weeks' old. Their first daughter, Plenty Medicine, had been a puny little baby not expected to live. A miracle child, she had failed to thrive until Has-Two-Spirits administered his healing arts. As a toddler, she trailed the medicine man, poking into his bag of herbs and mimicking his chants and dances. She escaped further sickness and emanated a charmed existence so that even as a three-year-old, she began to be called Plenty Medicine, and she was pegged to become a great medicine woman.

As soon as Horned Owl was able to crawl, Laughing Water freed him from his cradleboard to play with Song Bird. The two mothers watched the babies frolic like cubs on all fours. They grabbed at a caterpillar inching on a blade of grass or reached for a butterfly that fluttered over the head of a flower. Big sister, Plenty Medicine, would join them in their play. When they were able to sit up, she rolled a stitched deer-hide ball stuffed with hair to first one child and then the other. She cuddled the two chubby children like a little mother. When they fretted and cried, she soothed them with a song. Her ability to heal every distress and treat every scratch or cut, solidified the general belief that she was destined to be a medicine woman. She smelled and picked every herb in field and forest and brought bundles of plant leaves to Has-Two-Spirits, who instructed her from an early age in their names and uses.

Horned Owl was a two-year-old toddling around the encampment with Song Bird not far behind him when Laughing Water delivered her second child—a boy. From the day of his birth, he was querulous and colicky, a restless sleeper whose fists were curled as he nursed from his mother's breast until one day she exclaimed, trying to make light of this temperamental baby, "He kicks like a horse; he even kicked like that when he was still inside me." She patted her abdomen. "He was a wild one then and is a wild horse still. He bucks and then whinnies for attention all the time."

"His name is Wild Horse," Running Wolf said, and that is what he was called from that day forward.

Lone Wolf, pleased, observed the infant's disposition. "That is right. The spirit of the horse lives in him. I will train him like a horse, and in turn, I will teach him to train horses. He will carry on my work."

Since the Black Robes had established the church in the valley, they had built several workshops and taught the boys other kinds of work. The mission now included six log cabins, a flour mill, a sawmill, a blacksmith's shop, and a barn. The white brothers were teaching them farming, carpentry, blacksmithing, and saddlery. Such labor was for women, and by the time the boys were around nine years old, they preferred going hunting, trapping, and fishing with their fathers, grandfathers, and uncles. Small crops of wheat, beans, potatoes, and other vegetables had been produced from the Black Robe's efforts to make the Salish farmers. A few cows, sheep, and goats had been introduced to instruct them in animal husbandry. Running Wolf scorned the men who tried to farm or do the white men's kind of work. No son of his would do women's work. He saw too many of his brothers bending to the Black Robes' will and praying in their church. Too many beaver and other game were being killed for their purposes. Where once the beaver had built dams in every stream, now he was lucky to find one beaver lodge on the beloved Willow River. Buffalo herds were still to be found, but their numbers had dwindled to an alarming level. Only through the cunning, skill, and dexterity of their scouts and mounted marksmen were they able to obtain enough meat and hides to carry them through the winter. It was getting more difficult with each passing season. As far as he could tell, their life had not become any better under the auspices of the Black Robes. People still robbed, cheated, and lied. People still had to be whipped for their foul deeds.

    He was not the only one discontented with the state of affairs. Father De Smet had established a mission in Blackfeet country, which had contributed to the dissatisfaction. Although the Salish liked and welcomed him whenever he visited, he never stayed long enough in their midst. He was a trusted friend and ally who they knew acted on their behalf. The other Black Robes did not inspire in them the same confidence. They acted superior and gave the people to understand that they disapproved of their customs and argued that they must be abandoned for the salvation of their souls. They talked too much of something called sin and questioned the wisdom of their leaders. What was this sin? How could a baby be born bad? What was evil about that child cradled in his mother's arms? That was foolish talk. A newborn was fresh, innocent life, untainted by any vice.

There was less enthusiasm to attend catechism classes or church services. Some of the Salish pitched their teepees farther away from the mission. Faith faded that the white men's medicine was stronger than their own traditional methods of healing. Too often, the medicine Mengarini administered from his glass vials failed to cure a feverish child who died despite the Black Robe's ministrations. The Black Robes exerted their best efforts to rekindle the people's zeal, but the Salish continued to passively accept their presence while distancing themselves from the Black Robe's activities. Realizing that they could achieve no greater results, the Black Robes sold the mission buildings to Major John Owens and left for greener missionary pastures among other native populations who would be more receptive to the Christian religion. The tribe was not sorry to see them leave and went back to their traditional way of life. Still, they had imbibed some of the Christian message and observed a day of prayer. They just did not believe that the white men possessed a more powerful religion or magic that would make them indestructible. They would have gladly listened to Father De Smet, but he stayed away. He was one who truly talked with God.

The misgivings about the Black Robes' presence in their country that had plagued Rides-the-Wind, Lone Wolf, and Running Wolf dissipated during this period of relative calm. Even the Blackfeet incursions into their country were less frequent, and the good relations with the Nimiipuu to the west endured, although this tribe, having more exposure to pressures from white settlers, experienced increased belligerence and discontent. The Salish's reputation for peacefulness persisted, relatively isolated as they were, north of the major migration route of the whites. Could this protection last forever? Would they remain immune from the pressure of white society and their insatiable urge to claim land and resources for their own uses? For a while, Running Wolf could forget these concerns as he watched his two sons grow and thrive in the valley his ancestors had called home for generations, secure in the knowledge they were keepers of the earth. The Great Spirit, as in ages past, provided everything they needed; the people would preserve, honor, and praise the earth the Great Spirit had awarded them in perpetuity.

Running Wolf's penchant for exploration of the far reaches of their domain did not diminish. Now he went with his two sons to the sacred, towering mountains to the north—so high they scraped the clouds, and the clouds often bent to cover their sharp-pointed peaks. These were the first giants to tread the earth who were turned to stone before man came to guard the land. Here the Great Spirit hovered and sometimes thundered, driving his arrows down, striking the tallest timbers, and igniting the fire that swept plumes of smoke down the mountainsides. He taught his sons to walk softly through the forest floor carpeted with pine needles, to stealthily hunt the elusive deer and to identify every animal track. They could survive on the nuts and berries they found and the game they killed. They studied the stars that guided them in the right direction and discovered the caves where they took shelter from the rain. They went to regions where they encountered no other two-legged creatures, only four-footed denizens and birds awing in the air or flitting from limb to limb. Virgin and unsullied were the far reaches to which they tread.

Other times, mounted on fleet horses, they explored the uplands to the east and the eastern plains. Here they found buffalo and antelope. They camped along the rivers gurgling with the pure, clear water, bursting with trout and salmon, so abundant that they could spear fish from the bank. Then, with the fish impaled on a stick, they roasted it and ate the succulent red flesh. On racks, they dried their surplus and packed it to take home to Laughing Water and White Heron.

When the snows blew again, Running Wolf and his sons did not wander far from the warm circle of teepees pitched in the shadow of the Red Top Mountains. His father and mother huddled around the firepit inside the teepee and took turns telling legends of old. On clear mornings Lone Wolf and Running Wolf strapped on snowshoes to check the winter traps set for the fur-bearing animals. White Heron sat with Laughing Water mending garments. Her gnarled fingers worked at a slower pace than the younger woman's nimble hands, her chatter sounded as lively and animated as Laughing Water's. Running Wolf lovingly watched the two women as they skinned the rabbits they had caught and then roasted the meat on the spit. The rabbit fur would make good lining for their leggings. The company of family comforted him. Their wisdom fortified him, and he fully embraced his duty to pass on their stalwartness and courage to his sons. Peace dwelled with them in the valley. He was no man's enemy.

News of the Black Robes' return reached their ears the autumn his sons were ten and twelve years old. In the region to the south of the Broad Water, they had built another mission. Salish from his village had traveled north to live with them. They were folk who still clung to the teachings Father de Smet had brought and wanted to live with a few hundred Salish, Kootenai, and Kalispell who had migrated to this region where they had traditionally gone to hunt and fish. Red Feather was among the Salish from their village who decided to pack up and move to the new mission that was called St. Ignatius. For reasons inexplicable to Running Wolf, his father-in-law had embraced the white religion and adopted their mannerisms. Red Feather made the sign of the cross often on entering and leaving the house; he murmured the white man's grace before meals and observed their day of prayer. He cherished rosary beads that Father de Smet had given him when he first came to the valley. His wife, Laughing Water's mother, had died when she was a little girl, and he had taken a young Nimiipuu woman who was equally enamored with the white man's medicine. She had born him many children, too numerous to name, which he had baptized. Laughing Water brushed off her father's flirtation with the white man's religion.

"He is an old man . . . set in his ways. Who am I to tell him he is ridiculous? He thinks the white man has magic to make him live forever. He can go to the Jocko Valley and live with the Nimiipuu and Kootenai who are gathering there. They can think their lives will be easier there. It may be, or it may not be. I am happy here, Running Wolf. We should stay here. The land is good to us."

Red Feather took his young wife and train of children, one still in the cradleboard on his mother's back, and left for the new mission. His contingent could form a small village alone. Red Feather belonged to a group whose dedication to the white man's religion had never diminished, while most of the tribe became disenchanted when Father de Smet took his medicine to the Blackfeet. Nevertheless, the tribe had become dependent on the white man's goods and often went to Owen's trading post to barter furs for gunpowder, rifles, blankets, metal implements, fabric, ribbons, beads, and countless other objects they had learned to appreciate, recognizing their utility and durability. In addition, they bargained for the coffee, flour, sugar, and firewater Owen stocked. The Black Robes had warned them against the effects of firewater, or whiskey, as the tribe called it. However much the whiskey addled their heads, they asked for more, teetering on drunken feet until they passed out. When they awoke from their stupor, they claimed they liked the way the whiskey warmed their innards. While it circulated in their system, they could feel no pain, cold, or worry. It made all the difference in the world. It blotted out ugliness and unpleasantness. At this point, there were only a few warriors who drank too much. The traders were forbidden from bringing the firewater to the trading post. Despite the prohibition, some whiskey did make its way into the area. The fondness of weak men for the firewater underscored to Running Wolf that the arrival of the Black Robes had not made them better. There were drunkards among the white men, and they had spread their evil. If their religion was so wonderful, then the white men would not be evildoers.

Gradually these developments began to prey on Running Wolf's mind again, disrupting a period when he had been experiencing relative peace and unconcern in which he was occupied with his growing family and the traditional life of his people. The land had been good to them, just as Laughing Water had said. They worked, played, laughed, and told stories under the beauty of the sky, surrounded by the bounty of the land.

After Red Feather left to join the people living south of the Broad Water, other changes occurred. Chief Standing Grizzly died, and Many Horses took his place as the tribe's principal chief. He superficially observed the Black Robe's religion and was respected as a man of peace. As neighboring tribes began to speak of war to combat white settlement, he believed the earth was big enough to accommodate every living creature. Running Wolf was skeptical of his gullibility. Many Horses did not immediately perceive the duplicity in the white men's eyes. Something false inhabited their faces, pale and shallow. There lurked a coldness in that complexion, a lack of basic honesty. These feelings sent a shiver up his spine—a similar aversion that he would feel if he spotted a coiled rattlesnake sunning on a rock. Accompanying the change in leadership was the arrival of a short, bearded white man dressed in a black suit with gold buttons and epaulets, a long broadsword sheathed at his side decorated with red braided cord, and a wide-brimmed felt hat on his head. He rode into the encampment, dismounted, and in a courtly manner, greeted Many Horses who came out to meet him. He stood shorter than the Salish chiefs. Through the interpreter he brought with him, he introduced himself as Isaac Stevens, the Governor of the Washington Territory and Superintendent of Indian Affairs.

"What are these titles? What is this Washington? We are Salish. We take care of our affairs," the chiefs murmured among themselves.

Many Horses directed his remarks to the short, officious white man he judged was a horse soldier among those known to have built forts in the Sioux and Mandan country on the eastern plains. "I am Many Horses, caretaker of my people's affairs."

"I want to gather the peoples to make peace treaties," the little man with puffed-up chest declared.

"What peace to make? There is no war. No fight since the fur traders first came here. We greeted your people with hospitality, food, and supplies. We have furnished your travelers with horses and guides to lead them. There is no peace to make."

"It is my authority to tell you to gather the bands at the time and place I designate for the purpose of assigning territory to your peoples."

The translation did not clarify what assigning territory meant. The meaning came across to the chief as affirming what were the ancestral homelands of each band. A common understanding existed already between the Kootenai, Kalispell, and upper and lower Salish bands. They had no quarrel with their Kootenai neighbors and the bands who were their kindred, speaking the same language. Although dubious at the purpose of this gathering, in the end, Many Horses agreed to attend to maintain friendly relations.

Running Wolf did not like this development. He eyed with suspicion the maneuver of this man who acted as the big chief of the white men. He did not attend the council with Many Horses, only the sub-chiefs accompanied Many Horses to a place called Delimbed Tree, but that Isaac Stevens called Council Groves. Stevens made it clear he wanted Many Horses to move his people north to the Mission Valley where the Kalispell and Kootenai lived near the Broad Water and to cede his territory in the Bitterroot Valley to the white government. Many Horses adamantly refused to relocate and to sign the white man's paper. After several days of negotiations, Stevens hit on the plan to have the government conduct a survey to determine which was the best territory to establish the joint reservation for the tribes, giving the chiefs to believe there would be two reservations. Until the survey was completed, territory above the Bitterroot Valley, namely the Jocko and Mission valleys, would not be open to white settlement. Stevens sat behind a table under a tent while eighteen chiefs lined up to mark an 'X' on his paper, which he called the treaty. Some had Christian names, and others retained their native names. Many Horses used his Christian name, Victor. Others included Chief Alexander of the upper Kalispells, Chief Michelle of the Kootenai, Ambrose, Pah-soh, Bear Track, Adolphe, Thunder, Big Canoe, Kootel Chah, Paul, Andrew, Michelle, Battiste, Gun Flint, Little Michelle, Paul See, and Moses. Other provisions included installment payments totaling $120,000 over the next fifteen years, the erection and maintenance of an agricultural and industrial school, instruction in the trades, and salaries of $500 per year and housing for all the chiefs. In addition, alcohol was prohibited on native land, and the chiefs pledged that they would not war against white men or other tribes. Any offenders would be delivered to the United States government. Over the course of the negotiations, objections were raised, but were fogged over with vagaries and promises.

After the signing, Many Horses returned to his people, resolute that he would never surrender his homeland. He held a council at which he recounted the wrangling for eight days with Stevens. Running Wolf and Lone Wolf gathered outside in a circle with the elders to hear Many Horses' report.

"They dare to give our places their names. They dare to call us Flathead when that is not our name. They say Broad Water is Flathead Lake. Here in Wide Cottonwood Trees, our home, they call Bitterroot Valley, and the land of the Kalispell, they want to make the place of the Flathead reservation, which we have known since men first walked here as *Sinieleman*, the Place Where Something Was Surrounded, they rename the Mission Valley. They call us Flatheads, but our heads are not flat, and our name is Salish. They lump us together with the Kootenai and do not recognize that the Kootenai speak a completely different language than ours. The Kalispell, our relatives, they give the silly name of Pend d'Oreilles, which my tongue can hardly shape. Our good friends, the Nimiipuu, they say, are the Nez Perce. Have you ever heard anything so ridiculous? We are all people of the earth. We all call ourselves the first people. I was angered because they wanted to make us one big herd living all in one territory in the land of the Broad Water within the boundaries they draw on paper. But I refused to be driven like buffalo into a box canyon."

Heads nodded in assent to Many Horses's assertion. They would be unmovable, steadfast in devotion to the land where they were born and their ancestors were buried. They felt pride in their leader's steadfastness. Many Horses continued, "When I refused to sign the paper, the White Chief called me a dog and an old woman. I walked out. My hot temper cooled the next day, and I returned and told Stevens that the White Father in Washington can come and look at our valley and the Mission Valley and decide which is the better place for our people. Until he comes, my people and I do not move. I know the White Father will never come. We are secure here. The white chief said he added this stipulation to the paper. No Horses of the Kalispell signed the paper. He favors this so-called reservation in Sineleman because he is Christian and has been eager to learn more of the talking book. Big Canoe of the upper Kalispell agreed with me. He asked the White Chief, 'If I came into your land and asked you to give your land to me, would you sell it? No. I have nothing to say about selling land.' And he spoke no more. Moses, my brother here, spoke of our land of the Wide Cottonwood Trees and of his grandfathers buried here. He said he came here to talk of the White Chief's help with the Niitsitapi, the Blackfeet. He did not come here to talk of selling land. The fourteen chiefs were worn out with talk. Our throats were dry. Some things in the agreement we liked, for instance, promises of provisions, the right to hunt and fish as always, education in the white men's crafts to make useful things, and a ban on alcohol on our land. The things we did not like we put aside, because we wanted peace and did not want to fight. All the chiefs knew in their hearts, this race of men was stronger and numbered more than the stars in the sky. Each made an 'X' on the paper. That was what the White Chief wanted, and we honored his custom though strange to us."

"But you do not know what the paper says. You cannot read it," Running Wolf interjected.

"The Black Robe told me what it said."

"And you trust the Black Robe's words?" Running Wolf countered.

"He knows our language and does not speak with a forked tongue. He calls it sin to tell a lie."

"You give the white men one piece of land, and he will ask for another piece and another piece."

"Some fear that is so. Here I draw the line. Not one piece of my valley will I give or he will take."

Running Wolf shook his head and sadly rose to leave the council. Lone Wolf followed his son.

At a distance from the camp, they ascended a winding path to a rocky overlook. They sat on a ledge, surveying the Place of the Wide Cottonwood Trees. Its verdure was beautiful; the teepees beside the Willow River were white specks upon the valley's lush greenery. Overhead, an expanse of cloudless summer sky showered munificence on the world. Purity and cleanliness all around. All around earth's bounty and beauty. No rumbling cloud or dissonant sound disrupted the tranquility. Calming though the view was, it could not allay the tempest in Running Wolf's soul. He must speak his feelings to his father.

"I do not like the piece of paper the White Chief had Many Horses mark," Running Wolf said. "It is wrong. We are not long for this valley. The white men intend to remove us. Many Horses is right that to fight back will result in our extinction. Their feet will tramp us into the dust."

"I fear you are right, my son. I do not like it either, but do not know what is to be done."

"I have been thinking about it a long time, Father. There are places to hide from their hungry jaws."

"Hiding places? I know none. They can pursue us into our graves."

"I know such places. I have traveled to them . . . to ice caves in the north . . . to secluded canyons with narrow entry where only one man can slide through."

"What do you suggest?" Lone Wolf asked.

"To leave with our family. Those who are Christian can remain and see if they can survive through adoption of the white man's way. But they cannot stop being who they are—Salish—keepers of the earth. The white men come as destroyers. There is no meeting of waters with their kind. I am certain of that. I must go."

"Who would be willing to go where you lead?"

"Laughing Water, Horned Owl, and Wild Horse. I will take them with me."

"They are not enough to survive."

"Brave Bear, Laughing Water's brother, and Sage Hen will go with their children, Plenty Medicine and Song Bird."

"You need more men and women to do the work," Lone Wolf objected.

"I have spoken to my cousin Smoking Loon. He is a good fisherman. His wife, Half Moon, is a good worker. Their son, Sitting Crow, and their daughter, Painted Turtle, will add more helping hands."

"Have you spoken to them about your plans?"

"Yes and they said that, if things get worse they may agree to leave. And things have gotten worse with this treaty. I will speak to them again."

"I do not want you to leave. You are a warrior who must stay and fight if it comes to that," Lone Wolf said

"Many Horses is committed to peace. He is a Christian who believes that to spill blood is a grave sin. He will do anything to prevent war."

"But he swears he will not move to *Sinieleman* no matter what the White Chief wants. He gambles that the White Father in Washington will never come to say what place is better for a combined reservation. I do not like that white man's word, reservation. I can hardly pronounce it, but it is a word we must learn if we are to understand the white chief's intention."

"His intention is not good. I see it in his shifty eyes. His discourtesy to Many Horses. He called him dog and old woman. He pretends generosity and kindness to us, but evil hides under his smile."

"How are you sure that the white soldiers will not sniff you out of your hiding place?"

"They can try, but I will hide my tracks. I will preserve my way of life."

"You have courage, my son."

"I learned courage from you. You must go with us into the far north country."

"No, I cannot. I am too old and must be buried here where I was born. So must your mother, White Heron. We will not go with you."

"I am sorry for that. I will not argue with your decision if you choose to stay. The trip is hard and long. We must journey fast and settle before the snow is high."

"You must be certain the others will go along. You cannot survive without people to help hunt and make the things you need."

"I will speak to them again. They are not happy with the sale of land to the west and the borders the White Chief drew."

Wearily, Lone Wolf rose and lifted his gaze to the sky. The brightness spread over the land was deceptive. In his aging bones, he felt a change coming and wondered if he would live to see the removal of his people to *Sinieleman*. He could not divine the future. Perhaps the shaman Has-

Two-Spirits could prophesy if peace prevailed or the white man continued to take more than he gave. He trailed Running Wolf down the winding path to the village. They parted in front of his teepee, and Running Wolf went to seek Brave Bear and Smoking Loon. His plan to leave had to be finalized.

On the way to find the two men, he encountered Has-Two-Spirits seated in front of his teepee, crushing sage in a mortar. Running Wolf sat down beside him. The insights of the possessor of both male and female power would gird him on his journey. By sharing his intention to find refuge from white encroachment, he might induce the shaman to join the small group.

"Ho," the shaman acknowledged Running Wolf's presence. "What burden do you wish to lift from your heart?" Has-Two-Spirits asked, not shifting his gaze from mortar and pestle.

His prescience, always impressive, emboldened Running Wolf to speak.

"The signing of the White Chief's paper troubles me. The land cannot be bought and sold. My stomach sickens with the loss of our customs. Our chiefs have been swayed to trust in his lies. Too many wear their clothes and covet the white men's trinkets. They abandon the old ways and want to plant seeds, cut the earth into strips, and divide the land, saying this is yours and this is mine. They make roads over the ground where the bones of our fathers are buried. They want to bunch us together in one place, not our birthplace. The traders bring the firewater to poison and drive us mad, so our youth stumble and fall, and their tongues flap in their mouths. I do not like it. I yearn to dwell far from them. I feel we have been made dirty by the white men and sense nothing but darkness approach. I feel my people become an eagle without wings or talons. The white man is a vulture who would also feast on the dead."

His eyes still focused on grinding sage into fine powder, Has-Two-Spirits, in an even tone responded, "So you want to run like the wolf into its den?"

Impressed again by his prescience, Running Wolf did not know what to say for a moment. Then an urge to defend himself moved him to respond. "Isolation from their corruption is the solution. They contaminate everything that comes near them. Our people lose their sense of self, our traditions, and even our language. They give us new names; they rename the hills, valleys, and rivers to their liking. If I stay, I roll over like a dog in the dust." He paused in his speech, and, thinking better of his argument, changed his tactic. "Come with me," he urged Has-Two-Spirits. "Do you not see the white men are replacing your medicine with his medicine? The Black Robe wishes you gone and has no room in his heart for you. He damns the man/woman to his fiery hell—to his underground where the flames will eat your flesh without consuming it forever."

Running Wolf was surprised that Has-Two-Spirits chuckled at his description.

"I am not afraid," Has-Two-Spirits said. "You must go where your guardian spirit leads you. If it is to hide, I will not persuade you to act differently. I see it is your path. My path is to remain. My duty is to serve my people, to be the healer among nations. They will need me in the seasons ahead. I will not desert them in their time of tribulation."

"Then you do foresee trouble?"

"Ah," he sighed. The sage finally ground to his satisfaction, he scooped it into a leather pouch and tightened the cord to close it. His task completed, he turned his gaze upon Running Wolf.

"May peace follow on your journey." Then he rose and left Running Wolf with his thoughts. Running Wolf would have loved to have the medicine man part of his company, but that was not to be. He would not persuade him further. One did not argue with a shaman's strength of character. Once he had spoken, that ended the matter. He hoped he could count on the resolution of the others to accompany him. Now he must speak to the rest who shared his qualms—Brave Bear and Smoking Loon. Whatever these men decided, their women and children were bound to follow them.

The first man he found was Brave Bear, Laughing Water's brother. He needed his expertise as a tracker and hunter. Brave Bear saw Running Wolf approach and looked up from stringing his bow with fresh sinew.

"Ho, brother," Running Wolf greeted him and admired the craftmanship of his bow. He came right to the purpose of his visit. "Remember what we talked of earlier?"

Brave Bear nodded in acknowledgment of what Running Wolf referred to. He said, "The signing of the paper. It can get only worse."

"Aye, as we have talked about. Then you are prepared to go now?"

"After I heard Many Horses speak of what the paper said, I knew our path was set."

"We must leave in a few days. Summer is half spent. Get your woman and children ready for the journey."

"Do you have anyone else besides Smoking Loon to go with us?"

"He is the only one of like mind. Others are baptized and depend too much on the white men. I asked Has-Two-Spirits to go, but he stays to preserve the old ways."

"What of Lone Wolf and White Heron?"

"They want to die where they were born."

"I will tell Half Moon and Painted Turtle to begin packing our belongings for the journey."

"Now I go to tell Smoking Loon it is time to leave."

Running Wolf found his cousin fastening an iron head to his spear. This highly-prized, durable point had been obtained from the Owen's trading post, flint ones long since abandoned.

"My cousin, I am filled with disgust that Many Horses signed the paper. I cannot accept his leadership. It is folly to think the white men will relent. Wherever his shadow falls, there is misfortune. Eventually, they will take what Many Horses will not sell."

Smoking Loon set his spear aside and stood up. "I am with you. I prepare for the journey."

Sitting Crow, just returned from a reconnoiter of the valley, appeared, leading his horse to pasture. Almost a full-grown man, he was alert and keen to prove his prowess in the manly arts. Overhearing his father's last words, he asked, "What journey?"

"It is what we have spoken of before—making a new home where the white man's evil cannot reach us and where we can live as we have always lived—by our wits and the protection of our guardian spirits."

Tall and lean for his sixteen summers, Sitting Crow exuded the exuberance of youth. His eyes, black as the crow's feathers, sparkled at the prospect of the journey. Every muscle of Sitting Crow's body was strung like a taut bowstring, showing Running Wolf his preparation to participate in the bold adventure.

"Yes, the time to strike out on our own has come," Running Wolf said. "We cannot abide the despoilment and theft of our land and way of life. Young hands like yours are needed to carry on our culture."

"I have never liked the white man's ways. He is sly and not to be trusted. The White Chief looks down his nose at me like I am something rotten or a piece of wood to be thrown into the fire."

"You are wise beyond your years," Running Wolf said.

"Not so . . . just angry," the boy replied.

"We are all angry," his father added. "But we will put that anger to good use and venture to make a home far from this place that is doomed to be crushed under the white man's boot."

"Long ago, it was foretold," Running Wolf said, "but the prophet predicted a better life for us when the Black Robes should arrive, bringing a new religion. It has not turned out to be so because we see that the white Christian is not better than we are. In fact, our traditions ensured that the wicked are punished. But that is not so with the white men. They do not punish the men who kill us and take our land. They do not act better. They lie, cheat, steal, and take our women. If we did that to them, they would shoot us in the head in an instant."

"It is settled," Smoking Loon said. "When do we depart to where you lead us?"

"As soon as Half Moon and Painted Turtle take down your teepee and load your belongings on packhorses for the journey. At dawn the day after tomorrow be ready."

Sitting Crow gave a whoop, not able to contain his eagerness. "I will get the horses ready," he said.

Smoking Loon signed his son to hush, "Guard your emotions," he said to him. "It is not wise to show such excitement. We go quietly and in peace with our brothers who choose to remain." Then he turned to Running Wolf.

"What will Many Horses think of our departure?"

"I do not think he cares. He is ready to let anyone who does not accept his leadership leave. He embraces the peace the Black Robes preach of. He abhors bloodshed. He will play out his bet. It is his gamble that the white men will allow him to remain in the Place of the Wide Cottonwood Trees indefinitely. But I think he is mistaken. The whites are like the sands. They blow now from east and west and will eventually cover the earth. Like locusts, they swarm and will eat up everything in their path. So say I. Šey hoy. That is all."

Running Wolf, having made it clear that he had said all he wanted, Smoking Loon and Sitting Crow were given to understand that the conversation was ended. Tacitly, they had acknowledged the leadership of Running Wolf in the band they had formed and that would soon venture forth to establish a separate, smaller offshoot of the larger Salish tribe in a courageous effort to preserve their identity, their native culture, and their dignity. They were the holdouts to Christian baptism and the baptism into an alien way of life that would result in their divorce from the hunting and gathering way of lift that the Salish had followed from time immemorial.

Working steadily, the young girls Painted Turtle, Plenty Medicine, and Song Bird helped their mothers, Sage Hen and Half Moon, pack provisions and load them on travois and packhorses. The morning of departure dawned clear and bright with a cloudless sky and the peaks crowned in auras of light. Their neighbors assembled to bid them well on their journey, their sad faces revealing fear for the survival of such a small band in unknown territory. Many Horses did not shy away from seeing them off and did not withhold his blessings on their journey. He summoned the shaman to lead a farewell song:

> *May the wind blow softly,*
> *Soft the earth under your feet.*
> *May the sun shine kindly,*
> *Kind the earth where you go*
> *Where you go, where you go*
> *The Great Spirit goes,*
> *The cool water flows,*
> *Soft the wind blows.*

Sitting Crow rode behind the men—Running Wolf in the lead; next came Brave Bear and Smoking Loon. Behind them trailed the young boys on their horses—Horned Owl and Wild Horse. Next, the women on mounts pulling the travois. Lastly, the young girls Painted Turtle and the sisters Plenty Medicine and Song Bird rode, all smiles, excited at the commencement of the migration northward. Their route led past the confluence of the rivers over a pass into the Mission Valley. If they pastured and watered their horses three times a day, making sure they were well-rested in the morning, they could make twenty miles a day and arrive at St. Ignatius in four days. Their ultimate destination might take them three weeks of steady travel.

Laughing Water looked forward to the stop in Mission Valley, where she could see Red Feather again. She had not seen her father in many moons and hoped she would find him healthy and happy in the Christian community. There they would rest for a day before going onward. Perhaps some people, disgruntled with conditions, would want to join them in establishing a new community far from the influence of white men. Running Wolf shared that hope of gaining more recruits.

Their hopes were dashed when they reached St. Ignatius because the Kalispell and Salish living there were content with the Black Robes and were farming and raising cattle under the direction of the missionaries. The Black Robes were teaching the children to read and write their language but had few students because most of the children preferred to run freely and observe the elders engaged in traditional crafts. More girls than boys attended the schoolroom classes while the boys hunted and fished with their fathers.

Red Feather affably greeted his daughter and the rest of the company. He invited them into the log house that had been constructed for his family. His wife and seven children were squeezed into one room. Laughing Water preferred to sleep in the summer tule teepee because it was cooler and allowed the fresh breeze to blow through the reed, but for this one night she would sleep under Red Feather's roof. In her father's cabin, an iron stove stood against one wall, and on the opposite side was a stone fireplace. She could appreciate that the cabin might afford a warmer dwelling in winter. Even so, she believed the buffalo-hide teepee was as snug and cozy as this house constructed of trees. It appeared most of the people shared her opinion because they still camped in teepees in the general vicinity of the mission, dominated by the steepled church built of hewn logs.

"It is good here. We are treated well. You do not need to run and hide like foxes into a hole."

"Father, we do not change into white men," Laughing Water said. "Maybe for now you are well. Who knows what more disease they will bring."

"You have not listened to the words of the White Man's Book of Heaven. You have not learned how to cook the crops we grow from seeds or drink the milk the cows give or the eggs the tame birds lay. Their feathers are plucked, and the birds are boiled in an iron pot. The meat is good."

"We do not need those things."

"But the Great Spirit has brought these gifts for our use."

Running Wolf could not hold his tongue while father and daughter conversed. "What we had before the Black Robe came is sufficient. But it is more than a matter of what to eat or what to grow. They rob us of our language and our land. I cannot stand for their theft. In doing that, they steal my identity, my soul, who I am. Then I will become a hollowed-out tree that will crack and fall to the ground where the bears will come to eat the insects infesting my dead body. For a while, Red Feather, things may go well, but know, the vultures circle and will feed on the carcass of our people."

These words of doom did not ruffle Red Feather. He sat impervious to pessimistic prophecies. Red Feather, possessed of a sincere heart, had absorbed the essential mystery of Christianity, and had resolved to incorporate the virtues of faith, hope, and charity into his thoughts, words, and deeds. In all cultures, his type of man existed as the true believer, firmly adhering to the tenet that love conquers hatred. In whatever time or place he manifested as the perpetual optimist who believed that even from the greatest disaster or evil, ultimately good arose, that even from a divine prophet, the Son of God, crucified like a criminal, mankind could be redeemed from sin. That was the mystery embedded across cultures in which death was conquered.

Red Feather traced the sign of the cross, the sacred four directions the Salish cherished and recited the prayer. "Blessings on your journey."

There was nothing further to say. Neither side wanted to contend, so they spent the evening quietly, enjoying the peace of their last night together. Running Wolf and Laughing Water spread their robes on the wooden floor of the cabin and huddled with the mass of sleeping children. The rest of Running Wolf's company received hospitality and shelter with relatives who welcomed them into outlying teepees.

Early the next morning, they resumed the trek north. On the right, the Salish peaks towered; on their left were lower, more round-topped hills where hot springs spewed from the earth. The relatively straight, flat trail cut through grassland, making the going easy the first day. Late afternoon of the second day, they reached a promontory affording a grand vista of the Broad Water that glistened in a wide bowl beneath the height overlooking the huge lake whose farthest shore to the north they could not see. The water just dipped into the line of the horizon—the reason for its Salish name: Where the Lake Shore Tapers Down Like the Top of a Teepee. Descending the overlook, they veered to the northwest to skirt a large bay that bulged from the southeastern side of the Broad Water. After circling the bay, the ground began to rise, and they entered a heavily forested area that straddled the western shore of the Broad Water. For two days, they followed more rugged terrain on high cliffs. Through the treetops, sometimes they caught glimpses of the shimmering lake below. Ospreys, eagles, and hawks circled above. One night they camped in a sheltered cove near the water. Gradually, the terrain gave way to level ground again as the trees thinned at the northern end of the lake. Man and animal had defined a trail through lush grass. This was the land of the upper Kalispell. Many rivers drained into this flatland. They veered farther to the northwest, where a river flowed southeast into the basin. The clear day presented a spectacular view of the tallest, mightiest peaks in the country, the region where man began. Three jagged snowcapped peaks like spear points pierced the blue sky. Where they rode in the valley, the terrain was relatively level. Taking a cue from the river on their right that eons ago had cut a path through the lower reaches between mountain ranges, they kept to the narrow trail discernible through the undergrowth. The gait of their horses at a walk, they traced the course of the river. This was Kootenai territory, but they encountered no Kootenai in their travels. Known as the canoe people, the Kootenai would be fishing the abundant rivers that flowed west of the divide.

 The girls became restless. They had been three days on horseback since leaving the Kalispell country. "When will we get there?" Painted Turtle asked her mother.

 "Patience," Half Moon admonished. A skinny woman, she narrowed her slanted eyes at her daughter, who often stretched her own patience. Her gangly, bony structure bordered on gauntness and made her long, thin nose and high cheekbones more prominent.

But Painted Turtle was impatient and outspoken. She belied her name and was not known to withdraw her head into a shell and hide. Her colorful shell ensured she stood out from drabber turtles. When they camped that evening on the shore of a large lake, she boldly came up to Running Wolf and demanded.

"How much longer do we have to travel?"

Her commanding tone did not offend Running Wolf because he was not fond of shy, retiring females. He admired the feistiness and unflagging good spirits of women like Laughing Water. The thought flashed through his mind that someday a girl of Painted Turtle's temperament would make a good mate for his Wild Horse, who could benefit from an outspoken woman to rein him in.

"Patience," he repeated her mother's admonition, causing Painted Turtle to tartly respond.

"Grown-ups are all alike."

Running Wolf chuckled and said, "Not all little women are as pert as you are."

"When do we get to where we're going?" she insisted.

"Oh, I estimate three more days of riding. Enjoy it while it lasts because when we arrive, there will be much work to do."

Apparently, that satisfied the rambunctious Painted Turtle. Moving faster than a turtle is accustomed to moving, she scampered to join the women where they were preparing the evening meal over the campfire.

A soft rain fell the next morning as they resumed their journey. They stopped at midday to rest the horses. Men and beasts refreshed, they remounted. After riding a short distance, the trail turned directly north, and they traveled uphill and downhill through occasional clearings and stands of pines. Late in the afternoon, Running Wolf signaled the company to swerve northeast and follow a creek that led into dense forest. At times, the men had to chop down fallen limbs and brush to allow the travois to pass. Pine squirrels scurried across their path. They heard the drop of cones all around and the rustle of birds in the treetops. They felt a gentle rise as they rode. The climb was not steep, but at times they encountered a sharp incline. The clop-clop of the hooves added a percussive sound to the forest symphony. After two more days of travel through dense forest, any evidence of a trail had disappeared. They seemed to be meandering to the edge of the earth under Running Wolf's leadership. The climb had taken them to a higher altitude than they had traversed previously into the heart of the mountain range. On the third day of penetrating this thick forest, Running Wolf called a halt and told them to dismount and lead their horses. They were on a ridge overlooking a deep bowl set between two mountains. They went a short distance and saw an avalanche shoot that slid down into a small, turquoise-colored lake centered in a bowl formed by the surrounding mountains. It seemed the only route down was through the rubble of the avalanche shoot. Running Wolf continued a little farther. Through a series of switchbacks, he led them down into the declivity and brought them into the secluded canyon in the late afternoon. He stopped by the edge of the small lake. Trout leaped, cut the calm surface, and splashed back into the water. Abundant food, everyone thought.

"This is where we stop," Running Wolf announced.

Smiles of approval lit everyone's face. They surveyed the area, wondering what would make the best place for their permanent encampment. A vertical wall of rock blocked the north side of the box canyon, its white granite forming a shield against entry or exit from that approach. A stream entered from the eastern corner falling from a break in the rock wall, and trees populated a level area on the southeastern side, which extended to the slopes above the canyon floor.

"Follow me," Running Wolf said. He led them to where the stream dropped into the canyon, hurtling over a rocky ledge. Beyond the small waterfall, the mouth of a cave gaped, and he led the company into the bowels. Once inside, they discovered the cave to be larger than they at first thought. They could stand upright and walk around inside. There was no evidence of human or animal habitation. The cave penetrated deeper into the mountain, but they did not explore farther without more light. From the dim light that emanated from the outside, they could see stalactites suspended from the roof and conical stalagmites on the floor.

"Our buffalo-hide teepees will last another winter. There are no buffalo here, and we will not venture onto the plains again. Fish and other game are our food, along with what berries and roots we can find. For now, we unpack and set up our teepees in the grassy area near the stand of trees."

The men fed and watered the horses while the women assembled three teepees and immediately made the interior comfortable with all their belongings. The children gamboled like fawns, exploring their surroundings and discovering what animals shared the hidden canyon with them. Ducks, geese, and loons floated on the lake and nested in reedy areas along its shore. Shy deer came to drink, dipping their noses into the frigid waters. For bigger game such as elk and bear, they would have to trek up the switchbacks to hunt them.

"I name this place Big Hole," Running Wolf declared around the campfire that evening. "We will live and thrive here."

"Ho, it is so," Brave Bear and Smoking Loon assented.

Painted Turtle piped up. "We should dance thanksgiving to the Great Spirit."

"You are right," Running Wolf. "Let the women dance." Immediately, Laughing Water, Sage Hen, and Half Moon jumped to their feet and joined hands, beating out a rhythm with their feet. The pudgy Sage Hen, despite her extra weight, was as agile as the slimmer and taller Laughing Water and Half Moon. The three girls formed a line behind their mothers, and the six dancers snaked around the campfire. Then they began to chant:

*Great Spirit above*
*In clouds and sky*
*Great Spirit below*
*In rivers and streams*
*Great Spirit lives*
*In rocks and trees*
*Great Spirit everywhere*
*Great Spirit lives here.*

After the women and girls finished, the men and boys took their turn dancing, repeating the same rhythm and chants. Running Wolf became pensive. The others waited expectantly for him to speak because they perceived he had wisdom to share. He had become their acknowledged chief henceforth.

"You know one of the qualities I disliked about the white man?"

"His smell?" suggested Laughing Water. The group laughed.

"His upside-down face with hair at the bottom," Brave Bear added.

"His forked tongue," Sage Hen said.

"None of those," Running Wolf answered.

Smoking Loon, who had been mostly quiet that evening, guessed, "His greed."

"All those things are bad," Running Wolf agreed, "and I disliked all of them. But I was thinking of something else."

"We give up. What is it?" Laughing Water said.

"The white man talks too much."

Then they all laughed. It was true. He spoke many words to say little truth.

The laughter and jokes continued into the night. They retired to their beds of hides and blankets spread over a layer of grass, secure and happy in their mountain retreat, knowing that much work awaited them at morning's light. While summer lasted, they must gather and store up provisions for the winter and explore their new environment for the resources it could provide. In the following days, the women discovered where the chokecherry bushes thrived, ripening on the branches.

Disconcerted, Brave Bear came to Running Wolf. "There is not enough pastureland to feed twelve horses forever. What should we do?"

"Do not worry." He summoned Smoking Loon and Sitting Crow. "Follow me." He lighted a torch and led them into the cave. They walked a short distance through the tunnel. The roof rose higher than their heads but narrower in width providing a little space beyond a man's arm span. The tunnel broadened and light shone through the opening. They emerged into a meadow rife with lupine blooming amid the lush grasses. They immediately recognized that there was ample pastureland for more than twelve horses.

"We'll shelter the horses here for the winter," Running Wolf said.

Brave Bear looked on approvingly and beamed with pleasure. Even more so when he observed the buff-colored rump of a bull elk at the farther end of the meadow.

"Ah, maybe we will not have to roam too far for game," he mused.

Running Wolf smiled with satisfaction. "When the buffalo hides wear out, we will use elk hide for our teepees. The women will use the old hides to make soft moccasins and clothing." Pausing a moment, he concluded, "The Great Spirit provides."

Summer yielded a bountiful harvest of huckleberries and elderberries on the southern slopes. The women and girls tramped, singing as they went every morning to pick berries, returning later in the day with their bark baskets bursting. As summer gave way to autumn, the men hiked up the switchback path to the upper reaches of the mountains beyond Big Hole in search of deer and elk. They brought the quartered carcasses slung across the backs of their packhorses for the women and girls to prepare. dry some strips into jerky, and pound portions into a mash to mix with the berries in the pemmican that they stored in pouches. Their cache of food steadily increased, and the band was satisfied they could live on the gifts of the land as they had done for generations. Plenty Medicine was thrilled with the medicinal herbs and plants she found in the forest. She had the natural ability to concoct remedies for any ailment, whether it be a gash from a thorny bush, the bite of an insect, or a stomachache. Even though she was young, the band recognized she was one of their greatest resources. Maybe it was not so bad that Has-Two-Spirits refused to accompany them, Running Wolf thought, for little Plenty Medicine had imbibed all the wisdom and knowledge that the shaman had imparted to her.

Smoking Loon set his willow traps for fish in the reeds along the lake in Big Hole. He enjoyed his task and brought back trout for the women to smoke on racks. He also ventured farther afield where he knew salmon abounded in a big river that carved a wide swath to the southwest. On a rocky bank, he watched the fish in a whirlpool from where he bent forward to spear fish. His son, Sitting Crow, was not enthusiastic about fishing. He preferred to scout and hunt for big game and accompanied Running Wolf and Brave Bear on their expeditions. He was a dependable and industrious member of the band. Running Wolf wondered who Sitting Crow, the oldest of the boys, would take as a wife among their small number. Plenty Medicine was the girl closest in age to him, fourteen summers old. That lay in the future. For the present, the band must fashion all the implements and clothing necessary for survival and stockpile food for twelve people.

Horned Owl, eager to learn from his father, shadowed his every move. The art of chipping flint into arrowheads had to be relearned, since Running Wolf was committed to self-sufficiency and seclusion in a purposeful avoidance of contact with a trading post. Wild Horse paid little attention when his father demonstrated how to shape the flint into sharp points. They had retained iron axe blades that cut down trees faster and efficiently. These blades could be sharpened with flintstone when they grew dull. Wild Horse's inattention to detail irked Running Wolf. Losing his patience, he scolded Wild Horse and berated his inept work. "Look at the fine arrowhead your brother made," Running Wolf said, but Wild Horse only balked at the comparison, and the result was to pit one brother against the other. It was apparent to Wild Horse that Horned Owl was the favorite in his father's eye. "Then let him make bows and arrows if he's so good at it," he said defiantly. "I'll do what I like."

"And what is that, Wild Horse? Idle away the day? Not doing a man's work? I will put you to doing women's work."

"I will not do women's work. You cannot make me. I will run away before I do that."

"Oh, you will?" Running Wolf slapped him across the face. "You need a good whipping."

Wild Horse stood up. "I will not be whipped either."

"Sit down and behave yourself." The anger in his father's voice warned Wild Horse he had better obey, or he was in for a thorough thrashing. He clearly discerned the level of wrath in Running Wolf's demeanor and realized the punishment his father could unleash upon him in a second if he dared further defiance of his authority. Wild Horse sat down, sullen but not subdued.

"Every clan member must work. All hands are needed. Laziness has no place among us."

"Then I will take care of the horses."

Taken aback at first by this suggestion, Running Wolf pondered for a few moments. Maybe that was not a bad idea. It was an important task but was not enough to occupy Wild Horse's entire day.

Wild Horse saw that his father was seriously considering the suggestion and shrewdly offered another reason. "I like horses."

"From what I have seen, the horses do not share the same fondness for you. They prefer to be handled by Sitting Crow who understands their temperament. You can help Sitting Crow, but you cannot wheedle your way out of other work."

Wild Horse sulked but complied reluctantly. He was too young to kick up his heels and go his own way. In four or five more cycles of the season, he could assert his independence. Unenthusiastically, he fashioned weapons and hunted with the men, resentful always of his older brother's preference and jealous of his prowess.

Laughing Water worried about her younger son's laziness and obstreperous behavior. What would relax his recalcitrance? There was not an elder among them who could counsel him. Had not his father tried to curb his worst tendencies? Wild Horse had formed no bonds with his uncle Brave Bear or with Smoking Loon. He did not like fishing any more than he liked hunting. Both activities required too much exertion, and he would rather dither and dawdle around when he was not exercising the horses. He loved to lash the horse with a quirt into a gallop until the horse was lathered. Such treatment was universally abhorred. Sitting Crow vainly reprimanded him and tried to show him that horses responded to gentle chants and whispers, but Wild Horse ignored this instruction. Laughing Water thought she could use the same horse-training methods to soothe her son and tame his unruly nature. Because he was not empty of affection and respect for his mother, he would settle down and listen to her soft words, giving her the impression that these sessions had achieved some success, but she was deceived. Soon he would resume his harsh treatment of the horses and the pranks upon his older brother, putting nettles in Horned Owl's bed or recklessly scattering his tools. At first Laughing Water had found some of his mischief amusing, but as the pranks became more vicious like pelting Horned Owl with snowballs and throwing a dead skunk at him, she no longer laughed. There was only one person left in Big Hole who tolerated his presence—Painted Turtle, who happily tailed her cousin wherever he went. His behavior did not repel her because she shared his rebelliousness. Painted Turtle accompanied him to tend the horses. She joined him in races in the large meadow accessed through the cave. Her horsemanship surpassed his because she refused to whip her horse into exhaustion and practiced traditional Salish riding techniques using voice and touch cues. Thus, she became one with the animal and was able to win these races, holding the horse's energy in reserve for the last stretch. Painted Turtle could not convince Wild Horse to change his methods. He persisted in overusing the quirt and pressing his horse unmercifully. His stubbornness did not lessen Painted Turtle's regard for Wild Horse. She was willing to ignore his cruelty for the sake of the bravura he displayed. She admired his free-spiritedness because it corresponded with her nature that dictated self-assertion and expression of her opinion, even though they differed from her elders. A strong personality such as hers did not know what it was to cower or defer to authority. Smoking Loon was perplexed as well as proud of her fearlessness and often said that she should have been born a man. Her mother, Half Moon, just shook her hand and lamented that Painted Turtle preferred to do manly things, although Painted Turtle submitted and performed womanly chores without a fuss. Unlike Wild Horse, she did not balk at sewing, cooking, gathering wood, and tanning hides. Without complaint, she joined the women and girls in erecting and taking down the teepees.

 The prettiest of the three girls in the band was Song Bird. There was a fineness about her features that neither Painted Turtle nor Plenty Medicine possessed. Painted Turtle had a stocky figure, solid and thick-boned, square-faced, a broad nose, and wide mouth without the delicacy sought after in feminine beauty. Plenty Medicine was tall and gangling in limb, her illness as a baby had marred the luster of her complexion, which appeared pallid against her sister Song Bird's skin, but she wore a perpetual smile on her plain face and had the pleasing and gentle manner of a wise old woman, learned beyond her years in native medicine. Song Bird was aptly named, for even as she had babbled happily as a baby, she now went about warbling. She mimicked the call of every bird that inhabited the area. She chittered like a chickadee as she worked alongside the women and hummed to herself when she wandered, picking reeds to weave into mats. Sage Hen loved each of her daughters equally, feeling that she was greatly blessed in giving birth to sweet-natured children. Secretly, she considered herself lucky not to have a daughter like Painted Turtle. She sympathized with Half Moon's concern over Painted Turtle's outspokenness and preference to run about with Wild Horse, at whom everyone looked askance. When Sage Hen expressed the wish that Painted Turtle not spend so much time with him, Half Moon commented, "They are two halves of the same tree."

Half Moon, her thin face puckered in a frown, said, "I wish she would take an interest in Horned Owl. He grows into a good man."

"Yes," Sage Hen agreed. "But I think he has his eyes set on Song Bird."

"Aye, that is so," Laughing Water said, confirming readily her son's preference. "They suit each other like twin stars in the sky."

The other two women could not dispute the matter, and as is the custom of matrons, they could not resist engaging in matchmaking even though their choice of mates for their offspring did not often coincide with their children's inclinations.

Sage Hen, a stocky Salish woman, overweight but strong as any well-muscled man, consoled herself that Sitting Crow, a worthy young man, in contrast to Wild Horse, showed signs of liking her oldest daughter Plenty Medicine, and if Song Bird did eventually pair off with Horned Owl, her two daughters would have made the best matches possible in the small band. And if Wild Horse and Painted Turtle ended up in the same teepee, Laughing Water and Half Moon could expect no worse for two problem children.

Whatever the future held, perpetuation of the band in their isolated community must go on. The exiles intended to live and die at Big Hole. Return to regions that the white men continued to invade was out of the question. They would remain knit together for their mutual survival, living on the resources of the land as the Salish had done from the creation of the world.

For many seasons, they dwelled undisturbed, neither seeing nor hearing a gunshot in the woods, the clop of other horses' hooves, or the tracks of boots in the mountain passes—maybe because they assiduously avoided the routes that fur traders were likely to take. They did not encounter Kootenai either, because most of them had drifted south onto the Flathead Reservation, and Big Hole was located to the east of the trading posts along the Kootenai River. Big Hole was so sheltered in its bowl in the mountains that the winters were not severe. The weather was not extreme; the wind and snow did not buffet them unduly. Forays beyond their mountain basin were needed at times to pursue elk and deer while the women were kept busy tanning hides.

Wild Horse's behavior continued to upset the band's tranquility. After they had lived in Big Hole several cycles of the seasons, Running Wolf awoke one summer morning to find Wild Horse nowhere to be found. A little later, Smoking Loon emerged from his teepee and announced that Painted Turtle's bed was empty. She was nowhere in sight. Running Wolf and Smoking Loon immediately ran to where the horses were pastured and discovered two horses missing.

"They have gone off together," Running Wolf said.

"To what purpose?" Smoking Wolf asked.

Running Wolf at first did not want to suggest the most likely reason but felt compelled to offer the anxious father some explanation for Painted Turtle's disappearance.

"They fled to *Sinieleman*, to the Black Robes, or to the Place of the Wide Cottonwood Trees, wishing not to be ruled."

"It is true that they desired the things of the white men's world. Both are restless spirits, not content with what is here," Smoking Loon lamented and then grew hopeful. "Maybe they will return. Maybe they just wanted to explore."

"And so doing, they endanger us, exposing the outer world to our existence, and then the white men might force them to lead them to our hiding place."

"No, I don't think Painted Turtle would reveal it."

"I am sorry to admit that Wild Horse would betray us if the white warriors offered him horses, blankets, weapons, or anything else he wanted. Wild Horse is my bad seed, and Horned Owl is my good seed. I cannot say differently."

For days, they waited for the return of the prodigals. When they had given up hope that they would ever see Wild Horse and Painted Turtle, Half Moon was heard to give a shout. Everyone stopped what they were doing and came running to her.

"Look," she pointed to the switchback descent at the southern tip of Big Hole. All looked in that direction and discerned two figures on horseback in single file with a string of four horses behind them.

"That's them!" Running Wolf said.

The band watched in silence as the riders slowly descended into the bowl.

The two riders approached the cluster of people assembled to greet them. The reprobates dismounted and walked toward their families.

"Those are stolen horses!" Running Wolf exclaimed.

"Yes, why not?" Wild Horse brazenly admitted. "I have increased the herd. These mares are breeding stock . . . more foals to replace our horses who are getting old. We stole them from two Blackfeet camped along the Kootenai River," Wild Horse boasted.

"You fool!" Running Wolf shouted. "They will track you."

"They will not. I killed them and threw them into the rapids. I know how to cover tracks. I am not that stupid to leave a trail. With branches, we brushed our prints away for quite a distance and led the horses over pebble and rocks so that no one could track us."

"By your recklessness, you endangered all our lives! You deserve a flogging!" Running Wolf roared.

Wild Horse glared at his father. "Do not attempt to do that, or I will run away forever."

Running Wolf knew his son would make good his threat and had second thoughts. Wild Horse was more dangerous away from the band. At least here, he could try to control his son's indiscretions. He thought of Laughing Water and how distraught she would be if there should be a permanent rift between Wild Horse and him.

"No more horse stealing. You must promise never to do that again," Running Wolf said, modulating his tone. He accepted as assent Wild Horse's guttural sound and nod. For the present, the tension in the air dissipated as the father's wrath was mollified.

Smoking Loon turned to admonish Painted Turtle. "You were foolhardy to go with Wild Horse. You put our safety at risk. I am ashamed of your behavior."

Painted Turtle did not apologize. Rather than contrition, her stubborn expression exhibited pride in the escapade she and Wild Horse had executed together.

For a while, Wild Horse directed his energies toward the stolen mares. They were successfully bred with a big chestnut stallion. The foals, one colt and three fillies, were dropped the following spring, each had a white blaze in the middle of their face like the one their sire displayed. Thrilled with the outcome of the breeding, Wild Horse was content to turn over the long, arduous task of care and training to Sitting Crow, who was happy to assume responsibility for the foals because he disapproved of Wild Horse's handling of the horses. Furthermore, Wild Horse did not have the patience to persist. His lackadaisical and lazy attitude toward work earned Sitting Crow's scorn. Wild Horse liked riding the horses, but did not love the animals and treasure them as Sitting Crow did. The horse was a vehicle of Wild Horse's pleasure to use and abuse.

Wild Horse's idleness and desultory disposition toward the men's work soon overrode what transitory interest he had in increasing the herd. He was forced to accompany the men on the hunt, but his presence was tolerated if not considered a nuisance by the other men because his aim was poor, and he frequently missed the critical lung shot behind the deer's shoulder. If his aim hit the animal, it did not kill, allowing the animal to run into the thicket until it fell and died a slow death. Running Wolf was ashamed of his son's ineptitude. His other son's competence offset, to a certain degree, Wild Horse's failings. But could Horned

Owl's excellent qualities really compensate for his brother's glaring flaws? Could anything wash away his disappointment in Wild Horse? He was his blood. His duty was to countenance his behavior that he could and correct his intolerable conduct. So far, his efforts to correct had failed, but Running Wolf would not cease his admonishment and correction.

During the height of the summer, Wild Horse disappeared again—this time without Painted Turtle. She was questioned about her knowledge of his whereabouts but pleaded ignorance. She had no idea where he had gone.

"He must have said something to you," Smoking Loon grilled her. "You are his only friend. You break away from the women to run with him."

"He speaks of not being roped like a horse and of jumping on a cloud and riding it over the world." Painted Turtle laughed.

"This is serious," Running Wolf scolded her. "He can wander on his own somewhere and be captured and made to reveal our hiding place."

"What use does the white men have for us?" Painted Turtle jeered.

Her remark cut Running Wolf to the quick. Indeed, what use had the *suyapi* for them? No use. They think we are garbage, offal to be cast upon the fire.

"Wild Horse is not afraid of the white men like you are," she retorted.

Painted Turtle's accusation angered Running Wolf. He lurched toward her and then stopped. It was for Smoking Loon to discipline his daughter. Her rude words to the leader of the clan must be punished.

"Bite your tongue," Smoking Loon commanded. He struck her soundly across the cheek. "Honor and respect your elders."

Painted Turtle stepped backward with the blow. Tears rose in her eyes, but she did not cry out.

"Father, you do me wrong. I am your faithful daughter. Do not strike me if I speak the truth."

"The truth is you are disrespectful."

"If the truth is disrespectful, then, yes, I am justly disrespectful."

Running Wolf felt compelled to interpose. "You accuse me of fear. I defend the honor of my people. It is not fear but refusal to become like the *suyapi* who have neither honor nor respect." He spat on the ground. "That is what I have to say. *Šey hoy*." With an about-face, he left Smoking Loon to deal with his daughter. Disgust rose in his gorge for the girl, nearly a woman now, who dared to question his integrity and defend the behavior of his wayward son. If he never saw Wild Horse again, that would be good riddance to a bad seed. With that ugly thought, he stopped himself. Such a wish was unworthy of a father, even if his son was troublesome. Wild Horse would return, and then he would have one final cautionary talk with him.

Day after day, when Wild Horse failed to appear, the clan began to think that Wild Horse was dead, injured, or captured. His poor fighting capacity provided no defense against attack. "Ah," Laughing Water moaned, "he has gone to the spirit world. We will never see him again."

Hearing his mother's lament, Horned Owl vigorously shook his head.

"Nay, Mother, he is not dead."

Horned Owl's assertion could not easily be brushed off. Possessed of extraordinary perception and intuition, he penetrated the darkness that enveloped other people's minds and could see further than anyone in the darkness. He was not afraid of the night, but gloried in surveying constellations and shooting stars. He was wise beyond his years. His accuracy with bow and arrow received the respect and admiration of his elders. Honesty, integrity, and loyalty to traditional values governed his actions.

"Can you see when he will return?" Laughing Water asked.

"When he has nowhere else to go except home."

Running Wolf said bitterly, "His heart has never been here." Although he cynically dismissed belief in his son's return, he still harbored a hope that he would be proved wrong. Bad seed or not, Wild Horse was his son. But could the color of a horse be changed?

Painted Turtle nonchalantly shrugged off talk of doom, going about her tasks casually, indifferent to worry. Summer was coming to a close. An abundant crop of berries flourished on the slopes, ready to pick. The women busily hastened to the task. The men carved bows and arrows for the fall hunt. Smoking Loon hauled in fishing traps crammed with trout and speared salmon from the river banks. Preparations for winter proceeded even though one of their own had disappeared.

Two moons after Wild Horse's disappearance, he limped into the camp, leaning on a crutch constructed of pine. Smiling wanly, unapologetically, he described his narrow escape from death.

"Coming down a rocky hill, my horse stumbled, and I was thrown to the ground. The horse also fell and could not get up. Its right front leg was broken, and I had to kill it. My ankle was broken in the fall."

The clan gaped at him as if he were an apparition from the underworld. Running Wolf did not run to embrace his son but stood silently. His mother burst into joyous laughter as she had not laughed in a long time. "Welcome home. Horned Owl was right; you have returned to us." Painted Turtle hung back, a self-satisfied grin on her round face. "See, I told you so. There was nothing to worry about."

Plenty Medicine rushed forward to help. He accepted her support, leaning against her as she led him into her teepee where she applied a salve to his swollen ankle.

Running Wolf entered the teepee to see Wild Horse reclined against a reed backrest. "You disobeyed my order and traveled alone without my knowledge or consent. Why?"

"I do not want to be stuck here all my life—closed in. I did what you did as a young man. You explored distant terrain and found this hole to hide in. I will not hide my head. I will show my face to other men and ride wherever I want to. Walls and fences cannot keep me in."

"Brave words, my son, but unwise. You do not know what you say. When I was a young man, the white men were rare. Now their numbers overtake us. Where did you go? Did you not see them crossing the mountains?"

"I am not afraid of them. I wanted to reach the white men's fort and offer to scout for them."

"I forbid you to serve them. You are Salish! If you do not obey me, I will have to banish you. And I do not wish to expel you from the clan. Do not force me to take this measure."

At that moment, Painted Turtle entered the teepee to see how her friend was doing. She smiled and sat next to him. "Next time, do not go without taking me along for the adventure. I could have helped you when you fell."

"There will be no next time," Running Wolf said and sternly looked at Wild Horse, who seemed less inclined to resist his father's admonishment. Painted Turtle's presence had made him realize that he did not wish to live apart from her. His feelings for her had grown stronger with every passing season, and if he were to be banished, he was not sure she would be willing to leave her relatives to permanently live far away from them. She might like to accompany him on adventures, but exile was a different matter. For the present, Wild Horse thought it best to submit to his father's will rather than to risk losing the girl he intended to marry and consoled himself with the idea that if conditions became intolerable, confined to the area around Big Hole, Painted Turtle and he could strike out on their own. For now, discretion told him to play the obedient son.

Feigning submission, Wild Horse looked at his father and meekly agreed, "I will stay here and not leave without your permission."

"Good," Running Wolf said. Turning his back, he left the teepee.

Outside he met his favored oldest son. "Horned Owl, you must watch out for your brother. His rashness may not only bring about his downfall but ours as well. He has no caution. Keep an eye on him."

"What do you want me to do? Spy on him?"

"Trail him if you must. He has given me his word he will not roam without my permission. I am sorry to say I do not trust his word."

"He resents me. He knows I am the better hunter and tracker. My aim is keener than his. What rankles him the most is that you approve of me while he disappoints you at every turn."

"That cannot be helped. He does everything to irritate me and does not follow my instructions on how to treat the horses. Sometimes I think he has no love for any living creature. Some anger was born within him as if an evil spell was cast upon him."

"Perhaps he loves Painted Turtle. Perhaps she can free the evil in his spirit."

"More likely, it would take Plenty Medicine to cast out the demon."

"Have you asked her?"

"She has mixed potions and sung chants. None to any avail. She says her medicine is no good unless he is the one who asks for a cure, and he acknowledges no sickness in his soul."

"Then I will do as you ask and keep a watchful eye upon him. Even though he does not like me near him, I will be the spy."

## Horned Owl

The Salish had lived at Big Hole seven cycles of the seasons when the predictable pairings occurred. Sitting Crow and Plenty Medicine formed a couple, as did Horned Owl and Song Bird. Last to pair off were Wild Horse and Painted Turtle, being the youngest in the group. All the clan hoped these marriages would populate the community with more sons and daughters. Horned Owl and Song Bird were first to bless the clan with a child, a boy they named Standing Rock. Song Bird's water broke as she stood against a rock by the brook, watching a doe and fawn drink from the stream. Sitting Crow had come home after spearing many fish the day that Plenty Medicine felt the pangs of childbirth. She was in labor from noon to nightfall before she delivered a healthy, squalling baby boy they named Spears-Many-Fish in the expectation he would grow up to walk in his father's moccasins. Sitting Crow and Plenty Medicine proved the most prolific, producing the following year another son Burning Cloud, and eleven moons later a girl, Dream Weaver. Despite Plenty Medicine's administration of fertility concoctions for Painted Turtle, she failed to become pregnant. Song Bird also did not conceive again, but she stifled her disappointment, refusing to let her apparent barrenness dampen her habitual cheerfulness and retained the hope that in good season she would be fruitful again. Wild Horse and Painted Turtle, although troubled by not having children, eventually plotted to correct the situation by abducting an infant from their enemy.

"Be it a Blackfoot or a white, steal a baby for me, and I will raise the child as my own," Painted Turtle told Wild Horse.

"How can I do that? I promised my father that I would not venture away from Big Hole without his permission," Wild Horse said. "Am I to go back on my word because you desire a child? What do we need a child for? We are free spirits. If it is as my father fears that the white men will eventually kill all of us, why do we want our children to die?" he scornfully responded.

"Ah, but we will survive by adopting of the white men's ways."

"Then you are telling me to leave this place?"

"When the time is right."

"That means it does not disturb you to leave your mother and father."

"They cannot hide in this hole forever. Nor do I want to hide in this hole forever," Painted Turtle's tone was laced with contempt. "If we go back to the mission, I can also take an orphan as my own. Hasn't the white man made enough orphans among our people?"

Wild Horse could not deny that. Disease and war take many men and women.

"I will consider your words, woman, and decide when we go."

In the meanwhile, they stayed, storing away provisions for their departure when the weather would be favorable.

Horned Owl did not observe anything unusual in his brother's behavior and had followed his father's instructions to dog Wild Horse's steps. He made friendly overtures toward him, inviting Wild Horse to accompany him on his hunts. Wild Horse was wary at first of these invitations, but accepted occasionally to go with him. Although Horned Owl tried to establish a good relationship with his brother, he was not successful. Wild Horse was uncommunicative, and he was a nuisance more than a help on the hunt. His aim never improved, and he had no skill at stealth. Horned Owl tried to show him how to blend with his surroundings and tread softly, but Wild Horse's impatient rustlings in the underbrush revealed his presence to the deer, and he would release his arrow too soon.

A veneer of peace prevailed. Beneath that thin layer of amity, Wild Horse still envied his brother's prowess and resented his father's favoritism toward Horned Owl. He tolerated the situation because he did not want to give either of them cause for suspicion of his true intentions.

In search of game, Horned Owl ventured farther afield, following the creeks that fed into the Kootenai River, the torrent that rushed over rapids and falls to the southwest. Relieved that Wild Horse declined to go with him on this hunt, Horned Owl, lighthearted, set off on foot, leading his horse. He observed the needles on the larches were beginning to turn brown and would soon to line the forest floor. Yellow leaves mottled the aspens that grew in swampy areas along his route.

He had journeyed several days with no luck finding deer when he clearly discerned hoofprints in a thicket where deer had nibbled at willow tips. He set up camp nearby, planning to follow their trail. At first light the next morning, he walked along the creek, his ears attuned to the slightest sound of movement. At midmorning, he suddenly stopped, hearing a metallic rattle, nothing that he could immediately identify, but that reminded him of the sound that the pots and pans obtained from the white men made when the women scrubbed them clean. He crept nearer to the source of the noise. Then he heard the hiss of the white man's speech. Finding cover under a fir whose lowest branches swept the ground, he peered at two men crouched in the streambed, their backs bent over, dipping pans in the water. They scraped up gravel from the stream, shaking and rattling the contents. What did they hope to catch? Fish? They grumbled every so often, at times exchanging words incomprehensible to Horned Owl. What were they searching for in the water? Horned Owl could smell their stench even though he was a good two hundred paces from them. From his angle of vision, he observed the men in profile. Both had shaggy beards, were about the same age, young men but dirty and grizzled, wearing red plaid shirts, woolen pants, black felt hats, and worn boots. Around their waists were holsters. He watched their motions for a long time, keen to discover what these ragtag panners were about. Suddenly, from his kneeling position in the water, one man cried exultantly. From his pan, he picked up a pebble, glowed with victory, and held it up for his companion to examine. The other man beamed in delight, and then they resumed with renewed vigor their activity, unflagging in their sifting and grating until Horned Owl, weary of the sound, slinked silently into the dense forest.

This was a strange phenomenon in need of much more investigation. He removed his camp to a safe distance from the panners. For the rest of his hunt, their presence in his hunting ground continued to trouble him. He killed two deer, gutted them, and strapped them on his horse, trekking back to Big Hole. Laughing Water, Song Bird, Half Moon, and Sage Hen, on sighting his approach, ran to greet him. They unstrapped the deer from the horse and began the task of butchering and preparing the meat. Horned Owl, anxious to report what he had seen to the men, left the women to their work.

He had to wait until all the men returned from their respective tasks. Running Wolf was tending the horses; Brave Bear was setting traps in the woods, and Smoking Loon and Sitting Crow were off fishing in a high mountain lake. They assembled for the evening meal, but Wild Horse was absent. Concern for his tardiness occupied the group and prevented Horned Owl from launching into his account of what he had seen.

"Who has seen Wild Horse last?" Running Wolf asked.

"I saw him this morning in the meadow with the horses on my way to set the traps at that end of the canyon," Brave Bear said. "He was working with a colt."

Half Moon burst into the teepee. "Painted Turtle is gone. I cannot find her anywhere."

Running Wolf turned angrily at his son. "I told you to shadow your brother like a fox. You should not have let him out of your sights."

"He did not want to go with me on the hunt, and I did not think he would go back on his word to travel without your permission."

"He's betrayed our trust!" Running Wolf shouted. "Go check on the horses."

"I'll go," Sitting Crow said and hurried from the teepee.

Horned Owl, stung by his father's rebuke, sought to appease his anger. "Forgive me, Father. I will find him and bring him back."

"Find him, yes, but do not bother to bring him back. He is a curse. Demon-possessed."

"But Painted Turtle . . ." Half Moon pleaded, "I want her returned."

Running Wolf would not be pacified. "She is tainted. There is no man to be her husband here. She is tied to Wild Horse, so she must ride forever with him."

Tears welled in Half Moon's eyes, but she did not protest Running Wolf's verdict, schooled in obedience to the clan leader. What could she do but take solace in her good son Sitting Crow and the grandchildren that he and his worthy wife Plenty Medicine had given them—Spears-Many-Fish, Burning Cloud, and Dream Weaver. Acceptance was her mode. Partial happiness was still better than none whatsoever.

Swift of foot, Sitting Crow rushed into the teepee and exclaimed, "Two chestnuts with the white blazes are gone—the ones Wild Horse bred from the stolen mares."

"Find out where he has gone, Horned Owl," Running Wolf ordered.

"I promise I will learn that. I will leave at dawn."

By his lowered brow, Horned Owl could tell his father's anger still simmered, for he spoke no more, only sat and glowered, a silent, steaming hot spring. The others respectively observed silence, not wanting to stir his wrath. As the period of brooding lengthened, Horned Owl's anxiousness grew. He had other news to deliver but feared what he had to relate would worsen his father's distemper. But he could not withhold this important information. It affected their very existence. At the appropriate moment, he must tell Running Wolf. For a long time, out of the corner of his eye, Horned Owl observed his father's grim expression. Finally, he noticed a relaxation in Running Wolf's furrowed brow. A suitable interval had passed, and he felt he could no longer delay in speaking.

"Father, on my hunt, I saw two white men."

Running Wolf's head lifted, interest lighting his face, encouraging Horned Owl to continue. Horned Owl described how the two men sifted the gravel in the creek bed, moving the scooped-up grains and pebbles back and forth in pans.

"I have no idea what they were looking for, but it was clear they were determined to find something in the river . . . and they did at one point. One man held up a pebble, and both rejoiced at possessing it. What value it had I do not know, but it just made them work harder. I stole away."

Horned Owl looked in turn at Running Wolf, Brave Bear, Smoking Loon, and Sitting Crow. Puzzled expressions met his gaze. No one said anything. No one speculated on the white men's purpose. It was a mystery. As the clan leader, Running Wolf was expected to offer an opinion. The other men waited for him to say something. Horned Owl recognized that his father was deep in thought and was weighing his words. Emerging from his private reflection, Running Wolf turned to Horned Owl.

"You are the spy," he said. "It is your task to pierce the darkness, to solve mysteries. First, discover where Wild Horse goes, and second, track these white men to learn what their purpose is."

The commission was given and accepted. Horned Owl fully embraced his role. He vowed to answer both questions.

He went on the hunch that Wild Horse had traveled south because his brother had not hidden his desire to live among the white men. Horned Owl knew that Wild Horse admired their ingenuity and skill in making useful goods, tools, and clothing. They slept in beds, covered in woolen blankets. They never went hungry; their larders were full of beans and every kind of grain. Their cattle provided thick slabs of meat, and the cows produced milk. Stone fireplaces ablaze with logs warmed their dwellings in winter and sheltered them from buffeting winds. Wild Horse was impetuous, incautious, and rambunctious. He chose the easiest path, avoiding exertion whenever possible. He preferred to ride instead of walk, and if he could spend all day galloping around on a horse, he certainly would.

Horned Owl selected the sure-footed appaloosa for pursuit of Wild Horse. Once he reached the ridge overlooking Big Hole, he followed the spine of the mountain to the same creek that had guided the small Salish band to their secluded basin. The sun's position directed his route southward. The path zigzagged through the dense foliage along the creek, but the appaloosa did not lose footing on the rugged descent. Horned Owl ate pemmican from the parfleche slung to his shoulder. He dismounted at an opening in the trees that allowed access to the creek and stooped to cup the cool water into his palms and quench his thirst. In the evening he reached the valley where he camped for the night. Arising early, he resumed his journey. The fall morning was cool. A breeze shook yellow leaves from the aspens as he followed the river southward.

The wind faded away as the day lengthened, and the sun's warm rays penetrated the canopy of the trees. This was an area Horned Owl had not traversed before. His hunting expeditions had led him to the northeast and the southeast, forming an axis through Big Hole. He imagined his family plodding north on the same route before he was born to escape the baleful influence of the white men. He admired their determination to preserve their traditional way of life, which made him think of the panners and his second mission. It was a distinct disadvantage that he could not understand their speech. If he knew their language, he would know their intentions and how to deal with them. Language was the key to everything. The Salish language defined his people. It expressed their values, their beliefs, attitudes, and customs. The animals had their speech too. They communicated their wishes through sounds. So did men. Horned Owl ruminated long and hard as he rode, weighing how men were both different and the same, and considering how men were both alike and distinct from animals.

Toward evening, he stopped short, sniffing something in the air. Was that smoke? He studied the treetops and scanned both banks of the river ahead. Then he spotted a gray plume in the distance directly on his side of the river. Someone had made camp at that spot. There had been no storm to cause a lightning strike in the last few days, so it must be man-made. He walked his horse toward the location of the swirling smoke. It was about dusk, the time when any traveler would stop, make camp, and light a fire. Before he reached the campfire, he dismounted from his horse and approached the site on foot. He saw two chestnut horses tethered to trees and knew he had found what he sought.

"Ho!" he alerted the campers of his presence, not wanting to surprise them. His skill at stealth served him well. They had not heard his approach at all. Seated with their faces to the fire and their backs to Horned Owl as he walked toward them, they turned their heads, startled, to see who had surprised them. Surely, they must have recognized his voice, for they did not stand up but only gaped at Horned Owl for a moment.

"Well, well, who comes but my dear brother," Wild Horse greeted him with a smile that was half a sneer. "Worried about little brother, are you?"

Painted Turtle looked amused and anxious to witness the confrontation between the two brothers.

Wild Horse anticipated Horned Owl's intentions and said, "Here to take me back to Big Hole, I guess."

"No. Just to find out where you are going."

"To my people at Broad Water. Where I belong."

"True . . . all too true." He paused for a second and sat across from his brother. "Do not think I come to take you back . . . only to warn you not to reveal our hiding place to anyone. You endanger our lives, and we want to live free of the white men. If you want to dwell with them, go. But seal your lips and do not speak of us. We are dead to you, and you are dead to us. Is that clear?"

"I want to dwell with my people at the mission. From there I will go to the soldier's fort and be their scout."

"You are no scout."

"I know the land as well as you do. You think you are better than I am, but I am braver and stronger than you."

Horned Owl let his brother brag and claim virtues he did not possess. What was it to him that Wild Horse had an inflated opinion of his abilities? A dark premonition filled his soul at that moment. He would not see Wild Horse or Painted Turtle alive again. Their folly doomed them. Before his eyes passed a vision of their faces pitted and scarred, their teeth rotten, and flesh stripped from their faces revealing whitened skulls. The certainty overcame him that he would never hear from them again. He shook his head to dispel the horror.

"Will you spend the night with us?" Painted Turtle invited pleasantly. She could not imagine the horrible end that awaited her. Pitiful woman, Horned Owl thought. No harm in spending one last night with the doomed couple.

"Yes, but swear that you will keep the secret of Big Hole. We are dead to the world to where you go. Is that clear?"

Wild Horse did not hesitate to respond. "I swear gladly. Big Hole is wiped from my memory."

"Mine too," Painted Turtle said. "I swear to it."

"Cut your hand and swear it in blood," Horned Owl said. He unsheathed his knife from his side and handed it to them. Each in turn let blood from their wrists and repeated their oath to secrecy.

"Very well. I trust your oaths," Horned Owl said. "And I swear that if I hear you have violated your sworn words, I will cut both your throats." He knew his oath was unnecessary, because the white men's plague would get them. Nevertheless, he wanted to impress them with this threat. Scrutinizing their faces, he could not detect any guile. Maybe they succeeded in concealing malicious intentions. Horned Owl quickly dismissed that possibility.

They were too simple. Their motives were selfish and superficial. They wanted independence from authority and desired the white man's comforts, believing mistakenly that the white world afforded them protection.

"It is settled. We part in the morning. You go your way and I go mine," Horned Owl concluded.

Quietly, he stole away before dawn while Painted Turtle and Wild Horse were still asleep. They did not hear a rustle of blanket or a footfall. He softly trod to where he had tethered his horse at a distance from the camp. With a pat to its nose, he cautioned the appaloosa not to whinny. The horse, bonded to the man, instinctively understood.

Two days later, Horned Owl arrived at Big Hole. He stayed and delivered the news to Running Wolf that he had encountered the two runaways and had obtained their oaths drawn in blood to keep secret the clan's location.

"From Broad Water, he intends to journey south to the white men's fort where he will offer his services to the White Chief," Horned Owl informed him.

"Foolish man-child," Running Wolf said, "To think he can ally with the white man . . . to think he can be a scout."

"I do not think he will ever scout for the white soldiers. I foresee death overtake him," he somberly told his father.

The seriousness and certitude of this prediction struck Running Wolf, shaking him to his core and loosening his customary rigid, emotionless expression. Horned Owl perceived pain in his father's features and disbelief in his dark brown eyes that seemed to ask for further explanation.

Horned Owl continued, "I saw a dark cloud surround Wild Horse and Painted Turtle." He did not want to describe their emaciated, disease-scarred faces and just said, "They will die of the white man's pox."

Running Wolf's face stiffened and his lips tightened. Horned Owl imagined a wall of ice forming around Running Wolf's heart as his father's cold eyes stared, unfocused into space. For a long while, Running Wolf sat impassively, not speaking. Horned Owl held his tongue respectfully, not wishing to interrupt his father's meditation. Finally, Running Wolf uttered, "He is dead to us." He waved Horned Owl away, indicating he wanted to be alone.

"But, Father, tomorrow I go to spy on the panners."

"That can wait. Elk tracks have been sighted nearby. We must get more meat for the winter. I feel it will be a cold one," he murmured numbly.

As always, Horned Owl obeyed and joined the other men on the hunt the next day. His father's forecast proved correct because it was the coldest winter yet at Big Hole. The snow came unusually early and deep. They stored venison and other supplies in the cave and piled stacks of firewood to last the winter. In the heavy snowfall, they did not venture far from Big Hole. The children were toddlers now, frolicking as much as possible within the close quarters of the teepees covered double with elk hides. Horned Owl's own son, Standing Rock, surpassed Sitting Crow's two sons, Spears-Many-Fish and Burning Cloud, in stature and agility. Although the three boys were about the same age, it soon became apparent that Standing Rock led the games and displayed the greatest imagination and ingenuity. He was sturdy and solid like a rock, firm in expression of his desires and insistent upon their fulfillment to the point that Horned Owl thought Song Bird indulged him too much. As for Standing Rock, inheritor of his mother's happy disposition, he delighted in the songs she never ceased to croon and amply repaid the affection Song Bird lavished upon her cherished only child. Horned Owl loved the little boy no less than Song Bird, but would not coddle him, exercising the fatherly role to discipline and raise him up in the manly arts. He looked forward to the day, a year in the future, when he would begin instructing Standing Rock in the art of shooting arrows. In preparation for that time, he whittled arrows and a bow just the right size for a four-year-old boy.

Over the long and unusually cold winter, the women gathered in Laughing Water's and Running Wolf's teepee, the roomiest, to sew buckskin shirts and leggings for the men. Unlike the sorrowful Half Moon, Laughing Water had regained some of her humor and had reconciled herself to Wild Horse's departure. His absence meant she need not constantly worry about what he would do next. She commended him to the care of the Great Spirit and focused her love on Standing Rock, who caused her to forget all her younger son's deficiencies. Her sunny disposition prevailed, freeing her from dwelling on regrets and disappointments. Standing Rock represented hope for the future.

It was otherwise with Half Moon, who continued to mope, heartsick at Painted Turtle's departure. With Painted Turtle's absence, her hope vanished for more grandchildren. Sitting Crow and Plenty Medicine had added Spears-Many-Fish, Burning Cloud, and Dream Weaver to the small Salish band. Seeing how disconsolate Half Moon was over the loss of Painted Turtle, her daughter-in-law Plenty Medicine tried to shake her from her despondency.

"You cannot continue pining for Painted Turtle. She will not return. Life must go on. I have chanted the farewell song for her. Look at my little girl Dream Weaver. Does she not delight your soul? Look how her eyes sparkle and her chubby cheeks glow. Already she has the talent to lift spirits. Only once in a generation is such a precious child born. She will learn the healing arts from me. She will be a more powerful medicine woman than I am. If anyone can cure your sick soul, it is Dream Weaver."

Hearing her name, the three-year-old toddled toward her mother, clapping her hands. Already she had a large vocabulary and an insatiable curiosity to learn. She had her nose into everything, smelling the herbs her mother pressed and sniffing the boiling stews she cooked. She loved to dance and imitated the steps of the dancers, committing to memory many of Plenty Medicines' prayers and chants.

Gloomily, Half Moon gazed up from her needlework. Dream Weaver stood in front of her, her pudgy hands on her hips. "Grandmother, cheer up and play with me. You must not be sad."

The little girl was so cute and pert that Half Moon could not help smiling. Why had she not paid attention to this sprite of a child before? She was like dew on a dry leaf. She shone like the sun on newly fallen snow, and her voice trilled like birds greeting the morning. Half Moon awakened as if from a stupor, realizing that she had been so immersed in self-pity, that she had missed the beauty that still existed around her. She set aside her sewing and extended her arms to Dream Weaver, pulling her onto her lap. She took her hands and began to play a clapping, singing child's game with the little girl. The other women smiled happily at grandmother and granddaughter. Maybe

Half Moon's healing had begun, and she would no longer wear her long, sad face around the camp and would begin to live life to the fullest, no longer a moon on the wane but a moon waxing happier. From that day, Half Moon doted on Dream Weaver.

As for her grandsons, Spears-Many-Fish and Burning Cloud, she paid them no mind, brushing them aside, and they, in turn, gave no heed to their grandmother, largely finding her inconsequential. The two boys were so close in age, that they became inseparable companions, doing everything together. They even resembled each other and could be mistaken for twins. Both boys took an avid interest in fishing and had aptitude for it, quickly learning everything Smoking Loon could tell them about the habits of trout and salmon. Although Burning Cloud was younger, he achieved early the same height as Spears-Many-Fish, and the boys measured the same both in weight and stature as they grew. No rivalry or jealousy existed between them; they were partners in work and play.

When no more children were born to the Salish couples, Plenty Medicine identified a problem. She had tried every conceivable fertility potion on the women of childbearing age, but none had taken effect. She had explored every method she could think of to dispel the curse of infertility. She began to wonder why, who, or what had leveled this curse upon the clan. Was it the demon that inhabited Wild Horse, the obstreperous one who had wreaked so much distress and havoc on the clan? That demon was banished now, but evidently had left his evil influence among them.

Who were her two sturdy sons to marry when they reached manhood? Dream Weaver would then be the clan's only marriageable woman. Plenty Medicine broached the subject with Laughing Water, Sage Hen, and Half Moon, who were all too aware of the dilemma they faced.

"Clearly, Standing Rock, the oldest boy, should have first choice of Dream Weaver," Song Bird spoke up for her son.

"Then where will Spears-Many-Fish and Burning Cloud find wives?" Plenty Medicine asked.

"They can steal them," Sage Hen suggested.

"Be serious, Sage Hen," Half Moon scolded. "The men would not allow it for fear we would be discovered."

"I know," Laughing Water volunteered, "but Dream Weaver can quickly bear many daughters, and these girls can be given as soon as they can bear children to the old bachelors, Spears-Many-Fish and Burning Cloud." She giggled at her suggestion.

"That's not a serious idea either," Half Moon said. "It's not fair to expect them to wait that long to marry."

"What about finding orphans now to raise up for them?" asked Sage Hen.

"Where are we going to find orphans?" Laughing Water asked, skepticism in her tone.

"From the Kootenai. Could we not approach them? I think they would have a few orphans to spare," Sage Hen said. Apparently, because the two boys in question were her grandsons, she had a personal stake in finding a solution.

Plenty Medicine, more cautious of such a solution even though it was to the benefit of her sons, had reservations. "But can the Kootenai be trusted not to betray us? We have not had contact with them for as long as we have lived here. I do not think the men would agree to seeking them out. The Kootenai are in too deep with the white men. Many of them agreed to go live on the Broad Water reservation."

"I do not think the men would risk carrying out any of these plans," Laughing Water said. "I know you thought my idea ridiculous, and I laughed at it because I knew you would not think it serious. But the only solution is Dream Weaver's fertility. She will have daughters."

The men of the Big Hole had also thought of this problem and discussed it among themselves but had arrived at the same conclusion. Hopeful reliance on Dream Weaver's fecundity was preferable to risking exposure through contact with the white men, Kootenai, or the Salish. They were keenly aware that the Kootenai and Salish who lived in proximity to the white men were allied too closely with them to be altogether trustworthy. Besides, too many half-breeds dwelt among them, hopelessly dividing their loyalties. The clan must remain entrenched, a hidden stronghold against the white men's encroachment.

With the coming of warm weather, Horned Owl took up his mission to spy on the white men and ventured to the area southwest of Big Hole, where he had sighted the panners the season before. He traveled on foot, making it easier to maneuver through the forest and hide behind rocks or trees if necessary. Cautiously and silently, like a mountain lion, he prowled, searching for signs of white intruders. He knew how to slither through thickets, not snapping a twig, his ears alert to detect any human sound and his eyes keen to find any trace of a man's passing. He had been traveling for several days when he heard digging and the shoveling of dirt. He tiptoed closer to the noise, which was mixed with the staccato talk of men—next, the cacophonous chatter of more than two men, a company of at least twenty. Horned Owl found a tree at a safe distance to watch the activity. He counted ten men with pickaxes, chipping away at the side of a cliff. Ten other men were sawing lumber. Others were setting in place beams to support the entrance they had hacked open in the rock face, just high enough to allow the entry for a man of medium height. He identified two men as half-breeds from the clothes they wore—the motley garb of white men's floppy hats, feathers stuck in the brims, and woolen jackets and pants with beaded belts, their facial features a hybrid and their complexions having neither the lightness nor the duskiness of a true full-blood. They participated in pouring rubble from pans into a waist-high, wooden frame that had been constructed alongside the creek. It seemed they were washing the sand and gravel. The longer he observed this activity, the greater his perplexity. He wished to draw closer, hoping to overhear what the half-breeds were saying. Perhaps they spoke his tongue. If he dared to get them alone, they could tell him what this was all about. As the day lengthened, Horned Owl knew his spying must end, and he should find cover somewhere farther from the panners' camp. He found a secluded spot, sheltered by tall pines and a rocky outcropping at some distance from the creek. While the moon rose in the sky and slid behind a bank of clouds, he sat on his haunches and ruminated on the scene he had witnessed. How to unravel the mystery of the strange activity? His people were safe from discovery if these strangers stayed along this creek. They seemed intent on finding something in its waters and no other streams. Horned Owl did not know what else he could do except to return to Big Hole and report what he had seen. The troubling aspect was the number of men engaged in this peculiar activity had multiplied ten times. In the past, the appearance of one or two white men had heralded more to follow in their train, always proliferating like flies on a corpse. He would have to keep his eye on the panners from now on. So long as they did not move north, his people would be safe. His spying would continue. It was necessary that their every movement be monitored.

Running Wolf was concerned but not alarmed when Horned Owl told him that the number of panners had increased. "They are still at several days' journey from us, and we are well-secluded. Their interest is in those creeks feeding into the great river to the southwest. Our elevation is higher and not a likely location for what they seek."

"They seek nuggets. I have not learned why they consider them valuable," Horned Owl said.

"You are our eyes. Continue to spy on the white men. If by chance they come too near Big Hole, we will erase every trace of our camp and move everyone with our things into the cave and stay there until they are gone."

Horned Owl thought this a prudent plan. He accepted his role of spy with pride and humility—pride because of the confidence his father placed in his ability and humility that the responsibility for the safety of the clan rested upon his shoulders. He resolved to perform his duty.

Knowing that the cold and snow would probably prevent the white men from pursuing their activities along the creek beds, Horned Owl reconnoitered the area during the spring and summer where he had seen them. In the fall, his responsibilities shifted to hunting. When he next visited the site where they panned the creek, their numbers had doubled. Could this mean there were more of them working additional spots along other creeks that trickled down the mountain sides? Horned Owl feared that was the case, so he explored farther up the Kootenai River and wandered up streams that flowed into it. At a distance northeast of the original camp of the white men, he discovered another group of panners unlike the first group he had encountered. They were not white men or people of the earth. He stared in amazement at the strange appearance of six men dressed in shiny black tunics and loose-fitting pants of the same material. They bent over the water sifting gravel in the pans as intently involved in the process as the white men had been. Their skin was dark like his own but with a yellowish cast, and their faces had a roundness like the full moon, not usually characteristic of any people he had seen. Most unusual was the single long braid at the back of their heads that reached to the middle of their shoulder blades. They wore small hats that sat like boxes on top of their skulls. If he thought the white men's chatter hissed like snakes, the speech of these men chopped and clipped like crickets. Horned Owl watched this new breed of men for a while and then silently crept away. He decided to stay in the area and observe them longer the next day. He wondered if they had any connection with the other white group of panners or if they worked independently of them.

In the morning, he stealthily approached their camp. As he drew closer, cries of distress reached his ears. The scuffling of feet, the thud of bodies, the crash of objects, and the report of a gun ripped through the trees. Horned Owl inched closer, shielding himself behind tree trunks until he took cover behind a boulder. The clamor subsided, and he peeked around the rock situated about a hundred paces from a scene of devastation. Blood soaked the sand.

Six black-clad bodies were scattered across the creek bed. Ten white men, one with a smoking pistol in his hand, kicked at the side of one of the dead men. The others ransacked through the equipment in the camp, examined the pans of nuggets, and collected tools and any supplies they could find strewn about the canvas tent that had housed the six men. The two half-breeds he had seen before were not among the murderers. Horned Owl wished he could understand what the white men were saying. The massacre and destruction they had committed seemed to please them. They did nothing to bury the men. Horned Owl wondered if they would strip the bodies and dump them in the creek after he slipped away. He had to save his own skin and put distance quickly between himself and these vicious men. Because he had lived in isolation from warfare, other than the mutual slaughter that occurred during Blackfeet raids, his mind could not fathom the carnage. The old men had talked of the enemy raids and their skirmishes with the Blackfeet, leaving men dead on both sides. In this instance, attackers and victims were physically different, but they were engaged in the pursuit. What did they pursue? Their mutual goal eluded Horned Owl's comprehension.

    He fled deeper into the forest, his mind obsessed with the murderous scene. The trek back to Big Hole took several days. As he traveled, at times jogging across level ground and other times carefully making his way through thick woods and rocky terrain, his thoughts swirling, he tried to make sense of all he had witnessed. He needed to discuss this violent event and the presence of two kinds of panners with the older and wiser men of the clan.

Several days later, he arrived in the sheltered mountain basin where his family awaited his return from his spying mission. Running Wolf, Smoking Loon, and Brave Bear gathered around him, eager to hear his report. They could tell from the intense gleam in his eyes that he had stunning news to deliver. The young boys—Standing Rock, Spears-Many-Fish, and Burning Cloud—sidled closer to the cluster of men while the women, hearing the commotion of Horned Owl's arrival, emerged from the surrounding meadow to join the covey in the center of the camp.

After Horned Owl finished breathlessly telling his story of the slaughter, solemn expressions appeared on the men's faces. Indeed, this was disturbing, not only because of the warfare between the two camps but because a new race of men previously unknown had entered their world. First, it was the pale faces, then the black faces, and now men who were neither white nor black, but a mixture of brown, black, and white—yellowish like the clay of the earth. The Great Spirit had fashioned four colors in the same manner as he had fashioned four directions, four forces—water, fire, earth, and wind. Everything came in fours. Four colors to the circle of life—red, black, white, and yellow. The men were awed and stupefied by the colors. Silence reigned while each clansman considered the strangers. What action, if any, should they take? Were they endangered by the presence of these strangers? Running Wolf's opinion, as always, held sway. And after a long pause, he did not hesitate to voice his thoughts.

"Your spying must continue. We must observe and know if their numbers increase. We must find a way to discover their purpose. You say the white panners took what the yellow men had. They looked for what was in the pans. They took their tools. They searched for the same stones. What is it about the pebbles that is so important to them?"

"I forgot one detail," Horned Owl said. "There were two half-breeds in the *suyapi* camp."

"Ah, the false weasels, misbegotten children of the trappers. I do not trust them . . . traitors to the keepers of the earth. Neither this nor that, they do not know whom to ally with, nor do they know their best interests," Brave Bear sneered.

"Not all the half-breeds are bad. The blood of their mothers flows stronger in some of them," Smoking Loon said to moderate Brave Bear's harsh judgment.

"The truth is that none of them can be trusted until their word and actions are proven," Running Wolf asserted. His authority was not disputed. Horned Owl listened respectfully to his father's pronouncement.

"I am the spy, and I will test their mettle, "Horned Owl said.

"Wait a while before you spy further. Best to lay quietly in Big Hole. You will travel there when I tell you." Running Wolf signaled that the discussion was ended, and the people dispersed to resume their chores.

Horned Owl sought out the company of Song Bird. She had missed him in his long absences and welcomed him into their teepee. Standing Rock cavorted around him, happy to have his father's company. Song Bird bathed Horned Owl's face, arms, and legs, dipping a chamois in a bowl of water and wiping him with another dry cloth. From a pot on the firepit, she ladled broth into a wooden bowl and served it to Horned Owl. She did not question him about his adventures. Her role was to minister to her husband's needs, making him comfortable in his home after his arduous and worrisome journey. Horned Owl gladly received his wife's ministrations. The tender care she lavished upon him did much to ease his worry. He relaxed and resolved to enjoy the Great Spirit's bounty in the loving circle of his family. Standing Rock needed his guidance and direction. He would immediately start to instruct him in horsemanship and the use of the bow and arrow.

The next day the lessons began, and Standing Rock proved an apt learner. The little fellow mounted his pony with aplomb and soon pranced around his father, maintaining his balance. It was not long before he pleaded to shoot his bow on horseback, having proven his ability to hit a target after little training with his father. Horned Owl took him on all his hunting expeditions. They tracked deer and elk together and learned the habits of all the forest creatures.

Horned Owl passed several seasons, watching his son develop. The time came when Running Wolf told him it was time to spy on the panners again. Horned Owl was anxious to resume spying and considered whether he should take his young son, whose height now reached his breastbone. Song Bird did not favor the idea, arguing it was fraught with sufficient danger for one man. Having seen the brutality of the white man, Horned Owl had to agree with her. Spying required the stealth that was best pulled off by a lone man practiced in the skill of making himself invisible. If Standing Rock were to accompany him, Horned Owl would have to have eyes in the back of his head to keep watch on him and ensure that his movements were undetectable. Not exercising that extra vigilance might put both of their lives at greater risk.

"Take care of your mother while I am gone," he told Standing Rock. "Obey your grandfather in all matters."

He bade his son goodbye. Standing Rock looked ruefully after his father, hoping for the day when he could journey with him, but he was an obedient son and did not beg to go with him. Song Bird and Standing Rock were still waving him on his way as he disappeared up the winding path that led to the ridge overlooking Big Hole.

Late spring had blossomed in the mountains. A burst of woodland flowers surrounded him as he headed southwest, jogging at times where the ground leveled and treading carefully through tangled limbs where wind and snow had downed many trees during the winter. He shot a squirrel or grouse for his evening meal to vary his diet of pemmican packed in a parfleche slung over his shoulder. The forest was alive with the bird calls—stellar jays, pine siskins, crows, and ravens. The creeks he waded across gushed with the melting snow from higher elevations. All around, the mountain peaks towered. He paused on promontories to survey the scenery, tree-covered slopes, and lush valleys—beautiful virgin country upon which his people left no footprint because they blended in with nature. Not so, the white men. They were loud and raucous. They pounded and pitted the earth. He had found their trash around their abandoned campsites. What a mess they had left at the scene where they had massacred the six yellow men.

He trekked on, alert for any sound of human activity or sign of their passage. For days he hiked uphill and downhill, resting by a stream, cupping his hands to drink of the refreshing water, and resuming his journey. He observed the arc of the sun in the sky, his compass. Making camp at night, he sat and studied the constellations before falling asleep on a bed of grass.

After seven days, he reached the area where he had seen the panners. Slithering along the creek, he encountered camp after camp of men similarly occupied in sifting grit and sand in frames along the banks. He estimated there might be as many as five hundred men in the camps. Alarmed, he wanted to slink away. Did this mean they would move northward toward Big Hole? Fortunately, the density increased to the southward following the Kootenai River, but that did not bode well for his people. They were bound to fan out like a black cloud once they penetrated a region.

Horned Owl turned despondently away from the river, not knowing what to do next. Should he travel farther to the southwest and determine if they had built any villages? His mind roiled with plans to investigate further when he was arrested in his thoughts by the sound of voices—not just any voices but men speaking Salish, his tongue. He could not distinguish the words clearly, but carefully approached the source of the speech.

In an opening in the forest, he saw the two half-breeds, the same ones he had seen at the first panners' camp. They sat beside each other on a log, their faces toward him. They wore the same clothing as when he had first seen them—smudged and worn jackets, wide-brimmed hats with eagle feathers in the rim, and beaded belts around their waists. One was examining nuggets in his hand. He could make out what they were saying now. They clearly were dissatisfied.

"This won't amount to much at the Assayer's Office," one said.

Horned Owl wondered at the meaning of the words "Assayer's Office." He would have to deduce what all this meant from their conversation, Horned Owl thought.

"They're washed up. The pickings are too slim to continue working here. I'm for going west over the mountains where the diggings are plenty. I've heard there's plenty of gold there," the second half-breed said.

What was gold? Again, the word was spoken in English. The half-breed must be referring to the pebbles in his hand. What value did they carry? The white man coveted so many things. Everything the earth held, and this gold must be no different. It must bring him more things.

"I'm going west," the second half-breed repeated. "Are you coming with me or not?"

"Yeah, I'll go. It's no use. Those poor fools pan and think if they can't find gold, they can find silver or copper. I'm ready to move on. We ain't going to strike it any richer staying here," the first half-breed said.

"I give them a few more years, and the white men will give it up. This bit of gold is not worth a plugged nickel," the second half-breed said.

What was a "plugged nickel?" Regardless of what it was, Horned Owl got the gist. The nuggets were not worth much.

Horned Owl wondered if he should approach the man and introduce himself, speaking in Salish, and then quickly rejected the idea. He did not know if they would turn out to be friend or foe, and he could not risk finding out they were hostile. Had not Running Wolf believed them untrustworthy? He would err, then, on the side of caution, although he really wanted to obtain more information from the half-breeds. What he had learned was that the panners searched for the mineral they called gold; that this gold was very valuable to them; and that they had had limited success in finding the coveted mineral in the Kootenai River area. Maybe that meant they would all be moving on to richer areas far from the keepers of the earth. This was crucial information to deliver to his people.

He would have to keep spying and find out if the second half-breed's prediction would come true. Would their numbers dwindle? From what he was able to spy, their numbers had increased. Maybe it was the apex of a futile effort. He would have to see what happened in future seasons.

The two half-breeds opened tins of food and began to spoon out food. They gobbled the mush like hungry wolves and then tossed the empty cans into the woods—their slovenliness and sloppiness so typical of their father's blood. What a pity! They wiped their mouths with the back of their hands. Horned Owl, repelled, slipped away, anxious to return to his people. Was there anything more to learn about these despicable intruders into his country? He hoped they would depart as rapidly as they had appeared, never to return.

When Horned Owl reported his observations, Running Wolf approved of how he had refrained from revealing himself to the half-breeds. Their conduct proved that they had become infected with the white man's greed. The fact that the half-breeds were abandoning the diggings was cause for hope that the rest of the panners would one by one follow suit and look for their precious gold at places far away. Running Wolf was content to maintain a wait-and-see attitude. If the clan remained sequestered several days journey from the locus of white men's activity, they would survive. His calm demeanor reassured Horned Owl that his father's wise leadership would preserve them from harm.

"You have done well, my son," Running Wolf praised him. "From now on, you will return and investigate that area every so often. They must not approach our vicinity. From what you observed, they are headed in a different direction, but we cannot trust that it will always be so."

Nothing disturbed their peaceful routine. The daily chores to sustain life had to be performed—the gathering of wood, the berry-picking, the butchering of game, and the tanning of hides. The boys had to master the skill of tracking and hunting animals, and the only girl, Dream Weaver, under the tutelage of her mother, Plenty Medicine, learned the arts of healing. Surrounded by four older women, Dream Weaver benefited from their accumulated knowledge, becoming equally adept in sewing, cooking, and tanning hides.

Plenty Medicine's two boys, still inseparable, competed with Standing Rock in foot races and daring stunts on horseback—feats such as standing upright on the horse's back and leaping off the galloping horse. None of their antics resulted in broken bones. Their gymnastics only increased their physical prowess and strengthened their muscles. Spears-Many-Fish and Burning Cloud took greater risks than Standing Rock, although Standing Rock was far from timid. He just exercised more caution and exhibited wisdom beyond his years. In no degree was he prone to foolhardy behavior. Horned Owl had taught him well that watchfulness was the main ingredient of valor.

The cycle of the seasons continued in an uninterrupted round of their traditional activities. Horned Owl regularly reconnoitered the area where he had seen the panners. When he investigated along the tributaries of the Kootenai River, he found only vestiges of campsites and abandoned mine shafts cut into several hillsides. The panners had left their rubbish behind—scrap lumber, frames for washing and sifting through the grit and sand of the creek beds, rags, rusted nails, tin cans, and fish bones. Ashes lay in the fire pits. The white men had exhausted the small veins of ore they had managed to mine. For the time being, his people were safe from white encroachment, secure to enjoy peaceful seclusion.

That peace lasted at least until Standing Rock grew to manhood and started going with Horned Owl on his spying trips. Horned Owl taught him all he knew of stealth and living off what the land provided on these explorations of the surrounding territory. He told him that the white settlers had mostly congregated far to the south of Big Hole at the confluence of two great rivers in a region where their Salish forefathers had dwelt for generations. Situated in that region now was the reservation the white chiefs had designated for the remnants of their once prolific people that he estimated numbered only a few thousand souls now. He told him of the Black Robes who had tried to change his people and teach them new ways, to farm and to pray to their Jesus Christ and Mother Mary. His father, Running Wolf, had told him about how the Black Robes had worked to change tribal traditions, and in turn, Horned Owl impressed upon Standing Rock, the importance of preserving the Salish identity as keepers of the earth.

The disruption in their peaceful existence did not come from the white men but from their own kind. Spears-Many-Fish and Burning Cloud struck out to do their own explorations. They felt they possessed the same abilities as Standing Rock and should share the privileges and freedom of seeing other places. Horned Owl did not want more than one companion on his journeys, believing a pair of spies best traveled together, and his son already provided a good partner in that role. Determined to prove their competence and daring, the two brothers set off in the opposite direction to the southeast, telling Running Wolf they were tracking a herd of elk. Running Wolf had no cause to distrust them, for up until that point, they had followed his leadership and performed their duties in the clan.

When they returned to the camp several weeks later, he had reason to scold them severely. They wobbled into the camp, their speech garbled, and with a stench emanating from their flesh. It was as if their tongues were tied. Spears-Many-Fish extended a flask to Running Wolf.

"Sip this. You will like it," he said.

Burning Cloud, thick-tongued, grabbed the flask from his brother's hand before Running Wolf could clutch it and took a swig. He smiled stupidly. "Firewater in the gut. It makes me fly."

"Where did you get it?" Running Wolf demanded angrily and knocked the flask from Burning Cloud's grasp.

"From the Kootenai. They have lots of it. We met them going south, and they told us to try it. The firewater makes all pain go away. We had a good time with them. They spoke our language."

Running Wolf grabbed Burning Cloud by the shoulders and shook him. He released him and then slapped him across the face and pummeled him with his fist until his nose began to bleed and his right eye was blackened.

"Idiots! What have you done? Did you tell the Kootenai where we are? If so, I will kill you both now."

"No, no!" they both retained enough sense to shout, realizing the danger Running Wolf's wrath posed. "We said nothing about where we had come from," Spears-Many-Fish cried. "We just drank, joked, and laughed with them. Then they left us."

"You lie, you sneaking traitors!" Running Wolf menaced them with his clenched fists. "You idiots. Do you not know the firewater is the white men's poison to kill off all the Kootenai and all the Salish? The drink will wipe us from the earth."

"Please, do not beat us," Spears-Many-Fish pleaded. "We meant no harm."

"But you have done great harm and not just to yourself in your stupid state. Go from my sight. I do not want to look at either of you."

The two drunken Salish stumbled off to Smoking Loon's teepee. Their father stood shamefacedly as his sons wobbled past him to sleep off their inebriation. Plenty Medicine smudged their drunken bodies to expel the evil spirits from their reeking flesh. She took the empty flasks and threw them into Big Hole Lake. Dream Weaver watched these events from a distance, ashamed of her brothers' behavior. What would become of them? Would Running Wolf administer further punishment upon them? Would he tie them to a post and whip them until their bare backs were torn? She hoped not and prayed that their atrocious behavior was a one-time occurrence. Most of all, she prayed the Kootenai would not discover their location. Her wish was shared by everyone in the clan.

For many moons, Running Wolf scorned to talk to the offenders. Their father, Sitting Crow, admonished them, warning that terrible punishment would follow any repetition of their offense. To avoid further censure, the brothers adopted a docile demeanor and expressed remorse, renouncing their bad behavior and promising never to drink firewater again.

But the firewater had wreaked its damage and taken hold of the spirit of both men. The desire to feel the same burning sensation in the belly and the buzzing in the brain possessed them. For a while they managed to keep that lust at bay, but eventually it overpowered them. Self-control evaporated. They huddled together, sharing the desire to duplicate the feeling.

"We need to find the Kootenai again," Burning Cloud said.

"There is a *suyapi* trading post our father talked about near the land of the Nimiipuu. We could go there and trade for firewater," Spears-Many-Fish suggested.

"Trade what?"

"Beaver skins."

"They are hard to find."

"Elk hides are plentiful."

"How do we find the way?" Burning Cloud's interest was piqued.

Spears-Many-Fish replied confidently, "Remember how we journeyed along the great river to Kootenai Falls, catching fish? All we need to do is follow that river farther and then travel south to where a smaller river flows from the northwest and there at a bow in the river, Smoking

Loon says is a white trader's post where many goods can be obtained—clothing, tools, foodstuffs, weapons, and the firewater. He knows of it from the days when he dwelt in the Place of the Wide Cottonwoods before Running Wolf led the clan to Big Hole."

Burning Cloud's eyes glowed. "We can see the places our father talked of and walk wherever our ancestors chose to walk in freedom and joy. The firewater is not only to be drunk by white men but by us also, so we can drink what brings blissful ease. I believe it is the potion that gives the white men power, and when I drink it, I feel able to endure any pain or sorrow that may come my way."

"I feel the same way. It is strong medicine, powerful magic," Spears-Many-Fish agreed. "Besides, I do not think it is right that we be restricted to one corner of the earth. The earth is ours. Isn't that what our elders have always told us?"

"Running Wolf, Smoking Loon, and Brave Bear are opposed to anything the white man has, but I think differently," Burning Cloud said. "I think we cannot live separately. There is a burning now in my soul that tells me I must drink that liquor. It has taken over all my thoughts and desires. I must have it, no matter what the cost," Burning Cloud affirmed, a fire in his liquid, brown eyes.

It was settled. They would find a trading post where they could obtain all the firewater they desired. During the drunken interlude with the Kootenai when they had imbibed the firewater, their brains had become inflamed with the desire for more whiskey just as the panners were obsessed with the pursuit of golden nuggets.

One day the two brothers were nowhere to be found. Sitting Crow looked in consternation everywhere he could think of, around fishing holes, upstream and downstream, and through the surrounding valleys. Finally, dejected and tired, he returned to the camp where Running Wolf somberly met him.

"The contamination has spread," Running Wolf pronounced. "It is vain to pursue them. They have passed over to the other side, as did Wild Horse and Painted Turtle. They suffered the same sickness. We shall see them no more."

Plenty Medicine emerged from her teepee to greet her husband. With a grave expression on her face, she stopped before the two men and spoke. "The firewater caused their sickness. It is worse than what Wild Horse and Painted Turtle suffered."

"But we have lost all of them," Sitting Crow groaned.

Horned Owl and Song Bird joined the group. Slowly, the rest of the clan assembled around Smoking Loon, Sitting Crow, and Running Wolf. The older women—Laughing Water, Sage Hen, and Half Moon—clustered near Plenty Medicine, looking to her for counsel. The pall of sorrow was palpable; hearts were heavy with this latest calamity that had disastrous consequences for the survival of the clan. Their numbers were again reduced to the detriment of their welfare—fewer men to hunt and fish, to protect and defend the women. And what of children? Propagation was threatened.

Plenty Medicine spoke authoritatively, "Our hope and salvation reside in Standing Rock and Dream Weaver."

Where were the two youngest members of the tribe now? The women's heads turned, gazing around to catch a glimpse of them.

Anticipating their question, Plenty Medicine informed the women, "Dream Weaver is gathering willow branches, and Standing Rock is with the horses on the other side of the cave."

"It is time for them to marry," Song Bird said.

"So it will be," Horned Owl declared. "Let us replace our sorrow with joy."

Worry faded from all the faces because their spirits gravitated to happiness rather than the heaviness of hearts disposed to depression.

Laughing Water giggled delightfully, "A wedding! We will dance and sing!"

Song Bird trilled, "Oh, what fun, what fun!"

"I'll prepare the feast," Sage Hen chimed in.

When Dream Weaver and Standing Rock returned to the camp, unsuspecting of the plans that had been hatched for them without their presence, they were at first surprised. They smiled radiantly at each other, jubilant that they were now considered old enough to marry. They were in their late teens, and a man was not expected to take a wife until he was in his twenties. But the clan had more important concerns. Joy must succeed misfortune, and perpetuation of the clan was paramount after the loss of two members. The company was now reduced to twelve, the same number as when they had first settled at Big Hole. They could not idly succumb to extinction. As it was, aging members dominated their group. The three couples who had forged a path northward with their seven young children were entering their sixties. Among the children, Wild Horse,

Painted Turtle, Spears-Many-Fish, and Burning Cloud had succumbed to outside lures and had defected to the land being overrun by the white men. There they would learn whether their lives would be better with their defeated people who had been pushed onto reservations. No one expected to ever see these lost children again. With each passing season, even their mothers stopped hoping they would return. And they did not return.

For many moons after the panners abandoned their camps, Horned Owl discovered no traces of white men on his spying missions. The Salish lived in isolation, undisturbed by internal or external unrest, long enough for the young couple to present the clan with a fourth generation of Big Hole inhabitants. Dream Weaver gave birth to a set of twins—a boy and a girl. The boy soon earned the name of Song Dog as a toddler because he could imitate the sound of a coyote perfectly. And Moonbeam's chubby cheeks shone with the delightful sheen that the full moon had endowed her with on the night she was born. The Salish took it as a sign of good luck. Dream Weaver was fecund and would bless them with numerous sons and daughters. But as the cycle of seasons passed, and little Moonbeam and Song Dog grew old enough to follow in their parents' footsteps, Moonbeam learning to sew and cook and Song Dog to hunt and ride a horse, it became apparent that the curse of low fertility had been passed on. Other things had also been passed on—good things—the healing arts, how to live off the land, how to build teepees, and how to tan hides. Plenty Medicine passed on the healing arts to Dream Weaver, and Dream Weaver, in turn, began to instruct Moonbeam in the use of herbs. Song Dog soon was seen to possess an eye as keen as his father's.

That bode well for the survival of their clan, reduced in numbers, yet still clinging to the belief they would endure through any adversity. Unstated was the fact obvious to all: Siblings did not mate. Dream Weaver, when she came of age, might mate with an old man, but Song Dog could not father children with old matrons long past their childbearing years. It was a dilemma to be faced later, and one over which Running Wolf had to ponder. There were few options, and none appealed to him because they risked exposing his small band. It meant kidnapping a child from a neighboring tribe or adopting an orphan from the people he had left in the Place of the Wide Cottonwoods.

On one spying mission, Horned Owl and Standing Rock ventured to the northwest, crossing a verdant valley, the mountain range on their right shoulder and another range off to their left. Horned Owl paused in his tracks and held his forefinger to his lips, signaling to Standing Rock that he should also stop and perk up his ears for the sound he had detected emanating from the forest. They heard an axe striking wood, a crack, and then the thud of a tree falling in the forest. They crept closer and observed a clearing in the woods. A white man working with an axe had piled a stack of logs nearby. In the distance, they saw a cabin and a woman hanging clothes on a line stretched between poles. She wore a blue bonnet and gingham dress that reached to her ankles. A split rail fence enclosed a pair of cows munching the grass, and two horses grazed in a corral beyond the cabin. Stumps peppered another area, apparently awaiting removal. In a cleared section, a boy walked behind a plow cutting through the soil.

Horned Owl gaped. The first farmers had arrived in the valley. He knew of farming from stories Running Wolf told of the Black Robes who had tried to teach the Salish to use tools to plant and grow their own food. It was labor Running Wolf did not like and had refused to do. Were there more of these farmers in the valley? He did not know, but the presence of one farmer meant more were not far behind. His heart constricted. Had the inevitable arrived? Must they retreat farther away from this encroachment? Where could they flee to? Nowhere. They must remain in their hiding place and stand firm. He turned to Standing Rock and motioned that they should retreat. The concern in his eyes was visible to Standing Rock. After they had traveled for a while, they stopped to drink from a creek and to rest briefly.

"They will take everything from the land until it is naked," Horned Owl began. "You saw how they chop the trees and slash the earth. I can hear the trees cry."

"What can we do?" Standing Rock anxiously asked his father, his youthful indignation bursting to right wrongs.

"I do not know," Horned Owl answered and fell silent for a moment before adding, "Continue to watch and stay where we are. I, for one, will not retreat from this land."

Standing Rock admired his father's firmness. He would emulate his staunch refusal to be pushed further.

"Let us go now and report our findings to the elders," Horned Owl said, rising from the ground. Standing Rock stood up and followed his father. After several days' journey, they arrived back at Big Hole. Running Wolf received the news gravely.

"The day I have feared has come," Running Wolf said. "The farmers bring women and children. They are here to stay. Our numbers are few. We cannot chase them away." His voice weakened. There was resignation in his tone, as if he had finally met the inevitable, and he lacked the power to fend it off. Horned Owl could not believe his father would accept defeat. Running Wolf would have a plan; he would stand strong. If the white men found their hiding place, they would not retreat and not cede one bit of earth to the interlopers. No . . . never. The clan members were keepers of the earth. Finally, Running Wolf spoke, gathering determination and emphasis in his tone.

"We stand here. Big Hole is our home. We stay until we die and are buried here."

The conversation ended and the elders dispersed, resolved like Running Wolf to hold their ground.

A canopy of stars covered their secluded bowl between the mountains. Horned Owl gazed at the constellations and saw a shooting star, his eyes tracing its downward arc toward the horizon. Beauty above, beauty below, beauty all around. He admired his father's steadfastness. It was the steadfastness that he had inherited. Turning to observe his son follow Dream Weaver into their teepee, he knew that he had passed on that same quality to Standing Rock. The clan was in secure hands for succeeding generations as sure as the stars still decorated the sky.

On every successive spying trip, Horned Owl observed more ranchers settling in the valleys. More land was cleared. Once he came upon two men at standing at opposite ends of a bow-shaped saw, pushing and pulling back and forth so it cut a wedge through the trunk. Eventually, the saw cut through the trunk, and the stately tree crashed to the ground. Horned Owl realized this activity accounted for the many waist-high stumps dotting the clearings. He watched them fiercely cutting into the trunks. When they had a pile of logs, they chopped them into smaller, equal lengths. A horse dragged the logs to their building site. Horned Owl lingered in the area for several days, intent on observing their work. He surmised that they were father and son, laboring together. Around the partially constructed barn, a group of younger children tended chickens and cows. A woman worked a washboard over a tin tub in front of the rude cabin. Intermittently, she wiped her brow with her forearm. A dog chased pine squirrels around the yard. The family was here to stay, Horned Owl concluded, and they were prolific. He thought of Standing Rock's twins back at Big Hole, growing taller and stronger, oblivious to the need to procreate. Sadly, he turned away from the domestic scene.

Plenty Medicine's application of fertility potions had not helped Standing Rock and Dream Weaver. She persisted in her prayers and chants but nothing had availed. Even so, Horned Owl still hoped they would have more children, but with every passing year, it seemed less likely. His thoughts shifted to his father, Running Wolf. He could not ignore that his father's strength was failing. His face was wrinkled and weathered deep brown. His hair hung in gray strands, parted in the middle, and was held in place by a beaded headband. Around his neck, he still wore the bear claws and teeth won in his youth. His wisdom and sagacious judgments still ruled. His aged companions in the northern migration displayed the same ebbing vigor. Their eyes had witnessed great changes in their six decades and evinced both sorrow and sagacity. Sitting Crow, in his forties, was vigorous like Horned Owl. The older men relied increasingly upon them to perform the physical labor of the clan. It was expected that Horned Owl would inherit leadership from Running Wolf, succeeding him as chief.

But for the present, Running Wolf endured as the leader, and his word was law. Horned Owl approached his father with a heavy heart. He could no longer keep silent about his concerns.

"We know the white men have penetrated the valleys and are building houses. They have many children; we do not. We cannot delay going to the Place of Wide Cottonwoods for orphans. I ask that you send me on that errand. Standing Rock will go with me."

Running Wolf did not respond immediately, mulling the matter over for a while.

"How can you do it without the people asking where you will take the orphans?" he asked Horned Owl.

"Our tongue will be tight in our mouths. I will tell them they need not know and simply that we have a home in the far north, safe and secure."

"I have long thought that this eventually must be done no matter the danger. I hate to see you leave on such a mission. And you are right. It is best not to make the journey alone. Take Standing Rock with you. So say I, *Šey hoy*.

Horned Owl and Standing Rock set out on horseback, traveling south where they knew bands of Salish still dwelled on land the powerful white men had apportioned to them, some clustered around the mission churches the Black Robes had built years ago when Running Wolf was young. Reaching the southern tip of the Broad Water, they climbed a promontory overlooking the glistening expanse of the lake and realized why their people treasured this place and why so many refused to relinquish their ancestral land, still clinging to a tiny portion of the territory they once roamed unimpeded. Traveling on, they reached the outskirts of the second mission established in the valley and came upon three teepees. They dismounted from their horses and greeted the grandfather and grandmother seated in front of a teepee. The old couple looked haggard and worn, their faces wrinkled and emaciated. A few children milled around the teepees and gradually came forward to stare at the two strangers who spoke their language.

Horned Owl said they had been living with the traders, hunting and scouting for them, but had come to see the homeland of their forefathers. The old man grinned feebly, apologizing that he had no food to offer the travelers, but that they were welcome to stay and rest with them. The old woman asked if they had brought any food. They were hungry, in need of provisions the white men had promised and had not delivered. She moaned and rubbed her shrunken stomach. Six scrawny children stared wide-eyed at the visitors.

"You see our wretchedness," the old man croaked. "Disease swept through our village again and only recently has slackened so that those still strong enough can go in search of game. We have nothing to give you."

Horned Owl then spoke forthrightly. "What we seek, you have. We come looking for orphans. Our wives are barren, and they want children to raise as their own."

The old woman looked around. "We have more than enough mouths to feed and plenty orphans, little ones who have lost their parents to the disease." She motioned for a boy of about five to come forward. He limped; the right foot was twisted inward. "Take him."

"What happened to him?" Standing Rock asked.

"He was born that way. His mother had a bad dream before she went into labor. An evil spirit appeared to her, and she died shortly after she delivered him."

"We would rather have a girl. Do you have one to spare?" Horned Owl asked.

A girl of about the same age as the boy stood sheepishly behind the boy.

"That one you can have. Come here, Spotted Dove," the old woman said, pointing to the shy girl, her face covered in pockmarks. No wonder she wanted to hide. If not for the blemishes, she would have been a lovely child with the promise of blooming into a beautiful woman.

"Somehow she survived the illness," the old woman said.

Horned Owl considered the grandmother's proposal. They were now in the position of accepting other people's castoffs. "Are there other orphans to be found farther on?"

"None to be relinquished. The numbers in the villages have dwindled, and our brothers to the south will want to keep the children they have."

"We need another girl," Horned Owl insisted.

"There are none to spare. Be glad I have Spotted Dove to give you. She is a sweet child, and the boy has a good disposition too, eager to follow the example of the men."

The old man spoke up. "We are starving. We are weak. The Great Spirit has abandoned us."

Horned Owl's heart ached to hear the old man's piteous words, and he did not have the words to comfort him. Wisdom told him that they should accept the two children and cut short their mission. The old couple lacked curiosity, or perhaps it was just the energy to inquire about the visitors' origins. Encounters with more of their Salish kinsmen would elicit more about who Horned Owl and Standing Rock were and where they came from. The questioners would probably guess that they were descendants of Running Wolf who had departed from their midst almost fifty years ago. They would bombard them with questions about how they had survived those many years in a distant land.

But Horned Owl harbored his own curiosity and could not contain his desire to inquire about his long-lost brother, Wild Horse, who with his wife, Painted Turtle, had chosen to strike out on their own in the hopes of finding favor and happiness in their ancestral lands now being overridden by white men's cattle and ranches. He hesitated for a moment before posing his question. He had managed to suppress thoughts of his brother's fate over the years. Now the chance to discover what had happened to him prompted him to inquire.

"Do you know of a man called Wild Horse?"

"Aye," the old man answered. "He worked for the trader McDougal. He helped the white soldiers track down Salish accused of stealing. His wife, Painted Turtle, sold beaded bags and moccasins to the white settlers."

"Does he live at the trading post?"

The old woman's head jerked up, "They were the first to die of the plague, bringing the curse upon us from the dealings with the *suyapi*."

Horned Owl grew somber. He could not rejoice in their sad end and remained silent. Further questions risked revealing information that he did not want the old couple to know. There was no comfort in the knowledge that the couple may have received just recompense for the betrayal of their traditions. They were not those who had abandoned the ancient ways. Horned Owl recalled the reprobates, Spears-Many-Fish and Burning Cloud, besotted with the white man's firewater. Where were they now? Had they not also ventured south in search of the brew that befuddled their minds and left them in a stupor, inured to all pain and suffering? He had to ask about the drunkards too.

"Have you heard of a pair of brothers, Spears-Many-Fish and Burning Cloud?"

"Aye," again the old man responded, shaking his head disconsolately. "They froze together in the snow, locked in an embrace, ice stuck to their jaws, an empty jug at their feet. They were crazy with the drink, fell asleep, and never woke up."

The burden to tell of the four deaths lay heavy on Horned Owl's mind. He must carry the news back to their fathers and mothers. Who was there to sing them on the way to the other world when they passed? They died far away from their people, alone and unsung, as they passed to the land of the dead. A terrible fate he would not wish on any of his people. Sadly, he looked at the two orphans. He saw hope in their eyes. He motioned to Standing Rock that it was time to leave and thanked the old couple for handing the children into their care, but secretly his gratitude was greater for the information they had provided about his kinsmen.

Standing Rock took the two children in tow. He lifted Spotted Dove onto the horse in front of Horned Owl, and then placed the boy on his horse and remounted. They bade the old couple farewell and left at a trot the small encampment.

Neither child seemed reluctant to be taken away or saddened to bid farewell to the family they had known in their short lives. They shed not one tear. Hunger had made them listless, and to their young eyes, these men were stronger, healthier, and better fed than the people they were leaving. They were wanted, and the sense that they were needed inspired them with hope for a brighter future among strangers who meant them no harm.

"What are you called?" Horned Owl asked the boy who rode on the horse with him.

"Bent Arrow," the boy answered in a tone that indicated he was not ashamed of his name.

"That's a good name," Horned Owl said. "You will be sharp with the bow. I will teach you all I know. You are my grandson now."

On the long journey to Big Hole, the kindness and care of their foster fathers only increased their sense of security. Horned Owl and Standing Rock spoke lovingly to them, describing the beautiful hidden canyon they were going to. He named all the members of their band and enumerated the virtues of the six women who would all serve as their mothers. Was it not lucky to have so many mothers? The two children nodded their heads in agreement.

They were not prepared for the disappointed looks on the faces of the women when they reached the Big Hole camp. Only Dream Weaver clapped her hands in delight and hugged the orphans to her breast. The twins, at first, suspicious, stood aloof. When they saw their mother open her arms to Spotted Dove, they leaped forward. The twins took the newcomers, a good five cycles of the seasons younger, locked arms and showed them around the camp, readily recognizing how wonderful it was to have the companionship of other children. No longer would they be the only children at Big Hole. Pulling Spotted Dove by the hand, Moonbeam skipped into the marshy area at one end of the lake where pussy willows and reeds thrived, and ducks dipped and dived between the marsh grasses for minnows. Limping on his club foot, Bent Arrow bravely trailed Song Dog into the woods. Standing Rock watched his son take charge of the orphan boy, leading him into his favorite haunts, and contemplated the future arrangement of partnerships. Song Dog inevitably would pair off with Spotted Dove, who except for her scarred face, would equal Moonbeam's loveliness. Those pockmarks were also indicators of her resilience because she had survived the ravages of a terrible disease. Her disfigurement would not affect her ability to bear children. Bent Arrow displayed a spunkiness that would not keep him down. Although his foot was bent like a bow, his spirit was straight as an arrow. Character mattered, and the physical deformities of these two children had endowed them with extraordinary fortitude. The band would thrive and multiply.

Meanwhile, Horned Owl brooded over the fates of the four family members who had so unwisely broken away from the band. He hesitated in telling Running Wolf that they had died miserable deaths. He did not know how the old man would react to the news. More worrisome was how his mother, Laughing Water, might react. Not wishing to upset his parents, he held his tongue, waiting for the right moment. The calm of the evening was always a good time when everyone was relaxed, sitting outside, and observing the star-studded sky. And what about Plenty Medicine and Sitting Crow's reaction when they learned their two sons had frozen in the snow? Plenty Medicine, possessed of shamanic powers, was fortified against adversity. But what about Sage Hen, who had been inordinately attached to her daughter, Painted Turtle, and until this day had never accepted her loss? These were the elders of the village, the founders, and the pioneers who had left their country in search of a haven from white encroachment. Few moons remained to any of these gray heads. Their hopes lived in future generations. Could these aged parents bear to hear that their children were dead? He wondered if faith in the fertility of Song Dog and Moonbeam and now the orphans, Bent Arrow and Spotted Dove, would be sufficient to alleviate their sorrow and realize all their hopes for the future.

Horned Owl conferred with Standing Rock about how to break the news to the clan. They agreed to first tell only the men because they expected the women would burst into uncontrollable wailing. Plenty Medicine's expression of grief might be less vociferous than the other women's but no less painful at the tragic deaths of her two sons. When the women were all away berry-picking, Horned Owl approached Running Wolf and asked him to summon all the men together.

Running Wolf greeted each man as he entered his teepee and said, "My son has something to tell us. He has told me that he has learned where Wild Horse, Painted Turtle, Spears-Many-Fish, and Burning Cloud have gone. Therefore, we will hear him speak."

Horned Owl wished to deliver the news quickly and without mincing words. He began, "There is no easy way to say it. They are dead. The white man's disease killed Wild Horse and Painted Turtle. Filled with firewater, Spears-Many-Fish and Burning Cloud fell asleep in the snow and froze to death."

The men somberly received the news. None spoke. Well-acquainted with tragedy, they met it with silent stoicism. After a while, Running Wolf spoke in a grave tone, "We will not tell their mothers. They have long accepted that they are lost. To know nothing of their fate is kinder than for them to be upset by this news. It would be too cruel. I cannot allow it. Let them continue to believe their sons and daughter have just disappeared and will never return."

The men nodded their assent. And so it was. The secret was kept.

Horned Owl continued to spy on the white men's activities. After most of the panners disappeared for more lucrative lodes, one mine remained where apparently valuable minerals were still being extracted. Settlers trickled into the area but at a slower pace than in the Broad Water or the Place of the Wide Cottonwoods. Here the terrain was rougher, and there were fewer wide fertile valleys on which to graze livestock. The white men did not come in droves in covered wagons drawn by oxen, yet they insidiously occupied clearings and river banks, spreading thinly across reaches of the Kootenai region. On every exploratory mission, Horned Owl discovered another farmer planting seed or hewing logs for his dwelling. Sometimes a man worked alone, and other times women and children accompanied the squatter.

On one expedition, he heard a cacophony of hammering. Approaching the source of the noise, he saw a large crew of men working with sledgehammers and axes. A horse-drawn wagon contained lumber cut into square beams, which men lugged from the wagon onto a raised bed. At the top of the bed, the ground was level forming a road. Down this road, other workers shoveled and leveled the earth to extend the track being laid farther into the distance where felled trees blocked the route. The hewn timbers were placed parallel on each side of the roadbed. Then men wielding sledgehammers pounded steel bars in place atop the timbers. What was this all about? What kind of road was this meant to be? What purpose did it serve? Did they intend for horses to ride between the beams? The labor struck Horned Owl as unnecessary for horses and the width of the road too narrow for a team of oxen pulling a big four-wheeled wagon.

When Horned Owl reported what he had seen to Running Wolf, his father muttered, "The devils are at work again."

For a long time, the clamor in the woods broke the serenity of the land, the road growing longer and longer, covering a great expanse of territory from east to west. Where would this road end? At the edge of the world where the earth fell into the big waters?

Running Wolf, although feeble, wanted to witness the incessant work of the white men with his own eyes, which were still as sharp as ever. "We will ride on horses, and you will show me this strange work," he told his son. With difficulty, Running Wolf mounted his horse and accompanied Horned Owl. The ride to the southwest tired him, but his old bones told him that something earth-shattering was occurring, and he had to be fully informed in order to wisely guide his people whose fragile existence was once again in imminent danger. His son was no longer a young man either. Gray hairs peppered his long black mane held in place by a band with an eagle feather attached at the back. He was still strong as a bull buffalo; leadership of the clan would soon devolve upon Horned Owl's sturdy shoulders. Whether in the morning or the evening, Running Wolf envisioned that the sun was setting for him.

From a high cliff overlooking the Kootenai River, they observed a large swath of land stripped of trees on the southern side of the river. A few wooden houses set on square plots dotted the denuded landscape. In the middle of this expanse, a long building had been constructed adjacent to the mysterious track of beams and steel that Horned Owl had seen. Now the road extended into this huge clearing. They could see wagons loaded with barrels and crates and a sprinkling of white men walking about the main building along the tracks. Their hearts constricted in sadness at the scarred earth. They sat upon their horses, mournfully gazing on the scene below. At once, they felt powerless and naked like the earth that had been raped. For a while, they grieved, holding back the tears and shrieks of outrage. Then an ear-splitting screech ripped the air. It was rumble and thunder, an earthquake, and an avalanche of crashing rock all at once. Loud and deafening, the roar assaulted their ears. Toward the east, a black metal monster chugged toward the building, moving along the track, belching a billow of ash-filled smoke. Rods turned the massive wheels along the steel rails that had been bolted onto the wooden beams. A shrill whistle sounded as it slowed to a stop. White men assembled on the platform around the large building and greeted passengers who alighted from the cars. Women in bustled dresses and feathered hats, held reticules and parasols. Men in round hats like bowls, girls in pinafores, and boys in overalls stepped lively from the bowels of the behemoth. Other men hurried to the rear of the monstrosity, where doors slid open and they began to unload cargo.

Running Wolf clucked to his horse, directing it away from the scene. Horned Owl followed suit. Neither man said anything; the horrible scene had rendered them mute. Ahead of him, Horned Owl observed his father's slumped shoulders and bowed back. The eagle feather still stood erect at the back of his head. It was a melancholy journey back to Big Hole.

Safely returned to their teepee, Running Wolf sat wrapped in a buffalo robe around the firepit. He felt inordinately cold for this time of late spring. Horned Owl and Standing Rock sat cross-legged at either side of the old man. The women and children had gone to pick berries, and the rest of the men were outside, engaged in their assigned tasks.

Running Wolf withdrew his withered hand from under his buffalo robe, plucked the eagle feather from his headband, and handed it to Horned Owl.

"I pass on the chiefdom of the clan to you."

Horned Owl knew this moment was inevitable. He quietly accepted the leadership. Standing Rock gazed somberly at his elders, realizing fully that one day that responsibility would also be passed on to him, and he, in turn, would transfer leadership to his son Song Dog. That was the ancient way of the Salish, and so it was in the beginning and would be forever.

After he had seen the belching mechanical conveyance clatter along the road specially made for it, Running Wolf declined rapidly. He ate little and said even less, his loss of vigor apparent to all. Laughing Water tended to him, bringing him bowls of warm soup, which he tentatively tasted and then set aside. This latest manifestation of the white intruder's power seemed to have drained the last ounce of strength from his body. He was a larch with the wind about to blow its last needles from its branches.

"Old man, take some soup," Laughing Water prodded him. She spooned some between his wrinkled lips. He managed to swallow the small portion, and murmured weakly, "Leave me, woman. I want to sleep now."

Laughing Water had to brace his back as she helped him lower himself on his bearskin pallet. Old age had been kinder to Laughing Water. She still participated in all the women's work, cooked, sewed, and skinned hides. Her mobility was not restricted, although she walked less rapidly and rested more often. She found herself enjoying just sitting and watching the children play. Bent Arrow and Spotted Dove thrived under her tutelage and loving attention. She treated them the same as Song Dog and Moonbeam. Young and old sought out her wisdom in matters large and small.

One morning after the first snowfall, Laughing Water awoke, crept toward Running Wolf's pallet where she thought he still slept and tapped his shoulder. A shiver ran through her body. He was cold to the touch. Instantly, she realized his spirit had flown in the night. Quietly, she went from teepee to teepee, telling everyone their leader had died.

Horned Owl took the news gravely. It was no surprise to him or anyone else, and they accepted the inevitable. The old women immediately began their keening. Plenty Medicine smudged the body and chanted the song to speed Running Wolf on his way to the spirit world. Her daughter, Dream Weaver, joined her in the funerary tasks. They dressed him in his best clothes and carried him to the meadow to be buried.

"Ah, my mother," Horned Owl murmured as they left the burial site. "I heard the wolf pack howl last night."

"Aye, my son, I heard them too. It was the ghost pack welcoming him to the land of the dead."

"They were not ghosts. I got up and saw the gray wolf silhouetted against the moon on yonder ridge." He pointed to where the trail switchbacked above Big Hole. "His spirit travels to the Place of the Wide Cottonwoods where he was born," he added.

Laughing Water nodded her agreement. "I think so too." She chuckled softly in memory of the days when they were young and frolicked there by the waterfall.

They walked together back to the circle of teepees, deep in their personal memories of the man who had led a small band to this country far away from the land of their birth. He was brave; he was strong; he was intrepid. Could there ever be such another visionary leader, one who foresaw the dehumanization of his people and refused to accept their annihilation? Horned Owl vowed he would be a fit carrier of his father's vision.

The adoption of the two orphans had increased the band to fourteen members, but five of them were advanced in age. Running Wolf had led them and their six children to Big Hole. It was fitting that with his death, he lead his generation to pass over into the spirit world. Brave Bear and Smoking Loon, their faces sagging with the seasons, their flesh leathery, hovered by the fire, the light lending a faint sparkle to their otherwise dim eyes. Sage Hen and Half Moon shuffled about the camp doing what chores they could, hauling small bundles of twigs for the fire. Of the old women, Laughing Water retained the most vigor. Strangely, as she aged, she recovered some of the effervescence of her youth. She was heard to laugh and chatter as she was known to do in her younger days. Did she think she had to raise the spirits of the others? Her manner suggested that she wished to assume her husband's leadership role. She told stories of the old days more frequently. When the story had a tragic end, she finished with a whimsical chuckle as if to dismiss the vagaries of fortune, an end note conveying "such is life" and that one's only recourse is to laugh at evil. In that way, misfortune was brushed away. The three matriarchs no longer went with Plenty Medicine, Song Bird, Dream Weaver, and the children to pick berries. Their stiff fingers struggled to ply the bone needles that fashioned tunics and loincloths. Their movements had slowed but not their interest in the young life around them, watching with pleasure Song Dog, Bent Arrow, Moonbeam, and Spotted Dove romp and play together.

The winter after Running Wolf died, Brave Bear, and Smoking Loon followed him in quick succession to the spirit world, leaving Sage Hen, Half Moon, and Laughing Water to sing them on to the land of the dead. Laughing Water gathered the widows around her, saying, "Ah, my three sisters. Our tears stream down our cheeks. In rivulets, they run through our wrinkles. They will dry. The seasons turn. We will smile again. And surely, we will cry again. And surely, we will laugh once more. And surely our turn to die will come. For now, look to the children."

In the seasons that followed, Laughing Water became the wise old woman of the clan. Everyone turned to her for sage counsel. She delighted in her position as the old crone, delivering adages and recounting fables. She talked more and did less physical labor. She lived now to communicate the wisdom of the ages.

Her talk and laughter ceased when Sage Hen and Half Moon passed in the night, both having died in their sleep. Sobered and calm, she helped to dismantle the teepees they had shared with their husbands. She took charge of distributing their belongings to the younger members of the band. Then she retreated to her teepee to chant prayers and meditate. Her period of mourning lasted for a month. One bright morning in early spring, when the chickadees were alive with chatter, and the blue jays had appeared on the budding limbs, she emerged, smiling, from her teepee and raised her arms to the sky. "Rejoice and be glad!" she exclaimed and resumed her life in the village as the sage old crone.

Similarly, Horned Owl was passing on valuable knowledge to his son Standing Rock, increasingly relying on him to accompany him in his spying forays. A time came when he did not venture into areas the white men inhabited without Standing Rock. They saw the settlement along the Kootenai grow each passing spring, the string of iron horses bringing more families to the town. On one trip, they stopped to hear the loud buzz of saws and stealthily approached a large building. Through a wide doorway, they observed long timbers being cut into planks. Lumber was stacked at the entrance, and men were loading and unloading logs from wagons. The whir of the saws emanating from the interior frayed every nerve in their bodies. The wood's lacerated flesh cried out to them in anguish. But they were powerless to rescue the wood. The trees had been mercilessly uprooted and taken to be dismembered.

The sawmill was constructed at a larger scale than the one that the Black Robes had built in the Place of the Wide Cottonwoods. As a boy, Horned Owl, had witnessed carpenters at work at the mission. Running Wolf had told him how the Black Robes had tried to make them farmers and carpenters, but he had refused to do the white men's work. That is why they had traveled to the north country. He worried whether their small band could remain isolated forever. To his last breath, he would stave off that day. He would preserve his people's traditional way of life.

"What are we to do?" Standing Rock asked his father.

"Live," he answered.

To Standing Rock, that was not much of an answer, and then after a pause, his father succinctly added, ". . . until we die."

Was his father, whom he admired, embittered? Standing Rock's spirit resisted passivity. The urge for action stirred in him; he wanted to protest, to fight. The realization that they did not have the numbers to overcome the white men and repossess their stolen land quickly checked his impulse to fight. It availed nothing. He must be cagey and cautious like his father and follow his example.

When they returned to Big Hole, they recounted what they had seen. Sitting Crow, Plenty Medicine, and Dream Weaver listened with great interest to their description, recognizing that the sawmill boded ill. The destruction of more woodland was inevitable. Houses and farms would proliferate. More roads would bisect the forest. Unnatural noise would disturb nature's harmony. Plenty Medicine sank into silence that deepened into a trance while the others expressed distress and consternation at this latest desecration of the earth. Only Dream Weaver noticed her mother begin to rock almost imperceptibly. Long after the others had retired to their pallets for the night, Plenty Medicine sat up, her back moving in a slow rhythm. Dream Weaver's eyes grew tired watching and wondering when Plenty Medicine would emerge from her trance. Finally, Dream Weaver crept to her mat and fell asleep.

With the incursions of the white men advancing closer to their mountain redoubt, the Salish tried not to wander too far from its safety. Horned Owl was less inclined to spy on the settlers. He knew plenty already. They were cutting roads into the wilderness season after season, threatening discovery of the band's presence in the northeast reaches of the territory.

"What is the use?" Horned Owl lamented. "Their settlement on the river grows. It is a hornet's nest. If we step too close, a thousand stinging insects will cover us. We must hide like the foxes in their dens."

"Can we find a safer hiding place in the sacred peaks around Big Chief Mountain?"

"The white men are there too, traveling from the ice fields of the north. They surround us."

"I do not want to be caught in a trap," Standing Rock said.

"Nor do I, but our only hope is to stay here and survive. We do not have to accept the ways of the white men even if they discover us. They cannot force us to live as they do, cutting and digging away at the bounty of the earth until there is nothing left but naked hills. We stand our ground. We stay here. Never will I abandon our home."

"Father, I also pledge to live and die here. So say I, *Šey hoy*."

"There is nothing more to say or do. We are immovable keepers of the earth."

But curiosity got the better of Standing Rock, and one day he came to his father and said, "It has been a long time since we scouted the valleys to the southwest. Do you not think it is wise to see what the white men are doing in the town by the river?'

"Aye, it is time we know what more they have done to the land. We will go," Horned Owl said.

It would be Horned Owl's last spying trip.

Before they reached the settlement, the smell reached their nostrils. Approaching the settlement from the east, they saw plumes of smoke rising from the town's center. Men scurried back and forth, hurling buckets of water at three burning buildings. Frantic shouts filled the air. Horned Owl and Standing Rock watched the white men fight the fire for hours from a promontory on the other side of the river. They managed to save the rest of town by tearing down a circle of buildings around where the fire blazed. In the end, the three main buildings were burned to the ground, stopping the fire from spreading. Even with this destruction, they judged that the town had quadrupled in size since their last visit. Horned Owl estimated that at least a thousand people now occupied it.

"We cannot rejoice at their misfortune, although they all deserve to be burned. The Great Spirit spared them, but he has not seen fit to spare us from their depredations," Horned Owl said.

"Fire is a purifier. Perhaps it will cleanse them of their evil spirits," Standing Rock offered.

"So I hope. I do not wish to lay eyes upon the paleface again. You shall spy in my place." Horned Owl clucked to his horse, and they left the smoke and ashes behind.

After Standing Rock had described the fire to Dream Weaver, she sat pensively for a while. He wondered if she felt pity for the white men's destructive fire. How had the fire started? By the hand of nature or a careless man? No lightning had struck recently. In fact, it had been a particularly wet spring.

"You are thinking too much. Why such a long face that their buildings burned?"

She responded, "It is not a twist of fate."

"No, it is not, but something the Great Spirit willed," Standing Rock agreed.

Dream Weaver refrained from sharing her thoughts further, but at the first opportunity, she approached her mother, Plenty Medicine, in private.

"I remember your nightlong trance when Horned Owl told us of the sawmill. Tell me, mother, did you pray for this fire?"

Plenty Medicine smiled. "I did not know my chants had the power to work." She knew she had been found out and did not deny the magic she had invoked. "Yes, I prayed for fire to cleanse them. It took a long time, but who knows if the cause was my incantations or happenstance."

"This is the first time you have used your power for harm," Dream Weaver said, disappointment in her tone.

"More harm has been done to our people and the earth," Plenty Medicine said. "From the ashes left in the path of fire, the earth is restored. Mushrooms spring up in the blackened earth. Saplings sprout at the feet of the torched trees, and deer come to nibble on new grass shoots. That is the vision I received in my trance."

Dream Weaver acknowledged in her mind the truth her mother spoke. She had seen fire sweep over the mountaintop in late summer and the next spring had seen flowers poking their heads from the scorched soil. Yet she had been taught to heal. If it took fire to heal the earth, perhaps her mother was right to chant her prayer for fire. She knew she wanted to follow in her mother's footsteps. She had imbibed her wisdom from childhood. From her, she had received all her knowledge of medicinal plants. She had learned to respect the visions delivered in dreams. In the region between wakefulness and sleep, the vivid dreams came, so that she must respect Plenty Medicine's explanation that she was not the direct agent of the fire. As far as the Salish knew, no people had perished in the fire. From Horned Owl's report, everyone had fled before the buildings became an inferno.

After her conversation with Plenty Medicine, Dream Weaver went to talk to Standing Rock.

"Do you think the fire purged greed from their hearts?" she asked him.

"No." He scrutinized her for a moment and said, "Ah, do you know of a medicine that can?"

"Not yet, but someday I will find the right combination of aromatic herbs and spices to accomplish that."

"If you do, it will wear off over time, and then the white man's heart will darken again."

Dream Weaver appreciated that she had inherited her mother's shamanic powers, and it seemed proper that she carry on the medicine woman's healing art. The creative feminine force of the woman shaman was sought after and valued. Her parents' generation would pass away as had her grandparents, and she would become the keeper of shamanic wisdom.

The seasons continued in their cycles, with the Salish ensconced in the bowl of the mountain, crafting items for their sustenance, using the resources nature provided, rejoicing at the colors of autumn, the intimacy of winters by the fire, and the harvest of berries in the spring and summer. Elk and deer still ranged in numbers sufficient to fulfill the clan's needs for clothing and hides for their teepees, but not nearly enough for the larger tribe from which they had broken away.

The hottest summer that the Salish could remember descended upon them. Streams slowed to a trickle. No freshening breeze blew from the west. Dry twigs snapped under the horses' hooves. Flowers budded, only to wither shortly on their stems. They welcomed the advent of night, bringing some relief from the heat of the day. Heads tilted upward more often to catch the movement of clouds or a tinge of gray in the sky's light blue.

Dream Weaver and Plenty Medicine called for a rain dance. Gourd rattles in hand and stone amulets around their necks, they led the line of dancers to summon the storm clouds. On wobbly legs now, Plenty Medicine circled around, her arms outspread, chanting behind Dream Weaver, while Song Dog and Bent Arrow beat a steady rhythm on drums. Song Bird was first to get up and join the two women. Even the old matron Laughing Water danced briefly before resuming her seat beside Horned Owl. The dancing continued long into the night with the members of the clan taking turns in the dancing. Plenty Medicine kept up the pace for a good while, but finally had to cede her place to Moonbeam and Spotted Dove, adding their voices to the rain song:

> *Thunder, thunder,*
> *Ground shakes, mountain quakes.*
> *Thunder, thunder,*
> *Beat the drum, the rains come*
> *Black cloud, black cloud breaks.*
> *Let the rain come, quench our thirst.*

A few days later, a sprinkle came and stopped as suddenly as it had begun, leaving not a dark cloud in its wake. The dome of the sky shone clear and bright. The hot weather stubbornly refused to abate. Consoled by the thought that the heat could not last forever, the Salish went about their daily tasks.

One morning Dream Weaver arose from her pallet to fetch water in a cedar-bark bucket from the creek. As she stepped out of the teepee, she sniffed the air. The odor of wood smoke reached her nostrils. Raising her eyes, she perceived flecks of ash, sparse though they were, floating lazily to the earth. The sky was perceptibly gray to the southwest. Most different, the doldrums of days without a breeze were gone. Instead, a strong wind from the northwest rippled the tassels on her buckskin dress and bent the boughs of the tallest pines. The whoosh of the wind through the treetops awakened Standing Rock, and he emerged from the teepee. Taking one whiff of the air, he turned to Dream Weaver and spoke.

"The forest is burning to the southwest."

"But there has been no thunder or lightning," Dream Weaver said.

"It must be the white man's doing, careless with his campfire. In this heat, the forest is a bundle of kindling ready for a small spark."

"Will the fire reach here?"

"It depends on how long the wind blows or whether the rain cloud opens. The flames dance where they may, and the sparks land hither and thither. The wind could kick the fire toward us. For now, we are safe."

Dream Weaver reflected that "for now, we are safe" were words she had heard too often from the men's mouths. In what did safety consist? Immunity from sorrow and danger? No one who walked the earth was, but she was determined to alleviate suffering wherever she encountered it. Avoidance of danger was another matter, and now a huge forest fire threatened like none other she had ever witnessed.

Neither rain came nor wind slackened for a week. Ashes were borne upon the wind from long distances where the fire raged. When would it burn itself out? Horned Owl and Standing Rock decided to scout southward to determine if there was danger of the fire reaching them. They rode out one morning, the smoke thicker in the air, the horses snorting at intervals.

With each day they traveled, the heavy odor of burned bark increased. They could taste wood resin on their lips. It nipped rather than stung while their eyes began to water, but they continued, wondering if the town where they had seen the chugging engine was still there. Nothing they imagined could burn down that iron horse. Maybe some powerful magic that Coyote concocted could do it, but nothing in their legends told of such an occurrence. Along their route that paralleled the mighty river, they encountered more animals than usual. Both large and small creatures were fleeing the conflagration. They spied moose fording the water. Rabbits, squirrels, foxes, and badgers skittered, trying to outrun the fire, and here they rode, two men, bound to discover how far the hot arms of the fire had penetrated the forest.

In time they came upon the town. Veiled in smoke until now, it had survived intact, but there was a flurry of activity. The people were hauling barrels of water. Wagons full of men equipped with shovels and pickaxes moved out of the town toward the southeast. Horned Owl decided to circle around the town, and at a safe distance, follow them. Less than an hour's ride away, they saw a few smoldering treetops. Sparks flying from the edge of the main fire had ignited them. Men leaped from the wagons and chopped down nearby trees in danger of catching fire from the burning trees. Propelled by the wind and the fury of the fire, the flying sparks threatened to engulf the town in flames too. As they watched the firefighters' frantic work, Horned Owl detected a perceptible change in the weather. He held up a hand and gauged the wind, perceiving a difference. The wind had shifted, its force diminished—a good sign that the threat to the town might be reduced.

Carefully, they rode on, flanking the area where the men worked to contain the blaze. The peculiar character of the forest fire left some patches of forest intact and other sections devastated where charred trunks remained among the blackened timber that littered the ground—a forest uprooted. Sadly, they rode on, examining the graveyard of trees interspersed with expanses of untouched woods. They steered their horses clear of the hot earth. Weary with the scorched scene, their lungs filled with smoke, their noses and mouths tingling with the feel of ashy flakes, they turned their mounts back in the direction in which they had come. They paused to let their horses drink from a creek as soon as they reached an area that had escaped the fire's advance. Through the smoky atmosphere, the sun appeared like a brilliant orange ball behind a screen of gray. The smoke hung so thickly that the outline of the mountaintops was barely visible.

"By nightfall, we should be well beyond the town. We will make camp at a safe distance to the northeast."

Two hours later, they rested beside the river after eating a meal of pemmican. Each man was enveloped in his personal ruminations. Although the odor of smoke clung to their hair and clothes, they had become somewhat acclimated to breathing the noxious fumes. Darkness had obscured the gray pallor that surrounded them. They sat in silence until Standing Rock suddenly exclaimed, "It is raining! I just felt drops on my arms."

Horned Owl opened his palms, waited a moment, and felt a few raindrops. "You are right. It is a gentle rain, but rain it is. Praise to the Great Spirit!"

"And the wind has completely died down," Standing Rock said.

The men rejoiced. Dream Weaver's rain dance had finally taken effect. They were safe for now.

Echoing Standing Rock's thought, Horned Owl rose to his feet and said, "We are safe. The people will give thanks."

The next morning, they rose, invigorated, happy to head home to their people.

But Standing Rock could not shake off the feeling that the white men were the source of this calamity. The settlers had brought with them not only the seeds for new plants but had planted the seeds of destruction. The land cried out for reparation, justice, and mercy. How long would the earth sustain the gouging, the digging, the cutting, the extraction of its resources, the killing of its buffalo herds, and leaving all creatures with not enough food to survive?

Song Dog and Moonbeam were past their twentieth summer. Both of marriageable age, the elders deemed it time for them to pair off with their intended mates. Although Bent Arrow and Spotted Dove were several years younger than Moonbeam and Song Dong, the difference in age was not considered an obstacle. They were old enough to produce offspring, and that was of utmost importance if the band were to survive unto the fifth generation. Laughing Water, now in her nineties, wished to see the couples married before she died. Indications were that she likely could live longer because all her faculties were as sharp as ever. Only her body had grown fragile, her back bowed, and her limbs stiff. The wrinkles on her face could not hide her habitual smile. But when Sitting Crow suddenly dropped to his feet as if an arrow had struck his heart, she stopped smiling to mourn his death for the required number of days. Then she put away her mourning and said, "It is the way of the world." His wife, Plenty Medicine, distributed his possessions to the young couples.

No special marriage ceremonies were performed. The couples began simply to live together. Smiles reappeared on Laughing Water's face as she waited nine moons in anticipation of the expected births. Her patience was rewarded, and Spotted Dove had a daughter, and Moonbeam delivered a boy. The future of the band seemed in healthy hands. The grandmother, Dream Weaver, hovered around the babies. She cradled them in her arms and cooed to them. The grandfather, Standing Rock, beamed proudly, delighted that his children had blessed him rapidly with grandchildren. The curse of infertility seemed to have been eradicated with the infusion of new blood that the adoption of Bent Arrow and Spotted Dove, despite their defects, had brought into the band. The great grandparents, Horned Owl and Song Bird, thought the future of the band had been secured. The fathers' scrutiny of the infants determined the names they would receive. For the present, they were Baby Boy and Baby Girl. When their little eyes opened to the world around them, what would their eyes first fix upon? Or when they grew older, would some important act mark them for a different name? Baby Boy could not take his eyes off his grandfather's band of owl feathers, so he was quickly called Little Owl. Baby Girl's little fingers seized upon the shell necklace around Plenty Medicine's neck. The chubby baby clutched it, gurgling as she refused to release the necklace. Her grandmother obliged her, removing it from her neck, and dangled it before the infant, letting her eyes follow its movement. From then on, she was called Plays-With-Shells.

Horned Owl and Standing Rock, now respectively the chief and sub-chief, communicated aloud the assurance "We are safe," but in their hearts they knew that they stood on shaky ground because they had heard the rumblings of the iron horses and the explosions when tunnels ripped through mountains in their path. They had heard the creak and groan of majestic pines being felled. They had heard the wagon wheels lumbering down roads cutting through the valleys. They had heard the lowing sheep and cattle that grazed where once numerous elk and deer had fed. They had seen the smoke rise from chimneys where white settlers had taken possession of their former hunting grounds. They had seen boats on the river, bigger than canoes, and people ferried across the river on flat boats. In all honesty, they did not think for a moment that they could enjoy complacency. That they had managed to stay hidden for more than years in their mountain redoubt bordered on miraculous. Only the sagacity and caution of their founding fathers—Running Wolf, Brave Bear, and Smoking Loon—had made their seclusion possible. Like wily animals that had learned to elude hunters, they had escaped detection, blending into their environment or scurrying into dens and burrows, out of sight of predators.

When the men went hunting, it became increasingly difficult to avoid contact with white men or the Kootenai. All were competing for land and resources. Horned Owl and Standing Rock ventured cautiously even into territory they had previously known was unoccupied. It was unpredictable when and where an outsider would penetrate what they considered their domain. Time, as it was measured in the cycle of the seasons, in the growth of children, or the aging of parents, passed. The babes were walking; the babes were talking. Little Owl and Plays-With-Shells were learning their parents' crafts; they were listening to the legends of their grandparents. At the feet of Horned Owl and Song Bird, they heard the history of their people and the story of their great-grandfathers leading them to Big Hole.

**Standing Rock**

Every so often, Horned Owl and Standing Rock patrolled the dusty road that traced the route the band had taken north when they emigrated from the Place of the Wide Cottonwoods. On a hot summer day, scouting along this road, hearing a new sound, they stopped their horses to listen. There was a vibrating, a clunking, and a thumping on the earth that they could not identify—neither a wagon nor the noisy vehicle that moved along the iron rails. The source of the sound appeared down the road, kicking up dust in its wake. It was a four-wheeled, covered contraption, pulled neither by horses nor riding on rails. Smoke puffed from its rear. They distinguished two passengers inside, a man in a bowl-shaped hat whose hands gripped a wheel, and a woman in a broad-brimmed hat from which draped a thin veil to cover her face. They watched the black wagon that ran on its own power rattle past their secluded observation point and marveled again at the seemingly unbounded diabolical genius of the white man.

"It will not end," Horned Owl sighed. "I am tired."

Standing Rock turned his worried eyes to his father. Was he surrendering spiritually to the onslaught of the white man? Had he had enough of this world? No, it could not be. His father was strong; his courage was unstoppable.

"Father, we have to hold fast to the land and not let the monsters they create scare us."

"No, I do not mean I am defeated. I mean I am weary and rely on you to struggle on and keep our traditions."

"You know that I will, Father."

"I trust you to preserve that knowledge."

Despite Standing Rock's outward bravura, doubt gnawed at his belief that he could elude the burgeoning settlements of white men. They gobbled up land, and they crawled over mountains like voracious ants on hills. He could not grasp from where their lust to transform the land into fields, roads, and buildings sprang. They were men like the Salish; they walked and talked, ate, slept, procreated, and raised families the same way. Why did they always take more than they needed? Why did they lay waste the land—tree stumps everywhere? They created all kinds of devices to aid them in their destruction. This wagon that moved without horses to pull it was just another instance of their evil genius. It scared away animals in its path. It needed room to run, so it was necessary to cut down more trees and tunnel through more hills. It made the air stink wherever it went. Oh, Great Spirit! Why have you not freed us from this scourge?

Standing Rock knew he could not succumb to despair. He had misgivings about his ability to avoid contact with the intruder, but his duty was to safeguard his people who depended upon his and Horned Owl's strength. If they weakened in their determination to endure, the clan would lose heart. Standing Rock inhaled a deep breath, straightened his back, and nudged his horse forward. The two men rode in silence back to Big Hole.

Laughing Water hobbled to give them a cheerful greeting as they reached the cluster of teepees. Little Owl and Plays-With-Shells scampered toward the men and quickly bombarded them with questions about their trip. Bent Arrow and Song Dog approached to tend to the horses. Later, when all the clan members sat gathered in a circle around the two men, they recounted what they had seen. The women shook their heads in distress, knowing that what the men saw portended more vehicles of that type to come. The children marveled at the description, fearless in their eagerness to hear about such a wonder. Standing Rock studied the glowing faces of the young ones, and disquiet filled him for what the future held for them in a world changing faster than he could grasp.

"Next, the white men will invent something that will fly in the air," Laughing Water chortled. "I put nothing past them."

"It is not funny," Plenty Medicine said. "Their magic is harmful. They do not practice good medicine."

"Ah, but you know," Laughing Water counseled benevolently, "Coyote gets caught eventually in his own trap. They will go too far."

"Meanwhile, what are we supposed to do? Let it happen?" Plenty Medicine retorted.

Crinkles deepened around her eyes as Laughing Water responded, "Sometimes doing nothing is the best thing. Who can beat the wind to stop blowing? It will blow until it blows itself out."

With that, no one said anything, but pondered her words to themselves. They recognized the old woman's years endowed her with wisdom that they must heed even if they did not comprehend it.

Dream Weaver considered Laughing Water's words longest, mulling them over as she fell asleep that night. From her mother Plenty Medicine, she had learned to make potions from various plants, but laughter was a medicine that also had a calming effect. Its healing power she had learned at Laughing Water's knees. Dream Weaver desired to use the healing arts to benefit every man. She thought there must be some medicine that could heal the poison in the white man's soul. From her perspective, there was something misshapen in his spirit that caused him to wreak destruction on the land and his fellow man.

Only three members of the band remained who could remember seeing the buffalo. As very young children, Horned Owl and Plenty Medicine had accompanied their parents on a hunt to the eastern plains, but their memories of the mighty beast were vague. As a grown woman, Laughing Water had joined the hunt many times to butcher the carcasses and tan the hides. Now she felt it was her duty to teach Little Owl and Plays-With-Shells about the days when life centered around the buffalo and using every part of the animal. The teepees were now all made of deer and elk hides, the original buffalo-hide teepees having long since deteriorated as protective covering. Some objects made from the buffalo remained. The buffalo headpiece was a treasured possession. Laughing Water placed it on her head and showed how the buffalo, its horns pointed toward them, would stampede, imitating its thundering sound.

"I will go to the plains and see a buffalo," Little Owl said, his eyes wide with wonder.

"Before I left my birthplace, they were getting harder to find," Laughing Water said. "Who knows if any remain?"

"Where would they go?"

"The white men traded us the things they had made in exchange for buffalo hides. The people wanted pots and pans, beads and colored cloth, axes and knives, fire sticks and bullets . . . all kinds of goods to kill the buffalo. They did not eat the meat; they did not save the tongue, bladder, sinew, or bones."

Little Owl's narrowed his eyes and curled his lip in disapproval. "I do not think I would trade with the white men."

"Ah, but the people could not resist the usefulness of the white men's things. They made better tools."

"Then why did you leave your people?"

"We knew we had traded more than buffalo hides. We traded our language and our customs to them. They wanted to make us farmers. The Black Robes told us that their god who was nailed to a cross would give us eternal life. Some of our people believed that the white men possessed powerful medicine so our enemies could not kill us. They listened to the Black Robes and let them sprinkle them with their holy water, but Running Wolf and I did not. We heard the spirits of the dead whisper in the trees because spirits cannot die. To stay in our ancestral land meant we could no longer be Salish, and we would not change our ways."

Little Owl seemed to understand and accepted his great-great grandmother's explanation. She was so brown, wrinkled, and dry like a walnut. She appeared as ancient as trees in the old-growth forest, her skin as rugged and lined like bark. How could she have lived so long? She must be a hundred winters old. He begged her to tell him more about the old days and the land where she was born. Laughing Water chuckled and obliged, filling his ears with the difficult but idyllic days before a white man set foot in their lush valley far to the south.

"When I am a man, I want to see the Place of the Wide Cottonwoods."

"Ah, what will the world be like when you are a grown man," Laughing Water mused. "If you go there, my spirit will walk with you," she smiled benevolently and then said. "That is enough talking for today. I must rest." She waved away Little Owl and Plays-With-Shells. The little girl had listened in awe the entire time, absorbing the tales Laughing Water told. She was a quiet, demure child with ears keen to comprehend but with lips closed to express what her active mind was thinking. Laughing Water recognized her character. She was a stargazer and a muser, one who thought more than she spoke. In the old woman's estimation, those were valuable traits, and she did not prod the child to speak. Both children would grow according to their natural bents.

The clatter of horseless carts and lumberjacks' boisterous voices resounded frequently. Explosions rocked the mountainsides, leaving rubble and gaping holes. Logs floated on the rivers directed by men on rafts steering them downstream and breaking up logjams, relentlessly moving them to the sawmill where they were cut into planks. In winter, large sledges pulled by heavy horses, bigger in body than the sleek Salish horses, transported the logs through the snow. All this Standing Rock observed, sometimes with Horned Owl and sometimes alone. When Horned Owl's back ached from a fall from his horse that had lost its footing on a steep descent down rocky terrain, he chose to stay at Big Hole. After years of spying on the activities of the white man, a pall seemed to have fallen over Horned Owl's spirit. He often preferred to ponder and sit alone, avoiding the company even of Song Bird. She realized the future of the band weighed on his mind. The advance of white settlement deepened his sense of impending ruin. She tried to sing songs to ease his worry. He smiled wanly and thanked her for her effort and then sank into thought again. Only Little Owl cheered him. How could he languish in sad contemplation when the boy thrived in front of his eyes, reveling in the discovery of nature all around him? Horned Owl looked at the child and wondered how many more seasons of freedom from encroachment the band would have. The game was getting scarce, and they had to venture farther from Big Hole to track sufficient deer and elk to supply their needs for food, shelter, and clothing. The streams were unsafe; there was no predicting when a boat filled with white men could surprise them while they checked their fishing traps.

Standing Rock encouraged his father to come with him, but he respected his mood if he wished to stay behind and was happy for the infrequent times when Horned Owl agreed to go along on a spying trip. They were still shadows slithering between the trees, hiding behind boulders, and scanning the landscape from high cliffs. Skilled at evasion, they had managed to elude detection for decades. The vast wilderness had facilitated their movement like phantoms. The risk of encounter became greater with the ever-expanding population. Standing Rock knew he had to exercise proportionately greater care.

In late summer, Standing Rock and Horned Owl surveyed the area a little to the east of the burgeoning town that the forest fire had almost consumed several seasons ago. They came upon one of the first ranches that had been established in the region. Haystacks were aligned in two long rows in a spacious pasture. A pitchfork stood idle, poked in one haystack. The barn door was wide open, and a man in buckskin and wearing a black top hat with a feather stuck in the band emerged leading a chestnut horse, saddled and ready to ride. Standing Rock guessed that the swarthy man was a half-breed. Curious, he crept closer to the farm buildings. The man was about to mount the horse when a little girl of about five winters ran crying from the ranch house. The man shouted at the child first in the white man's language and then uttered a command in Salish to go back to her mother. His curiosity aroused even more, Standing Rock could not repress his urge to know who this man was, what caused the child's distress, and why the half-breed ordered the child away. The half-breed nudged his horse in the direction where Standing Rock lurked. As the horse and rider passed the underbrush where he crouched, Standing Rock leaped from the bushes and grabbed the half-breed's leg, pulling him off the horse, shouting at him to halt.

Astounded to hear Salish spoken, the half-breed staggered to his feet and confronted his assailant.

"That is no way to greet a brother," he grinned in an ingratiating manner. Clearly, he did not desire a fight, although Standing Rock spied a knife strapped to his side. He yanked the knife from its sheath and held it to the half-breed's throat.

"Tell me what you are doing here," he demanded. "Stealing horses?"

"No, I am no thief. The horse belongs to me. I worked for the rancher."

"Then why are you fleeing? Why do you abandon that crying child?"

"She is sick. Her mother is dead or dying of the plague. She is contaminated. I saw the two dark spots start on the girl's cheeks. She coughs and her nose runs. Do not go near them, or you will sicken too."

"And you think you are not infected already?" Standing Rock scornfully asked. "You fool, go on your way. The sight of you sickens me. No brave would leave that child alone."

The child still stood wailing in front of the ranch house. Between her sobs, she called after the man.

Horned Owl had silently watched Standing Rock's impetuous encounter. "Do not be hasty, my son. We need that man to translate." Turning to the half-breed, he said, "Lead us back to the house and tell us what the little girl says."

"I am not going back into that house of the dead," he retorted.

"Tie his hands behind his back."

Standing Rock and Horned Owl quickly overpowered the half-breed and shoved him to the ground face down. Subdued, he thought it wiser not to put up a struggle, and bawled, "All right. I will go with you, but do not tie me up. After I do what you want, let me leave this place."

They pulled him to his feet, and with Standing Rock and Horned Owl each firmly gripping an arm, the three men walked back to the house. The terror on the little girl's face relaxed when she saw them approach, and she stopped crying.

Standing Rock poked the man's back, indicating to him that he should enter the house, and the little girl trailed after them. Three steps led to a covered porch that stretched the length of the clapboard house with a peaked roof of shake shingles. They entered a cozy room spacious enough to hold a kitchen area with trestle table and a wood stove. Placed next to the stove was a box of kindling, and on top of one burner sat a black, cast-iron kettle. Enamel crockery occupied a shelf, and checkered white and red curtains adorned windows on three walls. A rocking chair was set by the fireplace at the center of the living space. To one side of the hearth, a ladder led to a bedroom loft. An oval braided rug covered the plank floor. Against the wall opposite to the kitchen was a bed with a metal frame on which a woman lay under a patchwork quilt. The little girl ran to the bed, flung her body across the woman's breast, and exclaimed, "Mama, Mama, get well," which words the half-breed had to translate. He went on to explain what had transpired on the ranch in the last few weeks.

"She and the girl are the last of the family to remain. The father and older son were the first to fall ill shortly after they returned from a trip to town to buy supplies. Disease had swept through the town, and the doctors were all busy. I could not get one to come to the ranch, so the father and son steadily got worse with chills and fever. They died five days ago, and I buried them. The woman was still up and about, doing the best she could with the work around the farm, but it was too much for her. She took to her bed with coughing and vomiting. I saw that she and the child were doomed and that there was nothing I could do. I wore my medicine bundle around my neck and luckily did not sicken. I cannot count on my luck anymore. I knew I had to get out of here—and fast. I advise you to do the same before you take the evil with you back to your village."

Standing Rock looked with disgust at the man. "I would have you gone from my sight now, coward, except that I need you to translate."

The half-breed was all too willing to oblige and scurried to the open door, but Horned Owl restrained him. "Stay—or I bind your hands and hobble your feet." The knife that menaced the half-breed's throat left no doubt that Horned Owl would make good his threat instantly, for the coward he truly was perceived that two against one was no match he was willing to test. Horned Owl shoved him down into the rocking chair.

Horned Owl approached the bed to determine if the woman was alive or just sleeping. The girl had slipped to the floor and was seated by the bed, her hands steepled together in the manner he remembered from long ago when, as a boy, he had seen the Black Robe pray. He placed his hand over the woman's mouth and felt her labored breathing. Her eyes were closed, but she moaned and sometimes stirred with a hacking cough. Sweat poured from her forehead. Her long blond hair lay in tangled strands against the pillow. She was neither very young nor very old, not yet in her middle years. If her face had not been discolored in a grayish-blue tinge, she would have been considered pretty, for her features were delicate and fine. Afraid that his appearance might frighten her if she should suddenly summon the energy to open her eyelids, he moved away from the bed.

"She lives, but I fear not for long. Maybe the little girl can be saved. How, I do not know. This looks different from the disease that plagued our people," Horned Owl murmured.

"I know of only one who may have the power to save the girl," Standing Rock said.

"Who?'

"Father, you must fetch Dream Weaver here. She will know what to do. She will know what songs to sing and what medicine to give."

"When the white man's sickness struck in the past, not even our greatest shamans could stop the curse. What makes you think she is any different?'

"She is my wife. I have felt her power. Evil flees from her presence."

"That is great faith to place in a mere woman."

"Female power will save us. It gave us life; mothers nurture and preserve life. What is needed is the feminine spirit."

Horned Owl considered his son's words. He did not feel any animosity toward these two white females. They were alone and vulnerable and had not injured them. Rather, he felt pity for their helplessness. Desire to wreak vengeance upon them for the manifold crimes their race had committed did not occur to him. He only sensed their common humanity and felt universal sorrow at mankind's susceptibility to disease and unwelcome death.

"I will go get Dream Weaver," Horned Owl agreed.

"While you are gone, I will keep watch here," Standing Rock said.

"May I leave now?" The half-breed rose from the chair.

"Wait. Not yet," Standing Rock commanded. "I have more need of you. You must assure the woman when she wakes, that I mean no harm, and my father has gone to bring a medicine woman. It is no good for you to run away. You have breathed the same air the sick ones have breathed in and out. It is the Great Spirit's will now if you stay well or sicken. Understand that I am not your enemy. I am your brother."

All menace was gone from Standing Rock's voice. His calm tone served to allay the half-breed's fear. It was true that he had already been exposed to the disease and that he could do nothing to prevent his also coming down with the same illness whether he stayed or fled.

"All right. I will stay until the medicine woman arrives."

"Good. Let us sit together and talk. You can tell me how you came to live with the white man."

Horned Owl did not wait to hear the story. He was already out the door. He whistled for his horse, mounted up, and started back to Big Hole.

Curious, the little girl eyed the two men who now sat face-to-face, cross-legged on the braided rug. Her wondering glance passed from man to man as they spoke in their strange guttural language back and forth. Intrigued, she watched them from where she sat at the side of her mother's bed.

Standing Rock learned that the half-breed's name was Angus Campbell. His father, Duncan Campbell, was the son of a Scottish trapper who had married a Salish woman of the Kalispell band. His Salish grandmother had raised him after both his parents died of consumption, another white man's disease. He left the reservation to work on a white man's cattle ranch when he was thirteen. He drifted across the mountains, finding jobs at different ranches and spent time panning for gold in Alaska before returning to the Kootenai River country. He knew of the old chiefs who moved to the reservation south of the Broad Water. He knew of the people who had accepted the Black Robes' religion. His grandmother was one of those who tried to teach him, but he was a vagabond, not accepting anyone's rules. He wanted to go his own way. He was neither this nor that and was open to learning how his father's people lived and worked, so he circulated in the white man's world and stayed there, never marrying, never having a family.

"You might say I am a loner, a lone wolf," he told Standing Rock, who nodded, understanding what Angus Campbell meant.

Angus continued, "I wanted to be free, which was not hard for me to do because I was not this or that."

"It is important to know who you are and where you come from," Standing Rock said.

"Important, too, is knowing where you are going, and that is something I have never learned," Angus said sadly.

"The land knows your name," Standing Rock said.

A confused look rose on Angus's face, not understanding what Standing Rock meant. He stared at his companion and said in a subdued tone, "You are lucky you know who you are."

"Aye, I do."

The little girl started to cough uncontrollably. Angus rose and went to the kitchen cupboard where he retrieved a jar and a spoon. "This is what her mother gives her to stop the hacking cough. It is honey." He spooned the syrupy substance into the girl's mouth between coughs.

Standing Rock felt her forehead, "She is burning with fever. Where is her bed?"

Angus pointed to the loft, whereupon Standing Rock lifted the child into his arms and climbed the ladder to the loft. He flipped the woolen blanket aside, while holding the child with his other arm, and gently laid her on the bed and covered her. The little girl whimpered and weakly repeated the words, "Mama, Mama," gradually fading, until weariness overcame her, and she fell silent.

Standing Rock descended the stairs and asked Angus what she meant by mama.

"She wants her mother," Angus replied.

Mention of the mother turned Standing Rock's attention to the woman in bed. He walked over to see how she was doing, hoping she had not expired and would survive until Dreamer Weaver arrived. He leaned over and saw that she still sweated. Now blood dripped from her nose. He looked around for a rag or wet cloth to wipe her forehead and nose. His eyes darted around the room, and noticing the curtains, he ripped a piece of cloth from a curtain. Angus watched his actions in silence, not rising to assist because he considered the woman doomed. While Standing Rock ministered to the woman, she moaned but did not rouse from her lethargy. Near delirium, she did not care whose hand tended her.

"Water," she finally murmured.

Hearing her, Angus stood up and walked to the kitchen sink, where he pumped water into a tin cup. He took the cup to Standing Rock, who bent down, propped the woman's head, and placed the cup to her lips. She took a few sips, her eyes opening into slits, but apparently not taking in the imposing native man who held it to her mouth.

Finished, she sank her head back on the pillow and murmured, "Thank you."

"Ah, she is aware of kindness," Angus said as he took the cup from Standing Rock's hands.

When they resumed their seats on the braided rug, Standing Rock said, "Tell me of this woman and child."

"The woman is Sarah McDonald. Her daughter is Abigail. As I told you, the husband and the older boy died. The man treated me well. I slept in the barn but ate my meals with the family. He wanted to get rich digging for gold, but that did not work out, so he sent for a wife from the east who traveled here on the railroad—"

"Railroad?" Standing Rock interrupted.

"The wagon that runs on the iron track. You must have heard the trains."

Standing Rock nodded in understanding. "The iron horses."

"Yes. Caleb, the husband, worked at the sawmill for a while. I met him at the mill. He bought his parcel of land to raise dairy cows and said he needed a farmhand and that I could work for him. He carted the milk to town, and that is why he picked up the disease. He was not that healthy because he had a lot of dust in his lungs from working in mines and at the mill. There was another son, the oldest one, who went to fight in a faraway place across the eastern ocean. A lot of young men signed up to go. Caleb did not want his oldest son to go because he needed him on the ranch. He had bought more land and wanted to build a bigger house. But Jack wanted to fight so bad that he did not listen to his father. He was killed in the first battle. I was here when the telegram was delivered to the house. Caleb crumpled the paper up and went back to work. He never forgave his son for disobeying him and going off to war anyhow. The younger lad, Frank, sought the father's favor and did everything he wanted him to do. Like I said, I buried them side by side. I cried when they died. Caleb was a good man but was hard on his oldest son."

The friendship grew between Angus and Standing Rock during the days they waited for Horned Owl to return with Dream Weaver. From Angus, Standing Rock learned many new things about the white man's world. Angus explained the innovations that white men had brought, giving him the names of their inventions. Standing Rock described the horseless wagons that he had seen puffing down the roads that had been cut through the mountain passes.

"Caleb was planning to buy one of those cars. A shipment was expected to arrive on the railroad from Mr. Ford's factory. The town's business men had all put in orders for a Model-T—that is what they call them. Already the richest men in town owned one, and they are parked along the main street in front of the stores. Some are trucks, that is, with room to haul supplies, lumber, boxes, and crates of all kinds of goods."

In the process of telling Standing Rock about the white world, Standing Rock also was learning words in their language. Angus had Standing Rock repeat the words until he could pronounce them well enough to be understood.

"What you describe is all well and good, but I am not sure it is good for my people," Standing Rock said. "For several generations, we have dwelled apart because we did not want to become like the *suyapi*—that is what my people call the white men. How do you stand their greed?"

"I stand apart, neither this nor that. I see their greed, but I do not become greedy. Because the things they have invented are good and make life easier, I work but not as hard as I would have to without their tools."

Sarah was seized with a bout of coughing so prolonged and grating that they thought she was choking. They hovered over her face that contorted with every cough. Her coughing stopped abruptly; she gasped for breath and heaved a sigh.

"She lives," Standing Rock said and started to wipe the phlegm that had issued from her mouth. He soothed her forehead with a cloth, and whispered to himself, "Dream Weaver, come quickly." Turning to Angus, he said, "Get her some syrup."

Angus brought the jar and gave her a spoonful of honey. Gratitude flickered momentarily in her eyes rimmed in a ghostly gray, and then she rasped, "Abby, where is Abby?"

Angus answered, "In bed . . .upstairs."

"See to Abby. See to Abby. Do not let her die."

"No, no, Sarah, we are taking care of her."

Listening to Angus's exchange with Abby, Standing Rock deduced the mother's anxiety for her daughter dwarfed any concern for herself. Realizing that they had heard no sound from upstairs for some time, both men now peered up at the bedroom loft, fear gripping their hearts. Standing Rock was the first to climb the ladder to check on the little girl. He found her sleeping, one cheek against the pillow, the other cheek exposed to view was grayish-blue, but she breathed. He tiptoed to the ladder and joined Angus, who sat in the rocking chair, gazing somberly at the bedridden woman across the room.

"We're all going to get sick here," he said. "Unless this medicine woman of yours has some powerful medicine, we're all going to die."

Standing Rock did not respond. If Angus wanted to sit under a black cloud and think the worst, Standing Rock could not cure his pessimism. As for himself, he chose hope instead of despair. He believed in life even after death. Dream Weaver would arrive in time. Dream Weaver knew what to do.

She arrived the next morning with Horned Owl, who anxiously entered the house, his face brightening when he saw that everyone still lived. His son and the half-breed stood robustly on two feet, no sign of illness in their faces that exuded only joy to see Dream Weaver and him. Although the little girl and her mother lay in bed, they still breathed. Dream Weaver got to work immediately, opened her pouch, and set out her medicinal plants and herbs. She first burned cedar leaves and smudged around the woman from her head to her foot, chanting a healing song. Sarah remained listless and lethargic all the while, even though she was awake. The sweet aroma soon filled the small house. Dream Weaver repeated the smudging ceremony in the girl's loft. Abby glanced up, pleased with the scent, and smiled at Dream Weaver, whose placid expression and benevolent dark brown eyes dispelled her fears. To the child, an angelic aura surrounded the medicine woman. Abby watched the cedar smudge that circled from her head to foot. Dream Weaver's chant and dance that accompanied the smudging fascinated her. Horned Owl, Standing Rock, and Angus observed the ceremony, hoping that Abby's reactions presaged the beginning of her recovery.

After the smudging, Dream Weaver prepared a wild rose tea and administered the drink to Sarah. She sipped the tea and grew more alert, her weak smile reflecting gratitude for Dream Weaver's ministrations. She drew sufficient strength to utter, "You are an Indian. Why should you care for me?"

Angus translated the words for Dream Weaver, who smiled benignly and said to him, "Tell her I care for all creatures."

In the following days, she administered other healing brews—teas made from sweet grass and crushed aster roots, everything that would soothe sore throats and relieve hacking coughs. Amazingly, Abby and Sarah improved a little bit more every day. After weeks of suffering, they cautiously got out of bed and took tentative steps around the house, gazing out the window and asking about the cows and hens. Angus assured them that he had tended well to the animals, he had milked the cows, and gathered the eggs from the hen house. They accepted the presence of the three Salish in their household and developed a particular attachment to Dream Weaver. Awed by her curative powers and serene demeanor, they treated her with infinite respect. As they recovered, Sarah and Abby regained their appetites. Dream Weaver wished to linger to make sure they had fully recuperated. They resumed their household tasks and joined with Angus in teaching the Salish more English vocabulary.

The happiness that the Salish and Angus shared at Abby's and Sarah's restoration to health was shattered a few days later when Horned Owl started coughing and vomited. They placed him in Abby's bed, and Dream Weaver performed her healing arts. Unfortunately, the course of Horned Owl's illness was rapid. The next morning, they found him lifeless, the breath all escaped from his body. A peaceful expression covered his dead face. Sorrowfully, they conducted the funeral rites and buried him in a stand of pines at a distance from the house.

Standing Rock was devastated and brooded inconsolably after the burial. How could a strong tree like his father be leveled in one fell swoop? Who would be cut down next? Dream Weaver came to sit beside him and comforted him, saying, "My husband, stir yourself to do what must be done. You must hold a sweat lodge to purify body and soul. In that way, everything will be made clear and clean again. The foul air must be dispelled. This must be done before we leave this place. It will be good for the white woman and her daughter too. So stand up and gather the rocks."

He looked at Dream Weaver and immediately understood she spoke truly. The sweat would clear his mind and soul. Work began to construct the sweat lodge. Standing Rock heaped smooth rocks into the pit that Angus had dug a short distance in front of the lodge entrance. Around this pit, he stacked wood in the shape of a teepee. The rocks would be heated in this pit and then carried into the lodge. Standing Rock selected twelve large rocks almost the size of a man's head, each representing a grandfather. Dream Weaver built a dome-shaped hut framed with bent saplings and covered with skins and blankets she found in the ranch house. Closed with a flap, the low entrance faced east to welcome the sunrise. In the center of the lodge, she dug another pit to receive the heated rocks. Dream Weaver brought cedar and sage into the lodge to be used as smudges. She placed a pot of water inside. When everything was ready and the rocks were hot on the sacred fire directly outside the lodge, the ceremony was ready to begin. Stooping, they entered the lodge. Standing Rock, Angus, Dream Weaver, and Sarah took places, sitting cross-legged around the pit with Standing Rock facing the entrance. Abby was considered too young for the ceremony. The participants were lightly but modestly clad. The men wore only breechcloths, and the women light cotton shifts. They sat around the firepit while Dreamweaver smudged them with cedar and sage. After opening prayers, Angus brought in three hot rocks from the outside fire and placed them in the pit. The flap of the lodge was closed, leaving them in darkness. Dream Weaver splashed water on the rocks, and steam hissed forth from the rocks. She sprinkled sage and sweet grass on the rocks and intoned prayers to the spirits of the three grandfathers. Each participant said a round of prayers. Dream Weaver then directed Angus to retrieve three more grandfather rocks for second round of the ceremony. Water was again sprinkled on the rocks, releasing more steam into the darkened interior, and the heat intensified. Correspondingly, perspiration trickled down the sides of their faces. Each person in turn recited prayers and chants, invoking the spirits of their grandfathers who lived in the rocks. In similar fashion, they huddled in the womb of their grandmother, symbolized by the dark interior of the dome-shaped sweat lodge where they connected with their beginnings in the earth. By sweating out all impurities, they could be reborn and renewed. Four rounds were repeated, the entire ceremony lasting several hours. One by one, they emerged from the sweat lodge. Night had fallen; the evening star was visible in the sky. Standing Rock was the last to step out of the sweat lodge. He straightened his back, stood erect, and raised his arms to the sky.

"I had a vision," he said. He lowered his arms and walked toward the others who stood in a circle around the sacred fire, letting the experience of the sweat lodge permeate their consciousness, awash in a universal feeling of well-being and union with the creative force.

An aura of serenity surrounded the tall figure, barechested, his moist skin glistened in the light cast from the teepee-shaped fire. He began, "In my vision, four men clad only in loincloths appeared—one white, one red, one black, and one yellow. They joined hands in a circle and danced around a cedar sapling. As they chanted in praise of the Great Spirit, the tree grew taller, and its branches extended outward. It grew so tall that its crown scraped a cloud. The men continued to dance and sing. The sun shone brightly, and birds sang from every branch. Then feathers began to rain down upon the dancers. They looked up at the falling feathers, and each man caught one." Standing Rock paused to let them picture the vision in their own minds.

After a few moments of silence, he continued in a solemn voice. "Separation of the races is no longer possible. All must live in peace together or all die together. The earth rises to preserve all its creatures and provides sustenance for all. The Great Spirit tells us to love the earth; she is our mother and loves us. If men hurt the earth, she will rise someday to devour them by flood, fire, and wind. Listen to me."

They pondered his words and offered no thoughts of their own, realizing that Standing Rock's vision contained a powerful message meant to have an impact on their lives.

Dream Weaver, reluctant to present her personal reaction, posed the question that was on everyone's mind.

"What, then, does your vision mean for our people?"

"It means we must return to the land of our grandfathers, our ancestral home, and live in brotherhood. The grandfathers have spoken."

Sarah, of course, understood not a word of this exchange but watched respectfully while Standing Rock and Dream Weaver spoke. Abby had been instructed to stay in the house during the four-hour ceremony. She had run gleefully out of the house when she saw the four adults emerge from the sweat lodge and now happily clung to her mother's skirt.

"I am hungry, Mama. Can we eat supper now?"

Sarah smiled down at Abby. "Certainly. Come everyone . . . into the house, and I will cook us a good meal."

During supper, Angus explained to Sarah that Standing Rock and Dream Weaver would leave at first light the next morning. She expressed regret at their departure but thanked them profusely for healing them. Angus related to her Standing Rock's vision, which moved her to tears. After they finished eating, Sarah went to the sink to wash the dishes. Dream Weaver helped her dry and stack the plates and cups.

Standing Rock and Angus remained at the table, engaged in a private conversation. The men had developed a friendship that Standing Rock would miss if they had to separate.

He asked Angus, "Will you journey with us? I take you as my brother into our tribe. Accept your mother's people as the blood that runs thickest and truest in your body and soul."

"Ah, I do feel it strongly after the sweat lodge. There is a closeness to my mother I have not felt as keenly before. But I am not white or red. I am mixed."

"You are a bridge then. You speak for white men and red men. You will be a valuable member of our tribe from whom we can learn much and grow to live together in harmony."

"That is true," he agreed.

"You have not answered my question. I invite you to come and live with us. Will you?"

Angus fixed a steady, friendly gaze at Standing Rock, "That would be an honor, but I cannot."

"Why?"

"The woman and child need me. I wanted to flee my duty as a man to help the widow and orphan. They have no one except me now. You have Dream Weaver, your children, and grandchildren."

A mischievous grin spread on Standing Rock's face. "Ho, I understand." He chuckled. "You fancy Sarah. I think she has captured and tied your heart."

Angus did not deny Standing Rock's assertion. "Aye, she has roped me. I will stay here."

Standing Rock accepted his decision and abandoned any idea to persuade him any differently. The sweat lodge had clarified purposes for him as well as for Angus. They had separate journeys but were united in determination to live in love within the family of man.

In the morning, fond farewells were said. Sarah and Dream Weaver embraced, while Standing Rock and Angus hooked opposite elbows together and lightly slapped each other on the shoulder. Dream Weaver bent to pick up Abby and hugged her. She set her on the ground and placed a thong around her neck on which a small leather pouch hung. She spoke a few Salish words to Abby, who fondled the pouch, wondering if it contained anything. She opened the bag and drew out a bluebird's feather. Her eyes lit up with delight as she oozed "ohs" of pleasure at the gift.

Angus stooped to her height and gently explained, "This is where you put all your treasures. It is a medicine bag. Here you put special things you find in nature."

Dream Weaver and Standing Rock turned to mount their horses. Astraddle their horses, they bid farewell and waved goodbye to Angus, Sarah, and Abby. Heading northeast, they followed the river to retrace their route back to Big Hole. After a three-day journey, they would reunite with their family. Standing Rock had no compunction about the length of their stay because he had felt a compulsion to aid the helpless. His sojourn there seemed to demarcate a turning point, if not a guidepost for the future. With the death of Horned Owl, their band had been reduced from twelve to eleven. So many countless years ago, their grandfather, Running Wolf, had led them into the mountain bowl. Standing Rock had to be the sad bearer of the news that their chief had passed into the spirit world. On his shoulders now rode responsibility for the four men and six women, one of whom was the ancient grandmother, Laughing Water. He was the chief of these ten people and must relay to them his vision that dominated his thoughts as he rode uphill and downhill, on trails through dense conifer forests and across streams.

Bent Arrow spotted the two riders as they descended the winding path to the camp. The entire band ran to greet the travelers. The younger members met them first—Song Dog and his wife Spotted Dove along with Bent Arrow and Moonbeam, now in their forties. Little Owl and Plays-With Shells, both age twenty, followed closely behind them. Song Bird, Horned Owl's widow, in her sixties, came up next and stopped short in her tracks, immediately alarmed at his absence. And last, the elderly women hobbled forward—eighty-year-old Plenty Medicine followed by the centenarian, Laughing Water, supported by a walking stick.

The group bombarded them with questions—one voice drowning out another in a tumult of curiosity and anxiety about the outcome of Dream Weaver's mission. Standing Rock dismounted and dispatched Song Dog to tend to the horses. He cut a path through the clamor toward his teepee with Dream Weaver behind him. Before entering the teepee, he turned to his people.

"I will refresh myself first and then call a council and tell you everything." The clamor for information subsided. Song Bird stooped to enter the teepee, intent on immediately obtaining the information that she had an indisputable right to receive first. Where was her husband? Would he arrive shortly behind them? Did he have to linger in the white man's house?

Dream Weaver ladled water from a cedar bucket, and Standing Rock drank several swallows. Then Dream Weaver took a drink. From a storage pouch, she drew some jerky, and they each ate a piece. All the while, Song Bird waited patiently. When she saw that Standing Rock had finished and was ready to talk, she looked at him expectantly, not needing to ask the question uppermost in her mind—where was Horned Owl?

"My mother, you want to know where he is. Your heart must tell you his spirit is here, but his body has returned to his mother, the earth."

Standing Rock was astonished that Song Bird did not instantly break into wailing but took the news calmly, not shedding a tear. He felt an urge to ask her why she did not cry and stared uncomprehendingly at her. Clear-eyed, she returned his gaze and said, "Several days ago, a vision came to me. A knife stabbed my heart. There was no blood, but I knew in that instant Horned Owl had flown. I looked up and saw the great gray owl rise from a tree stump and soar higher than it is possible for an owl to fly. His eyes were wide and golden, its wingspan enormous. It screeched and disappeared in the treetops. That was my vision. It was true. I feared he was in danger when he came for Dream Weaver. I did not like that he went near foul disease. I have never thought any good could come from being close to white men. I have already grieved. I have no more tears to shed."

Her voice grew faint as her words ended. Standing Rock felt he had to fill in the blanks.

"He caught the plague, and it killed him more rapidly than a snake strikes."

What would his mother think when he told his own vision? How would the rest of the band receive his interpretation of the vision? It weighed upon his mind to tell them everything that had happened at the ranch. He must speak of the half-breed Angus Campbell and the illness that had threatened the lives of Sarah and Abby McDonald.

Throughout the interchange, Dream Weaver had hovered in a corner, not wishing to reveal anything about her stay at the McDonald ranch. It was Standing Rock's place to recount the events to the council. She waited quietly for him to call the members. He signaled to her that he was ready to begin the council, and she went outside to summon the rest of the band into Standing Rock's teepee. Song Bird waited inside with him while each person entered the teepee and took a seat in the circle. Laughing Water stooped into the tent last and found a place between Plenty Medicine and Song Bird. Song Dog sat at Standing Rock's right side and Bent Arrow on his left side. Little Owl sat at Song Dog's side. Moonbeam, Spotted Dove, and Plays-With-Shells were seated with their backs to the entrance. Standing Rock faced the entrance at the head of the circle. Seeing that everyone was seated, Dream Weaver squeezed in a space left for her between Song Dog and Plenty Medicine. The meeting could begin now that everyone's attention was focused on the chief.

Standing Rock picked up the talking stick in his lap.

"Many moons ago our grandfather Running Wolf brought us here so that we would be safe from the white men's ways. I have seen how the white men live. I have lived in his house. In the vision that came to me, I saw all races living together no matter the color of their skin." Standing Rock proceeded to recount in detail what he saw in his vision and the tree of life that grew and thrived as the races joined hands and lived together in peace . . . the rain of feathers . . . the dancing and singing together.

"The vision showed me a new path. Wounds cannot be healed by separation. Dream Weaver came to the woman and child who were so sick that only a powerful medicine could save them. And Dream Weaver gave them that medicine. The half-breed Angus, Dream Weaver, and I were spared sickness. Alas, not my father. Why it was so, I do not know. The vision spoke to me, telling me the time for separation is past. Hiding from the white men cannot go on forever. I hear the trains and cars; I hear the buzz of their tools and the crash of the trees. They approached nearer and nearer over the generations we have spent at Big Hole. Even the bear cannot hide in his den forever. The bear after his long sleep comes out to forage for food. Small numbers have meant our food supply has been sufficient, but if our numbers were to grow, we eventually would have to come out of hiding and look for food where the white men have taken over most of the land. Without enough young couples to have children, we cannot multiply our numbers. Therefore, I declare we must return to the place of our origin in the Place of the Wide Cottonwoods. We will preserve what is valuable of our heritage even though we wear the white man's clothes, eat his food, and use his tools. We will take what is good in his religion and ignore what is absurd. So say I."

He passed the talking stick to his son, Song Dog, on his right side. "I was born at Big Hole," Song Dog began. "I know no other place, but my grandfathers have told me of our beautiful valley and how our people ranged wide and far . . . over the eastern mountains . . . how the buffalo darkened the plains. I am not afraid of the white man who has taken over the land, stripping the hills and dirtying the waters. I will go where my father leads."

Bent Arrow gestured for the talking stick, anxious to take his turn at speaking. His face glowed with expectation. "I, for one, as a little boy, was born in our ancestral homeland. I have lived into four tens of winter and want to walk on that sacred ground again. I want my son, Little

Owl, to tread that earth too, to see where I netted my first fish and shot my first arrow at a rabbit before Horned Owl came to take me as an orphan. I have been happy and content here, but there has always been a hole in my heart for the place I left behind. Memories are faint of that time. I was a boy of five winters, but I remember that the valley and surrounding mountains were beautiful."

He handed the talking stick back to Standing Rock who said, "The oldest men have spoken. Let us now hear from our oldest woman who remembers well the journey of six tens of winters past. She is our great mother, Laughing Water.

Laughing Water chuckled. "Aye, that is me. I am a wrinkled old pumpkin. I have seen so much that it is too long to tell, but I will speak my mind of this vision you spoke of."

The walking stick was passed around the circle from hand to hand until it reached Laughing Water where she sat across from Standing Rock.

"Few moons remain for me. I wake every morning and give thanks for the sunrise. The sun, the moon, the stars, the forest, mountains, streams, and all my people are beautiful. Soon I will be a part of it all. You will see my spirit pass in the clouds; you will feel me under your feet, you will hear me sigh in the wind; my shadow shall rustle as it moves among the trees. We have tried to hide from what must be. I do not know why the Great Spirit allowed the white men to populate our land. I do not know why he made their numbers grow so large and strong. What I know is that there is a reason for it. I know that peace is better than war, and the Great Spirit intends that eventually the war parties come home, put down their arms, and seek a better way, and that is the path of peace. The vision shows us the way to peace. The circle unites. I agree with Standing Rock that separation is no longer the way." Laughing Water lowered the talking stick to indicate that was all she had to say.

Plenty Medicine held out her hand for the talking stick, and Laughing Water gave it to her.

"I have seen eight tens of winter. I came as a child with my sister, Song Bird, and my parents, Brave Bear and Sage Hen. When I was old enough, I married Sitting Crow and bore two sons and one daughter. My sons are dead, but my daughter Dream Weaver lives. Now I am an old crone who has passed on her knowledge to Dream Weaver. Like Laughing Water, I believe what Standing Rock says is the meaning of his vision." She paused and concluded, "So say I."

Standing Rock gazed around the circle. "Does anyone else wish to speak?" he asked.

Song Bird spoke up, taking the talking stick from Plenty Medicine. "My sister Plenty Medicine has spoken. I share her words."

The eldest members of the band had all spoken, and now the younger members deferred in silence to the thoughts that had already been shared. Standing Rock, seeing there were no further comments, spoke again.

"Good. It is settled. We will make preparations tomorrow to travel."

One by one, they left the teepee, leaving Standing Rock and Dream Weaver seated together. Finally, Dream Weaver was moved to speak.

"We, too, were born here at Big Hole and have never known any other home. I am filled with a great desire to see the land our grandfathers and grandmothers described. I wish to know if any of our people are left in the valley where they were born. How can we know how many survive if we do not travel there? It is wise that we go and see for ourselves how they have fared under the white man's fist."

"Aye, that is what I think too. Those who remain have no choice but to try and live in peace. Then perhaps our people can flourish again," Standing Rock said

"I pray so," Dream Weaver said.

Then the old couple curled up together under their bearskin blanket, old flesh huddled against old flesh in an embrace of understanding. Both their dreams were of the Broad Water and the Place of the Wide Cottonwoods.

The next day the work of packing up their belongings began. The teepees were disassembled. The backs of packhorses were loaded with stacks of skins and utensils, and travois were fixed to two other horses to pull additional supplies. Laughing Water sat atop the bundle on one travois. Such an old woman could not be expected to make the entire journey on foot or straddle a horse for many hours a day. Everyone else mounted a horse. Before setting forth, they surveyed the beautiful bowl that had been their home for several generations. Each in their heart bid a silent farewell to this haven. The forces of history that inevitably brought change had converged, making it impossible for them to survive apart from the rest of humanity. They recognized that they were a dying breed if they did not reunite with their kind, even if it meant living in proximity to an alien culture. The process of integration would inexorably hold sway. The parting was bittersweet. They loathed the thought of leaving but looked forward to reuniting with their kinfolk. Curiosity pulled them forward to see what changes had occurred in their ancestral homeland during their absence of almost seven tens of winters.

    The line of horses slowly ascended the switchback trail. In order not to shed a tear or let regret overtake them, none of the party looked backward. If they did, they would see circles devoid of grass where their teepees had stood and the firepit ringed with stones where they had listened to stories by the evening fire. They pushed on steadily until they reached the ridge and the point where the trail led over the ridge of the mountains to the headwaters of a stream. The path followed the rivulet down the heights to the valley below. A graded road running north and south bisected the valley. At intervals between stands of trees, cattle grazed in cleared fields. They spotted a two-story clapboard house with a peaked roof. Like a tiny insect, a black vehicle sputtered along the road, which once had been a narrow trail used by the original inhabitants. They selected a spot to camp for the night far enough from the highway where passersbys might not sight them.

    Meeting other travelers on the road was inevitable. The virgin country sparsely inhabited by Kootenai and Salish several generations ago was now populated. The farther south they traveled, the more evidence of white habitation they met. They passed a sawmill with huge stacks of logs in the lumberyard. Vehicles were parked in front of a long building. The workmen in the yard paid no attention to them, although they must have seen them. Perhaps it was not unusual to see a stray band of a race they considered inferior and routinely ignored as insignificant, not worthy of notice, harmless and pitiful at best, so the white men continued to work like beavers on a dam.

In the distance, they heard the chug of a train. Traveling farther, on their left, they saw a man-made embankment. As they rode closer, they could see railroad tracks had been laid on the level surface of the embankment. The train rounded a bend and came into view on the track. They stopped their horses to watch it steam past. In the engine compartment at the front of the cars, they saw a man in a red neckerchief and gray-striped hat wave at them. They were too astounded to wave in return. The chug-chug of the huge steam locomotive faded, and they resumed their journey, coming upon more houses and barns along the route. They passed lakes on either side of the road and traversed stretches of forest and large clearings that had been transformed into grazing land. Occasionally, a Model-T car rolled in a rattling rhythm toward them from the south, at which time they moved off the road to make way for the passage of the car. Sometimes the driver waved, but most often they looked straight ahead, not deigning to acknowledge the eleven traditionally clad Salish alongside the road.

"We do not exist for him," Standing Rock said bitterly, watching the exhaust pipe of the Tin Lizzy (that is what Angus had called the contraption) leave a trail of smoke as it receded and disappeared around a bend in the road.

The band stepped onto the road again. They traveled for two days more and reached a point in the road where they saw a trestle over the road. Reluctantly, they rode under this structure and discerned steel tracks were laid over the top of this bridge apparently constructed to overpass the road. A journey of two days more brought them to a town tucked at the foot of a mountain lake with a high peak towering above it. This was the point that Laughing Water remembered that the trail led south to the Broad Water. Amazed, she gasped at the sight of a grid of houses where once tall pines had reared their mighty crowns.

"How are we to go around this place?" she asked Standing Rock.

"We will ride proudly through it. Let them gawk at us if they like. We ride through what is ours. Onward." He nudged his horse to proceed.

A shopkeeper sweeping the boardwalk in front of his mercantile exchange stopped to stare as the Salish rode through town. A female shopper, frightened by their appearance, scurried into a store, but most of the townsfolk ignored them as they passed through the town. Most likely, they were accustomed to seeing random natives wandering about the area, hardly a threat to their well-being anymore because they knew most of them were submissive, drunk, or safely shoved onto the reservation. This was their town; they built it, and they owned it. Standing Rock surmised all these things in his mind. He sensed a dominant, arrogant race as he rode by. The realization did not anger him; it saddened him that they were so deluded as to think that they were a superior race. His mission was to show them they were wrong—to ride with dignity, leading his people, his head held high, and an eagle feather in his headband.

After they passed through the town, the ground sloped into a broad valley. Laughing Water burst out, "Where has all the forest gone? Have the trees grown feet and walked away? Surely not. The white man's destruction again. My soul is sick."

Patches of trees remained, but not as she remembered. In the hazy distance, another cluster of buildings appeared that gradually emerged as a bigger town than the one they had just passed through. Roads crisscrossed blocks of houses, and a street running east to west bisected the town. Standing Rock reined in his horse and said, "We will bypass the town, flank it on the west where there seems to be less activity, and circle back to where the river empties into the Broad Water."

That night they camped west of the town and resumed their journey in the morning. Another surprise met Laughing Water's eyes when they reached the northern end of the Broad Water. From a promontory overlooking the lake, they saw hundreds of logs jammed into a bay. Apparently, the logs had floated down the big river from the mountains into the lake.

"Ah, the land weeps," Laughing Water sighed. "How everything is changed!"

"Oh, if my parents were alive to see, they would cry a lake of tears," Plenty Medicine exclaimed.

"Their spirits see it," Laughing Water added. "The land knows their names."

Standing Rock turned to them and said, "Let us not lament long here. The earth will find its own revenge for the white man's greed and destruction. Justice may take time, but it will come like the storms. The mountain will shake and the water rise. We are a patient people and can wait for the righteous to prevail."

They traveled on the higher western side of the great lake where cliffs lined the shore and trees still stood majestically in hollows and steep slopes. The trail of former days was now a wide gravel road carved out by the white men. Travel was easier over this terrain, but it saddened those who had known it in its virginal state.

Reaching the lake's southern tip, they encountered another town of about five hundred inhabitants. Also, they met several wretched Salish who informed them that they had not received the promised allotments from the white government. They often had to wander from house to house, begging a few morsels from the housewives, who were more likely to give them food than were their husbands, the merchants and farmers who had overtaken the land. Standing Rock was perplexed by what they meant by allotments. It was not the white men's place to bestow gifts upon them. Since when did they replace the Great Spirit who had given the Salish all they needed from time immemorial? It was a grotesque perversion.

"How did this happen?" Standing Rock asked a young man clad in the trousers and woolen shirt of the white man. "The government divided the reservation land into allotments for each Salish man, but purposely there was a lot of excess land that they opened for settlers to buy. They allotted us an amount of 160 acres. What are acres to us? Nothing, when all this land is ours. As if the land could be divided up and sold in bits and pieces. Then we were overrun with white farmers and ranchers." The young Salish man stared uncomprehendingly at Standing Rock.

"How is it that you do not know this?"

"We have lived apart in the far north country," Standing Rock answered, not caring to give more information.

"You dress in skins. It is easier to wear the white man's clothes. There are no buffalo to hunt, and our women prefer to sew clothes with fabric, ribbons, thread, and metal needles. Where are you headed now?'

"We go to the Black Robes' mission."

The young man laughed. "You will find a sorry bunch of people living off the scraps the white men throw them, like dogs gnawing bones after a feast. Good fortune to you, but we have had none since the first white men entered this valley."

He walked away, churlish and embittered at life in general.

Standing Rock was sad that the young man lacked vigor and purpose. He struck Standing Rock as an aimless vagabond with nowhere to lay his head. How had the Salish youth arrived at such a sorry state? In contrast, his grandson, Little Owl, exuded the vitality and strength characteristic of the Salish brave. Neither of those qualities were diminished in his middle-aged son, Song Dog, who would, in his turn, succeed to leadership of the band.

Perched atop the bundle on the travois, Laughing Water exclaimed, "There are signs and symbols everywhere!" She pointed to the billboards and sign posts seen on both sides of the road as they continued south. "The white man has to plant signs and fences to let us know he owns everything." She cackled an old woman's laugh at what she judged utter foolishness.

The road dipped into a broad valley. Large tracts were sectioned into ranches and fenced off into pastureland for cattle or wheat fields. A man rode on a motorized contraption that cut the grass, bound the sheaves, and then spread the bundles in the field.

"Ah, the white men are so clever at making monsters that spew smoke," Laughing Water said. "The monsters are greedy like their makers, eating up the grain."

They had already traveled two weeks before they entered the Mission Valley. On their left, the snow-capped peaks towered, and on the right, stood lower mountains less densely forested. They passed through marshy land where ducks and long-legged cranes moved through the reeds. The elevation dropped gradually toward St. Ignatius Mission. Bent Arrow and Spotted Dove squealed in delight, recognizing familiar natural landmarks as the party drew closer to the center of the reservation. They veered left onto a road that led to a cluster of shanties. Children and women dressed in a motley of European and native custom loitered around the rude dwelling. Above a cluster of trees, a church spire topped with a crucifix appeared, and they moved toward the imposing brick building.

"I do not remember that church. It was not here when I was born. There was a small, wooden church," Bent Arrow said. Looking to the north side of the church, he added, "Like those small wooden cabins over there."

They passed the mission church. Sprinkled among the rude shacks were a few teepees. News of the arrival of visitors had spread through the settlement, carried on the tongues of ragtag children. They came upon a slightly larger dwelling of planed wood with a covered porch in front. There sat a dignified Salish in feathered headdress. There was no doubt he was the head chief. Standing Rock's company all dismounted save for Laughing Water, who remained seated on the travois. Formal greetings were exchanged.

"Ho, I am Standing Rock, grandson of Running Wolf, who left here many, many seasons ago."

"I am Chief Martin Charlo, son of Claw of the Small Grizzly Bear, also called Chief Charlo. My father resisted long and hard our removal here, but in the end the people were forced to march north. It was the season of tears. Welcome. We will share with you the little we have. Long have we thought that Running Wolf and all who went with him perished."

"I am alive," Laughing Water piped up. "She got up from the travois and toddled toward Chief Charlo. "I am Laughing Water, daughter of Red Feather, who settled here after the paper was signed with the white Chief Stevens. Red Feather came here with his young wife and many children."

"I know his family. He was so prolific that almost all the people claim kinship to his sons and daughters. His descendants run wild here, but some are good Christians."

"Aye, my father, Red Feather, took their religion. I refused and believed with Running Wolf that the Salish ways were better because we saw that the white men did not act as their God told them to behave. Before I die, I come to see where I was born."

"My sister," the chief said, "You will find it not as when you were born. Where our people camped are villages and farms. We were pushed out because the valley was rich, and the land flourished with crops white farmers planted. They have changed the names of all the places we loved. They reserved for themselves the best land and reserved the less-fertile soil for our people, expecting us to farm without even the implements and supplies they promised. My father held out for a long time, refusing to depart, although some of the people did comply, drifting here in smaller numbers. Finally, Chief Charlo reluctantly agreed to lead his people here after a general from Fort Missoula arrived to escort them to the reservation. Our Salish words sounded on the white men's ear like 'Missoula.' In our language it is the Place of the Cold Water. So, they misnamed everything, calling us Flathead. Our heads are not flat. We are the Salish. They call our ancestral homeland the Bitterroot and not the Place of the Wide Cottonwoods. They do not respect the Black Robes either. The place the Black Robes named St. Mary they now call Stevensville, in memory of the terrible white Chief Isaac Stevens who tricked our chiefs into signing the paper that the white men claim gave the land to them. And that Stevens was not an honorable man. Our people were not as many nor warlike like the Blackfeet. We did not go to war like the Nimiipuu they called the Nez Perce. My father always sought to live in peace with the white men. When they were lost and hungry, we fed them and showed them the way over the mountains. And this is how we have been repaid." Chief Charlo gestured in a wide circle. "Confined . . . cast aside . . . the buffalo slaughtered so we could starve to death. My father did not want his people to be slaughtered in a war that could not be won against overwhelming numbers, so he strived to live in peace. I will do the same. There is no other course."

Questions teemed in Standing Rock's mind still, reeling with all he had seen on the journey to St. Ignatius.

"But if this wide valley was supposed to be set aside for our people, why are there so many towns and ranches? Why did I see white men walking around as if they were owners of the land? Why have they cut down trees and planted fields of alien grain?"

"Removal to the reservation was bad, but the worse came nineteen winters later. For the first ten years, we farmed and raised livestock, thinking to make the best of a bad situation. Then the white government proposed the land be divided up into very small sections and allotted to each Salish with his name on a piece of paper. So much reservation land was left over because we numbered a few thousand, so they opened the rest of the land to white buyers. We have only one-fifth of the Flathead Reservation now. They quickly bought the land not allotted to us, moved in, and built fences so we could not ride our horses straight across to where we wished to hunt and fish. What is worse, our allotments were rocky with the poorest soil. We no longer had good harvests. The land was only good for grazing. We grew poorer instead of richer. We lived in drafty shacks, while the white ranchers lived in big houses. It was better in the Place of the Wide Cottonwoods—what they call the Bitterroot Valley. The grass was greener; the berries and camas more abundant. The game roamed freely everywhere. They knew it was the best place to live, so they pushed us off that land onto this less desirable place, and then here they took the very best land and shoved us to the worse ground."

"We want to see where our grandfathers lived in peace," Standing Rock said. "We will travel south to the Place of the Cold Water and follow the river that runs through our ancestral valley."

"You will not like everything you see," Chief Charlo said. "But go and return here. We welcome you back into your family. Cross over by the confluence of rivers and ride the east side of the Bitterroot River. The place where Owen had his trading post is where you will find the town of Stevensville. Old Mother Laughing Water may help you find it by Red-Top Mountain."

They rested a few days at St. Ignatius before they resumed their journey over another mountain pass to the Jocko Valley, where they met scattered Indians living in rude houses who invited them to spend the night. They listened to bitter tales of ill-treatment and hard winters without resources. The next day they ascended the higher mountain pass. As they descended into the valley, in the distance, they saw the Place of the Cold Water, which Chief Charlo had told them the white man called Missoula. It was where the rivers came together. The closer they approached, the more farm wagons and automobiles they encountered. They were largely ignored because Salish, either singly or in groups, were at that time not an uncommon sight in the surrounding communities. Sometimes pitied, they were deemed harmless for the most part, unless one was unruly and drunken. Then he was jailed. Any accused of thievery were also promptly handcuffed and thrown into a jail cell.

It was a two-day ride from the confluence of the rivers to Stevensville. They stopped to fish in the Bitterroot River. Although they caught several trout, the fish were noticeably less abundant, and they did not immediately achieve success. The beaver, of course, were not to be seen, which Laughing Water remarked on, and kept up a stream of commentary on creatures that in the past she had spotted routinely skitter among the willows and cottonwoods.

As they approached the northern rim of Stevensville, Laughing Water directed them toward the northwest. They passed over rubble from crumbling mud-brick walls. Amid the overgrown grass, the partial foundation of a building could be seen.

"Nothing is the same," Laughing Water said, pointing to fields where cows grazed. This is where John Owen's trading post stood. We came here to exchange hides for white men's goods. There were walls on all four sides." She surveyed the area. "Now there are cattle and farm buildings. No church. No cabins the Black Robes built. They are gone. The earth has reclaimed what is hers. The Black Robes sold their building to Owen before we left the valley. Owen built a cabin for Chief Many Horses a little bit south of here. The Black Robes called him Chief Victor because he was a good Christian who practiced the white man's religion when some of us did not. Maybe the cabin of Chief Many Horses is still there. Let us go on."

They did not have to travel very far before they caught sight of the spire atop a wooden church dominating the area at the town's western edge. Several other cabins were scattered around the church. About five hundred paces behind the church was a cemetery. They reached the church and dismounted. Laughing Water hobbled off her travois and stood looking at the church. The door opened, and a priest in black beretta and cassock emerged on the low threshold. He greeted them in English.

"What can I do for you, my sons and daughters? If you are looking for food, Brother Sebastian can provide you some from my kitchen you will find just behind the church."

None of them understood a word he said. Realizing this, the pastor motioned them to follow him around the side of the church. They complied and were led to a back door where another Black Robe appeared and handed them sacks of flour and smoked ham. Standing Rock did not know what to do, so he accepted the gifts. He wished he had something to give in return, but he did not. The two Black Robes exchanged a few words, apparently the pastor informing the brother that they did not understand the language, whereupon Brother Sebastian greeted them in Salish and explained to them that they were happy to share with them what they had. Brother Sebastian introduced the priest as Father James O'Shea, telling them the priest had come to restore the church after a period of neglect that followed the Salish removal to the Flathead Reservation. A community of Catholics, both native and white, had grown, and now there were a few hundred who attended Mass every Sunday. Father O'Shea invited them to stay at the mission for however long they wished to stay.

Standing Rock said, "We have been away for a long, long time. My grandmother was born here. She has come to see once more her birthplace. This is Laughing Water. She and her husband, Running Wolf, left this place many, many seasons ago after it was clear that the white Chief Stevens intended to rob them of all their land, and it was no good to try to fight the hordes of white men overrunning the land. They had powerful weapons. If we fought them, we would be slaughtered. We are back because in a vision I saw that separation was not a solution either. For my sons to survive, we must return and live in peace, or my lineage will disappear from the earth."

"That is the way of Our Lord, my friend. Peace be with you and yours," Father O'Shea said, and Brother Sebastian translated the words for Standing Rock.

"We will camp by the willows tonight," Standing Rock said. He had not thought to ask permission, for this land belonged to them both.

The priest made no protest, his silence tacitly granted them permission. Laughing Water regained her seat on the travois, and they moved toward the river, crossing a grassy plot of ground before the fenced cemetery of gravestones and crosses. Bordering the west side of the cemetery was another unfenced rectangular section marked by one crude wooden cross. Laughing Water signaled to halt. Pointing to the area behind the fenced-in cemetery, she said, "This is where some of our people were buried in the time of the Black Robes. The bones of others are buried here and there among the hollows and hills of this valley. Put me here."

"Do not talk of that now. I will take you back to Chief Martin Charlo, and he will say where you are to be buried."

"I am the one to say that," she affirmed.

"Who knows if it is possible? The white man claims even the place where we are to be buried."

"There is room for me in this burial ground. So say I."

"This is not the time to talk of your dying day. Now is the time to remember the happy days when you were young."

"Aye, those were happy days when I ran with Running Wolf; he pursued me until I said yes. No girl could say no to a brave such as he." She laughed softly, a smile of reminiscence lighting her wizened face.

They found a spot close to the river. Plenty Medicine was dispatched to draw water from the river while Song Bird and Dream Weaver went off to collect dry branches for the fire. Moonbeam and Spotted Dove got to work immediately erecting a teepee. Because of her advanced age, Laughing Water was excused from any work, but insisted on gathering a few twigs for kindling to start the campfire. Idleness was not part of a Salish woman's nature, regardless of her age. She had to mind children, and if her eyesight was still good—and Laughing Water's vision was still good—mend clothing. The exertion of bending to pick up lightweight sticks from the ground had left her out of breath. For a minute, she could not straighten up her stiff back. She shuffled back to the firepit the younger women had already dug, dropped her small bundle nearby, and hobbled toward a cottonwood a few paces away from the teepee. She leaned her body against the trunk and slid down into a sitting position, her back against the tree. From her vantage point beneath the cottonwood, she contemplated Red-Top Peak, what the Black Robes had renamed St. Mary's Peak. How beautiful it looked now framed against the setting sun. In late summer, only patches of last winter's snow remained. Soon that would change as surely the snow would fly again. How beautiful, how sacred was this valley. Big Hole never could fill her spirit with the peace that she felt in this moment of dying day. The earth had been kind to her, sheltering her in fat and in lean times. The white man had destroyed a lot, but he could never move Red-Top from its place. Changing its name did not change its sacred place in her heart. How puny man was; how arrogant he was to think he could overpower the earth mother. Laughing Water smiled to herself. She chanted a song of thankfulness for the mountain's beauty, rejoicing that she had been able to return to the cradle of her birth. Ah, it was a good place to have lived! Ah, it was a good place to die!

When Laughing Water did not return to the camp, the other women looked about, wondering where she had gone. Plays-With-Shells was sent to search for her. Maybe she had slipped and fallen on the muddy bank into the river. When Plays-With-Shells found her under the tree, her head was uplifted, her eyes still open, and her hands crossed over her breast. "Grandmother, I am here. We are all looking for you. Time to come to the camp and eat." Laughing Water's eyes did not shift to the young woman but continued their fixed stare at the mountain. Alarmed, Plays-With-Shells waved her hand in front of her face. Laughing Water did not stir. Then she grasped Laughing Water's shoulder and shook her. "Come, Grandmother. Rouse yourself," she said, thinking to wake Laughing Water from her trance-like state.

Laughing Water finally stirred, and she looked at Plays-With-Shells. "Then help an old woman to her feet," she said. With that, Plays-With-Shells, relieved, clasped Laughing Water's gnarled hand and pulled her to unsteady feet.

"I feel a little faint," Laughing Water murmured.

At that moment, Song Bird and Plenty Medicine came upon them.

"Oh, there you are," Song Bird exclaimed. "We were beginning to get worried about you."

"Do not make a fuss over me. Hand an old woman her walking stick." Plenty Medicine retrieved the stick where Laughing Water had laid it on the ground under the tree. "I can manage on three legs." Plays-With-Shells released her hold of Laughing Water's arm and let her make her way back to the teepee on her own power.

Before retiring for the night into the teepee shared by all eleven of them, Standing Rock announced. "Tomorrow, we return to St. Ignatius and take with us our ancestor's spirits. I feel them hovering in this valley."

Laughing Water smiled placidly. "Running Wolf is here too. He accompanies me. He waits for me."

The others understood well what Laughing Water meant but did not want to dwell on her meaning. Each member spread their blanket in the teepee and tucked together with little space between them, fell asleep with Laughing Water's blanket nearest the entrance.

In the morning, after supplies had been packed on the travois and they were all ready to mount their horses, Standing Rock looked around for Laughing Water who he expected to have seen seated atop the bundle on the travois.

"Now where has the old woman wandered off to?" he said impatiently. The rest of the party again set off in search of Laughing Water. Standing Rock began to wonder if her mind was failing. Legs and arms already enfeebled; she might be getting a bit crazy.

The women ran to the cottonwood tree, thinking they would find her sitting there again. Their hunch was correct, for they quickly sighted the huddled form of the woman. Coming closer, they saw that her head had sunk into her chest, and her hands hung limply by her sides, her walking stick laid across her lap. Before he reached her, Standing Rock knew what had happened.

Her body was still warm to the touch, but no breath escaped her mouth. Standing Rock picked her up in his arms and carried her back to the campsite where the horses waited for their riders. The women began to keen. Standing Rock sat for a long time holding the old woman, then delivered the body to the women for washing and preparation for burial.

"Will we hold the burial ceremony here or carry her back to the reservation?" Plenty Medicine asked.

"Her wish was to be buried with her grandmothers and grandfathers in the Place of the Wide Cottonwoods," he answered.

"Will the white man allow it?" Song Bird asked.

"I will go ask the white father for permission to bury her in the Salish plot beyond the church." Standing Rock strode back to the church, leaving the women to dress the body. He went alone, determined that Laughing Water's bones would rest with her ancestors.

Standing Rock spotted Brother Sebastian in front of the church. He hurried toward him and told him his old grandmother had died that morning. Her last wish was to buried where she had been born. He wanted to fulfill that wish and bury her in the Salish burial ground of unmarked graves located at the west end of the fenced Catholic cemetery. Brother Sebastian sympathized with Standing Rock's request and said he saw no reason that it could not be done, but he must first check with Father O'Shea. They would find him inside the church where he had just finished celebrating morning Mass.

They entered the small nave. A potbellied woodstove split nine rows of rude pews each side of the center aisle that led up to the altar railing. A statue of a lady dressed in blue was at the right side of the altar, and a statue of a Black Robe holding a cross and a book was on the left side. The wall behind the altar was painted a turquoise blue. Father O'Shea was kneeling before a large oil painting hung on the wall to the left of the altar. The painting, taller and wider than a man, depicted a Salish boy kneeling before the lady dressed in a blue mantle that veiled her head and a white robe surrounded by stars. The boy's hands were steepled in prayer, and so were the hands of the beautiful lady who looked lovingly down at the boy. When Father O'Shea heard their footsteps, he immediately rose and greeted them with a smile. Brother Sebastian repeated Standing Rock's request. They engaged in conversation for a few moments, and then Brother Sebastian turned to translate for Standing Rock.

"He gives his permission to bury your grandmother here. Father O'Shea and I will help you dig the grave. He asks if he can say prayers."

Standing Rock nodded his agreement. It would do no harm to add the white man's prayers to the prayers his own people sang to send their loved ones on their journey to the spirit world.

They left the church together, Father O'Shea and Brother Sebastian, dipping their hands in a water font at the door and signing their forehead, heart, and both sides of their chest as they left. Thinking this was a good ceremony, Standing Rock mimicked the gestures and followed them out of the church. He understood that the white man's religious use of symbols and ceremony had captured the imaginations of many of his people. The different colors of the vestments during their prayer ceremony pleased them because the colors were also sacred to them, and they all carried meaning. So there were some good things about the white man's religion, and in many ways, it was not that different from their own. He vowed to keep, then and there, what was good in the Salish religion and take what he thought good in the white man's religion. He believed he could make peace with them. Perhaps they could share the land after all. That was to be seen. Now he had to bury his grandmother.

Brother Sebastian retrieved shovels from a shed. Father O'Shea took one, and the two of them headed for the far reaches of the field where the burial ground was located while Standing Rock walked back to the Salish camp near the river. He dispatched the other men to help dig the grave. Song Bird and Plenty Medicine had prepared the body for burial and wrapped it in a deerskin blanket. Spotted Dove, Moonbeam, and Plays-With-Shells carried the body on a pallet to the burial ground, chanting as they walked. The day was uncommonly gorgeous for a funeral, the sky an unbroken blue, the sun sending beneficent rays upon every plant, tree, blade of grass, and the heads of the two Black Robes and eleven Salish. The mourners stood by the gaping hole ready to receive the wrapped corpse. At the graveside, they continued their prayers for the dead as the men finished digging the grave. The corpse was lowered into the ground. Father O'Shea, a white stole around his neck, sprinkled water over the body with a shaker and recited a prayer for the dead. The men shoveled dirt upon the body. The people filed away and left Brother Sebastian to smooth the mound of dirt.

Father O'Shea invited them to share a meal with him at his house, and Standing Rock accepted the invitation. The Black Robe occupied a nicer house than the rude cabin that had been built for Chief Charlo at the mission. It was a one-story clapboard house painted white with a picket fence around it in a block of similar houses to the east of the mission. Lace curtains covered the two front windows. They stepped through the door into a comfortable parlor with sofa and chairs. A silver-haired woman, a curled bun of hair topping her head, bustled about setting platters of food on a long table in an adjoining room separated from the parlor by a wide archway. Father O'Shea invited them to take seats around the table. There was room for thirteen people, but Standing Rock declined, indicating that his people preferred to sit on the floor, so they all sat cross-legged on the parlor rug. Father O'Shea looked at Brother Sebastian, and they moved to take a seat with the Salish on the floor. The woman in a pinafore filled plates with food and scurried to serve each guest. They were offered knives and forks. Although not used to these utensils, they gamely copied the Black Robe's eating custom. They ate in silence. Every so often, a Salish would emit a sound of pleasure at the taste of the food. Other times, a grimace of distaste would appear on another face, but in general, they ate the food politely and respectfully. When the woman, apparently a servant, had collected the plates, not one plate had a morsel of food remaining on it. Standing Rock lighted a pipe.

"It is our custom to smoke as a sign of friendship," he said. He drew a puff on the pipe, and passed it on to Father O'Shea on his right, who obligingly smoked the pipe. It went around the circle in turn. Again, Father O'Shea invited the Salish to remain at the mission. He would find useful work for them and teach them about Jesus Christ. Lessons in his language would be given. They would be fed and clothed well.

"Most of our people are gone from here, having been forced to the Flathead Reservation where our chief now lives. We thank you for your kindness, but we wish to live with our people and speak our language. We will make our home with them," Standing Rock said.

"Will you farm?" Brother Sebastian asked.

"I do not know. I will do what I must do to take care of my people. What work that is, I do not know. The horse soldiers and white riflemen have purposely killed all the buffalo."

Father O'Shea and Brother Sebastian could not refute the truth of that, so they said nothing.

"At St. Ignatius is a priest who speaks Salish," Father O'Shea said. "Seek out Father Louis Taelman, and he will help you find work and a place to live."

"Will he teach me the white man's language?" Standing Rock asked. He was weary of the necessity for a translator to conduct daily activities. If he was to live successfully in the new world around him, he must not receive information secondhand. It was essential that no deception or misunderstandings occur through faulty translations.

On the way back to St. Ignatius, he took Dream Weaver aside and shared his firm belief that they must learn the language of the dominant culture.

"That may be so," Dream Weaver said, "but I will speak to my grandchildren in my native tongue. They must not forget who they are."

"We cannot let that happen, even though we are surrounded."

They reached St. Ignatius and reported immediately to Chief Martin Charlo the details of their visit to the Place of the Wide Cottonwoods.

"It is as you said it would be," Standing Rock said. "Laughing Water had difficulty recognizing places, but she guided us to the sites she remembered. I am happy that her spirit hovers there."

In the shadow of the Mission Mountains, Standing Rock and Dream Weaver moved into a hut abandoned by a couple who had gone to Missoula to find work. On the white man's day of prayer, they watched many of their neighbors walk to the tall brick building at the center of the scattered community of humble Salish shacks. At first, they were reluctant to join them, but finally, Chief Charlo, who was a devout adherent of the new faith, induced them to attend a service. The priest delivered the sermon in Salish and impressed them with his gentle demeanor. He spoke to the congregation, which also included a few whites, as equals. Hymns were sung in both Salish and English. Standing Rock watched his kinsmen kneel at the altar railing while the priest placed a round piece of bread on their tongues. This surely was a sign of special grace, of profound benevolence. He felt no evil intent in the church. In fact, a deep peace enveloped him as he gazed upon the grandeur of the rounded ceiling hung with glorious paintings of Jesus Christ, his prophets, martyrs, and saints. There was some wisdom to be obtained from this church. Again, he vowed to accept what was good and reject what he found to be lies and hypocrisy.

After the ceremony, Standing Rock and Dream Weaver approached the priest whom they supposed to be Father Louis Taelman, who the priest at St. Mary's Church had mentioned.

"Ho, I am Standing Rock," he greeted the priest. "Will you teach me your tongue?"

"Of course," the priest answered, smiling. His eyes projected kindness behind his rimless glasses.

Standing Rock continued, "Of all your people, you express no deceit. Your presence does not cause me alarm or revulsion to my spirit. In my vision, I saw I cannot avoid the white man. I have come to see that they rule the land. We are brothers and must live as brothers even though your people tried to kill off or starve my people to death. That cannot be; that will not be. Though they come to take and destroy and dirty the waters and strip the mountains, I pledge to defend the earth until the day I die."

"I wish to do the same," Father Taelman assured him. "It is my mission. I love this land and all its people."

Tears appeared in Dream Weaver's eyes. "I believe you," she said. "We are home."

"We are home," Standing Rock repeated.

Resolved to assimilate what was best from European culture, the Big Hole men pooled their land allotments to produce crops and raise livestock sufficient to support them. The women became particularly adept at making bead jewelry—earrings, bracelets, and necklaces. They also made garments, moccasins, belts, and purses with fine beadwork. Plays-With-Shells took to the native craft enthusiastically and was particularly skilled with her goods highly sought after by the merchants in town. Song Dog succeeded his father as head of the Big Hole clan and was elected to the Intertribal Council. In the years after their migration, Little Owl and Plays-With-Shells found mates among the original inhabitants of St. Ignatius, and their descendants intermarried with Salish and Kootenai residents of the area. After Song Dog died, Little Owl emerged as head of the clan.

Standing Rock lived well into nine tens of winter, loved, and respected by whites, Salish, Kootenai, and clergymen of all faiths. He kept alive the Salish language, gathering preschoolers around him to repeat Salish songs and listen to tales of the old days before the white men came. An alphabet had been created for the language. He wrote the letters on a blackboard for the children and spoke to them only in Salish. Even though he had been in his late sixties when he learned to communicate satisfactorily to be understood in English, he loved to hear his native tongue on the lips of the little ones.

One day he called Dream Weaver to his side. He was seated at the window, gazing at the Mission Mountains. They lived in a better house, insulated, electrically heated, constructed of planed wood, and roofed with slate shingles. It was painted a baby-blue color and trimmed in white. There was a carport to protect his Ford Fairlane from the weather. When he was seventy, Little Owl had insisted that he learn to drive and had bought the car for him, but he used it little, still preferring to keep a horse in the large backyard with pastureland sufficient to feed one horse.

"I had a dream last night," he told her. She waited for him to relate it.

"The face of Running Wolf appeared on the mountain, dwarfing the top. Then the face of Horned Owl appeared next to him, and next to him Lone Wolf, and then Rides-the-Wind, all in a line. Horned Owl spoke and said, 'What are you waiting for?' Running Wolf spoke next, 'We are waiting.'"

Dream Weaver chuckled. "I had the same dream."

"Ah, it is lucky we had the same dream," Standing Rock said. His face crinkled into a hundred smile lines.

"Luckier that we make the last journey together," she said.

"I save the last word for the woman. That is all. *Šey hoy*," Standing Rock said, looking into Dream Weaver's serene old eyes.

"But will the peoples save the earth?" Dream Weaver mused. Her question remained unanswered as the winter solstice sun set the Mission Mountains aglow in the last light of day.

## Acknowledgments

I am grateful to my husband, Rod Rogers, and my sister, Marianne Stephens, who accompanied me in my travels around Montana. Their support in my imaginative flights into Native-Americans encountering white culture spurred my resolve to complete this fictional conception of a small band of Salish determined to preserve their traditional way of life. Special thanks go to Alice Kane who read the manuscript and offered many valuable suggestions based on her experience working on a reservation. Christian Nelson contributed enormously to the novel's final form, first in his copyediting skill and then in design of the map, the lineage chart, and the cover. The map serves to locate relative positions of principal places mentioned in the narrative but is not drawn to scale. The attractive presentation of my work is entirely due to his editorial and graphic art skills. Characters on the lineage chart are products of my imagination, although historical characters appear. I claim fictional license and acknowledge that I took liberties in telling my story.

**About the Author**
Olivia Diamond's novels include *Inland Waters, Never the Same, Giselle, The Wheels of Being, Delayed Reaction, The Pluperfect Phantom, Gardens Under Which Rivers Flow*. Her trilogy (*Voice of Stone, Conquistadora*, and *Daughter of the Conquest*) dramatizes the story of the Inca Empire from the period immediately before Francisco Pizarro's arrival through the Spanish conquest and colonization of Peru. Her poetry books are: *Women at the Well, Land of the Four Quarters: A Poetic History of the Incas, Geography of My Bones: Collected Poems, Playground, Be Thou a Man, Please Trespass Here, Al-Andaulus, Grant Me a Cloud,* and *Stranger in My Own Land*. Her roots are in Illinois, but she now makes her home in northwestern Montana. Visit the author's website at mountainofdreamsbooks.

Printed in Great Britain
by Amazon